f^3, devoted to novels-in-progress
F Magazine, Inc.

Editor
John Schultz

The f issues are published twice yearly by F Magazine, Inc., 1405 W. Belle Plaine, Chicago, Illinois, 60613. F Magazine, Inc., is a not-for-profit corporation under the laws of the State of Illinois. Currently the f series is devoted to sections of novels-in-progress, or other longer works of imaginative prose. The editor invites submissions of excerpts of reasonable length. No manuscripts will be returned unless accompanied by a stamped, self-addressed envelope. All manuscripts accepted for publication become the property of F Magazine, Inc., unless otherwise indicated. Copyright © 1987 by F Magazine, Inc.

The publication of f^3 was made possible by grants and gifts from:

    The Illinois Arts Council, program grant
    Erwin A. Salk
    Mirron Alexandroff, Columbia College
    Yale Wexler
    Chicago Office of Fine Arts, City Arts I Program made possible by the City of Chicago, the Illinois Arts Council, the MacArthur Foundation, and the Woods Charitable Fund

and of contributions of up to $200 by:

    Susan Rue Braden
    Betty Brisch
    Mary Brophy
    Richard Cantrall
    Kathryn Devereaux
    Dr. and Mrs. David Edelberg
    Kathryn E. Jonas
    Mary Zoe Keithley
    Marie Leadaman
    Mitchell and Erin Omori
    Richard Riemer
    Marian Stern
    Richard and Ruth Talaber
    Mary Walker

Cover Photo: Nathan Lerner "Closed Eye" (1940) from the permanent collection of the Museum of Contemporary Photography of Columbia College, Chicago
Cover Design: Gerry Gall

ISBN 0-936959-01-0

Editor's Statement

F Magazine, with the publication of f^2—and now f^3—and subsequent book-issues, seeks to be the spearhead for novels-in-progress that will emphasize story—content, imagery, character, voice, and a rich exploration of points of view and style and dimensions of time, dramatic as well as self relationships, the mixing of the private and the self with the public and social and historical, the way life happens for all of us no matter how we wish it to be. Years ago, f^1 carried on its cover the statement "Here we begin again with story, image, word, and people." We are continuing the beginning.

If you're a poet or a writer of short fiction—and these days that often means very short fiction—you may write a piece in comparatively little time and see it published, get some audience response relatively quickly, if only from the audience of your resonating spirit. If you're a novelist you can go a long, long time in writing a novel before you get the audience and the life-giving audience response, the sort of response that can help sustain the novelist.

Historically, novelists have often had the great advantage of audience response to their novels-in-progress, published in the form of serialization or in sections. For many reasons, historical and economic, this is no longer so. If we examine even recent literary history, we find that prior publication of sections of works-in-progress has played an important part in many novelists' development and shaping of their novels. In many cases the novels were far from finished and the prior publication stimulated the author and whetted the audience's sense of contribution.

With realism and sometimes parody, the sections of novels-in-progress published in f^3 address some of the "common secrets" of American life—of power, family, job, institutions, sex, money, class, personality, racial relations, and much more. The "common secrets" of our lives have always been the fascinating stuff of story.

F Magazine will be devoted to novels-in-progress that are part of a movement towards invention through a synthesis of novelistic techniques, seeking ways to reclaim the author's function, place, potential, and responsibility in telling the dramatic tale, in this case the novel.

With this issue, we begin a Guest Editor program, in which issues from time to time will publish materials selected and edited by a guest editor who will bring her or his perspective to representing the novel as it is developing in this country and elsewhere. We are pleased that Shawn Shiflett, who writes a vigorous new realism, has found a striking variety of works-in-progress for f^3.

John Schultz
Editor

Guest Editor's Introduction

Without exception the writers whose works appear in f^3 have plunged head-first into the risky endeavor of committing themselves to long-term writing projects with nothing more to cling to than their own belief that story, steeped in the social and private ambiguities of life, will win out in the current squeeze of the literary market and eventually find a path that will lead to the reader. Yet in spite of all the obstacles that the novelist must overcome, the novel excerpts in f^3 stand as testimony that writers have not abandoned what Charles Johnson has called "the queen of the verbal arts."

My main objective in editing f^3 was to find original writing that demanded my attention from the first word to the last. Of the many manuscripts I read while selecting the pieces, these are the ones that most strikingly explore and exploit the truth within ourselves and our society, sometimes with stark realism, other times with the wicked humor of parody. From a story about a freed black man who stows away on a nineteenth-century slave ship and must use his wits to survive from moment to moment; to a Greek American who returns home to Chicago after being tortured and jailed for years by the military junta in Greece, only to find his former life shattered; to a young married couple engaged in playing a destructive game of trying to control what the other one sees in the mind; to a black man with dreams of building a black army to defend blacks against the racist society in which he lives; to a family coping with the deterioration of an alcoholic mother; to a tongue-in-cheek handbook on how women can become more exquisitely and "traditionally" feminine, more "pink"; to a man who wakes up with no elbows and must, quite naturally, find them at all costs—these works catapult the reader into the worlds, situations, and confrontations created by the authors. Perhaps just as importantly, the novel excerpts in f^3 tease the reader into asking the question that has compelled generation after generation of readers: *What happens next?*

I would like to thank John Schultz for giving me the opportunity to be the Guest Editor of f^3. Also, special thanks to Oakley Hall III for copy editing assistance, and to Robin Campbell for copy editing and help with innumerable other tasks of publication.

I believe that the novels represented in f^3 will have the same comprehensive effect upon you as they did upon me. "We read," says Schultz, "to be taken out of ourselves and, paradoxically, into ourselves, while being carried into an imaginative state of mind of experiencing the story." These stories accomplish just that.

Shawn Shiflett
Guest Editor

Contents

Editor's Statement
Guest Editor's Introduction

Works-in-Progress

From *Rutherford's Travels* 1
Entry the Second
Charles Johnson

From *Ghost of the Sun* 16
Harry Mark Petrakis

From *Phantom Rider* 29
Act I: Shopping
Betty Shiflett

From *Winter House* 52
So Why Let Love Die of Hunger?
Andrew Allegretti

From *The Adventures of Al* 68
The Spanish Friars Thing
Glen Ross

From *Hey, Liberal* 85
Lunchroom
Shawn Shiflett

From *The Elbows* 98
Disjointed
Bill Burck

From *One Anonymous Mourning* 114
Paul Carter Harrison

From *The Pink Lady Primer* 130
The Sunshine Inspiration Committee's
   Guide for True Ladies Everywhere
Beverlye Brown

From *Marquette Park* 146
The Porch
Gary Johnson

From *Act of God* 156
Zoe Keithley

From *A Chocolate Soldier* 166
Cyrus Colter

Contributors 187

From *Rutherford's Travels*

Charles Johnson

© Charles Johnson, 1987

Rutherford's Travels *is a nineteenth-century sea adventure story for modern readers, told in the form of a ship's log kept by Rutherford Calhoun, a young black thief who stows away aboard the* Republic, *a slaving vessel, at a time when trans-Atlantic slave-trading to the United States was illegal. Rutherford hides aboard the ship in order to escape a marriage he can't avoid to a prim schoolteacher, Isadora Bailey, in New Orleans. Set in 1832, many years after the legal ending of the slave trade, the novel details the terrifying passage of African slaves from the Gold Coast to the Americas—a passage that changes Rutherford as well—but here the slaves in question come from a mysterious tribe, the Allmuseri, known only to a handful of European explorers.*

Entry the second
June 20, 1832

    It wasn't the *Republic* sailing east for the Gulf of Guinea, skimming along easily in a six-knot breeze, that awoke me (I've been known to sleep through gunshots and tavern brawls), or even the chatter of Captain Falcon's flea-infested, foul-tongued crew, but rather the cold barrel of a firelock shoved under my shirt and against my belly by Peter Cringle, the first mate and quartermaster, that brought me back to full consciousness from the deepest sleep I'd had in years. An hour out of port, he'd thrown back the tarp fashioned from old sail, uncovering me, and I stared up, my mouth and eyes partly sealed and phlegmed by sleep, at a silvery-gray sky aswirl with honking seagulls, the elaborate webbing of the foremast entangled with low-bellying clouds, and the faces of five men you'd hardly care to stumble upon during an evening stroll: black eyepatches, I saw, beards like tangled bushes, hooks where hands should be—I speak the truth—and between them all they had, like the monocular witches outwitted by Perseus, only two good teeth among them. "A black stowaway, is he now, Mr. Cringle?" said one, whose mouth could have doubled for the Black Hole of Calcutta. "Let us 'ave him, sir. We'll throw the blighter overboard and save you the powder—we wouldn't want you exertin' yerself too much, y'know, you bein' an officer and all."

Laughter exploded round me, but the Mate's expression did not change.

"On your feet, you," Cringle ordered, and I obeyed because of all the faces present his seemed the most sympathetic. In other words, he had the only one not pitted by smallpox, split by Saturday night knifescar, disfigured by Polynesian tattoos, or distorted by dropsy. Indeed, First Mate Cringle's whole air spoke of New England gentility. He was tall and straight as a door, an officer and a gentleman from his powdered white wig right down to the spit-polished boots that reflected back winces and dead-eyes on deck. His skin was as white as wax, which made him seem like nothing less than a tightly wound toy soldier. "You've less than a minute," said he, shaking with rage, or more like fear, "to explain what you're doing aboard this ship."

Quickly, I pulled Squibb's papers from my waistcoat, unfolded them, then thrust them toward him. "I didn't mean to be asleep, sir," I said, maneuvering. "I'm ready now to report for work."

Cringle frowned irritably down the first page. The other sailors, this blustering, braying gang of tormentors, looked over his shoulder like an infernal chorus, and seemed to enjoy the agitation my discovery brought him; they watched him more closely than they watched me, elbowing each other and winking, like bullies having fun at the expense of a new kid—a sissy in short pants—at school. Above us birds veered, then vanished into diaphanous layers of mist high as the mizzenpole. The deck was silent. So quiet I could hear blood hammering in my ears and the hungry gurgle of gastric fluids in my belly. At length, Cringle shut his eyes. He crumpled the papers in his fist.

"Josiah Squibb is down *below,* you bloody imposter!"

"'Oh." My breath stopped. "Odd coincidence, that. Imagine! Two of us with the same na . . ." He leveled the firelock straight at my forehead, but less to frighten me, I thought than to make a point with the others. "Sir, my name isn't Squibb. You've guessed that already? Uh, right. It's Rutherford Calhoun, and I only came aboard to return these papers to . . ."

"Hold your tongue." He faced round to the others. "And stop your row, alla you, and get back to work. I can handle this myself."

Under Cringle's stare, the crew turned back, laughing less at me than the Mate, to their business—belaying sheets and halyards—and Cringle's bunched shoulders lowered a little. He put away his pistol, wiped his forehead with his sleeve, whispered, "Hoodlums, every blinkin' one of them," then shoved me aft toward Captain Falcon's cabin. "It's the Devil, I do believe, as sends us the toothache, the east wind, and rumpots like these!" We passed small pens of Berkshire pigs and chickens the captain kept on board for himself, but as we neared the cabin door my stomach dropped. I felt uneasy in my spine. Sweat began to stream into my clothes. The deck beneath me dipped and rose dizzily, and with that motion my center of gravity was instantly gone. My last meal, too, over the railing, which I ran to and gripped with all my strength as the ship—or so my confused inner ear told me—careened left. "Now, that's a pretty sight. And you say you're a midshipman, eh? Methinks you're a farmer, Calhoun."

Between heaves, I said, "Illinois!"

A softening and sort of pity came into Cringle's voice. He withdrew his handkerchief, handed it to me, then watched as my belly turned inside-out, like a shirtcuff. "But you'll feel a lot worse if the Skipper's in a mood for cobbing. What on earth prompted you to stow away on a ship run by Ebenezer Falcon?"

"Debts," I said, my eyes still swimming. "A woman. Maybe a jail sentence, or . . ."

The Mate smiled, and from out of his flash of even white teeth there flowered the relaxed, boyish grin, it struck me, of a young Presbyterian minister, or perhaps a child prodigy, someone who'd grown up with a great deal of wealth, privileges, or personal gifts, and felt guilty about them in the presence of those who hadn't: a man who'd maybe been a concert pianist at age five, or at twelve entered Harvard, or at fifteen solved some theoretical enigma in physics that had puzzled scientists twice his age, and who never spoke of these things without a touch of endearing humiliation because he hated not to be "regular," yet who, it was clear, carried a core of aloneness within him that nothing on shore could touch. Cringle had, I was to learn, an almost psychotic total recall of everything he'd read. He was also the only man I'd ever met who carried verses from the Sermon on the Mount on scraps of paper in his pockets so he could memorize them when he was on watch. Had he been a woman—he certainly had a feminine air—he'd be the kind who could do Leibnitzean logic, or Ptolemaic astronomy, but hid the fact in order not to frighten off suitors; or, if a slave, one who could bend spoons with his mind, but didn't so white people wouldn't get panicky.

"Half the crew's here for those reasons, or some other social failure on shore," he laughed. "But I'll tell you true: Jail's better. Being on a ship *is* being in jail with the chance of being drowned to boot."

"I can't go back . . ."

"None of us can. Come along. Maybe the captain can use someone in the galley. Can you cook?"

"Yes."

"Liar," said he. "Doesn't matter, though. We've all gotten used to the taste of maggots in everything."

At the captain's door, which had three bullet holes in it, Cringle tried the latch. It was unbolted, but he decided against barging in and rapped instead, and a good thing this was, because from within the cabin, whose curtained windows were pulled shut, I heard the squeaking of mattress springs, then a stifled whimper, and at last a venereal moan so odd in its commingling of pleasure and complaint that I had, of a sudden, the vision of not being aboard ship but instead in a bordello. It made no sense then, those Venusian groans, that gasping yip of orgasmic stings, but soon enough it would. "Has he a woman aboard?" I looked to Cringle for an answer, but the Mate wouldn't look me in the eye; he chewed the inside of his cheek, and politely pulled the door shut. "Didn't I say this was worse than prison?" For another minute we stood waiting, looking at the door, at each other, and finally it opened and a heartbreakingly handsome cabin-boy, with curly hair like wood-shavings, young but hardly in long pants (and barely in these, for he was pulling up his striped duck pantaloons, tripping on the cuffs) came scrambling out, closing the door behind him, his jerkin unfastened, his face drained of color, and eyes crossed by what he'd been through.

"Good day to you, Mr. Cringle." He kept his eyes low.

Cringle rubbed his face with one hand, peeking at the boy through his fingers.

"Are you and the captain finished, Tom?"

"Yessir . . . I'm sorry, sir, you kin go in now."

The Mate forced a smile that must have been harder to lift than a sledgehammer, looking down at the boy as you might a younger brother (or sister) you'd just glimpsed in a stranger's set of pornographic pictures, pained by his shivering and rubbing his arms and standing bowlegged as if his bum was cemented shut by dried semen, as it probably was (mind you now, I have no quarrel with homosexuals, but I do flinch when I see a child forced into something he can't rightly understand). Cringle tousled the boy's hair, his lips tight, and moved Tom aside. "Tell Squibb"—his voice quivered—"I said he's to fix you the finest meal he can, Tom." And then to me: "Of course, you'll say nothing of this to anyone."

"Of course," I said.

"It would not help morale, if the men knew . . ."

"I've seen nothing," I said, "but I wonder: Is my silence worth a word in my favor with the captain?"

His fingertips pushed the door inward. "Just go inside, Calhoun."

Ducking my head, I stepped down into a low-studded room, aware of Cringle's breath and bodily warmth behind me, but of little else, for the cabin of Captain Falcon had the dank, ancient dampness of old ships, or a cave—that, and the clamlike, bacterial odor of tabooed pleasures. The air was denser inside, difficult for my throatpipes to draw. To my left, a small voice, like that of a genie in a jug, said, "Draw the curtains a bit, Mr. Cringle," and when the Mate did so, suddenly raying the room with bright light, a high-post bedstead with valences and knotted with dirty sheets sprang forth in the glare. Now I was rivering sweat. From the ceiling a pyramid-shaped poop lantern with horn windows swung low enough to crack your head, and to the right of that were a washbasin and clawlegged bathtub bolted to the floorboards—perhaps the only other landside luxury in the room. Across from this was a cluttered chart-table. Seated at this, with his back to me, a big-shouldered man was barricaded in by maps of the sea and African bush. On his table lay a gilded, ornamental Bible, a quadrant, chronometer, spyglass, and the log in which I now write (but this months later after mutiny and death, with the ship lost in Space and Time, the reporting on which I must put off for a while). He kept to his business, refusing to turn, and said in that shocking voice thin and shrill and strung like catgut, "All right, stand at ease and state yer business."

Cringle cleared his throat, coughing into one hand.

"We found this boy in the longboat, Skipper. He says he's Rutherford Calhoun, a friend of Squibb. I thought perhaps..."

"You've rung the bell to change watch?"

The Mate paused. "I was about to when I discovered th..."

"See to it then. And shut the door behind you."

The Mate left, glancing helplessly at me and, standing alone, looking at the back of Captain Falcon's sloping head, shining my boots on the back of my breeches to polish them, I thought that maybe racial savvy might see me through this interview. Maybe I shouldn't say this, but we all know it anyway: namely, that a crafty Negro, a shrewd black strategist, can work a prospective white employer around, if he's smart, by playing poor mouth, or greasing his guilt with a hard luck story. At least it always worked for me before. In my most plaintive voice, I told the captain how desperate I was for work, that I'd stowed away because gainful employment was systematically denied black men back home, that New Orleans was so bigoted a Negro couldn't even buy vanilla ice cream.

"So?" said Falcon.

I told him about my mother's death from overwork in the fields of Illinois when I was three (she died in bed, actually, but I could trade on this version and liked it better).

"So?"

And then I related the hardships I'd received at the hands of my religiously stern master, Peleg Chandler, who gave all his slaves two teaspoons of castor oil *every* Saturday morning, whether they were sick or not, and called that "preventative medicine." (It may not seem like much to you, but to me, at age twelve, it was torture.)

"So?" he said again, this time swiveling full around to face me, his elbows splashed on the leather arms of the chair, and as his gaze crossed mine in the crepuscular cabin light, as I saw his face, I felt skin at the nape of my neck tingling like when you're being photographed, because the Master of the *Republic,* the man known for his daring exploits and subjugation of the colored races from Africa to the West Indies, was a *dwarf.* True enough, no one in 1832 was very tall, the average height of men being five-feet-six, both at sea and on shore, but Ebenezer Falcon, I saw, was shorter even than the poor, buggered cabin-boy Tom. Regardless, he was a dwarf to reckon with. Though his legs measured less than those of his chart-table, Captain Falcon had a shoulder-span like that of Santos, and between this knot of monstrously developed deltoids and latissmus dorsi a long head rose with an explosion of hair so black his face seemed dead in contrast: eye sockets like clefts in rock, medieval lines more complex than tracery on his maps, a nose slightly to one side, and a great bulging forehead that looked harder than whalebone, but intelligent, too—a thinker's brow, it was, the kind fantasy writers put on spacemen far ahead of us in science and philosophy. His belly was unspeakable. His hands, like roots. More remarkable, I'd seen drawings of this gnarled little man's face before in newspapers in New Orleans, though I never paid them much attention, or noted the name. He was famous. In point of fact, infamous. That special breed of empire-builder, explorer, and imperialist that sculptors loved to elongate, El Greco-like, in city park statues until they achieved Brobdingnagian proportions. Sir Richard Francis Burton, I read, carried Ebenezer Falcon's portrait, clipped from the Press, on every expedition he made.

Now . . . yes, now I remembered those stories well. Falcon, the papers said, knew seven African coastal dialects and, in fact, could learn any new tongue in two weeks' time. More, even, he'd proven it with Hottentot, and lived incognito among their tribe for a month, plundering their most sacred religious shrines. He'd gone hunting for the source of the Nile, failed, but even his miscarried exploits made him raw material for myths spun in brandy and Cavendish smoke in clubs along the eastern seaboard. He'd translated the *Bardo Thodol*— this, after stealing the only scroll from a remote temple in Tibet—and if the papers can be believed, he was a patriot whose burning passion was the manifest destiny of the United States to Americanize the entire planet. Really, I wanted to take off my hat in his presence, but I hadn't worn a hat. Never mind that his sins were scarlet. He was living history. Of course, he only stood as high as my hips, and I had to fight the urge to pat him on his head, but I was, as I say, impressed.

"Sit," said he, motioning to the chair at his chart-table. "I don't like people looking down at me."

I could understand that; I sat.

Falcon toddled over to his washbasin, poured water from a bucket half his size, and began to sponge-bathe under his nightshirt, speaking over his left shoulder at me. "And, generally speaking, I don't like Negroes either."

"Sorry." He was frank; I liked that. With bigots a man knew where he stood. "But I can't help that, sir."

Falcon half-turned, his eyebrows lifting.

"I *know* you can't, Calhoun. It's one of the things I learned about Negroes after living with the Lotophagi on the African coast. You don't think too well, or too often. I don't blame *you* for stowing aboard." He squeezed out his sponge. "Poor creature, you probably thought we were a riverboat, didn't you?"

I fell back against the seat. "This *isn't* a riverboat?"

"I thought so." Falcon wet his hands, then finger-combed his hair, shook off the water, and carried his basin to the door, throwing it out on a midshipman who began cursing like ... well, like a sailor until he saw the captain's face, and meekly tipped his hat. Slamming the door, Falcon fixed me again with both eyes. " 'Tis a *slaver,* Mr. Calhoun, and the cargo awaiting us at Bangalang is forty Allmuseri tribesmen, hides, prime ivory teeth, gold and bullocks, which comes to a total caravan value of nearly ninety thousand pounds, of which the officers and I have a profitable share—quite enough to let me retire after this run, or finance an expedition I have in mind to Tortuga, or, if I've a mind, see my share tripled at the gaming-tables of Franscatis in Paris —but if you sail with us to Guinea—that is, if I don't decide to nail your feet to the floor—it will have to be without pay. Do you see that, Calhoun?"

"Yessir." I nodded. "Thank you."

"Good." After toweling his hands, he took a shirt with frills down the front and a pair of pantaloons from a chest by the door. "I don't hold it against you for being here. Or for being black, but I believe in *excellence*—an unfashionable thing these days, I know, what with headmasters giving illiterate Negroes degrees because they feel too guilty to fail them, then employers giving that same boy a place in the firm since he's got the degree in hand and saying no will bring a gang of Abolitionists down on their necks. But no," he looked pained, "not on *my* ship, Mr. Calhoun. Eighty percent of the crews on other ships, damn near anywhere in America, are *incompetent,* and all because everyone's ready to lower standards of excellence to make up for slavery, or discrimination, and the problem ... the *problem,* Mr. Calhoun, is, I say, that most of these minorities aren't ready for the titles of quartermaster or first mate precisely because discrimination denied them the training that makes for true excellence—ready to be mediocre mates, I'll grant you that, or middle-brow functionaries, or run-of-the-mill employees, but not to *advance* the position, or make a lasting breakthrough of any kind. O, 'tis a scandal on the ships I've seen, and hardly the fault of the poor, half-trained Negro who hungers like anyone else these days for the glamour of titles and position." He was grimly quiet for a second, lost in thought, and though it troubles me to tell you this, I almost saw his point, yet only for an instant, for what he said next was enough to straighten a sane man's hair. "Now that I think of it, you remind me of a colored cabin-boy named Fortunata who was aboard on my first trip to Madagascar."

"He's aboard now?"

"Hell no ... Christ, no." Falcon's brows slammed together. "We ate him."

Slowly, I sat forward in my chair. "Sir?"

"Don't look at me like that. I believe in Christian decency and doing right as much as the next man. I have a family, you know, in Virginia, and the man-eating savages I've seen, who make it a practice, disgust me. But there's not a civilized law that holds water," Falcon's smile flickered briefly, "once you've put to sea." He held the slow, hurt sidelong look he'd given me, then began finger-stuffing his nightshirt into breeches that might have been tailored for a child. "We ran into a Spanish galleon, and sank her, thank God—we'd have swung for smuggling if we hadn't—but she left us damaged and with half the crew dead. The foremast was gone, the main-yard sprung, and our rigging hung in elf-locks. 'Twas an awful fight, I tell you, and we drifted for days without food or fresh water." Falcon squirreled closer to me, his eyes brighter, wilder than I'd seen them yet. "The sea does things to yer head, Calhoun, terrible unravelings of belief that ain't in a cultured man's metaphysic. We ate tallow first, then sawdust, stopped up our noses and slurped foul water from the pumps before barbecuing that Negro boy. He was freshly dead, of course, crushed by a falling mast," added Falcon sadly, I thought. "He tasted ... stringy."

Shivering, I rubbed my arms, wondering if just maybe the crew-list for this voyage and the menu might be the same thing for this man. "I'm sorry."

"So was I."

It was silent then, Captain Falcon peering back into his memory of deep-sea cannibalism, a faintly bitter smile twisting his lips and jaw to one side, and I saw something—or thought I did—of myself in him and hated that. Cannibalism at sea was common enough, I knew, but he *enjoyed* telling this tale—enjoyed, as I did, any experience that disrupted the fragile, artificial pattern of life on land. Once at home, I realized, he'd probably boast of his "experiences" at sea, use them to pull rank on those more timid and less vital (so he'd view them) than himself, interrupting a dinner with his wife's parson—some psalm-singing milquetoast—to say, "I've no taste for chicken dumplings tonight after eating cabin-boy, dear," and they'd look at him in both horror and fascination, yes, this above all else did Captain Falcon and his species of world-conquerors thrive upon: the desire to be fascinating objects in the eyes of others.

Even then, as he quietly reflected and paced, tapping the end of his nose, he sneaked a look at me to see with how much reverence or revulsion—it didn't matter either way since both fed the ego—I regarded him. More of the latter, I daresay, but for a man like this, who was so full of himself that he could not speak slowly, or without collapsing one sentence into another, the words spilling out in a rush of brilliant confusion—for an American empire-builder even my revulsion was enough to make him feel singular, special, unique.

"Have that mama's boy Mr. Cringle find you a hammock," said he, "and tell Squibb to put you to work in the kitchen. You'll be his shifter and keep the coppers supplied with water and clean. You won't turn a guinea on this trip, Calhoun, but I'll wager you'll be a man's man when we dock again in New Orleans."

"Thank you, sir." I extended my hand. "Like you, sir?"

"Like me?" It seemed to startle him. "Don't be silly." He barely touched my palm with his fingers. "No, never like me, Calhoun."

That was reassuring to me, though he'd never realize it. I turned and walked slowly to where Cringle stood on watch, for I was still very weak in the knees, and my stomach hadn't stabilized either, continuing to chew upon itself as the Mate led me through a hatchway on the main deck, then farther down, well below the ship's waterline, to a soggy pit that assaulted my senses with the odor of old piss riding on the air beside the sickly sweet stench of decaying timbers. This wet cavity had a name: the orlop, an ammonia-smelling hold with little light and less air, where hammocks swung from mildewed beams and where cargo—sea chests and cable—was stored. He gave me a footlocker and gear, and showed me how to fashion a hammock from sailcloth, but seeing these berths I felt sicker than before. Isadora's cat-ridden rooms were intolerable, no question of that, but in the *Republic*'s orlop only an inch of plank separated my boots from the bottom of the sea. "It's bloody dangerous below," Cringle said, and you didn't need a degree in maritime science to see why.

Down there, in the leaking, wishbone-shaped hull, the fusty hold looked darker than the belly of Jonah's whale; it was divided into a maze of low, layered compartments much like the cross-section of an archaeological dig—level upon level of crawl spaces, galleys, and cramped cells so small we barely had enough room to turn around—and, once the forge was going, the forecastle cookroom, where I was to work, was hotter than the griddles of Hell. Cockroaches I saw everywhere. And rats. All this, however, was like a hotel suite when compared to the Head. It consisted of twelve splintery boards in the bows—a shipboard *pissoir* impossible to use on a rough sea because the foul, malarial soup of human feces from intestines twisted by flux flew up round your feet and splattered overhead when the ship met a head sea. "Either this," Cringle kept his mouth covered with one hand, "or swing your black arse over the side, as the Skipper and I do." His eyes watering, he motioned me to climb back up. "After a month that side of the ship's so rank the authorities at Bangalang make us clean it before we can put to port."

All in all, she was a typical ship, I learned those first few days from Cringle, and by this he meant she was stinking and wet, with sea scurvy and god-awful diseases rampant, but even queerer than all this —strange to me, at least—the *Republic* was physically unstable. She was perpetually flying apart and reforming during the voyage, falling to pieces beneath us, the great sails ripping to rags in high winds, the rot, cracks, and parasites in old wood so cancerously swift, springing up where least expected, that Captain Falcon's crew spent most of their time literally rebuilding the *Republic* as we crawled along the waves. In a word, she was from stem to stern a process. She would not be, Cringle warned me, the same vessel that left New Orleans, it not being in the nature of any ship to remain the same on that thrashing Void called the Atlantic. (Also called the Ethiopic Ocean by some, owing to the trade.) And a seaman's first duty was to keep her afloat at any cost.

His second duty was to stay drunk. Every man "knew the ropes"— specifically, the sheets and halyards that controlled the sails; each knew the ship's parts and principles, and any one of them, from the boatswain's mate to the cabin-boy Tom, could undertake the various duties involved—to hand, reef, or steer—but only a fool would stay sober when he wasn't on watch. The whole Middle Passage, you might say, was one long hangover. It had the character of a four-month binge. And the biggest sot of all, I discovered—the most pitiful rumpot—was Josiah Squibb. Stepping timidly into the grimy cookroom after Cringle left me, my arms over my head in case Squibb pegged something at me for stealing his papers, I found the adjacent spirit-room open and Squibb as polluted as I'd left him in the tavern. The poor devil's head lay on a long table littered with strips of salt pork and brick-like biscuits double-baked back on shore. His parrot was drunk, too, but his voice was not as faint as Squibb's, who was in that advanced stage of alcoholic stupor that severs mind from body, both his eyeballs large as eggs, and glaring blankly into a mug of warm beer, as drunks often do, talking to his reflection. "Josiah," he sniffed. Then answered: "Yes?" "If yuh wants respect, darlin', yuh got to leave the ruddy cup alone, yes yuh do. Yuh wants 'em to respect yuh now, don't yuh?" "Yes," he said, "yes, I do . . ."

'H'lo?" I stepped closer. "Mr. Squibb, are you alright, sir?"

"Do I *look* alright?" He sat scratching under one arm, squinting to see me more clearly. "I'm a wee bit drunk, with dinner to fix, and so help me I can't *do* it!" The movement of looking up tipped him backwards (the ship veering larboard didn't help either), and I was obliged to catch him under his armpits, then pitch him forward. He let his head hang. "Fix me some blackstrap, will ye, then finish up this mess."

"But I've never . . ."

"*Do* it." Squibb filled his cheeks with wind, then he swallowed. "I'll show ye how."

Following his orders, I helped him prepare mess, and mess it was, for the biscuits were hard and full of weevils ("I left two teeth in one of 'em this morning," said Squibb), the salt beef tasted of the barrel in which it had been packed, wasn't helped a whole lot by the onions and peppers I added, and would have been intolerable if not for the beer— each crewman, he said, consumed a gallon a day, but in Squibb's case it was more like three. He was, had been, an alcoholic since his first voyage at the age of eleven, though he wasn't exactly certain of his age, and precious little else when he was pickled, which was every waking hour as it turned out. His lips kept the set smile of a lush. There was no risk in his recognizing me from the tavern; he had trouble keeping track of my identity from one hour to the next. And, sad to say, this was probably Squibb's last voyage. Only a slaver would have him. His right foot was dead. He'd drunkenly stepped off a mizzentop during his last trip, having forgotten where he was, fell nine fathoms, and miraculously landed on his right foot. Which shattered. Where bone had been Squibb now had a metal rod. He limped, of course. Like most fat people he wore his shirt outside his trousers whenever possible. He was slow, useless except in the cookroom, with lumps and udders from liquor in his face: a liability at sea, but what sailor could not see in Josiah Squibb his own portrait in years to come if Providence turned her back? As for his parrot, he was more or less the cook's shadow, having his bawdy humor, and even asked me occasionally, "You had any lately, Mate?"

"Aye," said Squibb, sipping blackstrap as I slopped salmagundy into buckets to haul to the great cabin. "I've *seen* some things, laddie. Reason I look so bad is 'cause I've been livin'."

That made me pause in the doorway. Like Captain Falcon, like me and so many other modern people (except Isadora) he seemed to hunger for "experience" as the bourgeois Creoles desired possessions. Believing ourselves better than that, too refined to crave gross, physical things, we heaped and hived "experiences" instead, as Madame Toulouse, I'd heard, filled her rooms with imported furniture, as if *life* was a commodity, a *thing* we could cram into ourselves. I was tempted to ask him about his "experiences," to have him share and display them before me like show-and-tell at school. Instead, I asked:

"Was it worth it?"

He flinched back. "How do you mean?"

"Are you a better man for all that fast living?"

Squibb stared at me, growing sober now. "Yer a strange one, Illinois. Naw, darlin', I can't say better." He laughed suddenly, but with little humor. "Ask my wives—all five of 'em—and they'd probably say I'm worse for it."

"Five, is it now?"

"Or six." Squibb shrugged. "I lose count. I gets drunk, ye know, and I forgets I'm married, and a woman comes along, and before I knows it I've proposed again, and do ye know what's odd? I keeps fallin' in love with the same kinda woman ovah and ovah again. They all look like my wife Maud—God rest her—when we first met. She was a pretty li'l thing. She ruined me, ye know. Spoiled me. I mean, Maud didn't even mind when I broke wind under the bedsheets: you *know* that's love, darlin'. She had long, dark hair, a waist no bigger than that," he snapped his fingers, "and eyes dark as wine—they all do. They could be her sisters, for all the diff'rence, and damned if I don't slip sometimes 'n' call 'em by the pet name I give her—Stinky." He sighed, perplexed, and rapped his temples with the heel of his palm, as if to shake his brain back in place. "Ain't the quantity of experiences that count I sometimes think, Illinois, but the quality. It's sorta like I keep lookin' for Stinky when she was seventeen so I kin do right by her this time."

I left him still mumbling into his cup, and Squibb, I'm sure, didn't notice my absence for an hour. But what he'd said stuck to me like a barnacle. It seemed so Sisyphean, this endless seeking of a single woman's love—the vision of the first girl who snared his heart—in all others, because they would change, grow old, and he'd again be on a quixotic, Parmenidian quest for beauty beyond the reach of Becoming. Yet, he seemed ironically faithful, too, despite his several wives, his devotion to Stinky as deep as any monk's for the Virgin. A peculiar man, this Josiah Squibb, I thought, though really no stranger than the others in Captain Falcon's ragtag crew. We were forty of a company. And we'd all blundered, failed at bourgeois life in one way or another —we were, to tell the truth, all refugees from responsibility and, like social misfits ever pushing westward to escape citified life, took to the sea as the last frontier that welcomed miscreants, dreamers, and fools. Only one sailor the Mate warned me to stay away from, a dark midshipman, clean-shaven, with thin brown hair and the air of a parson about him. Cringle pointed him out to me as he tied dead-eyes down the deck from where we stood. "That'll be Nathaniel Meadows," whispered Cringle, "and I'd not cross him, if I were you."

I turned to give him a better look; Cringle swung me around.

"Don't *stare* at him, fool!"

"He doesn't look dangerous," I said.

"Then," said he, "your judgment of character is worse than your cooking. Meadows signed on to escape the authorities in Kentucky. He murdered his whole family while they slept, according to the Skipper. Axed them all. The family dog, two cows, and a goat, too."

I tried to swallow. Failed. "Why?"

"D'ye care to stroll up 'n' ask him?"

"Oh no... wouldn't think of prying. Hardly my business, you know, that sort of thing..."

The Mate smiled. "Smart boy."

Slowly, I gained my sea legs. By and by, I learned to keep my dinner down and keep up my end in the cookroom and on deck with this crew of American degenerates and dregs; but there's little point in describing individually the other men on board, for the voyage to Africa was uneventful, the men on ship capable at their specialties, and not one of them would live to again see New Orleans.

Only Cringle, I suppose, sensed what was coming. He had a sixth sense about disaster. Ankle-deep in deckwash, he'd stand by the bowsprit some nights in the light of a candle lanthorn, wearing a woolen fearnaught to blunt the teeth of the wind, and stare. Just stare. The matter of fact is that Cringle, more than all the others, was out of place: an officer by accident, he seemed, whose precise speech the crew saw as pomposity, whose sensitivity Captain Falcon read as weakness. The *Republic* was, above all else, a ship of *men*. Without the civilizing presence of women, everyone felt the pressure, the locker-room imperative to prove himself equal to a vague standard of manliness in order to be judged "regular." To fail at this in the eyes of the other men could, I needn't tell you, make your life at sea (in prison or a boy's orphanage) quite miserable. Who wanted to be known as a wimp? It led to posturing among the crew, a tendency to turn themselves into caricatures of the concept of maleness: to strut, keep their chests stuck out and stomachs sucked in, and talk monosyllabically in surly mumbles or grunts because being good at language was—or so male virtues said—womanly. Lord knows, this front was hard to maintain for very long. You had to *work* at being manly; it took more effort, in a way, than rigging sails. The crewmen had drinking contests. They gambled on who could piss the farthest over the rail, or on whose uncircumcized schlong was the longest, and far into the night lie awake in their hammocks swapping jokes about nuns sitting on candles (and some of these, I must confess, weren't all that bad, even memorable, such as one Squibb told one night:

Q: What's the difference between a dog and a fox?

A: About four drinks).

But Cringle kept his distance; the competition to prove the purity of one's gender, I'm guessing, made him uncomfortable, even melancholy, and this cost him the respect of the others, who claimed the Mate, at age twenty-nine, was canned goods. A virgin. Little wonder then that he was relaxed only when alone, there on watch, or reading, or talking with me once he learned that I'd grown up in the household of a (Thomist) theologian.

"They can't feel it," he said the night before we sighted land, looking back from the rail to where two men were carousing around a lantern. His gaze drifted from me back toward row after row of white-maned, foamy waves. That night the sea was full of explosions, rumblings deep as the earth tremors I'd learned to fear in southern Illinois, like the Devil knocking on the ground's thin crust. "Three-quarters of the world's surface," said Cringle, "is covered by that formless Naught, and I dislike it, Calhoun, being hemmed in by Nothing, this bottomless chaos breeding all manner of monstrosities and creatures that defy civilized law. These waters are littered with wrecked vessels. And I've seen monsters, oh yes, such things are real down there." He laughed, bleakly. "Down there, reality fits more the dreams of slugs and snakes than men. 'Tis frightening to me sometimes," he added, looking from me to his feet, "that all our reasoning and works are so provisional, so damned fragile, and someday we pass away like the stain of breath on a mirror and sink back into *that* from whence we've come." He fumbled through his pockets for his pipe, then puffed hard to get it going. "They skim along the surface, the others, they have no feeling for what the sea *is*." He gave a slow, Byronic sigh. "Sometimes I envy them for their stupidity."

When he talked like this he frightened me. I wondered if the others were right about him being weak, or enfeebled somehow, and I hardly knew how to reply. "We'll be on land soon enough. I heard Squibb say we'd put to at the factory within the week."

The Mate smiled gently as if I'd said something stupid. "We're taking on Allmuseri tribesmen, Calhoun. Not Ashanti. Nor even Kru or Hausa—them, at least, I can understand. Have you ever seen an Allmuseri?"

I had to admit that I had not.

"Don't feel bad." His smile vanished. "Few men have. Arab traders will bring them from the interior, I'm told, because no European has been to their village and lived to tell of it. They are an old people. Older, some say, than the world itself, people who existed when the planet—the galaxy, even—was a ball of fire and steam. And not like us at all. No, not like you either, though you are black. In all the records, there is but one sentence about these Allmuseri, and that from a Spanish explorer named Rafael Garcia, whose home is now an institution for the incurably insane in Havana." He was silent again, biting down hard on the stem of his pipe. "I do not feel good about this cargo, Calhoun."

"That sentence," I asked him. "What did Garcia say?"

Cringle stared back to the sea, leaning on the rail, his voice blurred, then obliterated by the wind; I had to strain to hear him. "Sorcerers!" he said. "They're a whole tribe—men, women, and tykes—of devil-worshipping, spell-casting wizards."

from *Ghost of the Sun*

Harry Mark Petrakis

    Autumn of the year, 1974. An Olympic Airways flight spanning the ocean from Greece to America. Matsoukas passed the hours reading, twisting fitfully in the window seat that was too cramped for his big body. Every hour he rose, squeezing past the taciturn man and anxious old woman who occupied the center and aisle seats in his row. For a while he exercised his aching feet and legs by limping up and down the aisle. When he pressed back into his seat, apologizing to his rowmates, the man grunted and the old woman sighed.
    Midway across the ocean the attendants served dinner and he drank a split of wine. Afterwards he drifted into restless sleep dismembered by visions of great silver wings plummeting toward the earth. He woke gratefully as the pilot's voice announced their impending arrival in Chicago.
    The plane began its descent, shattering the dense, swirling clouds. For a buoyant moment he felt their cabin floating on a cushion of foam. When they cleared the clouds, his view encompassed the city he hadn't seen in eight years.
    With his forehead pressed against the window he tracked the jagged shoreline of the lake running south and east to the steelmills in Gary where he'd once labored. Following the shoreline back to the city, the downtown area flourished with skyscrapers he couldn't remember. Fanning out from the Loop were the residential neighborhoods, and

the parks where they picnicked in summer when his children were young. He was shaken at the nostalgia suddenly evoked in his heart.

The wheels of the plane struck the ground with a jolt and then bumped along the runway. When the thrust of the jets was reversed, noise roaring through the cabin, the old woman beside him fervently made her cross. As their plane taxied toward the terminal, he patted her arm in reassurance.

Matsoukas remained seated until the aisles were clear before he rose and pulled down his cap and jacket. The hours of confinement aggravating his limp, he lurched stiffly from the plane.

Avoiding the surge of passengers moving toward the baggage areas, he sat down in a deserted boarding section. Staring out the high windows, he watched planes arriving and departing. The tumult of loudspeakers faded and he slipped back to a garlanded dawn eight years earlier when he'd carried his seven-year-old son, Stavros, aboard a plane for Greece.

The doctors had told him his son was dying but Matsoukas scorned their dark prognosis. He believed the resurrective fire of the Aegean sun would heal his child of the illness and the dreadful seizures he had suffered since his birth.

For a while it seemed his faith would prevail. Each day they sat for hours in the sun, overlooking the radiance of the sea, and it seemed to him that his son was a little stronger. Then, on a night when he slept beside him, his son's strangled shriek woke Matsoukas. When he embraced him he felt the small body fiery with fever. Almost at once the child suffered a seizure. Matsoukas held his heaving, thrashing body for only an instant before he felt the frail arms and legs go limp. When he realized his son was dead, he screamed so piercing and spirit-wrenching a cry, he thought he'd never utter any sound on earth again.

The villagers knocked on the doors and windows but he warned them away. He sat with his son through the night, kissing and caressing the boy's face and fingers. At daylight he left the room to make secret arrangements to have his son cremated. Later he chartered a boat and, at dawn, he sailed beyond the harbor as the ascending, grieving sun turned the sea into flame. He scattered his son's ashes across the water so the wind and tides might carry the boy's soul in eternal journeys around the earth he'd never traveled in life.

Matsoukas picked up his single suitcase from the baggage claim and cleared through customs. He rode a bus to the Palmer House and took a taxi from there to Halsted Street. Arriving in the neighborhood where he'd spent so many years, he was shocked because everything was changed. The Tegea grocery owned by the dyspeptic Akragas from whom he'd rented his second floor counseling office had been replaced by a souvenir shop selling brass and plaster replicas of the gods and heroes of Greece. The Delphian coffeehouse had been transformed into a garish restaurant whose windows held blown-up photographs of belly-dancers with fleshy, alabaster thighs. The bakery from which the Widow Anthoula had once sweetened the bitter hungers of the world was now a travel agency, cerulean posters of sunny Aegean seaports beckoning from the window. Standing before the glass, Matsoukas nodded at the dour young woman who sat at a desk inside the shop.

"I've been there," Matsoukas said. In the glass his reflection shrugged.

He rented a room for a week in the Royal Arms hotel on Jackson Boulevard. He remembered that shabby establishment because his friend, the dealer, Cicero, had resided there for a while. Emerging from the elevator onto the fifth floor, he inhaled the familiar odors of garlic and wine. That primal aroma hadn't changed. He also recalled a phonograph scratching a Greek ballad while, in another enclosure, a man and woman argued vehemently. As he unlocked the door of his room at the end of the corridor, from the adjoining room he heard a baby crying, its voice echoing plaintively through the thin walls.

His own chamber was musty as a tomb and he hurried to raise the solitary window for air. Afterwards, he sprawled wearily across the bed, inhaling the odors of futility and spent desire that rose from the lumpy mattress. Staring at the ceiling, he had an eerie feeling he was still suspended in the sky between Greece and America.

"You're on the ground, Matsoukas," he muttered. "The earth and your battered carcass have once more been joined."

For a while then he slept and was quickly betrayed by a dream that brought him a horde from his past, as if furious they'd missed him at the airport. There was his former wife Caliope (her dark beauty loomed before the rest), his daughters, Faith and Hope, the Widow Anthoula, Falconis, Youssouf the Turk, others whose faces he remembered but whose names he'd forgotten. They swarmed about his bed, clamoring for reasons why he'd returned. He was relieved when the baby crying in the next room woke him.

His room had grown dark except for tracings of light from the window through the railings of the fire escape. He rose from the bed and stared down at Halsted Street. The gleaming neon signs of the restaurants flashed scarlet and yellow streamers into the sky.

Showered and dressed in clean underwear and a fresh shirt, as he left his room he heard the baby still crying, its voice grown hoarser. For an uneasy moment he listened outside the door, wondering if the infant were alone. He was reassured when he heard a lulling voice between the baby's cries.

He ate macaroni and salad in one of the Greek restaurants. At an adjoining table a granite-faced old man had finished his dinner and was reading a Greek newspaper. From time to time, he stared at Matsoukas.

"To your good health, Barba," Matsoukas raised his glass of wine in a greeting to the old man.

"Drink to your own health," the old man answered gruffly. "I saw you limping in."

"You're right, Barba," Matsoukas smiled. "In a Delphian footrace, you'd lap me twice. Let me buy you a drink then so we'll toast my health."

The old man ordered an ouzo and folded his paper.

"I've just returned to this city after a long absence," Matsoukas said. "What's happening here now?"

"The politicians remain corrupt and the inhabitants violent," the old man said.

"That's the same then," Matsoukas said. "What else?"

"Nothing that concerns me as long as I can eat, drink and shit."

Matsoukas nodded, admiring that lucid summary of life.

"Tell me, Barba, have you lived in this neighborhood for long?"

"Long enough."

"Do you recall a bakery owned by a blooming widow named Anthoula?"

The old man shook his head.

"What about a grocery owned by a wretch named Akragas?"

The old man stared at him in silence.

"You must remember a horsebetting establishment run by a nervous Macedonian named Falconis," Matsoukas said, growing desperate. "A music store in front was a concealment for gambling in the back room."

The old man finished his ouzo and rose, jamming his folded newspaper under his arm.

"Never heard of any of them," he said. "How long have you been gone?"

"About eight years," Matsoukas said.

"If nothing you remember is left here, why did you bother coming back?"

Why had he come back? Perhaps the truth wasn't clear but manyfaceted and ambiguous. He ordered another cognac and coffee, reluctant to leave the warmth and light of the restaurant. Many of the patrons were young people casually dressed in jackets and sweaters. He noticed a pretty blonde girl near the age of his daughters, Faith and Hope. He'd be seeing them for the first time as young women. How would they respond to the reappearance of a father they thought had abandoned them and who they might have begun to believe was dead?

After his son's death, he stayed on in Greece. In her letters to him, held for him at a hotel in Athens, his wife, Caliope, enclosed snapshots of their daughters while pleading for him to return. In less than a year he hardly recognized the children he'd left behind. He yearned to see them but he senselessly kept postponing the journey. He knew it was because he still mourned his son and the vistas of mountains and sky and sea were somehow consoling.

In his moments of wild grief, the sight of a tiny bird still alive while his son was dead could make him weep. He contrived an obdurate fantasy that his son was with his mother and sisters in America. They'd all be reunited when Matsoukas returned home. To maintain that illusion he avoided going home. He wandered across Greece, working for farmers in orchards and fields, relishing the exhaustion of his body at night that let him sleep soundly.

When he had been in Greece a little less than two years, a junta of colonels overthrew the government and took power. All these fulminations took place in Athens, a world away from the village near Kalavryta where he dwelt. In that hamlet little seemed changed except for the appearance of a number of oversized banners proclaiming GOD, NATION, FAMILY. In addition, the policemen in the village walked with additional swagger and bravado, as if they'd just inherited the earth.

He felt ready, suddenly, to return to America. He started to write Caliope and then decided he would surprise her and his daughters. Before departing for Athens and then America, he made a farewell visit to the rugged mountains of Epirus where he had fought with the partisans against the Nazis during their occupation of Greece. He placed wildflowers at the site of battles where he'd lost comrades, brave men borne to heaven in the volcano's breath of the struggle for freedom.

He descended to the old city of Ioannina, on his way back to Athens. In the hotel where he stayed he met a zestful Bulgarian named Rashgora who persuaded Matsoukas to join a game of poker he had set up with several extremely solvent sheiks from Saudi Arabia and Yemen. The sheiks were canny players but Matsoukas was better and, as he began to win, his passion for the cards returned. For several days, cloistered in one of the suites of the hotel, Matsoukas abandoned any desire for food or need to sleep in the whirlwind of wagering larger and larger stakes. Rashgora had been winning, as well, and when the game finally broke up on the fourth day, each man had won almost $25,000.

Matsoukas was delighted at being able to return to his family with his new wealth. The money seemed to justify his having remained in Greece. He deposited his winnings in dollars into an American bank and, after a final heartfelt binge with Rashgora, he flew to Athens.

His last evening in Greece, he celebrated by buying rounds of drinks for the patrons of a taverna in Piraeus. The festivities were disrupted when several oversized louts began abusing a young farmer who refused to give up his table to them. Matsoukas had gone genially to the young farmer's aid and briskly hurled the louts into the street. The taverna owner warned Matsoukas that the hoodlums worked for the local police and would probably return with them. The farmer fled but some perverse pride made Matsoukas remain, basking in the dipsomanic admiration of the taverna patrons who praised his fearlessness. A short while later the louts returned with a squad of police who hauled him off to the station. When they checked his fingerprints and military record and discovered he'd fought with the partisans, they questioned him zealously about his Communist affiliations and how often he'd visited the Soviet Union. He scorned and defied them until they beat and kicked him unconscious. When he wakened, bleeding and sore, he was being transported in a truck with a group of silent, wretched prisoners. One of them mustered the courage to whisper to Matsoukas they were being transported to the dreaded Bouboulinas prison.

For nearly five years, an interminable, nightmarish span of time, Matsoukas remained in prison. In the beginning he raged against his captors, demanding they bring him to trial or else release him. When he asked for a lawyer or to see a representative of the American Embassy, they laughed at him. He came to understand that the prison was filled with political prisoners without hope for a trial or freedom.

As the months extended into years and he wasn't permitted to write a letter to his family, his rage turned to despair and he feared he'd go mad. He spent hours thinking of his daughters and Caliope, recalling every holiday and picnic they'd shared. As he envisioned them, he exercised his arms and legs, doing push-ups and deep knee bends. Realizing it was important to occupy his thoughts, he recalled and recited poetry and plays he knew by heart. Near the end of his first year of imprisonment, he salvaged the fragment of a broken cup and used it to scratch the outline of a chessboard on the stone floor of his cell. He settled the squares with imaginary pawns, bishops, knights and queens. In the beginning he could not encompass the pieces but as he disciplined his concentration, he was able to play the phantom pieces against illusory opponents. Sometimes these ghostly games lasted for days and nights.

All this time his interrogations continued, conducted once or twice a week by different policemen who asked identical questions about his affiliation with radicals plotting the overthrow of the government. When he denied those charges, they beat him for lying. If he remained silent, they beat him for obstinacy. On those days they left him alone, hearing the screams from other cells, he knew the brutes remained busy.

Some policemen beat him routinely and some beat him zealously but, at the beginning of his fourth year of imprisonment, a new interrogator appeared, a monster sergeant of police named Farmakis.

The first time Farmakis questioned Matsoukas, he greeted him as warmly as if they had been old friends, praising Matsoukas for his obdurance and resolve.

"You're a remarkable man," he said with a droll wink. "All my associates admit they haven't been able to obtain a shred of any confession from you about your guilt. We're all Greeks, God be praised, and can admire courage even in our enemies and the enemies of our beloved Nation. Don't you agree?"

"I'm not your enemy or the enemy of our beloved Nation," Matsoukas tried to match the man's amiability of voice. "I candidly feel I've had enough of your hospitality, God be praised, and would like to be set free."

"You have wit as well as courage!" Farmakis laughed buoyantly. "You know, I must also tell you you bear an uncanny resemblance to the actor, Anthony Quinn. Same size physique, same majestic head. Did you see him in *Zorba?*" Without waiting for Matsoukas to respond, Farmakis continued. "I enjoyed his splendid performance but his philosophy was grossly in error. The beginning and end of life must be order, discipline, obedience to authority."

"You have forgotten freedom," Matsoukas said.

"Wonderful!" Farmakis cried. "You even think like Zorba! But believe me, my friend, we'll change that. Providence has brought us together for your reformation. Up to now you've been beaten by peasants in shiny buttons. But in me you will find an artist of chastisement, a Picasso of persuasion! My area of incomparable skill is the Falanga."

That first day he demonstrated his craftsmanship to Matsoukas the way a master would display his technique to an apprentice. Matsoukas was strapped to a bench and his shoes and socks removed. Using sticks of varying thickness and, from time to time, a narrow iron bar, Farmakis briskly beat the soles of his bare feet. After about a dozen blows the pain became so piercing Matsoukas believed he was being battered on the crown of his head.

"That's the beauty of the Falanga!" Farmakis told him proudly at the end of their first session. "The feet shoot impulses of pain through every nerve and muscle until you feel your eyeballs about to explode! The secret, you understand, is to alternate light and hard blows, spacing them enough to keep the subject conscious. I tell you with unqualified admiration I couldn't believe how many blows you took before passing out! I suspect Zorba too would have shown such endurance! Most of these cowardly pisspots pass out after a few blows!"

In the sessions which followed, two or three times a week, Farmakis beat Matsoukas with unflagging dedication. During intervals between beatings, Farmakis allowed him to sit up, offering him a cigarette and a cup of coffee, while speaking to him passionately about his craft.

"The Falanga, I admit, was creatively initiated among the followers of General Franco in Spain. But in the beloved motherland of our revered leader, Colonel Papadopoulos, I am unquestioned master! I could show you letters from the Commissioner of Police commending me for the hundreds of confessions I've obtained from obdurate prisoners!"

The recital of his accomplishments so moved Farmakis that, for the first time, Matsoukas caught a glint of tears in his tormentor's eyes.

Meanwhile, his hours of punishment continued through a purgatory of pain. As he grew weaker, he began losing consciousness earlier in the beatings. Farmakis and an aide hauled him to his feet and made him wave his arms like windmills to restore his circulation.

"Pull yourself together, man!" Farmakis pleaded. "Everyone in the prison is talking about your fortitude and courage! Prisoners and guards are wagering that you'll be my first failure by dying before confessing! Let's provide them, I implore you, an epic contest they'll never forget! For the sake of the Greece we both love, don't give up on me now!"

Matsoukas no longer understood why he endured the punishment and torture without breaking down and begging for mercy. In some enigmatic violation of sanity, he felt he couldn't let Greece and Farmakis down. Meanwhile, desperate to avoid further suffering, he was eager to confess to anything they wished him to say. His confession, he discovered to his despair, wasn't relevant any longer. Farmakis and he were engaged in a battle of Titans and the Falanga continued.

He felt his spirit waning, his soul shuddering like a broken lyre. Resigning himself to dying he thought with thankfulness of being reunited with his son. A small human remorse remained when he considered that even after he had ceased to exist, olives would ripen again, almond trees would blossom, and harvests would be reaped.

When his last hope and fear were gone, soldiers opened the door of his cell one morning and told him he was liberated. He contemplated them mutely, thinking them some fiendish variation of the Falanga. Finally, hearing the cries and shouts of other prisoners, he understood he was really free. Later, he heard the news that the junta had attempted a coup against Archbishop Makarios of Cyprus, trying to unite that island with Greece. The action had provoked Turkey to invade Cyprus, driving tens of thousands of Greek Cypriots from their farms and homes. The threat of war with Turkey caused the junta's collapse. A new government was being formed under the exiled, democratic Constantine Karamanlis.

Matsoukas asked about Farmakis. But while a number of the prison police had been arrested by the soldiers, that elusive artist and patriot had escaped.

Matsoukas was transferred to a hospital where he remained for about a month. He had been in such fine physical condition before his imprisonment that he had escaped mortal injury. But he had lost forty pounds, had incurred injury to his kidneys and the bones and nerves in both his feet had been shattered. The doctors told him he'd limp and endure severe pain from those extremities for the rest of his life.

He brooded about his misfortune and the years he'd spent in prison until he read newspaper stories of the suffering of the refugees on Cyprus. From other patients he also heard something of what Greece had endured during his years in prison including the massacre of thirty-two young students and the wounding of hundreds of others when the junta sent tanks against the Athens Polytechnic school in 1973. He suddenly felt his own afflictions trivial beside the agony and suffering of others.

Meanwhile, during his first days in the hospital he had sent a messenger to inquire for letters at the hotel that had held his mail in the past. No correspondence from his family could be found. He tried to phone Caliope in America but there wasn't any record of her residence in Chicago. He sent her a wire at the last address he had from her, but heard nothing in reply.

When he was discharged from the hospital, he returned to the hotel a second time and implored the owner to make another search. After foraging among boxes in the basement, the owner's wife discovered a packet of about a dozen letters addressed to him. All of them were from Caliope.

Seated in a corner of the lobby, his fingers trembling, he opened them in order of their postmarks. His wife's first letters were pleas for him to return and bewildered queries about the reason for his silence. Her letters grew bitter and then angry when she wrote she'd asked the U.S. State Department to communicate with the Greek government about him. They found no record of his whereabouts in Greece but cited a report from the Greek police who confirmed they'd located a prostitute who confessed Matsoukas had been her lover and had told her he never wished to return to America.

The last two letters informed Matsoukas that Caliope had filed for divorce by reason of his desertion. Her final letter, dated a year later, tersely let him know she was being remarried to a real estate broker named Sophocles Gravoulis, an honest, decent man who'd look after her and the children.

For a long time Matsoukas didn't move from the lobby chair. He read the letters again, with disbelief, then with indignation, and, finally, with outrage. Not satisfied with imprisoning him unjustly, with his torture at the cudgels of Farmakis, the perverse and pitiless authorities had contrived to destroy his memory for his family by producing a harlot to make false witness against him. He was enraged at them and then transferred his rage to the usurper who'd exploited his misfortunes and stolen his wife and children. For an instant his hate for that man matched his hate for Farmakis.

He vowed he'd fly at once to America and search out Caliope. He'd inform her of his imprisonment, insist her remarriage wasn't legal or fair and demand the marauder be banished from her life. He fervently rehearsed the words he'd use to shame her lack of faith.

Then a melancholy wind of reason and resignation dispersed his anger. He'd had almost two years to return from Greece to his family before he'd been imprisoned. All that time Caliope had pleaded with him to come home. The grim truth was that while the woman the police claimed to have found was a lie, he hadn't been totally faithful to his wife. There'd been a few lonely, desperate nights when he couldn't resist the warmth of a fleeting human contact. Yet, in his heart, he never ceased loving Caliope and knew she'd remained virtuous and devoted to him until her divorce. If she were happy now and settled into a new life, it would be inhuman to make a tardy and harsh claim upon her. There was even a murderous justice in losing her. In a classical period, another Sophocles had written, "Men of ill judgment oft ignore the good that lies within their hands until they have lost it."

The restaurant had filled with late-evening patrons. Matsoukas ignored the young waiter glaring at him to relinquish his table and lit another cigarette, blowing rings of smoke into the air.

Why had he come back? At first, he rationalized, it was to pursue Farmakis, who had fled, he was told, with other police officials to America. He spent hours relishing the dark joy of his vengeance when he located that monster.

But he understood there were other compelling reasons besides vengeance. Although only a few months had passed since he had read the letters from Caliope, and despite his decision not to intrude into her life, he hadn't anticipated the pervasive loneliness of his days and nights. He felt spiritless and unmoored, the years in prison making him aware how fragile was a man's life on earth. He yearned to see and hold his daughters in his arms, and to explain the reason for his silence to Caliope. She might be grateful to know he was alive.

Finally, he'd always conceived of his life as an epic journey and himself as a mortal, despite his flaws, darkly wise and rudely great. Believing that by indignities men might come to dignity, he vowed not to allow the prison nightmare to deflect him from living out his destiny. By returning to America, he might reinforce the power and vision of his dreams.

When he returned to the hotel, the baby in the adjoining room was quiet. He stretched out across his bed, restlessly resisting sleep. When the baby cried again, he understood he'd been waiting for that cry. The infant's wails carried through the walls and, from the corridor, a door banged open and a man shouted a curse.

Matsoukas left his room, bristling at the sight of a stocky Neanderthal in an undershirt further down the hall.

"Is that damn kid gonna squawk all night?" the man asked with a snarl.

"Crying is therapeutic in an infant's life, old sport," Matsoukas said brusquely. "Stuff a little cotton into your tender drums and remember even you were once a bawling baby."

The man glared at him and went back into his room, banging the door once more.

Matsoukas knocked gently on the door of the baby's room. When there wasn't any response, he knocked again. Between the baby's cries, he heard a tense, muffled voice.

"I'm your neighbor," Matsoukas said. "I'm in the room next door."

The door opened on a chain. He glimpsed a girl's cautious face, pale in the shadows, under tousled brown hair. He smiled to reassure her.

"Can I help in any way?"

"My baby has a cold and a little fever," she said nervously. "We'll be all right, thank you." She started to close the door and paused. "I'm sorry if his crying is disturbing you."

"His crying isn't bothering me at all," Matsoukas said. "Perhaps I could go down and bring him some hot tea. That may soothe him."

Without waiting for the girl to consent, he took the elevator to the lobby and walked a block to an all-night lunchroom. He bought a container of tea with sugar and lemon and a packet of aspirin. Anxious to keep the tea warm, he hurried back to the hotel, aggravated at his limp, which impeded his speed.

When he knocked on the girl's door a second time, she opened it again on the chain.

"I've brought the child some tea and aspirin," he said and he tried to slip the bag through the opening but it wouldn't fit. She made no move to unlatch the chain.

"I think he'll be all right," she said. "Thanks anyway."

"The tea and aspirin will help him if he has a fever," Matsoukas said. He gestured in reassurance. "I'll leave the bag here on the floor outside your room and go back to my own room. When I knock on your wall you can take it inside."

He placed the bag on the floor and felt her watching him.

"Wait, please," she said in a low voice. She closed the door and he heard her release the chain. As he picked up the bag, she opened the door. She was young, no more than nineteen or twenty, barefooted and clad in a yellow cotton robe over her nightgown. Her pale face was almost obscured within clusters of chestnut brown hair that tumbled about her shoulders. Her eyes were large and also brown and wary as the eyes of a doe.

He started to hand her the bag. She stepped back, opening the door wider.

"You can come in."

"Are you sure?" he asked.

"Yes," she said. "I was just nervous. I'm sorry."

"You should be careful," Matsoukas said. He stepped into the room that was as cramped and bleak as his own cubicle, the stale air holding the odors of the baby's excretions.

He stepped closer to the child who lay in the center of the double bed. Matsoukas knew at once it was a boy, his head crowned with light, silky hair, his eyes a softer brown than the girl's eyes. The fever and crying had wearied him and puffs of air fluttered through his throat as soundless as a sparrow's breath.

"I'll crush one of the aspirin into a spoon of tea," the girl said. After she had prepared it, she brought it to the bed.

"I can hold the baby for you," Matsoukas said.

She stared at him in a mute plea that his kindness be sincere.

"It will be all right," he smiled. "During the American Revolutionary War, I was a father too."

Her tension seemed to ease. Matsoukas carefully raised the child in his arms, hoping he wouldn't begin to cry again. He was surprised how weightlessly the infant rested in his grasp. He cradled him gently while the girl slipped a spoonful of tea between the baby's lips. A trickle ran down his chin.

He felt reluctant to put the child back on the bed. At that moment, from the street below the hotel, tires squealed and glass shattered. The girl trembled and moved to take the child from his arms. She placed him again in the bed, adjusting his blanket gently, her fingers softly and slowly caressing the baby's temples and cheeks. Feeling suddenly as if he were an intruder, Matsoukas turned to leave.

"You were kind to help us," the girl said. "Thank you."

"Babies are the future of our species and must always be helped," Matsoukas said gravely. "Now, if you need me, just knock on that wall. I'm a light sleeper and I'll hear you."

He stepped into the corridor and closed the door behind him. He heard her hesitate just an instant and then she slipped on the chain.

Matsoukas undressed and climbed into bed. From the adjoining room he heard the bedsprings creaking and imagined the young mother and infant nestled together. He recalled the girl's warm eyes and the way her fingers caressed her son. The lines from a poem came to him, "... and peasant girls with youthful eyes and hands that offer early flowers."

He recalled with delight holding the baby. He wondered what they were doing in the dismal hotel, unable to fathom any father willingly separating himself from such a child.

Still clinging to the baby's warmth, he settled to sleep. Trying to relax, he became conscious of his feet aching, pain knifing up his legs. He twisted vainly for a more comfortable position, longing for rest. Then his drowsiness was banished as the chess pieces of his prison years sprang at him from the darkness. Around his bed whirled the stabbing bishops and swooping rooks, the leaping knights and nimble queens. They renewed the ritual of games he'd played a thousand times while, in their midst, a vision of his dead son drifted like the ghost of a glowing star.

from *Phantom Rider,* a novella in play form

Act I: Shopping

Betty Shiflett

© Betty Shiflett, 1987

Introduction: Rules of the Road

(On a mirror-black, "three-quarter thrust" stage stand three silver touring bicycles at elegant attention. From beneath their wheels, "radiating" stripes of astro-turf *zoom* outward toward us creating an illusion of direction and *speed!* The stage is built in two overlapping levels connected at either side by ramps. At Upper Level, Stage Left, our Stage Mechanic emerges from the blur of shadows, resplendent in his white jump-suit, and immediately busies himself replenishing the Eau de Lilac on the lavender chiffon scarf attached to the old-fashioned stand-up fan with silver grill, which blows in the direction of the bicycles. With artfully economical motions, he sprays scent from a silver-veined perfume bottle directly, proudly into the fan, then leaps to Lower Level, and, coming down to the foot-lights, addresses us with the flourishes of a "carnie barker.")

Prologue

(DRUMROLL...)
Ladies and Gentlemen!
The Rules of the Road!

(CYMBAL!)
In three minutes exactly,
On this very stage,
It will be my pleasure
To present to you —
A "nice" young couple!,
> (Spotlight at Upper Level reveals Woman and Man in leotards and seated on the Stage Right and Center bicycles, respectively.)

Not too young, and not too old
To learn new tricks.

This winsome twosome
(A pair after your own heart)
Will attempt to put together
Those *amazing pieces,*
The puzzle of their lives! — *using,*
Or ignoring, certain "hints"
Dropped by Yours Truly
Into their heated game.

If, when the show is over
(I keep a tight schedule),
Our couple have knit a whole garment
From these events —
> (Strains of "carousel" music accompany the projection of a "brass ring" against the *rear* wall. Man and Woman rise on pedals, reach forward, turning gradually sideways *away from* each other as each grabs for the "brass ring" and misses.)

They win! They get the "brass ring,"
The PERFECT HOUSE in which to
Reign as King and Queen
Happily Ever After!

But if their struggling
Fails to join these bits
In some useful cloak —
Ladies and Gentlemen, this sphere of
Rosy lights will
Take a different shade.

> (Lights on couple dim, then go to BLACK. Man and Woman exit; lights flow up again on empty bicycles. Stage Mechanic leaps to Upper Level and furiously works bicycle bells. Their jingling induces in him a rapt, ecstatic mood in which he continues.)

The "Demo"

From spokes to sprockets,
Handgrips to handlebar bells,
Everything about them rings
Divinely silver!
>(Gives bell a final *prrrrrring!*, jumps to Lower Level where he resumes.)

Nothing else moves... except
>(Snaps his fingers overhead and "clouds" made of nylon parachuting, quilted to puff in all the right places, begin creaking along on the oval track to which they are attached with wires.)

"Blue Cloud"... and "White Cloud"!
Ahh... serenity!
When "Blue" disappears,
"White" returns!

>(Stage Mechanic sweepingly indicates:)

An old-fashioned stand-up fan!
>(Snaps his fingers again, and fan hums as he leaps once more to Upper Level, takes perfume atomizer from his hip pocket and puffs it into the fan. He rushes to exit at Stage Right, and almost immediately re-enters dragging a potted, artificial "lilac bush" with showy, indiscriminate blooms, some of lavender, others of white, depositing it with a *thud!*, opposite fan.)

An artificial Lilac Bush,
Excited by the breeze!
>(Toys with the lavender chiffon scarf as it streams toward the bicycles.)

Very feminine!
>(Producing atomizer, he replenishes scent on the scarf, then sprays it into the fan, enjoying the scented breeze on his face.)

The tantalizing scent
of "Eau de Lilac,"
Ladies and Gentlemen!
Take a whiff!
One... two... three... *SNIFF!*
Very good! Now watch this!
>(He snaps his fingers at the fan; it instantly hums *louder* and begins to oscillate.)

And this... and this!

>(Stage Mechanic rushes over to tinker with the fan... "off," "on," *listens* to it as if to a "heartbeat." Then he jumps down to the Lower Level, points *upward*, snaps his fingers, and both

"clouds" *halt!;* snaps his fingers again, and they resume creaking around on their circuit. He bows deeply, with a sweeping gesture all around, as if to say, *"More good things to come!"* He straightens, and the stage lights begin to come up on one item or area at a time, as he has need of them. He calls for each "item" with a *snap!,* or other gesture.)

The *Black... Skyscraper!*
Looms like perpetual night!
> (He leads us in "hissing!" at a "glowering" building in the background which is a slide projection of a line of skyscrapers, most prominently, this dark building and a "pristine" looking white building topped with spires.)

In glittering contrast—
The *Wrigley Building!*
Shines like a palace!
Verges on doing something
Sensationally beneficial! —
Burst open any minute!
Shower goodness everywhere!

At her joyous, rollicking
Best — Lake Michigan!
> (With another snap of his fingers, a shady, flat-topped Pleasure Excursion Launch filled with customers and replete with flags and a jaunty little uniformed Captain at the helm, rides back and forth parallel to the Chicago skyline, the frothy "wake" and myriad "flags" indicating a direction aiming straight for the foreboding skyscraper.)

Barely controlled "optimism"!,
That's our style!
Van der Rohe, Sullivan, Wright!
The "Cradle of Architecture"!
This is where it'll happen!
ME? TIME'S my specialty,
I keep things movin'!
(Property's a sideline of mine.)

Real estate's the game,
Movin's my "middle name"!
—A livin'?
I don't *make* one, I *take* one!
(Wanna buy a house?)
> (Looks at his watch.)

TIME'S UP!

Ladies and Gentlemen!—Filth! Fireworks!—FUN!

(Our Stage Mechanic at the fan looks into the wings, Stage Right; snaps his fingers, the lights go out!)

Shopping

("Yippieee!!!"—trills from off-stage, in "soprano" tones. Light springs up on a Woman in a red bathing suit pedaling hard on the Stage Right bike, her wheels two blurs of silver spokes, her longish dark hair swinging. She leans determinedly over the handlebars in frowning concentration, though not in irritation or worry. From this moment, we're sucked up in her will and purpose, the whirling of her spokes as she builds an enormous momentum—she stands up, leaning forward pumping, her eyes widen as all three bikes slant up, up, up on their tiltable panels UP!, we expect something *un*-expected to happen and perhaps are a little fearful as she tops the hill. Now her hill's achieved, she switches to easy no-hands pedaling, waving her outstretched arms to touch the very sunshine, balancing, delighted with herself, looking about and beaming everywhere from side to side.... A Man, in a red jump-suit, runs up to the top of the ramp at Stage Right, and mimes eager running at an angle to catch up with her for a moment or two, but then rapidly crosses behind her bike, with a final *hop* to the seat of *his* bike, at Center Stage. Behind him the spotlighted Wrigley Building with its munificent sparkles speeds him into wise decisions and grants him a perfect day. Under the lights the magnificently empty Stage Left bike gleams sparklingly silver. Where the other bikes go, it will accompany; when they tilt, it tilts also, elegantly.)

Woman: (Lightly guiding the silver handlebars, as she drifts back against the *pull* of her bike. With just an *edge* of worry.) I thought you'd never get here! We may be late, you know.

Man: (With cocky, lazy, one-handed pedaling as his voice stays innocent of *any* edge.) Let the asshole wait. All real estate agents are alike, just one thing on the brain: They want to sell you a house. (He taps his temple knowingly, not as a put-down of real estate agents, but rather as one of the world's less arguable facts. *"Asshole"* has been almost a term of endearment.)

Woman: I'd hoped this one would be a little different...

Man: Look! (Jabs the air.) A cardinal!

Woman: I don't see it . . . (She strains every lithe line of her body to see it, following the arc of his arm, as they both try to re-capture the flash of the bird.)

Man: I saw a cardinal up there!, fluttering red . . . (He is awed and honored by the sight as he checks her out for the effects of the scarlet echoes of birds.)

Woman: I wish I'd seen it.

Man: He just exploded off that branch! All red and soaring!

Woman: That branch?

Man: The one next to it.

Woman: That wasn't a cardinal, that was a scarlet tanager.

Man: No way!

Woman: (Bridling.) And why not? My *Birds of Our Nation* says they've been "sighted" this far north. It says, "If you want to *see* scarlet tanagers, you have to *look* for them!"

Man: Is that a fact! (Unwilling to concede her "point," but nonetheless trying to "recoup" his own.) Hey!—We'll see another soon! (Punches her on the arm, "man-to-man"!)

Woman: Maybe . . . (She looks ahead not at the tree-line now, but into this day, rather savoring her first sight of the real estate agent, the chosen implement of her *dreams come true.*)

>(The Stage Mechanic, in the spotless white jump-suit, but not seen by the couple is busy at Stage Left, tinkers with the fan. Stoops, head, ear, close to the whirring blades, like a car mechanic listening "under the hood.")

Woman: I hope the real estate man is nice! . . . and doesn't have a mustache, or smoke cigars, or wear big jazzy class rings, or— (We see she's more salaciously excited by what he *will* do than by these things he "shouldn't" do.)

>(The Stage Mechanic laughs loudly on *"class ring,"* but the couple obviously do not hear him. He stands up, turns the fan finally to *"on,"* and from a small black bag at his feet produces,

with stylized flourishes, the perfume atomizer which he sprays directly into the whirring blades, turning his head a bit with grave practicality to avoid the direct force of the mist. He is not foppish, but hearty and efficient, enjoying what he does and amused by what he hears. He stands honestly admiring the Woman as if she is an essential part of this gorgeous day, and smilingly shakes his head, grinning big.)

Woman: Oooo—(inhaling Eau de Lilac)—I smell something good!—

Man: There it went—(Springing on the pedals, he describes an arc with one hand.)

Woman: What?

Man: Too late! A bluebird.

Woman: (Smugly.) Not a chance.

Man: Ohhhh?

Woman: A "California *jay*." Twice the size! You don't recognize it?

Man: Nice geography! (Exaggeratedly to himself.) I wonder what *Birds of Our Nation* says about *that.*

(The Stage Mechanic slaps his knee, laughing at the Woman's audacity, the Man's wry "come-back," and the resulting "escalation" of their game. He whips the lavender scarf off the fan, copiously dries "tears" of mirth with it, then partially stuffs it into his hip pocket and, deliberately waggling the visible portion of it behind him, exits, Stage Left. Reappears almost immediately, Stage Right, wearing a black derby, checkered coat, huge green class ring which he displays to the front rows suggestively, and a fresh red carnation in his lapel. He has achieved a barrel-chested look. Out of the black bag at his feet he now takes a mustache, applies it to his upper lip, asks us, by pointing silently and mugging, if it's "okay," and, assured that it *is,* "walks" the potted lilac bush over to a position nearer to the couple and "hides" behind it—actually *waiting to be seen,* "leaning" back without visible support, arms folded, one leg jauntily crossed over the other. From time to time, he peeks ostentatiously over the parted branches of the lilac bush, or, *that* failing, cranes head and torso around from behind the bush inviting the attention of the Man and Woman, both totally engrossed in winning the next "point"; both oblivious to the subtle blandishments of the Mechanic. Seeing no results from his "build-up" of maneuvers, he steps out from behind the potted lilac in black derby and full agent's regalia, and raises his black bag forward at attention in an attitude of service. Still *"no dice."* He takes from his black bag a small cellophane-covered package of cigars, unzips the cellophane, crushes it, relishing the crackling noise, and slips three fresh cigars into his outside breast pocket, patting them conspicuously. He looks at the couple curiously—open-faced, intelligent, and alert.)

Man: It's the house that counts.

(The Stage Mechanic as Real Estate Agent "lights up," and, brandishing his cigar, alternately sings and shouts:)

> Houses? Did I hear "HOUSES"?
> (Property's a sideline of mine!)
> What's in a house?
> *Shelter??!!—*
> *Madam!,*
> *Get off the "bottom line"!*

(Taps his temple "knowingly," mocking the Man's earlier gesture, and unfurls from his black bag a small "scroll" from which he announces his "listings":)

> *Have I got houses!* I got houses,
> *Lovely* Houses, *Perfect* Houses,
> Houses of Your *Dreams Come True!*
> House of the Century!
> *Chance of a Life-time!*
> Houses that'll knock your eye out!
> Nothin' showy, (strictly "CLASS"!)
> "Homes of Distinction"!
> Set you apart from the crowd!
> (Nothing radical.)
> Give you that *"leading edge"!*
> Here's something even better,
> *The IDEAL HOU—!*

(He shrugs off the Woman's interruption while lighting a cigar, and, taking a big puff, turns to her; while he makes a great show of smoking, he listens to her attentively; though *she,* apparently, has neither seen nor heard *him.*)

Woman: (Bursting into song.)
> I want a white one.

A big low white house,
With Greek pillars in front,
And crickets playing through
The deep summer nights . . .

And rosy cantaloupe for breakfast
At our big round table,
With sunlight flooding through
White organdy cottage curtains,
And gingerbread balconies!

And out in back,
We'll have a crystal brook running
Over smooth brown stones . . .
You know the kind of stones,
With speckles on them. . . ?

Man: We can't ride that far. They don't sell those in the city.

(He has begun mild calisthenics on the bicycle, using his time well at all times, and they require a certain amount, no more, no less, of his attention, his hands now only rarely on the handlebars as he does stylized versions of calisthenics, waist bends dipping forward then side-to-side . . . now hands on hips, energetically rotating his head to exercise neck muscles. Suddenly the Woman, with only a gurgle of warning, *lurches,* forfeits her balance, and almost takes a nasty spill. The Man suddenly grabs his handlebars and they both vigorously steer toward Stage Left. After a brief but violent struggle with balance, during which, by the Man's gestures and expression, we are somehow made to feel that *he* is largely responsible for keeping them upright, the pair is back on course!

(The Stage Mechanic all this while has warned them of the turn they must make, gesticulating vigorously and pointing them in the right direction, ultimately throwing an arm across his eyes to blank out the awful spill he sees impending. But now he peers out sheepishly at the upright, pedaling couple, exclaims, "My God!", picks up his black bag where he's dropped it on the shoulder of the road, and giving it a little shake up next to his ear to check it—even in the back rows, we hear metallic rattles—returns to his former sunny, alert disposition though it is still apparent that *neither* of the pair has seen him.)

Woman: What do *you* want? (Anxious and afraid that *his* opinion on houses will cancel out *hers.*)

Man: Oh... I'd like some place with a pool table. A long *green* pool table with a Tiffany lamp. They're pretty big, those tables. We might have to hunt for a house with *really big doors!* (He boyishly takes both hands off the handlebars and with arms outstretched, describes *huge doors,* his face brightening then reddening deliberately with the effort, his little joke.)

>(The Stage Mechanic breaks into a loud laugh, slaps a knee again, and takes from his pocket a heavy key ring with many keys, selects *one* with a distinct jangling gesture and resulting noise, inserts it in an imaginary keyhole at Stage Right, and gustily pulls open two huge doors, indicating with a beckoning smile and flourish of his free hand that they should step right inside. When they fail as usual to see him, he closes the double doors ruefully but stoically, locks them, and dusts off his hands, exiting with his black bag, a last sad jangle of his keys.)

Woman: Listen... I think my chain is slipping. (She tests it, gingerly pedaling backward, it slips, and we hear the familiar abrasive rattling noise.) *Damn!*

>(Off she hops at the precise magic point where the Stage Mechanic made his previous attempt to "usher" them in. The Man jumps off, too. As he gallantly swings his straight-kneed leg off his bike, on a sudden mood-switch he offers her his arm, and they enter together the house created by the Stage Mechanic. They are a little "out of sync" with the Stage Mechanic's earlier open-palmed gesture, but still act as if at his command, though they rigorously do not see him waiting watchfully in the shadows at Stage Left. The Woman sails into an immediate inspection of the "house," while the Man trails after her, still intent on his pool conjecture and talking volubly with full gesticulation.)

Man: Boy, oh boy! I'd be good with just a little practice! I could get you a Hobbie Culp pool cue for your birthday, you'd like that, wouldn't you?

Woman: A what...?

>(She strolls preening about the new house, dusting silkily with her fingertips the tops of furniture, window sills, thoughtfully pausing with a sort of pirouette to shake out drapes—then she spies her bicycle over her shoulder and back-tracks abruptly to the spot

where they first entered the new house.

(The Stage Mechanic has just repeated his now more stylized, open-palmed gesture, sweeping *low* before her as the Man trails curiously after, and now he exits with *arch* disappointment when they do not notice. He rattles his keys and swings them promisingly from his index finger as the Woman, squatting at her bike while his feet pass by, examines her chain, runs a finger along it and shakes her head, absently wiping grease from her finger down one bare thigh.)

Woman: It's shot! (She stands up suddenly, pointing at the Man because her chain is shot.) Big doors and pool tables and *winning!*—Is that all you care about? Don't you want to see something nice and pleasant on the *outside* when you come home at night? *You* know . . .

(During her subsequent rapid naming of architectural details, the Stage Mechanic, who has optimistically and usefully re-entered at Stage Left, takes up a playing position in his most elegantly poised manner, and stoops over the table sighting along his cue, opposite the Man at Stage Right side of the imaginary pool table. Our Man not only sees him fully, but is mesmerized instantly into the game, and responds as the Stage Mechanic beckons, *Your turn.* The Mechanic stands back admiring the Man's shot. We hear the crack! of balls, their smooth clacking tumult and chatter, as both men watch the path of the purple ball spinning neatly into the far Downstage Right pocket. The Man stands back, this time agilely—fine, light dancing rhythms bursting for attention in every line of his body—oh he's doing something he likes and he's winning! Both men in their performance of the game seem to emanate peak physical levels. The Stage Mechanic crosses to the other side of the table while the Man leans back on his staff-like cue and watches him aim with elaborate flourishes of his elbows as he stretches far out over the table to take a cracking mean long-shot, which they both then grinningly admire, standing back in gracefully relaxed poses that become a shade more stylized now. The game seems to *gel* and *set* into its own rhythms, as they, like good fellows, lean angularly on their cues. The balls roll and clack, the Man more challenged than chagrined when the Stage Mechanic's shot sinks balls in both Upstage pockets. He snaps his fingers—"Damn!"—but airily, every ounce the superb loser! Within the rakish, dancing framework of the game, they have become rather buddies, their movements at once clipped, "civilized," and boyishly genial. The Woman, at the head of the table, is impervious to their game, and speeds on with her endless enumeration of architectural assets that the new house shall have. She fires her words straight at the Man, who continues to play pool and does not look at her.)

Woman: ... a red brick chimney for our open fireplace, climbing the side of our white-washed house—built-in birdbath—Dutch roof—mansard eaves—brass door-knocker that's a lion's head—dormer windows (clasps her hands low under her belly like a ho-ho-ho Santa Claus to describe dormer windows)—lots of cupolas, of course (talking faster with busy hands, almost breathless)—a widow's walk with false parapets—gargoyle rainspouts—a few galleries thrown in from old Southern show boats—Creeping Bent lawn like a regular emerald of a golf green, and, and, and—(she points sharply heavenward, triumphant)—a rooster for a weathervane! (Her hips simply *twitching,* she moves to the rear of her bike, while the Man leans listlessly on his imaginary cue, waiting his turn as the Stage Mechanic plays: a *shot* like a pistol! and the Mechanic waves his cue over his head, jubilant, he's sunk two *more!)*

Man: (Flatly, to woman as he chalks his cue.) Is that all?

Woman: (She cutely continues, flouncing a hip at him.) ... and, maybe a little *ping-*pong out under the trees?

Man: (Emphatic, implacable.) Pool.

Woman: ... squeeze in one eency-weency game before dark? ... install an outdoor spotlight...?

Man: (Carefully lays his cue over the corner of the table and faces her.) Pool.

Woman: (Now at the rear of her bike, rifling through the satchel behind her seat.) God damn, my pliers are gone. Who takes things out of here? (Looks coldly at the Man, drawing into herself.) You can't trust anyone anymore. (She glares about as if to say, So that's the way the land lies! The Stage Mechanic hoists his cue like a balancing pole across his shoulders, and clowns Upstage on tiptoe where he meticulously stands the cue against the black Stage Wall and exits stiffly, a trifle sadly, though still clownish, on tiptoe.)

Man: (Hands her a pair of pliers from *his* bike's pouch, spanking them lazily into her palm.) Pool!

Woman: Aren't these my pliers? (She examines them closely.)

Man: They came with the bike.

Woman: Whose bike?

Man: (Noncommittally takes the pliers, stoops to tinker with the chain, his head lowered studiously, then grins up.) You could never fix this. How'd you get it in such a mess?

Woman: Oh nothing special—(airy but careful)—Look!—(jabbing at the sky)—a kite!

Man: I don't see anything... (Squatting by the bicycle, he scans the air following her pointing finger, rotating on the balls of his feet to trace the path her index finger makes through the sky.)

Woman: (Jumping up and down, hands clasped childlike beneath her chin.) Oh yes! an oriental one—

Man: (Shading his eyes to distinguish forms or *create* them, if he must.) There *is* something moving...

Woman: ... purple and red!—

Man: But *plain*—(Begins to rise with pliers, on one knee.)

Woman: ... with a tail like a dragon!

Man: ... with a faded *blue* tail...

Woman: (Her pleasure cresting)—Oh see how *grandly* it flies?

Man: ... sinking... can't quite clear the ground... it keeps thrashing ... (he cringes back)... a nosedive!... It's crashed! Stuck on a telephone pole, caught in the wires, blowing to smithereens. (His voice sinks with the kite, but travels even more distinctly out to us, as he throws his arm across his face and dodges with the movements of the kite.)

Woman: (Prancing a bit.) ... its back arching, and its tail floats so... (Makes a grand, liquid gesture with her hand, rapturous, mindful of her grace and effect on him when she peeks to see how he's taking her victory.)

Man: (Dull-eyed and resigned, his arms clap limply to his sides.) ... just shreds and rags popping in the breeze... (For a moment he looks haunted.) . . . Think of dying on a telephone pole, left to blow . . . (He flaps his hands dejectedly back and forth from the wrist, then exaggerates it so much that he brings himself close to amusement which can narrow her lead, and if not close the gap, at least diminish his loss.) There! That oughta hold you for a while! (He spanks the seat, all business and job well done, waves the pliers through the air as he starts to put them in the satchel behind *his* bike.)

Woman: (Palm up, arm extended.) Better let me keep them. . . . You misplace everything so. (He delivers the pliers to her open palm, an acknowledgement that he knows she is right.)

Man: (With a sly little bow.) I didn't know I had a helper . . . (They swing onto their bikes, and immediately resume medium, no-nonsense pedaling. Brisk faces and postures for both. A shipshape team they make.)

Man: I suppose he'll be all business, like my father. Pretend we're not late, and rush us into a contract. (He's whimsically resigned to a lousy contract, even forgiving, as he pedals lackadaisically, then brightens, sits back matter-of-factly on the seat.) After he gives all the right come-ons, of course, he'll know when to be honest.

Woman: (Leery.) Whad-do-you-mean?

Man: We'll be in the bathroom, probably, there's always trouble in the bathroom (quickly checks her expression) . . . and pretty soon he'll lift the toilet lid and point down (gestures *down,* pointing over the side between their bikes) . . . maybe sniff . . . then the tank lid, that's heavier, more trouble, and he has to take all kinds of junk off it first, you know (she nods, seeing it now in spite of her resistance) . . . tall stuff that falls when you move it: air sweeteners and bath salts and Pepsi bottles half full of brown gunk, and then the stuff that hangs over the edge and falls into the tank, or the *bowl*—a dirty pair of stockings, hairnet—that must be Grandma's—and *Time* magazine, *choke* a toilet!, *that* would, and of course what he misses is that yellow toothbrush some kid's forgot to put up in the perfectly good toothbrush rack over the sink.

Woman: (Anxiously.) Does he get it?

Man: But of course! He's brave and honest and puts his whole arm down there and pulls it out shining, and says the toilet needs new insides for sure—"Rotten insides!" he says, running hot water over the toothbrush, and shaking his head, moaning, "Probably got the original lead plumbing in this house, too," like our problem was his problem. (She groans loudly, as if this were the only house in the world, only bathroom, only chance.) Now he doesn't tell us that nearly every house in that end of town has lead plumbing and it holds all right, doesn't turn into a fountain or geyser or something, you know, in the middle of the night. (Shoots both arms upward . . . making a generous geyser-shaped fountain.) Nah. He doesn't tell us that. Perfect touch, too.

Woman: Why? (She's a little strung out, frightened by his confidence and animation, yet absorbed in the story.)

Man: He just scoops that dead bird (Woman starts) lying on a bloody paper towel on the back of the toilet—probably the same kid left it there that left his toothbrush—just *sco-oops* that ole bird, his eyes are cold and filmy-looking, into the wastebasket, little yellow lice creeping round on his head—

Woman: (Shrieks, claps her hand over her mouth, jerks her head away, then back). Why did you have to do that?

Man: . . . and washes his hands carefully, *thoroughly* . . . because of both "un-pleasant" episodes—lots of hot water, soap, nailbrush— Boy! Can he handle that nailbrush! Dries his hands sort of like a doctor after an operation, and plumb forgets to tell us the furnace is busted!

Woman: Wha-a-at?

Man: Nope, it's summer anyhow. Why should he tell us something we don't need to know yet? Spoil the sale? We *like* this house, we'd get *mad* if he blurted about the furnace—

Woman: (Regretfully, almost tearfully.) It did have lovely window-seats in the library where children could daydream after school . . . and those perfect, high pitched gables . . . (Shapes a gable to frame her pretty face.)

Man: He's gotta make a living, *too!* He has mouths to feed! (He grips the handlebars tighter.) They can't live on Franco-American Spaghetti —every *night?*

Woman: Oh no.

Man: They *sit,* his pale wife, and those *dir-*ty lit-tle kids (he shakes his head, by the tone of his voice creating a virtue out of *"dirt"*) . . .

gathered round that rickety kitchen table, in their nasty, crowded, cold-water walk-up apartment—

Woman: We live in a walk-up apartment... (She draws up into herself, but he pays her no mind, absently rings his bicycle bell, absorbed in the pathetic faces around the table.)

Man: ... and they wait! the smeary bibs tied round their poor thin necks, framing the scrawny little heart-shaped faces.... One of 'em pipes up like an angel, you know, his knife and fork planted on the table upright like a man, but in those skinny baby fists, and says "Maybe Daddy will bring us home some meat tonight!"—They hope! Can you beat it? They think he's coming up the stairs *right now,* a white butcher's package under his arm with a little good red blood oozing from it, and all he's got is another bag full of cold, canned spaghetti! "Here kids," he says, trying not to look at his wife, who's tryin' not to look at them—she knows, and has plates out with forks, *no* knives. "See what Daddy has shot on his way home from work? a real buffalo" he says, "here's your *real* buffalo steak, kiddies." The poor slob. Hasn't sold a single house today, but there's the wife passin' out orange floppy goop, makin' with the can opener like he taught her to do in emergencies—but sweetheart, this is every night!

Woman: Are you sure?

Man: Sure I'm sure. (Fired with assertiveness because of his "discovery.") He has to make a living!; and those kids?—*that* one, with his little head on the table hasn't got the strength to prop it up!, looks like he's got T.B.! Pasty-looking as the Franco-American they been eating! Our agent's got to do something, and quick! He's got to do *any*thing! (Earnestly *splams!* his fist down hard on the handlebars, the bell erratically jingles.)

Woman: (Tremulous.) What will he do?

Man: It's a good thing... (brrrrrrngs! the bell with his thumb)... he didn't tell us about the furnace!

Woman: Let me off, I'm sick. (They dismount quickly, and he, with careful attentiveness, eases her to the ground at Lower Stage Left. She curls up with her head in his lap. He strokes her forehead, smoothes her hair.)

Woman: Why do you always have to do that?

Man: Do what?

Woman: Let something like that happen . . .

Man: Let *what* happen?

Woman: That bird. So *warm* and squishy and just dead when he picks it up—the eyes black and shiny and bugs crawling over his little half-opened beak, as yellow as *it's* yellow. (Shudders uncontrollably.)

Man: Yes. (Sadly.)

Woman: It's no use scooping him into that wastebasket, you know. He'll just sit there, rotting in that plastic wastebasket under the sink, all the water pipes hung with rags overhead and only cans of scouring powder to keep him company . . . no one in that house will touch him until his sinews are dry and pulled hard in the rank flesh, a dark veiny red showing through the feathers when you open up the paper towel, his tiny feet drawn up under him like an unborn baby's and his little brown sparrow feathers so dull and dried to powder that if you touched him they'd fall away like ashes from a burned coal! (Shudders tenderly.) Oh it's no use your getting him thrown away!

Man: I suppose not. (She has moved her head out of his lap and he turns his back on her, pulling up grass and throwing it down.)

Woman: (Cheered.) And the little mother! At her table how carefully she plies the can opener! How beautifully she sees that no drop spills, no nourishment shall be wasted, and *gently,* she sli-i-des it onto their plates without a splatter! not vexing them with the long, hungry delay to heat their food, but stopping the pains in their little tummies as fast as she can! (She has risen rapturously on her elbow as if she's about to sing Christmas carols . . . to a needy audience.)

Man: Yeah, I guess you're right. (He stands now with his back to her, his legs spread, hands buried in his pockets. He jerks his head toward the brace of silver bicycles, barks:) Let's *go!* (He leaps onto his bike on the Upper Level and pedals furiously, paying no attention to the Woman, who, on the Lower Level, still sits directly in front of him, startled upright now because it looks like he will crush her under the wheels of his bike . . .)

>(The Stage Mechanic as Real Estate Agent enters Stage Left, jumps onto the Woman's unused bike and with a hell-bent, shit-eating grin pedals furiously with the Man, the black satchel

swinging animatedly from his handlebars. In derby and full regalia, his brilliant class ring flashing green under the lights, he's all Real Estate Agent now. The Man calls *back over his shoulder* to his wife, as if she's lingering tardily in the Stage Shadows behind, apparently unaware of the fact that she's in *front* of him.)

Man: Hurry—Hurry! We're almost too late!

(The Stage Mechanic as Real Estate Agent takes a cigar from his breast pocket, pedals no-handed rapidly, and attentively lights his cigar while the man beside him continues to call, cupping a hand to protect the words which seemingly must travel a *great distance* behind him.)

Man: Hu-u-urrry . . . We're la-a-ate! (He calls Left, calls Right, still pedaling furiously while the Stage Mechanic slacks off his pace with easy thrust of the pedals.)

Woman: (She kneels before them on the Lower Level, back to us, legs spread, calling with cupped hands upward to the Man:) Wa-ait for me-e-e, Howard, wait for *meeeee!*

Man: (Still calling backwards.) Hu-u-urrry . . . Pleeeeeeease hu-u-urrry . . . (Glancing at the Real Estate Agent, who seems suddenly evil, the Man looks bitten with fright. He slides off his bike and hops down to the Lower Level. He's chickening out of his search for the Woman and giving up riding as fast as the Agent, enduring his sharp quick laugh as the Agent pedals on. Our Man now stands alone at Lower Center Stage, clutching his collar to keep out encroaching cold, and trying to cheer himself with a little humor:) It's gettin' *dark* in these here hills . . . them *woods.* (Still protectively clutching his collar, he sizes up the steeply wooded small distances all around him, and with the other hand systematically stabs with his finger to point out trees growing fifteen feet above each of our waiting heads . . . He finishes on some inner logic of his own, without the "down-home" accent.) . . . And she'll be getting cold.

Stage Mechanic: (Grimly.) She has ways of keeping warm.

Man: You mean . . . I can't protect her? (Anguished, he resumes the effort to cheer himself up. Rubs his hands together.) We all gotta go sometime, hey!? *But—business is business!* (Spoken with resolve, evenly and quietly:) I'll take that house now. If you're ready.

(The Stage Mechanic is spotlighted on his bike, with gold underlighting so that eyes, nose, the upper planes of lips, all glow out from the lower planes of his face, which stay blacked out. He flicks cigar ash, then suddenly throws down his cigar, the sound of *whip cracks!* as he peers backward with a whiplike gesture of his arm.—*"Faster!* Gotta build up speed for that hill!"—He shakes his head with grim humor in appreciation for the steepness of the hill while the Man struggles reluctantly onto his bike. They lean back, pumping hard and slow on the bikes which are tilted *up*ward, the Woman's empty bike tilts, too.—*"There!"*—The Stage Mechanic crests the hill first as all three bike panels level out in sequence: They swiftly tip *down*hill as the Mechanic-as-Agent mimics a sports announcer's bland voice:—"Watch the gravel on the shoulder, and it's all the way dowwwwnn..." The sound of drumrolls, and they bear downhill as if they will spill right over the handlebars, staring at the spot down in front of their bikes where the Woman lies back with naive confidence, the lights flickering stormily about her. For a liquid moment as long as a flame leaping, we want to *warn* her...

(Lights like blue "moonlight"—chilly, spooky—sink slowly on the riders, out to *black,* as lurid red comes up on the woman reclining with her head propped on one arm. She bounces up with a cry! as if their speeding down on her is a nightmare, and she's awakened by the sheer silent velocity and *aim* of their ride.)

Woman: (Sitting up very straight, as if to say an incantation that will dispel her fright, her nightmare which now becomes *ours.*) My mother said, "Chew your fish in lit-tle bites, with your *front* teeth, to get all those ti-ny little bones out... before one jumps down your throat, and sticks"—and chokes me to death!

(She clutches her neck with one hand and we feel every fear-filled, dimly articulated, strident pang that has ever attacked us with warnings in the black waking hours of the night. We see her eyes popping and terrified, and it's as if we're looking inside-out at ourselves from the audience. Then she reprieves us, rolling rapidly, fluidly, to Stage Left, the outskirts of light, and disappears. But an instant later we are treated to the gaunt reassurance of the white-lit Wrigley Building in the dark background, its friend the Black Skyscraper a foreboding hulk on the skyline, as the snappy cruise-launch Captain steers less jauntily now in semi-shadow, cuts less of a figure, in sad diminishment at the helm.)

(As the Stage Lights come back up, they are the sunny lemon

lights of morning, the hour when people get a "good start" on the day, a new chance, a time to "do it better." The Stage Mechanic as the Man's Father in an old tweed coat and tie rides in a dignified if awkward fashion on the Woman's bike beside the Man, his Son. He is avuncular when he speaks, slow and deliberate in his movements, with the softening effects of age. He uses some business, pulling a newspaper out of his pocket, consults it economically folded, subway style, in one hand. Later he uses a nail-clipper with careful attention to road hazards which his no-hands pedaling occasions, a "defensive driver" at all times, we can see, then blows his nose on a large white handkerchief from his hip pocket, wipes it thoughtfully, side-to-side, pocketing the handkerchief with a curt hitch of his buttocks forward on the seat. We remember with longing the sharp, often stylized, sardonic movements of the Mechanic, the *let hell open up if it will* attitude which he frequently displays. This man is not *diminished,* but looms formidable and large before the yellow lights, and judging from the Son's deferential demeanor is to be reckoned with at all times. When he bangs his fist on the handlebars to emphasize a point, we get a brash echo of the Son's earlier, tinkling bell.)

Stage Mechanic as Man's Father: Now, Son (Son starts with guilty recognition), just let me tell you one thing. There's nothing I regret like not having an education. They don't pass you up, no sir, when you've got that ole degree. (Bangs his fist on handlebar.) No sir, they don't *dare!* (Son nods, respectfully, attentively.) You've got your future cut out for you! and they'll step aside gladly to make room for you going up! (Son smiles and nods to both sides, as if surrounded already by an aura of adulation and good will which his simple presence promotes and he welcomes. The Father's face darkens. Sometimes his voice goes raw with pleading earnestness, his jowls shake in vindication. . . . He fumbles, just *slightly,* getting the handkerchief back in his hip pocket, clears his throat garrulously, while his Son squares himself quietly for the next round of advice:) For *me,* not one raise in ten years while all the others took theirs, took it for granted, like they had it coming, it was their birthright! Stepped on my head goin' up! (He shakes his head as if freshly marveling at it all.) I sat there behind those invoices and bills of lading they *needed* from me, and they acted like they couldn't see me at my desk. Son, you get yourself a profession, you can write your own ticket, thumb your nose at 'em all the way up!

(The two men thumb their noses in unison, pedaling sedately, looking to neither side, and when the joke is over, "Son" salutes "Father" briskly with the air of tipping his hat, returning to a manner most deferential, his every earnest movement calculated to please, as he anticipates his old man's advice at every point. They ride steadily on, as *their* lights dim, then go out to black, and the Woman's flash up. She's sitting at Lower Stage Left with her back to the Top Level, leaning back on her arms for support in a studiedly child-like posture, her feet stuck out in front, bare soles toward us, her knees pulled up and spraddled.)

Woman: And in the long winter afternoons we made crepe paper roses, quietly, while Mother took her nap. She had T.B., before I was born, and needed her rest! So every winter afternoon the hired girl Alice and I, we'd sit on the floor cross-legged and make crepe paper roses (sits up eagerly and mimes scissor-work), and talk in whispers so we shouldn't wake Mama up. We'd tear and cut, cut and tear, long strips of red and pink and yellow crepe paper, and roll them, and crimp them, and spread them into roses ... We wrapped the long wire stems round and round with narrow strips of dark green. Sometimes we had pale blue roses with light green leaves. They would bounce and sway if you waved them, and we put them into vases. We made acres and *acres* of crepe paper roses and we put them into vases (she sees, wearily, acres of crepe paper roses and that many years), and we talked in low whispers so Mama shouldn't wake. We didn't want to get her T.B. back, did we? Alice the maid was young, a bohunk farm girl from a Czech family, and she thought the roses were as pretty as I did. She liked lipsticks, chewing gum, and she said "kink" for "king" when we played cards. (Ruefully looking out over the audience, as if the memories do not *give* her enough.) We crimped the edges of the petals to make them curl.

> (The lights die quickly on her. She changes place with the Stage Mechanic in pitch darkness and is back on her bike with the Man as light floods up on the pair. We see the Man, as a younger version of himself, bare-chested and wearing blue jeans.

> (The Woman now appears as the Man's Mother. In addition to her red bathing suit, she wears a pillbox hat topped with violets, perhaps carries a Bible in her free right hand, a lace-edged hankie in the other, which she frequently whisks at her nose—on her *way,* to church or Ladies Aid. Or, in an alternate, *housekeeping,* image, she wears over her bathing suit an apron, carries on her right arm a dish cloth or dusting rag, rides with an eggbeater or spatula brandished in one hand, occasionally gives a spat! with the springy, flexible end against her other palm, all executed with an efficient brand of no-hands pedaling for cockier female emphasis. Sometimes she tucks the eggbeater, spatula, Bible

under her arm to avoid an accident, flicks the dish towel, dust cloth snappily over her shoulder with just the glimmer of a proud-set smile, the thrill and attitude of rapidly getting things done. She speaks as though she's waited a long time to say this, also as if she may have said it many times, and warms to the opportunity of saying it again. She speaks with many arch little nods, and lifts of the chin, the very sort that make us forget she has long flowing dark hair tucked up under the violet-topped pillbox, a disturbingly pretty face . . .

Woman as Man's Mother: I won't have a bunch of naked men sitting round my house all summer. I told your father *and* your brothers and I'm telling *you,* if I have to be the only woman in that house, the least you can do is keep an undershirt on when you sweat. I will not look at all that naked flesh, I don't care *how* hot it gets! Men don't have to lie around half naked just because they're *hot!*

(She glances first at the Man to one side of her, then even more covertly flicks an attentive eye at the Stage Mechanic one level below. Her pleased "looks around" include a spry salaciousness and a certain sly pleasure. On the Lower Stage the Mechanic lolls, stripped to his muscular waist in a lawn chair, one leg impudently crossed, ankle propped on a raised knee, turning the pages of a magazine, holding it up so the centerfold falls out, evidently grinning at something in "full color" which this Mother would not fully approve of. In contrast to the Mechanic's behavior, the Man, obeying his Mother's order, adroitly snatches a skivvy from the black satchel behind his seat. He dodges through the neck and armholes quickly while keeping one well-trained eye on the flow of traffic. With a practiced yank! and mannish waggle of his elbows, he pops his head through, *grabs* those handlebars with a minimum of lurch and wobble, now the other arm!, and pulls down the vise-like shirt which his Mother requires. A shrug helps to work it down his body as he sits erect, still tugging and smoothing it over his belly with one hand, grinning wickedly, sheepishly, up at us to share the joke . . . but the light level falls quickly with a greenish caste, his expression smoothing over to one of loutish, jaunty anxiety as he pedals faster than Mother, who's lost in Stage Shadows by the time he turns his knees rakishly out. His transformation from the obedient Son to an anxious young lout complete, he smacks his gum.)

Stage Mechanic as Man's Older Brother, the Lout: (Jumps on vacated Woman's bike carrying rolled up *Playboy* magazine in his hand and speaks as if in mid-conversation.) No-no-no-no. . . ! Like I *said* (confidential, glances at Man as the Loutish Kid, then looks straight ahead again), you gotta watch the *tits!* The boobs, man!, the JUGS! (Gestures "jugs.") Any broad what's got somethin' good *up*-stairs (gestures), she gonna be worth da time she'll take, *DOWN*-stairs! Ya follow me? Ya gotta watch them *tits!* Dat's all ya got to *go* by—tits an' ass!, tits an' ass. Now ya take one a dese women what's got an ass dat don't wiggle—no wiggle at-tall!. *You* know da kind, looks like she's wearin' a straight-jacket? FERGIT IT, man. Dat straight-jacket goes ta *bed* wid 'er! (Kid starts to remove his T-shirt again.) No matta how *prom*-is-in' dose titties look, say ta yourself, *I know this number!* (Kid nods gratefully, trying to look wise.) Here! (Hands him the *Playboy* magazine just as Kid gets clear of his T-shirt, which he exchanges for the magazine, pouncing on the centerfold.) Betta read up! Ya got ya homework cut out for ya, Kid.

Kid: (Devouring the centerfold with his eyes.) Some swell dames in here!—I mean broads, er, chicks,—(Interrupted.)

Lout: Call 'em anything—de "ABC's of SEX!" But don't go sniffin' roun' fer no horse-flesh ta match dese "specimens"! Which brings us chest-ta-chest—shall we say "abreast"!?—wit my "point of depah-chure," ya *fuchure,* Kid: MAIN CHANCT! Da practical effects of sex!

(Both men laugh, the Stage Mechanic as Lout laughs uproariously, *lewdly;* he is having his own joke, with the Kid and with the play. They ride away lazily, knees out, the Kid engrossed in centerfold and smacking his gum–until suddenly:)

Stage Mechanic: (Drops "Lout" role. Yelling, brutal, with the force of a whip-crack.) *Faster!* Don't have all day! You want Marlene to get ahead of you?

(Lights go down on Act I as Man and Stage Mechanic ride furiously into descending darkness, the Man dropping his "Kid" role immediately the Stage Mechanic speaks; Man assumes a *driven* expression after glancing only once at the Stage Mechanic. Both men peering intently ahead, full forward motion and speed of the bicycles, racing on into the night.)

from *Winter House*

So Why Let Love Die of Hunger?

Andrew Allegretti

Wyatt Parsons kicked a cardboard box concealed behind a row of suits in his father's closet, heard the unmistakable sound of glass hitting glass, and stiffened for he recognized the sound instantly. He touched the shirt he had come to borrow, closed his eyes, opened them, expelled breath, gathered himself and pushed aside a row of suits.... Yes, bottles. Wyatt had never seen so many at one time. There they were extending far into Will's deep closet.

Bottles.

Carton after carton filled with bottles, bottles, bottles. A treasure trove of empty bottles: Johnny Walker Red (and Black), J&B (the Judge's brand; his grandfather's brand), Chivas Regal (Kaiser's brand; his brother-in-law's brand), Cutty Sark, Jack Daniels, Canadian Club, Seagram's, Old Grand Dad, Wild Turkey, Two Sisters Vodka, Smirnoff Vodka, Bombay Gin (Victoria glowered up at him), Beefeater Gin, Tanqueray Gin—Catherine's tastes, his mother's tastes, were universal, indiscriminate, democratic, and sometimes obscure. And there were fifths—for hiding behind the five blue volumes of Carl Sandburg's *The War Years* on the library shelves or in the cooking pots cabinet in the kitchen. And there were quarts—to nestle beneath blankets and towels in the linen closet. And there were pints and half-pints—for pocket, purse, or pillow.

Behind Wyatt, outside the delicate fretwork of the leaded glass window of the closet, the day lay bright, suspended, and soundless beneath a layer of thick snow under a cloudless blue sky. Looking at the bottles, Wyatt saw how they glittered and shone in the winter morning light, dazzled and wavered in this benediction of a day, this celebration of a day.

And the careful vision of what was to be a perfect Christmas vacation from college (the stark winter light and the bare trees at school making him think of the light and trees at home) slipped away. For at school he had sat propped back in his desk chair in the dorm and, looking out a tall window of the old building at the black winter branches of the trees against the white snow of the quad, he had seen the winter sun at home as it would flood his bedroom, when he would wake to it spread over his bed like a blanket, and then had seen in his imagination the top of the tall pussy willow tree outside his east window, the branches, feathered with new snow, glowing in the winter morning sunlight. He had seen those sights in his mind and he had seen his parents winter-time comfortable in the library, reading the newspapers, and he had seen himself stride into the room and how they would dip their heads and look at him over their glasses.

Sitting in the dormitory room at his desk with a text book open before him the day before his last class, he had dreamed of home, conjured it, made it perfect, taken this fragment of the truth and that fragment of the truth—the smell of roasting meat, the sun spilling over the carpets, the tangy cold smell of the fallow winter countryside, the crackle of creek water spilling over the log dam—he had taken those fragments and made something in his imagination that was quite untruthful, and then his roommate Thomas Clearfield had burst into the room, and, full of vacation delirium, had grabbed the arms of the wheeled desk chair in which Wyatt was sitting, and before Wyatt knew what had happened Thomas had propelled him out of the room and down the hallway past dodging senior men toward the fast-approaching stairway at the further end; but fat, elegant Jeff Farnsley had stepped from his room into their path and with the yellow and gold shaft of a Balkan Sobranie cigarette planted blowzily center mouth, had fixed Wyatt with his eyes and begun a playful, graceful side to side two-step towards him, a relic of a nickel plated martini shaker held high in two hands, and they had stopped for a drink.

But this morning and barely a day later all that was gone. The perfect dream of home had never been. He had forgotten it all and now he remembered it all. Yes, he was home. And looking at the bottles he thought, Yes, this is home. And he lightly tapped the nearest carton with the toe of his shoe, and leaned forward with sudden interest for he realized that his father Will had categorized the bottles according to the type of liquor and capacity of the bottles—at least some of the boxes were filled that way, but the more recent ones, that is the ones closest to the front of the closet, were all jumbled together higgedly-piggedly. Wyatt whistled, fascinated by the organizational sense his father had. Law school had taught his father something, for this was, Wyatt realized shrewdly, evidence, *courtroom* evidence, the kind of dramatic evidence that could be presented to a judge or jury, and it shocked Wyatt, and then he found himself laughing. Good God! he thought, this is a riot! This is a farce!

Why, this is *found art!* he thought suddenly and took up the idea. Yes, you could put this collection on plexiglass pedestals in an art gallery somewhere—grocery store boxes and all—and call it... What? Wyatt thought and then had it. You could title this work of art "Throw Mama from the Train, A Kiss, A Kiss" which is what Catherine said to them all when they ganged up on her, taking the title of a song popular in the fifties. She would shake her head sadly and say in a solemn, bitter voice, "That's it. Just throw Mama from the train!" Or you could call it, "Enough to Stupefy a Swedish Plumber," which was another one of Catherine's favorite sayings. Or you could call it, "Naked in Saks With a Checkbook," another one of his mother's sayings, applied to anything that excited her or made her happy.

"Bottles, bottles everywhere, and nary a drop to drink! Bottles, bottles everywhere, and oh, how this stinks!" Wyatt recited and laughed. But his laughter was all from the throat, choked there, and for a moment he was afraid he would not be able to stop laughing. And then he was faint. Almost fell. Had to steady himself against the doorjamb, and every time he looked at the bottles, he giggled and then he knew his sister must see this, too. Someone besides himself must see it and believe it.

Virginia must see this! Wyatt thought triumphantly. Ginny-Gin-Gin must see this! Chinny-Gin-Shin, the Sayonara Girl, must see this!

And then the obvious occurred to Wyatt. Why, his mother had actually drunk all this! Her veins had run with a river of booze floating on her blood. How many hundreds of gallons had pumped through the spongy membranes of her brain? Eyes fixed on the glimmer of the endless boxes of bottles, Wyatt said aloud, "This has drowned us!" And then, quite without reason, "Lord love a duck!"

But Virginia must see it.

And when he had roused his sleepy sister from bed and dragged her half-awake and protesting to the closet, Wyatt stood outside the door as Virginia peered around the jamb at the bottles.

"God!" Virginia said sleepily. "God!" And started back to bed, but Wyatt called, "Halt, Sayonara Girl!"

And he stepped into the middle of the room somber with mahogany, and as Virginia turned toward him, pulling her robe about her slender figure, he began:

"Now this is the set-up. We've decided to commit our Kate to some home for boozers—you know, one of those places with drying racks. And there's this big dramatic courtroom scene where Dad, arguing for commitment, presents these bottles as evidence." And Wyatt quickly dove into the closet and with a clamor of glass dragged one of the cartons into the bedroom.

"So we're all in the courtroom. You and me and Dad and Herself, and Dad's beginning his opening statement.

" 'Your Honor,' he says, 'I would like to enter as Exhibit A an accumulation of bottles that I assembled over the last year. I shall demonstrate, Your Honor, that my wife consumed the contents of these bottles.'

"And the Judge will say, 'Very well. Proceed.' "

And fully aware of his sister's eyes upon him, Wyatt continued: "Dad will go to the first box in front of the bench and the Judge will lean forward, and you and I will lean forward, and the defending attorney will lean forward, and Dad will tip a few of the bottles up one by one to show that every drop is gone, all the time saying, 'Yes, Your Honor, my wife drank all this.'

"But then," Wyatt said, jumping to one side and lowering his voice, "Johnny Graves, her lawyer—and she'd get Johnny to defend her if we really tried to commit her—Johnny Graves will stand up and say, 'I object, Your Honor. There is no question of my client's illness—and remember, Your Honor, alcoholism is an *illness*. What is in question is whether this poor woman should be punished, consigned to torture, if you will, by her family. Oh yes, my client admits she's a sodden drunk, but she is not the guilty one! Oh, no! He is the guilty one!' " And Wyatt pointed dramatically to an armchair over which Will's robe had been flung.

And there was a long silence in which Virginia gave a full-mouthed yawn, anchored a lock of hair behind one ear, her face uncertain as though she had not quite seen the joke.

And Wyatt looked at his sister, aware of her uncertainty and his own, but he continued as Virginia sat down on her father's unmade bed.

"Guess who the judge is!" Wyatt said. "Just guess!"

"Gramps. Grampa Parsons, of course," Virginia said and smiled.

"That's right!" Wyatt said triumphantly. "You've got it, baby! De old Judge himself. The old His Honor himself!"

And there was another silence and then Wyatt said quietly, the fun gone, "And Gramps will kind of wake up and look at Dad and say, 'Objection sustained.' And then he'll say to Mike Gill, the bailiff, 'Please remove this garbage from my courtroom!' " Then Wyatt looked at his sister and added, "And we'll all live happily ever after, of course."

Wyatt dropped his eyes then and looked at the sunlight playing over the rug and thought how miraculous and marvelous light is and how ironic sometimes, how it illuminates human activity—lies buttery and rich across battlefields piled high with the dead, and across courtyards in which men are hanged, and plays out the colors in the blankets of deathbeds, and makes white and intense the flames of burning houses and automobile wrecks.

"That was quite a performance," Virginia said quietly after a moment.

"Yeah," Wyatt answered her, "it was." And as she watched he thoughtfully opened the front of his jeans and tucked the shirt in with those assured masculine gestures which Virginia so admired—the wide-handed smoothing into the top of the pants, the slight backward push of the hips, the sharp pull of the zipper.

When he was finished Virginia said, "And you're quite an actor."

"Yeah," Wyatt said and she waited for him to say more. But he only sighed and shook his head and she kept on watching him and then he burst out, "This is so wasteful! They're such wasteful people! They lead such wasteful lives!"

"I know," Virginia said, "but there's nothing you can do about it. Don't *you* waste your life trying to solve it." But she knew that he had never been able to put it behind him, knew that it haunted his dreams, haunted his waking life, that he felt it always, that it was never far from his thoughts.

"I know what you do, Wyatt," she said. "You play around like this and then you try to *solve* it. I've given up on that, you know. And that's what you have to do. It's the only way."

But she saw him stiffen at her words, saw the stubbornness come over him and she said as gently as she could, "Don't come home too much, Wyatt. I know Mother will put pressure on you to, but don't come home. She did that to me all the time I was in college, and I came home and then worried all the time and my grades suffered. Don't give in. Stay away." Then she added after a moment's pause, "Leave them alone. They'll work it out or they won't, but there's nothing much you can do."

And Wyatt looked at her and from his stubbornness said, "You're home. You're sitting right there. You came home."

Virginia only sighed and stood and ignoring her brother's last words said, "I'm going to get dressed." And she crossed the room, stood in the doorway, looked first at the carton of bottles he had dragged from the closet, then at him, and added, "I'm home because I give them what I can spare. You try to give them everything. I just give them a little, because if I gave them one particle more my husband would divorce me."

But Wyatt did not answer her and so she left him and he sat a long time in the sunlight.

And it is the winter sun which holds them all. Sunlight cast through windows filmed with tobacco smoke, rich, slanting bars of sunlight touching old wood and frayed silk upholstery—dusty, silvery, shimmering.

The sun this late winter morning holds Will at his stamps. Snip, snip go the golden scissors. And the plate block envelopes are spread out on the wide desk. How carefully, how neatly he works! Snip, snip, snip. How the strain on his face eases, how the features soften, become gentle when Will works at his stamps. Snip, snip, snip go the golden scissors, gleaming in the light as though Will's fingers are wrapped in sun.

And the winter sun holds Virginia who is stretched on her bed, idly turning the pages of *Vogue,* dawdling until lunch, the door of her room open to the upstairs hall. Her eyes are thoughtful, appraising the clothes, and she twists a lock of hair in concentration as she slowly turns the pages thinking, Oh, I'd fly out of the top of that one! I'd have to glue my breasts down with rubber cement to wear that one! And, Oh, that enormous bow under the chin on that one—that's a soup catcher if I ever saw one!

But Wyatt cannot calm himself.

Wyatt cannot put the thought of those bottles out of his head. Wyatt cannot doze, or read, or walk, or wool-gather. He wanders from upstairs room to upstairs room. (Virginia sees him now and then as he prowls across the periphery of her vision like a shadow, or hears him creak on the boards, or clear his throat, and she thinks two things— one, that Wyatt is brooding, and two, that in three days she can go home.) Now he leans a little over the banisters in the upstairs hall and hears the sound of his father's scissors rising up the stairwell. Then from the bay of a south bedroom he sees, through the glass and the dusty mesh of the window screen, his mother wrapped in an ancient pie-bald fur coat, sprawled in the full, warm sunlight on a wooden chaise in the dilapidated summerhouse, sees her throwing her head from side to side, her breath coming silver as she moves her lips, and he knows that she is enumerating to the winter sun her endless list of grievances.

He thinks again of the bottles.

Feels himself tighten. Feels himself release. Then returns to his room, takes up and sets down almost immediately the text book foreign in color and smell to this house, belonging to a college room and a life not of this house. But the life of this house is never far from the other lives he lives. And he returns to the south bedroom and looks again at his mother sprawled in the sunlight in the windless air on the garden chaise. And squats down, raises the window to smell the winter air and the fainter smell of sun-warmed clapboard—a dry, powdery smell of old paint. He rests his chin on his arms, which rest on the cracked and yellowed varnish of the sill, and he can smell, too, beyond the screen, the acrid warmth of the copper flashing of the ledge, and he can hear faintly his mother's despairing voice; and turning his head to one side and resting his cheek against his hand he goes on listening and smelling and wants to weep but cannot, and so instead he *blames.* Thinks: She's a drunk. She's ruined him. He's a bankrupt. He's weak. I'm the son of a drunk and a bankrupt. Why . . . I'm invisible!

Then they were in the library: Wyatt, Virginia, and Will. Will sitting behind the desk, his stamp albums spread out before him; Virginia arranged on the couch, lying back in the faint stench of the exhausted cushions, a coffee cup and saucer resting on her stomach; and Wyatt sitting forward on the edge of a chair opposite his father near the fireplace, his elbows on his knees, his pose one of eager attention as though he might spring from the chair, yet his skin is drained of color and the agitation is apparent in him, but checked and held back by the careful and deliberate calm of his father. Virginia felt like a spectator at some gruesome match, or like the member of an audience at a play— the action of which she cannot join, alter, or end. This moment, she knew, would go on. Her brother's agitation and her father's calm would go on. If she said, "Wyatt, please, let it rest," he would not. If she left the room, he would let her go without a glance and so would her father. No, she thought, my father will not disallow this moment, nor will he protest it, either.

All this Virginia knew as Wyatt said to his father, "Those bottles in your closet, did she really drink all that?"

And Virginia closed her eyes, aware of the weight of the coffee cup on her stomach, aware of the faint smell of old sweat and hopelessness in the worn leather cushions of the couch, waiting for her father's answer; then opened her eyes at the sound of her father exhaling cigarette smoke like a sigh, and watched him tilt the desk chair back dangerously until it touched the glass doors of the shelves under the window behind him, taking his time answering. A page of the album flopped of its own accord, and Will turned it back, resting the brass circle of the magnifying glass on it—her gift, that marvelous and precisely ground lens. As he set it on the thick page of the album, it caught the rich light, and beyond the wide window behind Will, that same rich light lay over the snow and the summerhouse where Catherine is sprawled wrapped in the pie-bald fur, the dog there beside her.

And though none of them can see Catherine, they all know she is there, and Virginia realizes that she is waiting in a kind of awful suspension for her father to answer Wyatt's question.

Just when Virginia feels she cannot bear the hanging silence, Will nods, says, "Yes, she drank all that," says it as a fact of life.

Virginia thinks, We are drowning. And she steadies the cup and saucer on her stomach and stares up at the deep green of the ceiling. The room fills for a moment with the sound of a rushing wind come up suddenly singing between the storm window and casement and there is a patter of upthrown snow against the glass as the room darkens with sudden shadows—heavy clouds gathering there beyond the glass.

Then Wyatt asks his father, "How long have you been saving the bottles? How long did it take her to drink all that?"

"About a year and a half," Will answers both his son's questions.

"Why did you keep them?" Wyatt asks.

Without taking her eyes from the ceiling, it is Virginia who answers for her father, "Because she should know what she's doing."

Will glances at his daughter, crosses his arms on his chest and says to his son, "I thought she ought to see them."

"And has she seen them?" Wyatt asks.

"Yes," Will says. "She's seen them alright."

Virginia shakes her head from side to side and Will feels suddenly weary. Infinitely weary. Infinitely tired and very old.

"What did she do?" Wyatt asks, his eyes on his father, who tilts the chair forward suddenly, shakes his head, snorts, and answers, "I lined the boxes up in the upstairs hall one morning where she couldn't avoid seeing them and she just walked right past them and started down the stairs and I said to her, 'Don't you see those bottles, my girl?' And she kept right on going. And she has never said another word about them again—nor have I."

Virginia felt her eyes begin to fill with tears, felt the tears well and gather, blurring her vision of the room, and then run from the corners of her eyes and she made no move to stop them, only let them flow openly and evenly and continuously.

Will shook his head and made a disparaging sound in his throat, and glanced at his son and then at his daughter who had not moved and he felt some force from them pushing up against him and some equal (or perhaps greater) force that was his wife. Oh, he knew she was out there wrapped in fur and drunk in the summerhouse on the lawn. He had only to turn to the wide, tall window behind his desk to see her. He knew that she was there and he had kept his back to her all morning and he knew he'd have to go out presently and rouse her to keep her from freezing to death if she didn't come in on her own. He began nervously clicking his thumbnail against a thick corner of the album page, the sound rapid and sharp in the silence, merging with the suddenly audible hollow click of the pendulum of the mantle clock.

Presently the chime marking the hour released as Wyatt said, "Does she *believe* what she sees?"

When the clock finished striking, Virginia's sniffles startled both men, brought them up sharply, and they looked at her with astonishment. And they did not know what to do except to grope ineffectually for handkerchiefs none too clean, for they were suddenly men together with a weeping woman on their hands. But Virginia, in the way of many weeping women, had her own handkerchief, lace-bordered and scented, which she found in her skirt pocket and used to dry her eyes.

The wind came again in a hard gust, and they all heard it whistle, and heard the loose snow cast against the window glass, followed by the cold clutch of a creeping draft. Virginia blew her nose, controlled her tears, said, "Oh, this damned house! I'm always cold in this damned house!"

She looked at her brother and father and then toward the wide windows and beyond where Catherine was and said, "Well, I'm going to do something about lunch." And she stood, set the cup aside, smoothed her skirt, wiped her eyes, dismissed the moment, reminding herself in no uncertain terms of these facts: I have a husband, a house, a life which is my own. And then became an efficient swirl and flurry—a lunch-getter.

But on the lawn Catherine feels the wind divide around the chair from behind, sees it ruffle the collie's coat beside her, rushing down the lawn, curling the snow up and back as it hurries toward the creek where it touches the water, then sweeps on into the barren trees on the far side of the stream where it is lost. Catherine crooks her neck towards one shoulder and closes her eyes and feels the slip, tip, and whirl of the world which she can stop by simply opening her eyes, but she lets herself go into the spin.

Oh, how easy it is to spin and spin and spin!

The sun bursts through the heavy cloud cover and the trapped light behind Catherine's eyelids turns to blue and she is sitting on her mother's lap in a sleigh moving through blue snow, and her father is racing against Toby Yates—General Yates—at Greenlake in Wisconsin across the frozen ice of the lake, and there is the smart trot of the horses neck and neck and the jangle of the sleigh harness and the smell of her mother's perfume and the feel of the fox sleigh blanket under Catherine's tiny hands, and there are the Yateses beaming over at them, and the whole vast sky above them and the green pine rim around the shore broken only by the waterfronts of summer houses, and then one runner of her father's sleigh heaved up on some obstacle caught in the ice and hidden by the snow which her father, snow-blinded and intent upon the race, had not seen, and the sleigh poised on one runner at a sickening angle for a stomach-tightening interval too vast to measure, and then was flung back the other way, and Catherine felt herself leave her mother's lap and she was soaring in the winter air, weightless for a moment, smiling and surprised at being airborne, and then down she came with a slam that yanked the very air from her chest as though an invisible hand dived down her throat and jerked the air out of her lungs, and she landed in a drift just behind the Yates' veering sleigh which the General had abruptly angled away from the Shaws' when he saw it begin to spill, and then she opened her eyes, not to meet her mother and father's frightened eyes looking down at her, but to feel the collie's snout digging into her lap and she is home again and it is a December afternoon and she is weary and the sun has disappeared and she is cold and the booze spin is long gone—the bottle, lying at her side under the coat, is empty, quite empty, and she feels she cannot move so weighted down she feels. And she tells herself, "I'll go in presently. Presently I'll go in."

Once from the high-pointed windows of the attic dormer facing the creek, when Wyatt was nine, he had seen Catherine walking alone on the snowy lawn beneath the blue winter sky toward the creek which was glazed with ice like thin clear frosting. And from that high place, he had seen the collie, a puppy then, explode in a puppy run from under the porch roof far below where Wyatt stood, saw the dog running hard, bearing down on his mistress, hurling and streaking straight toward Catherine who had stopped to watch, but the dog veered off at the last moment and made a long loop and headed back, closing the gigantic figure eight of which Catherine was the center, continuing two, three, more passes, the loops of the vast eight tightening with each pass until at last the dog stopped, leaped up, paws out towards Catherine, then landed beside her to sniff and plow the snow with his long collie snout.

And Wyatt, standing at the attic window, the rafters of the roof pitched high above him, the air so paralyzingly cold that he could feel his fingers beginning to numb, fumbled with the stiff catch of the casement and pushed it open. And leaning into the warmer air outside, dislodging a line of snow on the sill, called to his mother across the vast space, watching her turning this way and that, trying to locate her son's voice which came to her high-pitched and clear across the winter air. Spotting him high above her, she had returned his wave with a vast, extravagant wave of her own, and they had played at that—exchanging extravagant waves, while the collie dropped on his forepaws, rump in the air, barking, playing too, until at last Catherine chopped off a last wave and turned and continued her solitary walk, the collie trotting ahead toward the creek. And Wyatt descended the narrow attic stairs to the warmer climate of the upstairs hall, like going from the Arctic to Palm Beach, his skin burning and tightening at the touch of the dry house heat.

Many years later then, following the talk in the library, Wyatt stood again in his father's closet looking out the delicate fretwork of the leaded glass window, and he remembered that moment when he had leaned from the attic window, and it was as though he were in both places and both ages at once—a boy of nine leaning out an attic dormer, and an adolescent—almost a man—of twenty, standing in another room in another winter season, for he was acutely aware of the winter sun on his face, and of the bottles glistening behind him, refracting thin rainbows on the walls and ceiling of the closet.

Then they were at lunch—Wyatt, Virginia, and Will—in the beamed dining room, clustered at one end of the table made long for the Christmas holiday. The screen of lilac bushes beyond the triple north window which made the room cool, green, and shadowy in the summer was barren now, the netting of naked branches intricate as old lace against the bright winter sky, the table surface filled with refracted light, the plates and glasses and silver seeming to float on an ice surface, and there was great effort of talk.

Wyatt, cutting cold chicken, said, "I hitch-hiked from school. Walked to the college gates, put my thumb out, and got a ride right to the front door." He was proud of the adventure, but disappointed that it had ended so quickly—the thumb gesture, the ride, home. What more was there to tell?

Virginia, wearing a bright luncheon smile, corrected her brother's arrangement of the dessert fork and spoon above her plate, and for a moment something in the angle with which she held her head—the unequivocal presenting of the face and eyes to the speaker at the table, the undivided attention given her brother—echoed Catherine. And Will, turned from the table, smoking already, though his plate was hardly touched, saw the echo of his wife in his daughter and knew the thing against which Catherine railed and fought, knew it certainly, nakedly, and without apology, just as he had known it earlier in the library and that morning when first he awoke, and for twenty-six years now.

"Indifference," Will, the realist, would call it. "Lack of love—lovelessness," Catherine would call it. And Will would concede, "Indifference, lovelessness, yes, all that—call it what you will." For Catherine believed this:

> Be not like a stream that brawls
> Loud with shallow waterfalls
> But in quiet self-control
> Link together soul and soul.

A bright girl with a nervous shingle-bob and soft eyes had taken to heart those words from Longfellow, scored them with violet ink in a school book, had whispered them to herself mornings on the varnished stairs at boarding school, applied them twice in her life: first, at age sixteen, to her brother's friend, an unresponsive Princeton man named Horton Conrad; then almost twenty years later—a svelte woman of thirty-five almost reconciled to maidenhood—to Will, recited the stanza to him in a low, clear voice at the foot of her father's walk one night as snow fell, the flakes glittering white and perfect on the velvet of her evening coat.

At the luncheon table, in the presence of the issue of his marriage to Catherine Shaw, Will remembered that snowy moment and drew deeply on his cigarette, for his indifference was as calculated and as objectively pursued as eating or sleeping. Long ago he had withdrawn from Catherine and she knew that he had and she could not reach that withdrawn part of him, could find no strategy to reach him save the daily reminder of her hurt, relentlessly and objectively pursued in her drinking. Will knew these things, was familiar with his wife's strategy, and though he fought the strategy remained indifferent. He sighed, thinking that in a moment he'd have to go outside and get her.

Then came the hob-goblin, a bundle of sticks and straw draped in fur so mangy one expected lice and buzzing things there, flaps of rips like lolling tongues revealing the purple silk of the lining. There stood Catherine in the entrance to the room—the puffy mask of the face, the black-rimmed, flat brown eyes without depth as though the substance of the woman had drained.

"Umph," the rattling bones said to the blur of light that was the room and the blurs which were her husband and children.

"Umph," Catherine repeated. And, "Oh, oh, oh—umph!" At the same time recalling the words of a college drinking song sung on the 20th Century Limited at holiday breaks, and applying it now to the spinning room:

> Around, around she goes! Around, around she goes!

But Will watched his wife shrewdly and coldly from behind his cigarette smoke; and Virginia set down her fork and stared beyond her brother's back at Catherine; and Wyatt, knowing who was behind him, hunched his shoulders, flinched as though against a blow, reached out his hand impulsively to top his wine glass against an imaginary refill, as Catherine stood waiting for the blur before her eyes to clear in order to take the steps necessary to get her from the hall archway to a place at the table. When the fog cleared she moved fast and comically, not in steps but in broad totters and fits, Virginia at the head of the table presiding in her mother's place, reaching out at the last moment to swing out a chair into which Catherine collapsed with a sickening shatter of Chinese cane, her bony behind sinking into the circle of the broken seat from which she attempted to disengage herself, but the chair held on relentlessly, and Catherine, attached to the chair, stood up and pawed it off, letting it drop, then looked for another vacancy, found one, sat down again more cautiously.

Then, when the astonished look disappeared from her face, Catherine gathered herself and kicked into her lady-at-lunch gear, shrugged out of the dead fur coat, smiled graciously to the assembly, spoke brightly to her children the old table manner rhyme, said of the non-existent soup: "Like the little ships going out to sea, I push my spoon away from me!" Then, that done, began an endless, nerve-racking search for cigarettes and matches—all the time her family watching in utter, stricken fascination the drunken and comic motions unfold—parodic of sobriety, exaggerated, but undeniably human and profound.

When the performance of the cigarette was done, Virginia had had enough and stood up abruptly from the table. Will glanced at his daughter and, ignoring his wife, turned to his son, met his son's eyes, waiting for his son's decision, and presently Wyatt stood, too—shaken, for he had seen for a flickering instant in his father's eyes an apology which Wyatt, filled with passionate blame, did not believe. Many years later though, long after his father was dead, quite unexpectedly one May morning as Wyatt was in the act of reaching into a stone-lined window well at a summer house to scoop out another handful of winter-accumulated leaves, he saw in his mind his father's eyes as they had been twenty years before on that winter afternoon, saw his father again offer the apology, and, unlike the first time, Wyatt accepted it. And then, as he leaned forward to grasp another handful of wet, matted leaves, he knew that though he had accepted the apology, there still remained some barrier, for no matter how carefully he searched those long-dead eyes, he could find no love in them. He shook off the discomfort this realization brought and went on with his task. Still he blamed—but it had become an empty blame. He was forty.

Then it was only Will and Catherine alone in the winter afternoon light in the beamed dining room. They sat in silence after the children had left them—Catherine near the head of the table, smoking, her pale face turned toward the pale light from the north windows and the snow-covered lawn; and Will at the foot of the table, smoking, gazing in the opposite direction through the archway to the hall and the long living room beyond, past the glass sheets of the sunporch, across more winter lawn, all the way to the distant stand of winter trees marking the woods and the Haggertys' tennis court canvas, a yellow speck like a postage stamp or flag breaking the white distance.

"Will."

She spoke his name and he came back, startled, not at the speaking of his name, but that his name had been spoken in a way that made him realize that Catherine was almost sober. And he thought, How has she found sobriety? What sheer act of will has allowed her to find sobriety?

"Will."

She spoke his name again and he could hear the great effort in her voice and he looked at her flat, brown, comprehending eyes and said, "Where do you get the strength, my girl, to pursue this after all this time?" And she drew up with great dignity at his question, intently listening, as he continued, "Where on earth do you get the *strength?* I don't have it. Why don't you let it and us and you and me and them *rest?* Why do you keep it up?" He looked at her quite mildly, quite without anger, quite without rancor or blame. "I'll tell you what you should do," he continued. "You should pull yourself together and get back on the track. Make it easier on yourself, Kate. Take a little vacation from this—and me. Just let it all be, let it be." And he pushed back slightly from the table and the plate of food before him and said, "Kate, I'm sixty-two years old. You're sixty. We've been married twenty-six years. What on earth, after all this time and at this late date, do you want from me?"

"That time at the Haggertys' . . ." Catherine began, her voice heavy with effort, but Will cut her off.

"Kate," he said with real feeling in his voice. "Oh Kate, Kate!"

But she ignored him. "That time at the Haggertys' before we were married you said you loved me and I made you swear that you did and you swore. Do you remember that time at the Haggertys'?" And she looked at him, but her question hung a long time between them, had hung for years between them, and he did not answer as she knew he would not.

And so she continued, "You said you loved me and I didn't quite believe you and so I made you swear and you swore and I believed you. You pledged your troth," Catherine added simply. And she laughed ruefully and said, "Do you know what they used to call an engagement? They used to call it a 'trothplight'! Imagine, you used to get engaged to a man and they'd call it a plight. I wonder who thought of *that?* A plight! Imagine that—a plight!"

And she looked at her husband and saw how drawn he was, how tired, and she wondered why it was that she could not simply let him alone, why she had to hound him like this. She'd told herself for years that the love was perhaps unequal but that she shouldn't withhold *her* love because of that. Yet she met it at every turn—not love, not hate, but a great void of indifference which absorbed every effort, every emotion. She knew all this, but at the same time she insisted to herself that he must in some way love her, that no love could be so unequal, that she could not be so given to him without a reason.

Even as she thought these things she heard someone—a woman—cry out. "Oh God!" the woman cried. "Oh God! Oh God!" And the sound was all around, outside Catherine and inside her, and she realized her mouth was forming words and the words were coming from her. "Oh God!" she cried again at the realization that it was she who was crying out.

Will started at the first sound, tightened progressively at each ensuing repetition and it was almost with relief that he watched Catherine stand suddenly, cross blindly to the sideboard, and with trembling hands open the wide drawer, shoving aside the green felt bags of silver there, looking for what he knew was a hidden bottle.

Yes, it was a relief to him when she found it. A relief when she unscrewed its cap and raised it to her lips and drank deeply—an odd relief which took him out of himself, released him from his secrets. But she plunged him back when she wailed her love for him, wailed it without words, wailed it in a terrible, tearing cry.

And he plunged back to this:

A heavy crash of shattering glass coming from the hall, followed by another and another. "What the hell!" Will yells. But at the first crash, Catherine had clung to the sideboard, her head down, her eyes, wide with realization, flinching at each new crash.

"What the hell!" Will yells again. He stands now in the archway to the hall, stands looking at a sea of shattered glass upon which float three torn cardboard boxes, not ten feet from him in the square well of the stairs. And even as he stands there, another box drops past his vision, hits heavily, with an upsurge of liquor bottles and another deafening shatter of glass.

"Wyatt!" Will bellows. "Goddamnit, Wyatt!" And Will is climbing the stairway, and as he rounds the first landing of the square, he looks up at his son who stands above, another box balanced on the rail. And father and son freeze their poses, looking at each other, and then Wyatt shouts, "You can't stop this!" And he hurls the box with all his might, and even before it explodes on the mass of shattered glass below, Will, flinching back from the sound, again bellows his son's name, and suddenly Wyatt gives in, feels the fierce defiance evaporate.

Then he hears a gentle sound—his name spoken through the afternoon shadows and he looks across the banisters of the stairwell and sees Virginia standing there in the doorway to her room.

"I'm sick of this!" Wyatt says fiercely to his sister, ignoring his father standing below, except to feel the defiance gathering again.

"I know," Virginia says quietly, ignoring her brother's fierceness. "So am I."

And Wyatt raises his arms high and slaps them down, hitting the banister with his open palms which sting immediately with pain, and he tucks them under his armpits and leans forward. "Jesus!" he says of the stinging pain. And Virginia glances down at her father, then quickly across at Wyatt and laughs gently. "Jesus!" Wyatt says again and smiles, seeing the humor suddenly—how silly he must look, what a maniac he must look. And he shakes the banister expecting it to be loose from the blow, but it does not move and he feels both relief and disappointment.

And then an inchoate wail of despair rises up the stairwell, and Wyatt looks down at his father who quickly turns his head in the direction of the cry. And they all freeze—Virginia and Wyatt standing at the banisters in the upstairs hall, Will at the first turning of the stairs below them. And when the cry comes again, Will looks up quickly at his son and says, "You'd better clean this mess up, boy." And he turns away quickly and goes down the stairs and Wyatt hears the library door close and again Catherine's wail rises up the stairwell, louder now. He looks wildly over at his sister who shakes her head as though in warning, and then they hear the library door open and Will bellows out, "Button up your lip, you old bat!" And there is an indignant silence from below followed, after a moment, by another long drawn-out wail which is cut off by the slamming of the library door.

Wyatt and Virginia exchange silent laughter across the banisters, and then they hear Catherine begin to mount the stairs, hear her uncertain pawing for the handrail, glance down to see her pause and turn her head in the general direction of the library door and give a loud, rude Bronx cheer, followed by sobs.

And Wyatt looks over at Virginia and says emphatically, "Tomorrow is Christmas *Eve!*" And he turns, strides quickly to his room—amazed that he searches the dresser top for money and keys; amazed that the emotion that rises from his stomach when he hears his mother collide with one of the boxes of bottles in the hall comes out as a laugh and not a sob; amazed that he laughs again when he hears his sister say quite distinctly, "If you're drunk like this tomorrow when my husband arrives, I'm leaving." Yes, these things amaze Wyatt and he goes on being amazed as he finds a heavy sweater and opens the window beside his bed, backs out, balances on the ledge to pull the window closed behind him before dropping lightly to the chimney ledge below, and then to the top of the electric meters, and then to the ground where he stands trembling for a moment in *utter amazement* before he sets off at a trot across the snowy lawn in the direction of Sallie Burnham's house a mile down Blackberry Road, followed for a time by the collie who stops at the edge of the Parsons' property, stands a moment with one paw raised and ears pointing up straight, then turns and trots back in the direction of the house—as Wyatt runs on, amazed that he feels no lack of breath, amazed that the orange sun casts his shadow so enormously on the snow beside him as he runs.

from *The Adventures of Al*

The Spanish Friars Thing

Glen Ross

The Spanish Friars was a sixty-unit motel on the Camino Real down by San Bruno. We left Benfield's apartment around midnight in Gerald's car and drove out Dorland Boulevard and turned south on the Camino. Al was tense and trying to display as much cool as possible. But I was scared and depressed, and Al kept trying to cheer me up.

"There's always some degree of risk in these jobs, Carlos," he said. "But that's true of any business. I think we've got a good sound plan for tonight. Do you see any problems?"

I can't foresee problems worth a damn or I wouldn't have been in that car. I didn't have anything specific, but I had a watery feeling in my bones that this Spanish Friars hold-up was too complicated. It wasn't just a matter of grabbing the cash from a drawer and taking off. According to Al's observations of the place, there would only be one clerk on duty after midnight. Al and I were going to force this guy into the office behind the lobby and get him to tell us where the week-end receipts were. Al said the clerk was a middle-aged Chinese man who would be shaking in his shoes. But if he wouldn't tell us where the money was we would search the place until we found it. We didn't plan to use anything more than threats on the clerk. We figured it would be a waste of time to twist his arm, and anyway it would take too long.

"In any case," Al said, "they'll have the Sunday receipts on hand. If we walk out with less than three hundred, I won't take a dime for myself."

We planned to tie up the clerk with pieces of clothesline Gerald had bought two days ago and which we'd cut to suitable lengths and carried in our pockets. We would also gag the man, and barring anything unusual, we'd have a walkaway. Thirty seconds after leaving the motel we would be on the side road between San Bruno and the city and on the freeway a minute later.

"You're going to be up front on this, Gerald," Al said. "We're counting on you."

Gerald was going to take the clerk's place at the desk for the five or ten minutes it took Al and me to do our part. He was supposed to turn on the NO VACANCY sign first. Then he was to take care of the switchboard if there were any outgoing calls. Incoming calls he was supposed to just ignore. Al had drilled him on the switchboard with a dummy model he'd sketched on a cardboard box.

"Get the no-vacancy sign on, and you shouldn't have any problem with people just dropping in. It still might happen that somebody shows up who has a reservation. If they do, then just act natural and try to find their name in the book so you can give them a key. If it gets complicated, tell them you're just filling in for the regular clerk. Say he'll be back in five minutes."

Gerald tried to sound confident. "No problem, Al," he said. "I got it all down cold." Like me, Gerald may have been thinking about that glass-and-redwood pad on Twin Peaks that we had lined up. The motel job would make up the rest of the lease money.

We passed the San Francisco State campus and were rolling along south on the Camino under rows of giant eucalyptus trees. It was cold and the highway looked wet, even though it wasn't raining, and I was all tight and shivery. I half listened to Al telling how the Spanish Friars had romantic associations for him, because he had spent the first night of his honeymoon there. "We were booked to go to Monterey," he said. "But we couldn't hold out that far."

As we were passing the race track north of Bruno, Al leaned forward in the back seat and shook Gerald's shoulder. "Gerald," he said. "If somebody comes in while we're there, and you yell at me, 'Hey, Al, this guy wants a room!' do you know what I'm going to do? I'm going to tie you up and leave you right there in the lobby." He chuckled, and Gerald laughed weakly. Then Al pointed out the side road we would take on our way back to the city. It went straight over to the Bayshore Freeway. And then we could see the motel sign up ahead, and all at once we were there. Al and I got out and walked into the lobby.

We were in trouble from that moment on. As soon as I saw the clerk I knew we ought to turn around and walk out, because it wasn't the middle-aged Chinese man Al had told us about. It was a middle-aged woman. And she wasn't the kind of woman you would want to rob, if you had any choice. She looked like a retired school teacher, one of those indestructible old ladies who are made up of pig iron and algebra. The kind that never give up at anything, no matter what. And we're going to hold a gun on her and try to get across the idea that she is being hijacked.

I couldn't ever have done it on my own. I would have just signed for a room and gone to bed. And even Al . . . well, it took some of the wind out of his sails when we walked in there expecting to meet a mild oriental fellow and came face to face with that old lady.

She spoke first, asking Al if he wanted a room. And he told her no, he wanted the cash box. She looked him straight in the eye, like he'd zapped her with a paper clip, and said, "No, sir! Certainly not! It's absolutely out of the question. Now, you put that gun away and get out of here. I don't want another word out of you!"

She didn't sound scared, or even very mad, but irritated—like she'd been putting up with would-be robbers all day, and it was getting on her nerves.

Al didn't hesitate long. He denied afterwards that he'd hesitated at all. But he did. Just for a minute there I could see he'd forgot who he was. But then the Al in him snapped back, and he was over the counter talking sense to that old Roman almost before she could grab a ledger and start slamming him over the head with it.

When I saw Al was having a problem, I kind of woke up and jumped over the counter too. We didn't want anybody to get hurt, because this job was already too damn complicated, as far as I was concerned. I got around the old lady and grabbed the ledger, and the two of us managed to push her back into the office behind the lobby, and she started to yell then so we had to gag her and tie her to a chair.

I hope I don't ever have to go through something like that again. Getting that old woman to set still and shut up was a job for a squad of riflemen, not for two guys who are all out of shape from too much drinking and smoking. Al and I did it, but it took the wind out of us. And while I was getting the clothesline around her ankles she kicked hell out of me—once in the groin and once under my chin so hard I chipped a front tooth.

We had one piece of good luck. She had a key that was on a cord around her neck. It wouldn't slip over her head, though, and we fumbled away five minutes trying to find something to cut the cord with. We used a nail clipper out of a desk drawer. And all this time we were getting a double whammy from old Iron Pants that made me wish I'd worn a ski mask. But we got the key and it unlocked a side drawer in the desk. Inside the drawer was a metal cash box, also locked, which Al took out and handed to me, saying, "Hang onto this, man. It's cost us a lot of trouble." He was never more right.

All of this didn't happen in a vacuum exactly, free of all other distractions. Gerald had hit the wrong button and instead of turning on the NO in front of the vacancy sign he had turned the whole sign off. We didn't know this at the time because that part of the sign wasn't visible from inside. And while we were struggling to tie up the old woman, we could hear Gerald *talking to somebody* out in the lobby. It wasn't the last thing to expect in a motel lobby, but under the circumstances it tore me up. My nerves, if I can call them that, felt like a roll of concertina barbed wire. I knew all along that Gerald wasn't any more qualified for that kind of work than old Bumble was. I got that frozen, fractured feeling—kind of like the feeling you get when you know you have been wounded in combat, only worse. Like a nightmare you can't wake up from.

Gerald had left his car in the driveway, right in front of the door, and he had to go out and move it so the guy he was talking to could get through in his own car. And the damn switchboard started buzzing and kept up a steady blatt all the time we were there.

As soon as we had the cash box, we cleared out of the office. The lobby was empty, and Al stopped behind the counter and cleaned out the money drawer there before vaulting over the counter after me. We came out through the front door just as Gerald was pulling his car around to the entrance, and we jumped in before he had stopped the car and told him to get the hell out of there.

We took off north on the Camino at top speed, and we hadn't gone half a mile before this cop car went screaming by in the opposite direction. Just before we got to the turn-off road to the freeway I looked back and saw the cherry-topper make a screeching U-turn in the empty lanes and head back our way. Al saw it too, and he told Gerald to kick that old Studebaker in the ass and get us off the two-lane road quick. Gerald did his best. The freeway was less than a mile from the Camino, and we hit the southlane ramp doing about seventy with the cop car flashing and wailing half a mile behind us.

For once Al didn't have much to say. The idea of trying to outrun the cops in a car like ours never even crossed our minds. If we could make it to an exit and drop off the freeway and get out of sight for a few seconds, we would have a chance. But we would have to leave the car.

We didn't quite make it. We came to an exit ramp and went down it fast, but we just barely got the car stopped in time to bail out, with the cop car so close behind that it damn near rammed Gerald's car when he hit the brakes. We took off in three directions, and I lost contact with Al and Gerald at that point. I was still carrying the motel's cash box when I took off, and I dodged in among the concrete freeway pillars, running hard with the cops yelling at me to stop. And I could hear that horrible frightening crackle of the patrol car's radio. I figured they were going to take a shot at me, and I was willing to risk it because I knew from experience how hard it is to hit a moving target at any distance. I was crouching and dodging and weaving, expecting to hear a bullet split the air any second. But they didn't shoot. Maybe because it was a poor chance of hitting me, but probably because there were houses in the line of fire across the frontage road and if they hit the freeway supports the bullets would ricochet in any direction.

When I was a hundred yards from the place where we left the car I leaped over a ditch full of water and sailed over a barbed wire fence onto the right-of-way alongside the frontage road. I pounded across two lanes of asphalt and cut across the corner of the concrete apron of a service station that was still open even at that ungodly hour. The guy inside stood up and looked out at me, but I was gone before he knew it.

Before we started out that night, I thought I was in bad shape, physically. I never knew I was such a good runner. When I passed that service station I was just getting warmed up. I sprinted down a side street into a residential neighborhood where there were houses with trees all along there, and in the first block I picked up a stupid goddamn dog that took out after me yap-yap-yapping at the top of his lungs. There must have been two dogs for every house along that street, and most of them were running loose. I don't need to describe what it was like before I got to the end of the block. They were yipping and yapping and barking and baying until I couldn't even hear my feet slap the concrete. They didn't try to bite me or anything, but the noise was nerve-racking. So I stopped at a corner and let the leaders of the pack catch up with me, then I turned around quick and kicked a few ribs, and the ones I connected with backed off and the others stopped to talk it over, which gave me time to gain half a block on them. But as soon as I was out of their territory I picked up another pack that yelped along after me. I was glad it was late at night and everybody was in bed, or I would have had dogs and kids strung out for a mile behind me.

I saw a moving red light cut across an intersection up ahead, and I knew they were cruising for me—probably two cars crisscrossing the area to get a fix. If they spotted me just once I might as well stop running and get used to the idea of jail. But they hadn't seen me yet, so I kept going and tried to scan in all directions. It was a good thing I did, because about two seconds later I glanced over my shoulder just in time to spot another prowl car as its light swept between a corner house and the house next to it, half a block behind me. I had about three seconds to get out of sight when it turned in my direction.

I ran across the corner of somebody's lawn, heading for the dark area between two houses. I put my arm up to shield my eyes as I pushed through some shrubbery, and ... *Wham!* I slammed full tilt into a cinder-block wall and staggered back, almost falling. I was still clutching the cash box, and I hugged it to my chest and scrambled over the wall—no choice, no planning in advance. The cop car's spotlight was already sweeping the yard of the next house toward me. I got a leg over the top row of blocks and rolled over.

I came down hard in a sandbox and hit my shin on a toy tractor or something lying there, which just barely registered as pain because at the same time I had woke up a dog that made all the others look like toy poodles. I heard this murderous growl and looked up and saw a dark bulk charging at me, and my reflexes took over and I rolled back into an angle of the fence where I tried to get into some kind of defensive position. Because this dog was a German shepherd about three feet tall that must have weighed more than I did. This was happening so fast that I didn't have time to think. Just when I knew I'd had it, I heard a *click-snap-clink* of a chain and the damn brute fell thud on his side about two feet away. It stunned him enough for me to get the hell out of his reach by way of the wall along the alley side, which I cleared in about two seconds.

I dropped down among some weeds and garbage racks and waited there a minute till I could get over the shock from that last dog. My legs were trembling, and I felt cold and my mouth was dry and my heart pounding. I had to lean against the wall until I stopped shaking, and by then the prowl car had gone out of sight. I went on down the alley, not running any more because it was too dark and there was too much junk back there, and I was still too weak to run anyway. But at least there weren't any dogs back there, so I stayed in the alleys and kept going south until I was out of the neighborhood. I caught sight of the patrol cars a couple of times, but they were farther away now, and I was sure they hadn't seen me.

After a while I was getting close to the main streets of some town—Millbrae or Burlingame—and when I had to leave the shelter of the alley and walk across the street I froze. I was afraid to show myself, even though it was late at night and there weren't any cars or people on the street. The cash box I was carrying felt like it was radioactive, and all I could think of was getting rid of it. But I wasn't ready to ditch it with the money still in it, so I tucked it under my arm to hide it the best I could, and struck out across the four-lane street, walking as fast as I could without running. And before long I was able to get into the alleys again and I felt a little better. By now I must have been a couple of miles from where we left the car. But that wasn't far enough for comfort.

I didn't know where I was going. If Al and Gerald had got away from the cops they would head for Benfield's place. There wasn't anything in Gerald's car that would lead the cops there, so we would have a chance to think about our next move. But getting back to Benfield's was the problem. I was ten miles from Dorland Boulevard, and I was still seeing cop cars all over the place. I guess my imagination made me think that every cop in the county was after me. Even the glimpse of a flashing red stop-light would give me a jolt of panic. I was afraid to stop at a phone booth and call a cab because I thought the cops would have alerted all the taxi companies.

I had to get rid of that cash box. I kept moving south away from the lighted streets, until I got to a junky part of town where there were salvage yards and tin sheds and cement block storage buildings. I ran into a pipe rack in some weeds and kept stumbling over things, so I knelt and groped in the weeds until I put my hand on a heavy chunk of steel—like a pinion gear or something—and I put the metal cash box on the ground and smashed the lid with the pinion gear until it twisted and broke the lock. I opened the box. There was money in it, all right, and all in bills. I didn't have any idea how much was there, but it was a good handful. I stuffed the bills in my inside coat pocket and threw the box into the weeds under the pipe rack and went on.

All I knew was to keep following my instincts, and they said keep moving, keep putting distance between me and the Spanish Friars. I'd lost all sense of time and hadn't once looked at my watch, but it must have been an hour later when I came to a clearing and looked out into the asphalt acres of a big shopping center that was all empty and lit up with those weird blue-green lights everywhere. I saw a sign over one of the stores that said SAN MATEO MUSIC MART and I remembered that Bert King lived in San Mateo. I thought about that for a minute, then I turned and went back into the alley and found a place where I could hide between some garbage-can racks.

My idea at first was to call Bert and ask him to pick me up at the shopping center on his way to work. But the longer I sat there the less I liked it. Bert had always been friendly because he liked and respected Al, and he would probably be willing to do me a favor with no questions asked. But I would have to have a believable story to account for being where I was without a car at that time of night, or any other time, without my car. Because the Spanish Friars was going to be a news story, and it might even come on the radio in Bert's car while we were on our way to the city. It would be hard even for somebody as innocent and unsuspecting as Bert not to wonder if there might not be a connection between me and the motel job. I decided to give it some more thought.

I sat in the alley smoking until I ran out of cigarettes, then I counted the money. I'll admit something I never admitted to Al. The only part of the armed robbery business I enjoyed was counting the money. It took me a long time to count the money from the motel cash box. It was so dark in the alley that I had to look close at every one of the bills to see the numbers. But the longer I worked the more interesting it got. There were only four denominations—ones, fives, tens, and twenties— so I sorted them out and put them in different pockets, then I counted each pocket separately and added it all up in my mind. It came to 994 dollars, more cash than I had ever held in my life. And like anybody else, I gave some thought to just walking straight away and never looking back. I could have got to L.A. easy, by myself, or even Mexico. But I knew that if Al had survived this night he would be counting on me to meet him, and he would be worried about me honestly, even more than about the money because he didn't know how much it was or even if it was there at all, or if I had been able to hang on to it. I had to go back, there wasn't any question about that.

When I had been stashing the bills in my pockets, I had felt a piece of cardboard which I had thrown on the ground at my feet. I could see it there, a little white rectangle on the dark ground, and I remembered that it was a business card that Grover Burns had give me. His name and office phone number were printed on the front, but he had written his private number on the back. He owed me a favor for helping him the night he wrecked his Cadillac—not to mention the dozens of lies I'd told for him to the characters who were always coming around to Dorland's looking for him. I got up and left the alley and went to find a phone to call Grover.

I couldn't bring myself to walk across that shopping center lot, under the cold blue-bleak light, but I went west along the empty street to an intersection that turned out to be the Camino Real again. A diner was open there, with a pay phone inside. A clock behind the counter said four o'clock. In a corner booth a couple of truckers and a girl were eating breakfast, and a man behind the counter was making coffee in a big stainless steel urn. God, that coffee smelled good. But I couldn't take the chance of stopping to drink a cup. I went to the phone and put in my dime, and after dialing the number on the card I heard the phone ring at the other end. No answer. I let it ring a long time—six, seven, eight, nine, ten, eleven, twelve times it must have rung, with my mind all out of gear and not willing to hang up. Then I heard Grover's voice come through strong and clear, and I could almost see him in that one word. "Yeah?"

I told him I had a problem and it would be worth a lot of Bibles to me if he would send Maylene or somebody down to San Mateo to pick me up.

He didn't ask any questions, just where I would be, and I told him the shopping center in front of the San Mateo Music Mart. "Thirty minutes," he said.

I bought a pack of cigarettes and walked back to the alley where I could keep an eye on the Music Mart while I waited. That was a long thirty minutes, and when Grover came he wasn't in his Cadillac. He was in a tan Dodge so nondescript that it was almost invisible, which I recognized as belonging to Maylene Burns. She was driving, and Grover was sitting in the back seat by himself. Early as it was, he had got dressed in a suit and wore a big hat and held a cane propped between his knees. He was smoking a cigar. He could have passed for an old-time Southern Congressman on his way to Washington—I mean, he looked that honest.

I got in the back seat beside Grover, and Maylene drove east to the Bayshore Freeway and merged with the early north-bound traffic. Grover was cool. He didn't have to ask any questions, he could figure out what had happened, more or less, from the circumstances. He didn't seem the least bit curious about what I was doing away to hell down in San Mateo at four o'clock in the morning without my car, or why I'd called him instead of a cab or somebody else. He didn't say anything until we were on the freeway, then he said, "You and Al still a' boll-weevilin' it up at Dorland's?"

"Yeah," I said. "Business has picked up since the first of the year. We been doing pretty good."

Grover chuckled and coughed and spit out a piece of the cigar he was fuming over. "You working your way up to a real estate license, like Al?"

"No, I'm just hanging on till I get on my feet. I'm going into the freight business as soon as something turns up." I told him a lot of other stuff, about how I had it all planned to get my road driver's card before I was thirty and buy my own rig and everything.

Grover would listen to a person, I'll say that for him. "Carlos," he said. "You got some brains, you ought to learn to use them. It'll take you ten years to get where you want to go, the way you're going about it. Do you mind if I make a suggestion?"

Of course I didn't mind, and he went on. "This ain't the right town for truckers. If I was you I'd want to be in L.A. Get to know some people down there and kind of learn the feel of the situation."

I said I knew that, but that I was strapped by lack of money and contacts. "I'll make it on my own," I said. "Like my dad, just sticking at a job and learning from experience."

Grover changed his tone and his tactics. "Of course that's the best way," he said. "But one way or another you're going to have to get to know some people. Can you handle a semi?"

"Sure," I said. "But I ain't got the papers to prove it."

He shrugged. "When you get ready to go south, look me up. Maybe I could put you on to something."

We were driving past the place where we had left Gerald's car, four or five hours earlier. The car was gone, but I recognized the service station I had run past. I kept talking to Grover but I wasn't following him very closely. My mind was busy with a problem that I hadn't been willing to face until now. I had about fifteen minutes to think it through. The problem was that the cops had Gerald's car, and the odds were ten to one that they had Gerald too. And Gerald was very persuadable. He would have to prove to the cops that he wasn't as dumb as they thought he was, and he would tell them everything he ever did in his whole life.

I said to Grover, "What has Bible sales got to do with the Teamsters Union?"

He laughed and slapped his knee and said, "You gotta get out of that cotton patch, old son. Them boll weevils are affecting your brains. What I mean is, a man never knows when he might need somebody to do him a favor. So I help out people when I can, and then I ain't too proud to ask a favor in turn."

I didn't know what he was driving at. "Damnit, Grover," I said. "You're too damn deep for me. If you got something in mind, why don't you spell it out for me?"

Some people are flattered when you tell them they're all that subtle. Not old clubfoot Burns. He puffed a cloud of stogie smoke and looked out over the bay, where everything was all silvery and misty cold. "Don't waste your time trying to figure people out, Carlos. What the hell? I don't understand nobody, but I get along better than most. Some people I like, and I help 'em out. If I happen to know a guy that might be able to use you, well. It don't cost me anything."

I didn't have much room to maneuver. Any kind of friend was worth holding on to, was how I felt then. I wanted to keep the line open to Grover because I was starting to realize that I might be going to L.A. sooner than I planned—like today. Because I was in deep water. While I was waiting for Grover to pick me up, sitting there in the alley, I had taken a deep breath and let myself sink down as far as I could. I could just barely touch bottom with my toes. I was treading water now, with no shore in sight.

When we got to California Street I told Grover that I would see him later, and I got out of the car a couple of blocks from Benfield's apartment. It was foggy and windy up there on Pacific Heights, and still dark in the early morning. I scouted the place as I walked up the hill and saw my car parked where I had left it the night before, and when I turned onto Sacramento I saw Al's car still there across the street. I had just turned in the driveway gate and was walking toward the door when I heard a car pull up and stop at the curb behind me. My heart started racing, and I looked around slow, expecting to see a police car. But it was a Yellow Cab. I saw Al get out and give the driver a bill and wave him on.

We didn't say anything until we had got upstairs to Ben's flat, and we held our voices down because he was asleep in his bedroom. Al picked up a bottle of bourbon from his room and we went out on the roof deck to the farthest corner over the alley. We had a couple of stiff shots of whiskey before we talked; after the second drink Al wiped his mouth and shook his head, trying to grin. "Whew!" was all he could say. We had another drink, then he said, "Chico, old buddy. I just realized something. You and me have got charmed lives. It's the only explanation."

77

I never enjoyed a drink as much as that one. The whiskey took hold fast, and in a minute or two that frozen, fractured feeling that came over me in the motel began to melt away. "I'll be honest with you, Al," I said. "I thought we'd had it this time, I honestly did. It looked like—well, like no way out, man."

"It was bleak," Al said. Then he chuckled and said, "You took off like a wild duck. I don't think your feet even touched ground. Those cops were really impressed at what a good runner you were. I guess it saved my neck, because one of them had to get on the radio and call for help, and they tried to zero in on you."

"I saw plenty of cop cars, all right," I said. "I guess they all concentrated on that side of the freeway."

Al told me he had found a culvert a little way from where we left the car. "I remembered that time in Korea when we got ambushed by those gooks in a culvert. We wouldn't ever have known they were there if they hadn't shot at us—so when I found that culvert I crawled in it and did a quick camouflage job over the end and waited it all out. When the area was clear I walked over to a cafe in Burlingame and ate breakfast, then I took a cab to Market Street and another cab out here."

I told him all about my flight through the alleys, without saying anything about the money box. Al didn't once ask about it. Under the circumstances he wouldn't have blamed me if I had lost it. I asked him if he had seen Gerald after we left the car, and he said, "I'm not sure, but it's ten to one he got picked up. The last I saw of him he was galloping along up the east side of the highway, headed north. I don't know how they could have missed him."

I said, "That's too bad." But I guess I was thinking more in terms of what was bad for me and Al.

"Well, there's no help for it," Al said. "I don't think it'll hurt Gerald's career much. It might even improve his attitude to do some time."

"It couldn't hurt it," I said.

"I'm kind of worried, though, about what he might tell the cops. What do you think?"

"He'll tell them everything he ever did in his entire life," I said. "Clear back to his childhood. And anything else they want to know about."

Al took a deep breath and looked kind of grim.

"It looks like we're going to have to pull back, Al," I said. "We're cut off, and the sooner we get out of town the better."

Al didn't say anything, and I knew he was feeling pretty low, in spite of the whiskey. I took the stacks of bills out of my coat pocket and said, "This ought to get us out of town easy enough."

It is a rare thing to see a person as happy as Al was. "You did it!" he said, and I'll be damned if he didn't give a rebel yell. "I was afraid to ask you about it," he said. "Have you counted it?"

I said I hadn't exactly counted it, because I knew Al liked to share the pleasure of the final tally. So we counted it out again there on the deck, and it was still 994 dollars.

"I take back everything I said about you being wishy-washy, Carlos," Al said. "I was sure you must have dropped the damn box or had to get rid of it somewhere."

Al had got more than two hundred out of the cash drawer in the motel, so we put it all together and split it between us, and Al figured a minute and said that if Gerald turned up we owed him a couple of hundred apiece. But that looked more and more remote as a possibility. I was itching to get on wheels and clear out.

Al said, "Let's hang on here till eight o'clock to give Gerald a chance to turn up. Even if he got away from the cops he'd be stranded here without his car. But if we don't hear from him at least by eight o'clock, we'll have to assume he's out of contact."

Since it was only five minutes till seven, that meant we would have to sweat out an hour, but I didn't feel like arguing with Al about it. He went down to the street to buy a paper, on the chance that it might have some information about the motel robbery that we didn't—such as something about Gerald.

He was back with the paper in five minutes. There was something in it, all right, but not about Gerald—about me. Thank God it wasn't on the front page, but on the inside with the police news was a picture of Gerald's car, and down below it was that awful goddamn picture of me that they took at Apex Freight when I went to work there. They had fingerprinted me at Apex too, and filed the prints with the police. I had made it about as easy as I could for them to identify me by leaving my paw prints all over Gerald's car. I was just sick about it. I had been worried about Gerald ratting on me, but it had been me that blew whatever cover we had left.

There was a story about the Spanish Friars too, and Al and I read it together silently.

Al laughed like he was a little bit embarrassed and said, "That old lady really has it in for you, Chico. It sounds like you raped her." He read that part out loud, and the way they had twisted the facts around made me mad as hell.

"I didn't assault that old witch, Al," I said. "Did I? All I did was hold her arms so she wouldn't bash our brains in with that goddamn ledger. That's not assault, man, that's self-defense."

"You don't need to prove it to me," Al said. "We can't afford to start worrying about minor injustices right now. Nobody who saw her would believe you tried to rape her. So forget it." But he couldn't help laughing a little bit.

"This goddamn paper has been nothing but bad news for us, Al," I said. "First they tried to put us out of the rental business, and now this! And look at that picture. And that description of me—they've even got it in about my ear."

The only sign of a lucky break in the whole sorry mess, as far as it concerned me, was that they had got my name off the Apex files too. And I had signed it in full, like I always do on anything official—Carlos Angel de Torres Quemanda—and they had shortened it to Carlos Quemanda. It wasn't much of a break, but Al saw a ray of hope in it.

"Nobody in San Francisco that knows you ever heard you called Carlos Quemanda," he said. "And I don't think anybody could recognize you from that picture. And as for the description, well, most people don't read that far. And even if they do, they don't remember the details. Nobody notices people's ears, anyway."

"That old lady at the motel noticed," I said. "And she noticed that I'm Spanish American, and she called my height to the inch—five feet four. Tell me the truth, Al. How many short Mexican guys do you know who are named Carlos and who have a notch in their left ear? How many, all together?"

Al tried to laugh it off, but I don't think he would have seen the humor of it, if he'd been in my shoes. "I'm trying to tell you not to panic," he said. "We got to stick around to see if Gerald is going to show. If the cops caught him it ought to be in the paper. So it looks like he might have made it. But we can't be sure, on account of the time lag. We got to give him a chance."

Al was right, of course. But Gerald wasn't any threat to us, regardless of what had happened to him. One thing was clear, the cops had his whole story from his car records, and they had a clear trail to me by way of Apex. It wouldn't take them more than a few hours to catch up with me, depending on how much else they had to do. But I was willing to wait around for an hour, partly for the pleasure of finishing off Al's bourbon, which we had been nipping on steadily.

I had got over that tight, shivery feeling that had clutched me for so long. Out there on the roof deck where Al and I were it was so cold we could see our breath in the air, but the damp wind felt good on my face, and I could smell the ocean like I used to sometimes in Japan. Every few seconds a foghorn blasted, out in the bay, like it was warning me to get the hell out of San Francisco. I still didn't know where I was going. I didn't want to go back to Santa Fe for a long time. And I didn't want to go to Las Vegas, though Al kept talking about it. That left L.A. as a possibility, and if Grover had been trying to tell me something it looked like that was my best bet. But I didn't mention it to Al because he hated L.A. and didn't like to hear me talk about truck driving.

As the minutes went by, Al kept up a one-sided conversation about the interesting possibilities in Nevada. But I couldn't see much in it. In Vegas, I figured our money would last us maybe three hours, depending on whether or not we ate supper before we hit the casinos. And we would end up in L.A. anyhow, only we would be flat broke in the bargain. I didn't argue with Al, because it only strengthened his mind to take his dreams as serious possibilities. I just kept nodding and half listening and getting more depressed all the time, until he said, "What's the matter with you, Chico?"

"I'm not feeling myself, Al," I told him. "I feel kind of numb. You know what I mean?"

"It'll pass," he said, with his usual cheerful acceptance of other people's problems. "You need sleep. Did you eat any breakfast?"

I said no, so Al went inside to get us something to eat and he was gone a long time. But when he came back he was carrying a couple of plates with scrambled eggs and bacon and a pot of coffee. "We might as well fill up," he mumbled, with a cigarette in his mouth. "If we're gonna march we might need it."

The food looked good, and I lit into it. I realized that I hadn't eaten anything for twelve hours, and during that time I had burned a lot of energy. I knew that was the cause of my mental tailspin—or part of it. The rest I could mark up to the lack of sleep and the general lousy situation I was in. My father used to call it the *ley de pan*—law of bread. He used to say that all any man had to do was eat and sleep. That this was the only law ever passed by nature. There is something to it.

It was almost eight o'clock by the time we finished eating. I was going to try to say adios to Al and take off. On my own, I would have about one-third as many problems as I was used to having, and I figured I could handle them.

We were still sitting there on the deck with our plates when all at once we heard a noise that froze us. I thought it was a telephone, then I thought it was a doorbell, and then I realized it wasn't either of those things—it was something else. It was louder and too clear to come from inside the apartment or downstairs. Al and I stared at each other with our minds racing over the same possibilities, trying to evaluate the whole thing and make our move quick without any mistakes. Then it stopped. I saw a funny look come over Al's face, and he got to his feet and walked toward the other side of the roof deck. I followed him over to where the sound had seemed to be coming from. We looked over a planter stand, where there were some flower pots and stuff, and there was Gerald crawling out of his sleeping bag. His alarm clock was on the deck beside him.

My legs—right behind the kneecaps—had turned to loose string, and I had to lean on the planter stand and catch my breath. Al stood there. He was pale and kind of sick-looking. But Gerald didn't look any worse than usual. He didn't even seem surprised or particularly glad to see us. We didn't bother to tell him that we had been planning to leave that very minute, or that he had given us both a nervous shock equal to about three months of infantry combat. As soon as I had recovered enough to think, I realized that everything was different again, and we'd have to think it through all over, with Gerald included.

"We better leave now, and make plans on the way," I told Al. "With Gerald's car and my prints and everything they'll be right behind us."

"Wait a minute," Al said. "Stop and think. Gerald, does anybody besides Angela know you're staying here?"

Gerald said no, but like me he wasn't going to hang around while Al was being logical. "I'm not taking any chances," he said. "I'm hauling it out of here."

"Me too," I said. I took out my billfold and counted out two hundred dollars and gave it to Gerald, expecting Al would follow suit. But he didn't, and Gerald was so distraught that he didn't even count the money. "You can ride with me," I told him. "We'll split when we get out of town." I had to say that, but I didn't feel happy about it.

Al looked at us like he couldn't believe his ears. "What's with you guys?" he said. "You're losing your heads. All we got to do is cool it, and it'll all be over in twenty-four hours. Believe me."

"Al," I said, taking a deep breath and trying to keep my voice down. "The cops could walk out here through that door and onto this deck at exactly any minute. Now, cool is cool, but we are hot. And that is not just my opinion, Al, it's a fact."

Gerald had put on his sport coat and was trying to straighten himself up. He ran his hand through his hair, which was standing at attention all over his head. "I can't understand you, Al," he said.

"It's not fun and games, Al," I said. "It's in the paper, man! It was *my* picture, and a description of *me*. And they've got Gerald's car to trace."

"But that wasn't your right name, was it?"

"Not exactly, but—"

"And Gerald didn't list this place as his address, did he?"

"No, but they've got our office address, because it was the only one I had to give them when I went to work for Apex."

"Well, nobody at the office is going to know who they are talking about. They will think it's another one of Grover's problems and they won't give it a thought. Besides, the cops aren't going to put Charlie Chan on a case like this. It's too simple. And it's not big enough for an all-points bulletin, so it looks to me like the best move is to just lie low and act like it never happened."

Gerald wasn't listening. "That was my car, Al," he said. "And I have had enough. My nerves are just flat stripped out, and . . . and that's all. I gotta get out of here."

Al dug in his pocket and fished out his car keys and tossed them to Gerald and said, "O.K., Gerald, if that's your decision, you can take my car. Keep it, you might need it to run away in, next time you're in a jam."

Gerald didn't respond, except to kneel and start to roll up his sleeping bag and blanket.

"Me too, Al," I said. "You can do what you like, and I hope you can keep clean of this mess. But they'll be looking for me. They're not gonna just put it in a hold basket, with the leads they've got. That's how I see it."

Al didn't look at me. He took time to light a cigarette like it was his last one on earth. He exhaled a stream of smoke and vapor and said, "You're gonna cut out on me, huh? You're going to play it safe and leave me without any transport. That's not like you, Carlos."

I was getting as crazy with nervous habits as Gerald. I kept brushing my hair back out of my eyes and rubbing my shoes on my pants legs to get some shine back into them. "You're twisting it around, Al," I told him. "You really are."

He got this bitter look. "What I'm wondering right now," he said, "is how I ever got hooked up with you two losers in the first place." He looked coldly at Gerald, who had rolled up his gear with a lot of magazines and stuff and was muttering to himself, "Man, I've had it. I gotta get out. If I don't get outa this creepy pad it'll total me out, I mean . . ."

The sight seemed to take something out of Al. He kind of gave up, and when he spoke again he sounded tired. "Well, I won't say any more," he said. "But I don't think you would be wise to leave right now, Carlos, and I will explain why. First, you are pretty drunk, and in your condition the least little thing—minor car problem, any false move—could do you in. In the second place, you need sleep bad. You want your judgment to be in as good a shape as possible, which it is not. And another thing, the papers with that motel story and your picture are on the streets at this moment and people are reading it right now. By tonight they'll have forgotten it, but, as you were the first to point out, there is a risk that you will be recognized."

What Al said went against every instinct in my bones, but it made sense. What he said was true. And I had got to the point where I didn't trust my feelings the way I once had.

Al went on. "It's too bad. But you've got to do what you feel is necessary. We had some laughs, eh?"

"Yeah, it's been a long party."

"Well, let it go, live it down, what the hell? You know, Chico, even now it's hard to believe it's over and I've gotta leave San Francisco. The only two places I ever wanted to be—Tokyo and here—I never felt at home anywhere else."

"That's how it goes, Al," I said. "You never can tell how things will work out. But you're right about waiting till dark before I make a move."

"Yeah, get some rest. The cops won't be here for a day or two. You shouldn't ever make a big decision on the spur of the moment, when your nerves are jangled."

Gerald had been standing there waiting for me to leave so he could go with me, and now he didn't know what to do. Al said he could keep our cover by picking up Angela, wherever she was, and keeping her out of sight before the cops got around to talking to her. That approach could be sealed off. So Gerald left in Al's car to look for Angela, and I went into the apartment, which was quiet and gloomy in the early light, and climbed up to the dining room gallery and stretched out on the floor. I tried to think. Before Gerald popped up, I'd had a clear line of thought, but that damn alarm clock had shook my mind so that I'd been rattled and confused ever since. I had an idea Al was going to be with me when I left town. That business of his giving his car keys to Gerald had baffled me, but then I realized that Al's car would be hotter than mine very soon, and it was Al's way of paying Gerald his two hundred of the Spanish Friars loot.

It was all so freakish and up-in-the-air that I had to stop thinking and get hold of myself. I told myself that since nobody was shooting at me I might as well get some sleep. I did, and when I woke up a couple of hours later Benfield was there, and it was one big monster of a scene.

from *Hey, Liberal*

Lunchroom

Shawn Shiflett

> *Mama come here quick*
> *and bring that'a lickin' stick*
> *Mama come here quick*
> *and bring that'a lickin' stick...*

Like it was the sureness of the next beat blaring from the P.A. that counted more than the music itself, the sureness that James Brown was right there with them, a soulful black man's scream screeching through the lunchroom:

> *Mama come here quick*
> *and bring that'a lickin' stick*
> *Mama come here quick*
> *and bring that'a lickin' stick...*

A girl sitting at a table screamed, "Gimme back ma quarta', mothafucka'; gimme back ma quarta' fo' I bust yo' mothafuckin' head." Her boyfriend just grinned, and then she grinned too, trying to slap his face, but he caught her wrist and held it loosely; she didn't seem to mind. Everywhere dudes threw fake punches as they yelled, "You a lie, bawh!" or knocked someone's hat off, or took a couple of steps back from a friend and shadowboxed, shuffling like Muhammad Ali. Black girls bobbed their heads in time with the music, and some of them stood on their chairs, and jerked their hips, and looked mean as a motha', because you got to look mean to be bad, and you got to be bad to be cool.

A Coke bottle crashed against the back wall. Over by the windows, Simon, one of maybe five white students in the entire high school lunchroom, looked up from his history book, his eyes focused straight ahead as he let his hearing scan the room to tell him what he needed to know. The black crowd's voice rose as one, "Ohhhhh," then sporadic sing-song voices, "Who did iiiiit? Who did iiiiit?"

Black dudes walked around whistling shrilly with their fingers in their mouths. Others pounded on tables, any kind of noise so that what wanted to happen would happen. Simon leaned farther over his history book and flipped through the pages faster. Adrenalin pumped through his temples, and his feet sweated in his gym shoes as he curled his toes in and out, digging into the soles.

Suddenly, he heard the chair across from him slide out; he tensed, a rush of heat rising to his head. It was OK, calm down, only Louis, another white. His face was unshaven, his eyes an empty ghostly gray with dark bags underneath. He wore an over-sized, un-ironed, white dress shirt with the tails untucked and a pair of khaki work pants. He plopped down in the chair, did not even look at Simon, and gazed out the windows into the barren courtyard that was enclosed on all four sides by the school.

Defying everything that had and would happen that day, Simon tried to sound cheerful.

"Say, Louis, what's goin' on!"

Louis just continued to stare out the windows, his face pale and his legs sprawled out in front of him, the rawhide shoelaces in his construction boots untied so that the ends were all black from being walked on. He took a long snorting sniff through his clogged nose, then let the air out through his mouth.

"Why ya mess with that shit?" Simon asked, Louis sitting there once again strung out on some drug or other; but Louis just blinked real slow as if to say, Not now, man, don't start that shit on me now.

Fuck him, Simon thought. He comes in here, sits next to me and then doesn't say a fuckin' word—looks out the goddamn window like a jagoff. But underneath his anger Simon wondered, why do people always get tired of me? Well, fuck him; fuck the whole goddamn place, fuck every...

"Say, man." A tall, skinny, black dude, his palms turned back bad-like, stood over Simon. "Loan m'a quarta'." He wore red pants and a black, silky-looking shirt, and what looked like some kind of a tooth hung from a silver chain around his neck. The bridge of his nose sunk way in, and his nostrils flared out, dominating his whole face.

Simon looked up, his anger erased just like that. He raised his eyebrows as if to say, "Who, me?" and, "Sure, man," all at the same time. He dug his hand into one of his front jean pockets and rubbed a couple of quarters hard between his fingers, then sat the coins back down without letting them jingle. He would risk it—no, don't be a fool —yeah, risk it, risk it, risk it. He took out a dime, his voice suddenly sounding black as he said, "Ah thought ah had a quarta', man, but ah guess ah just got a dime."

The black boy glared theatrically. "What you mean, *you guess?*"

"Really, man, come on, it's yours, that all ah got; take it." Simon raised his hands to either side of himself, "All ya find, all ya keep."

The black boy flipped his hands up and down for Simon to rise so that he could frisk Simon. "Awright, mothafucka', if you a lie, you a dead lie," and then the boy mumbled something about how he didn't take no shit from no hunky. Simon stood, and from another table where a group of black students sat, someone yelled, "Dig Jackson. What you gonna do ta dat white bawh, Jackson? If he ain't give it, dot dat hunky's eye, ma man."

Simon felt a nervous grin glued over his face. Three quarters lay at the bottom of his pocket—that's the kind of stuff people get killed over, trying to hide seventy-five cents. It didn't take long for Jackson to find them. He pinched the material of Simon's pant leg and held one of the coins sandwiched inside.

Oh fuck, Simon thought, a simple Oh fuck. So this was what everything had been building up to all day—he was going to be the *oh fuck* of the day. For the benefit of the lunchroom audience, the boy looked all around himself with a smirk until his eyes came right back around to Simon's grin. The boy glared even more and flared his nostrils. Simon knew it would only be a moment now, and he would do nothing but stand there as the black boy bopped him upside his head again and again. But just then Louis leaned forward with his fists clenched on the table top. He ran his nose close along the table and sniffed like a bloodhound.

"Damn, where's it comin' from; damn, do ya smell it, Simon? Damn!"

The black boy still pinched the quarter inside Simon's pocket. "What you call dis here, hunky?" He moved a step closer so that his warm chest smashed against Simon.

"Like maybe you didn't hear me, nigger," Louis yelled, "I SAID, DAMN, IT FUCKIN' STINKS! STINKS OF NIGGERS! YEAH, JESUS CHRIST, THERE'S JUST TOO MANY FUCKIN' NIGGERS IN HERE!"

James Brown alone didn't have sense enough to shut up:

Say it loud

I'm black and I'm proud
Say it loud
I'm black and I'm proud . . .

Everyone in the lunchroom stopped what they were doing and turned toward the white boy's screams of "nigger." The weight of all those eyes pressed down on Simon like he was in a feverish dream. "Louis," he whispered, yet his words seemed uncomfortably loud, "what have you done?" But Louis just grinned like the crazy fucker he was. There wasn't a teacher or another white student in sight, not even the German canteen lady: funny how people can always feel what's coming and split. Jackson, the black boy with the tooth hanging from his neck, looked up quickly as if to check if . . . yes, the world, at least his world, was watching. His hand fell away from Simon's pocket. He turned to face Louis sitting across the table. Jackson's lips moved, but the words wouldn't come quick enough nor accurate enough to express whatever he felt. For the first time Simon saw blood rise in a black man's face, and Simon's chest quivered with each breath, his grin just now disappearing. He looked around, wondering why the hell hadn't his father just let him go to Lane Technical High School with all of his other friends. He backed away until his ass pressed against the next table just behind Jackson and left Louis to stand on his own. Louis just looked up at Simon as if to say, It's OK, I understand, all with one calm look of the eye that made a half-assed attempt to release Simon from the guilt one feels when ignoring the responsibility of one's skin.

Suddenly, Jackson couldn't move fast enough. He bent down and sprang back up almost in the same instant with a red, pearl-handled switch blade in his hand that he had pulled from inside the top of one of his tall, polished combat boots. The blade flashed open and gleamed clean. He reached back for the first slash, and people knocked over chairs to get closer, and girls screamed with their hands over their faces, and lots of students jumped up on tables to get a better view. Just as Jackson swung his arm around and started to dive across the table for Louis, he inadvertently caught the blade on the inside of one of Simon's nostrils as Simon stood pressed back against the table directly behind Jackson. A fast, sharp, lacerating pain pulsated through Simon's face, and in a rush his body both plummeted and rose into a shock. With a thrust of his legs, Louis scooted back in his chair just as Jackson swung down with his knife, stabbing the air where Louis had been. Jackson didn't quite make it over the table and lay stranded on top of it, kicking his legs and waving his arms. That's when Louis reached under his shirt tail and pulled out a gun from the waist band of his khaki work pants, a short-barreled .357 Magnum. He pulled it out like he'd rehearsed that smooth draw all night. He placed the barrel of the gun right up against Jackson's forehead and cocked it.

"Move, nigger."

Jackson's arms and legs froze stiff in the air, and the crowd stopped dead in confusion. He dropped the knife, and it clicked on the floor. Louis grinned. "How 'bout that. You're not as stupid as you look, are ya, nigger?" He uncocked the gun and took it away from Jackson's head. He looked the other way as if about to get up and go attend to other more important business, but when Jackson started to move, Louis sprang from his chair, grabbed him by the afro, and banged his head down on the Formica table top so hard his chin bone must have cracked. Before Jackson could say or do anything, the gun was again cocked and pressed against his head. Thick warm blood ran down Simon's face and dripped to his shirt in deep red blotches. He reached up to feel his slit nostril, and as it throbbed, he relived that split second the blade had cut through his flesh over and over, until it seemed like the blade hadn't been sharp at all and had slowly torn, instead of cut, through every little bit of his flesh.

The crowd stood amazed at Louis, the crazy white boy. Simon picked up his books that felt so heavy and slung them under his arm. "Come on," he said, sure that Louis would follow. But Louis just stood there, grinning down at the black boy.

"Come on, Louis, let's go!" And then Simon realized Louis was perfectly capable of not doing the sensible thing at all. "Are you crazy? Let's go!"

"What's the hurry, hunky?" Louis said matter-of-factly. The crowd laughed, and the multitude of their numbers became painfully clear to Simon. It was as if, suddenly, Louis had the power to turn the crowd on Simon, to say, You want a hunky? Here's your hunky, letting the crowd do as it pleased with Simon just for one of Louis's crazy jokes, or maybe underneath all that coolness Louis was really scared and wanted to save his own skin. Still holding the barrel of the gun to Jackson's head, Louis grinned at Simon and laughed.

"Relax, liberal. Have a seat; the show's just beginning." He wiggled his eyebrows a couple of times and laughed some more. Simon came back to his seat and sat down. As long as he stayed near Louis, near the spell Louis held over the crowd, he was safe. Louis took the gun away from the black boy's head and, stepping around beside him, placed the barrel right in the crack of the boy's ass.

"Excuse me, ladies and gentlemen," Louis addressed the crowd, one and all, "but does this nigger have any relatives out there? Sheeeeeeit, I hear you're all brothas and sistas. Come on now, no relatives? Let's be honest, this nigger had a busy mama workin' late nights. Why, I bet all thirty of his brothas and sistas go to school right here. Sheeeeeeit, I bet they're all in the same grade, too!"

Some students giggled.

"Sheeeeeeit, I bet his mama's related to the whole fuckin' neighborhood. Do you know his fuckin' granddaddy still hasn't graduated—fucker's been goin' to school here for forty-five years. Oh, man, come on now, don't be laughin'; we shouldn't be talkin' about his relatives, especially his mama, since none of us, including him, know who his mama is."

Louis shoved the gun barrel harder into Jackson's ass. "Anyone could be this boy's mama." Louis pointed at a boy in the crowd. "You there, sir, are you his mama? Don't be shy now, are you his mama?" The boy mumbled something, and Louis cocked the gun and pointed it right at the boy's face. "Tell me you're not his mama again."

Just like THAT the crowd stopped laughing and parted away from the boy who backed up, smiling nervously, waving his hands in front of himself as he said, "I'm his mama, I'm his mama, come on, man, be coo'."

Jackson started to ease himself off of the table, but Louis shoved the barrel of the gun back into his ass, and he froze. The crowd laughed and slowly gathered around again. It was as if Louis were becoming a goddamn soul brother the more he talked. He stamped his foot, and yelled, "I knew it! I knew this nigger's mama was a brave man. Sheeeeeeit, I bet her beard's so thick she breaks her razor every morning when she shaves."

Simon's wound had numbed, the warm blood comforting to taste on his lips. Louis laughed with the crowd as he flipped open the gun's cylinder, and whereas maybe seconds before the crowd might have rushed him, now they just laughed and watched. He hit the gun against the heel of his palm, shook most of the bullets out onto the floor, and pranced up and down the aisle, shuffling his feet in an awkward dance step, always trying but never able to stay on beat with James Brown telling blacks to be proud over the P.A. As Louis passed by students, he'd show them the almost empty cylinder.

"See? One bullet. See? One bullet." The untied rawhide shoe strings of his construction boots flew every which way, and there was a drip of dried mustard on his white shirt just above the pocket. He stopped suddenly, snapped the cylinder shut, and put the gun to his head. He squinted his face and pulled the trigger real fast three times, CLICK CLICK CLICK.

Black girls nearby sucked in their breath and raised their hands over their faces, but they and everyone else wore a cross between a smile and an expectant wince on their faces. Even Simon smiled against his will. Again Louis shuffled up and down the aisle.

"See? One bullet. See? One bullet." He stopped, spun the chamber, put the gun to his head, and CLICK CLICK CLICK.

While Jackson had the chance he wormed off the table and didn't seem to notice Simon; if he had, he probably would have wished he never asked Simon for a goddamn quarter. Where the fuck are you goin', nigger? Simon heard his mind ask, and then, just as quickly, he blotted the thought out—yes, he was above thinking such thoughts.

Louis pranced back over to Simon, put his arm around Simon's shoulders, and hugged him tight. The fact that the hug felt comforting made Simon goddamn uncomfortable as Louis looked at him seriously, eye to eye.

"White men aren't afraid to die," he told Simon, and kissed him on the cheek, a kiss that could not be denied by Simon no matter how uncomfortable it made him. Louis looked out at the silent crowd.

"White men aren't afraid to die."

The grin fell from his face. "I said, WHITE MEN AREN'T AFRAID TO DIE! HOW 'BOUT YOU!" and he whirled every which way, pointing the gun at the crowd and pulling the trigger again and again, "OR YOU OR YOU OR YOU!"

Black girls ran with their hands out in back of their heads as if that would stop a bullet, and other students kicked chairs to the side like doll furniture. Tables crashed to the floor, and one boy stumbled and fell, a friend dragging him by the arm so he wouldn't get trampled. Louis squeezed the trigger one too many times, and a bullet went off, the noise from the blast ringing in Simon's ears like the high pitched sound of that test they do on radio and TV just after an announcer tells you, "This is a test: for the next sixty seconds" . . . goddamn, it was deafening, and a pair of fluorescent light tubes that the bullet hit exploded overhead like a bomb, sprinkling star dust down on the crowd as it streamed through the back exit door that banged again and again against the wall in the hallway. And then the lunchroom was empty except for Simon and Louis. Louis laughed his ass off as if he were watching an old Marx Brothers movie where all the blacks wave their light palms at the camera, or run scared from the farmer's dog.

James Brown still told blacks to be proud, because the person running the record player ran off and left the record to play over and over. Finally, wiping his tearing eyes, Louis sat back down in a chair and stared out the windows into the small courtyard the way he had before it all started. He let all the air out of his lungs. Simon looked down at the floor. He wanted to say something, but he wasn't sure if it was a thank you, fuck you, or maybe both, or maybe it was best not to say a thing. Yeah, he had to keep movin', keep thinkin'—what was he going to do next? Where was it safe to go? He picked up his books, his eyes still cast down toward the floor because there was something so strong between him and Louis that Simon wanted to try and ignore. He started down the aisle.

"Come on, man," Louis called out. "Sit down and stay awhile, you're always in such a fuckin' hurry. Whadaya runnin' from, me?"

Simon whirled around, "Stay for what?" He rubbed his hand hard against the back of his neck. "Fuck, man, you're crazy, you're absolutely positively a banana!" He looked up at the ceiling in total disbelief as the whole scene replayed in his mind: Louis with a gun, with a gun on the black boy, on the crowd, on himself. Simon's jaw twitched uncontrollably, a shiver running through him.

"Jesus, Louis, an absolute positive banana!"

"Well, this banana's askin' you to stay, OK?" Louis smiled at Simon for a long time, then laughed softly. "Come on, man, this won't take long." The way Louis's voice was so calm and sincere as he sat slumped in his chair pulled Simon back... back... back to the seat across the table from Louis. Louis propped his feet up on the table. "Good," he said, and nodded his head in approval. "Good." He didn't even have any socks on, and his hairy white legs made him look even more of a mess. Simon sat stiffly in his chair with his back straight, his feet flat on the floor and his palms flat on the smooth table top. He rubbed his index finger in slow circles over the Formica and felt his sticky blood mix with sweat. Louis pulled handfuls of little brass bullets from his coat pocket and flung them on the table where they scattered like beads and rolled in little circles, spilling to the floor. He flipped open the cylinder and began plugging the chamber with bullets, then snapped the cylinder shut. His easygoing expression turned hot and explosive and, "Jesus Christ!" He pointed the gun back over his shoulder and aimed at the P.A. speaker above the back door, firing again and again, and no matter how hard Simon tried, he couldn't keep from flinching with each deafening shot. At least one of the six bullets put a hole right in James Brown's vocal chords.

"Never tell a nigger he's *black* and *proud* more than three times a day, or it goes right to his head and he hears *black* is *better*," Louis said, and smiled.

"Don't start that shit!" Simon's ears rang so bad from the noise of the shots, he heard his voice as if it came from someone else. For a while, both he and Louis had to talk a little louder than usual just to hear each other.

"What shit?" Louis asked.

"You know what shit, that... that *nigger* shit."

Louis slapped the gun melodramatically over his heart. "Oh, excuse me, I mean Colored, I mean Negro, I mean Afro-American, I mean Black—fuck, talk about shit, fuck, don't give me that liberal shit about how that nigger I almost wasted not being a fuckin' nigger! Like he don't know any better 'cause he's uneducated, is that what you're gonna tell me? I don't need it, man. You wanna know what's racist? That's racist! Say he hasn't got the brains to know better. Suck the whazoo, baby! That nigger can kiss my sweet, white, cauliflower ass and you know it just like you know the only thing Aunt Jemima does is pour from a bottle."

What the fuck is that supposed to mean? Simon wondered. He listened to the silence. Out in the hall he heard the light tapping of street shoes running, and at the other end of the lunchroom a teetering lunch tray clattered from a table to the floor.

"Would you really have shot him?" Simon asked. "Would you really have shot him if he moved?"

"I don't know—I know I had the right, but I don't know if I would have. Maybe I don't have the right; maybe no one's got the right. Fuck—yes I do."

"But Jesus, Louis!" Simon tried to make Louis see the seriousness of the situation. "What would you have done if the gun went off when you were dancin' around?"

"Ahhhh, I don't know, man. I guess I would have laid down and acted dead—how the fuck should I know?" Louis slid his feet off the table and leaned forward like someone else might be listening. "I don't think about those things anymore, I really don't. Ya know, I hear when people die violent deaths they have an orgasm. Can you believe it—they come right in their pants—don't have to touch it or nothin'. It must be the ultimate fuck—a sweet succulent death."

Simon, still on another train of thought, pointed out the windows across the lunchroom, where the street lay outside. "Just because in here..." and then he finally realized it. "Just because in here we're the niggers, it ain't like that out there, and out there is always, man, out there is..."

"A nigger has the right to stand up for himself no matter where he is," Louis said. "Man, I'm here five hours a day, five days a week. You're fuckin' crazy, liberal. Just listen to what you're sayin': you're sayin' you're a nigger and you haven't got the right to be anything else 'cause of out there. Jesus, the ultimate in guilt; Jesus, I just can't fuckin' believe it."

"Don't be puttin' fuckin' words in my mouth," Simon said, glaring at Louis.

"You said it, man. I ain't puttin' nothin' in your mouth—I can't, it's too full of donkey dick. Just listen to me a second, OK? I say, you have the right to say *screw you* when someone cops a dime off you, *screw you* when six of them jump you, *screw you* when you're scared to fuckin' walk in a school bathroom to take a fuckin' piss. I mean, if you're still going to try and apply right and wrong to this shit, I suggest you give yourself the benefit of the doubt and live your life. Don't you ever get sick of politely askin' someone why they're shittin' on you when it's drippin' down your face? You tellin' me you can't because you're white? You don't think like that, man, ya just react, I mean... Oh, fuck, I don't know what I mean, all I know is it sure felt good to see those niggers run, didn't it?"

Just then the back door opened. First a gun stuck through the door,

93

and then a cop's head in a baby blue, Chicago police department riot helmet. "What the hell's goin' on in here?" The cop said it as if hoping the harshness of his voice would intimidate Louis and allow him to take control of the situation, but before he could say anything else, Louis spun around in his chair and pointed the empty gun right at the cop's head. The cop disappeared, the door slammed shut, and Simon could hear a lot of commotion out in the hall.

"Damn, Louis, what's a matter with you? Those are cops, man, real cops!" But Simon could see that his words drifted right through Louis, as if Louis could give a shit if it were fucking President Nixon himself out there. Someone called to them from a bullhorn out in the hallway.

"This is Sergeant Garzato. Come out with your hands up."

"Dragnet is your next door to the right, grease ball!" Louis yelled back. He rubbed his hand over his face.

"This is Sergeant Garzato. Come out with your hands up, I repeat, with your hands up."

Louis still rubbed his face. "OK, five minutes, grease ball! Five minutes and we come out and no one gets hurt and life can go on beautiful like a fart rising between your legs in the bathtub, OK?"

There was a pause from the hallway, "OK, son, five minutes . . . as of now."

Simon scooted his seat away from the table as if about to get up, a trapped expression on his face. "Come on, Louis, let's go."

"What for? He said it was OK for five minutes, and he's a reeeeeeal po-lice-man."

"Come on, let's go. What the fuck are you gonna do? They're gonna put your ass away—why make it any worse?"

"Five minutes. Goddamn, you're always in such a fuckin' hurry." Louis took out a cigarette and started to light it.

"What the fuck are you doing?" Simon asked, pointing at the cigarette.

"What's it look like I'm doin'? I'm lightin' a cigarette."

And then Simon realized how silly what he was about to say would sound, but he said it, anyway. "You can't smoke in here; you're in school."

Louis laughed, gobs of smoke blurting out from his mouth, but Simon still shook in spasms, his chest quivering with each breath. Louis flipped open the cylinder of the gun and put one bullet inside, then spun the cylinder again and again, waiting each time until it clicked to a halt.

"You know," he said, "I can honestly say that none of my best friends are black. I have never met a nigger in this school who felt comfortable with me unless I hated him or felt guilty because of him, and when I'm neither, he's scared shitless of me—now *that is sad.*" He spun the cylinder again.

"Damn, as soon as I copped a buzz this morning I knew something was gonna happen. I mean, I knew this was the day; can you understand that, liberal?"

"What the fuck is a buzz?" Simon asked.

Louis did a quick double-take on Simon. "Man, sometimes I don't know why the fuck I talk to you. I was smoking some mar-i-juany." His eyes glazed over, and, talking to himself, he said, "Shit, I wouldn't mind coppin' a quick buzz now."

He flipped the cylinder of the gun shut. Simon looked into Louis's eyes and felt so young, so incomplete. He picked up one of the brass bullets off the table and rubbed it between his fingers, trying to stabilize his shivering body. He wiped at the dried, caked-on blood on his lips, then said, "Yeah, yeah, I did enjoy watching them run. I really did, I really, really..."

Louis laughed, "Dig the liberal now, the truth speaks."

"Quit callin' me liberal!" Simon yelled, but Louis just grinned. "Come on, Louis, how come they can't see I'm tryin' to mind my own business?"

"Because there ain't nothin' more racist than a nigger. They must wake up in the cold morning and say, 'Hello, hunkies, do unto you just like you done screwed unto me, except I'm gonna do it ten times better.'"

"Yeah," Simon said, "niggers are racist. You're fuckin' right, niggers are racist... niggers are...." CLICK.

Simon looked back up at Louis to see that Louis had the gun pointed at his own temple.

"Quit fuckin' around, Louis!"

"Just keep talkin'," Louis said calmly. "Let's see, where were you ... oh, yeah, niggers are racist; sounds good," CLICK. "Almost promising, liberal," CLICK. "Don't stop now."

Simon raised his hands, wanting to do something with them but not sure if he should cover his eyes or reach across the table and try to wrestle the gun away from Louis.

"Goddamn it, Louis, you're fuckin' crazy, fuckin' positively crazy," and from out in the hallway came a loud scratchy, "Time's up son. Whadaya say, come on out, huh?"

Simon rose to his feet, still not knowing what to do with his hands. "Why, Louis, just tell me why?"

"Why the fuck not? It's time to try something new." CLICK CLICK. "Damn! That's five, can you believe it, liberal? Five times! Guess I'm just a lucky motherfucker."

Louis squinted up his face like it was going to really hurt. The blast picked him up more as if he were shot out of a gun than with one, and he flew down the aisle, ricocheting off chairs until his back smashed against the edge of a table. Blood showered down over Simon like millions of hot tingling freckles. Louis's feet slowly slid out from under him, and he fell into a sitting position with his arms hung up on chairs to either side of him. His eyes were bugged out, and one side of the top half of his head was missing like someone had scooped it out with an ice cream scoop—blood, bone, and brains splattered all over his body. Simon, deaf except for the ringing, the constant ringing. Blood everywhere, on his yellow pinstriped shirt, on the table he leaned on, the floor, the ceiling. Louis hung like that on the chairs, dead, dead, blew his brains out with a gun, at least that's what they say—yeah, that's what they say, all right, because he's dead, dead. Simon reached up and began to massage his temples. He couldn't feel his head, his fucking head! and now he rubbed violently with both hands, scratching his scalp—goddamn you, Louis. "GODDAMN YOU!" Suddenly he realized he wasn't alone—no, wait! spied on. He looked up across the courtyard at the black faces lining the windows of all the classrooms on all three floors, and he couldn't tell if they were satisfied or disappointed, all of them watching, moving around in front of him as if in a kaleidoscope. They had seen, seen everything. But still Simon could almost believe Louis might walk through one of the doors with a big grin on his face and a capgun in his hand, saying, "Fooled yo' ass, bawh."

Gotta... gotta keep movin', Simon thought. What to do now... what... He started to walk across the lunchroom toward the back door, his feet having trouble finding the floor with each step as everything in front of him seemed to move around like a puzzle trying to fit back together. Somehow his mind was drifting out the back of his skull—he was sure of it—drifting back to where he refused to look again, to where Louis sat hung up on the chairs. Gotta fight for control, Simon thought, fight for consciousness—you're OK, gonna be all right, just keep movin'.

Every door in the lunchroom crashed open, and cops burst in, crouched down with their guns drawn. Before Simon knew it someone was frisking him, then he heard someone else yell, "He ain't the one!" A far off "It's OK, son," let him know he could come back into the real world if he wanted to, because he was free and white, even if not proud. Yeah, he thought, it's OK, yeah, big fuck.

A cop held him up on either side with a firm grip on his limp body. They took him back over to where Louis hung on the chairs. Someone whistled as if to say, What a mess, and other cops reached up to adjust their baby blue riot helmets, because they had nothing better to do with their hands, and all was quiet. Until Simon took a breath, the first breath he could remember taking in a long, long time. And now, as he stared at the hulk that used to be his Louis, his crazy Louis, breath came to Simon in loud, sobbing gasps. He'd have to learn how to breathe all over again.

"I'm takin' this boy outa here, OK?" Simon recognized Huntly on his right, the black cop who had once given him a ride home in a squad car after he got jumped in the vacant lots. He figured maybe after a couple of more times getting jumped and a couple of more days like this one, Huntly would recognize him, too, just maybe.

In fact Huntly did recognize him. On days when the whole school was enveloped in a riot—when any white student with any sense at all knew he had better go home—Huntly would see Simon walking down a hallway. He's asking for trouble and he don't even know it, Huntly would think. No white boy who exuded as much middle-class pride as Simon could possibly survive at Dexter.

The white cop to whom Huntly had spoken said, "Yeah, take him to the hospital." All the time everyone stared at the hulk that used to be Simon's Louis, Simon's Louis—goddamn you, Louis! Huntly and a small white cop marched Simon out of the lunchroom. Things were becoming clear now.

"It's OK, son, it's OK," Huntly kept saying, "it's all over now." But the sobbing would not stop.

from *The Elbows*

Disjointed

Bill Burck

Elbows are elbows, a man is a man, and a tale is a tale—that much seems clear. But when elbows become more than just elbows, a man becomes less than a man, and a tale becomes... well, that remains to be seen. Without further ado, then, here it is, the tale of an extraordinary pair of elbows.

The back door slammed, its window rattling, and George Jenkins snapped awake. He was lying in bed with the covers pulled up to his chin, and the first thing he noticed was that he had a rock-hard boner. A boner, he thought to himself. Hmmm.

The heavy tread of construction boots thud, thud, thudded across the kitchen floor, and George flinched as his wife's bowling bag landed with an authoritative clunk. Rolling over as quickly as he could, he yelled out, "Dearie, I left the change from the groceries on the kitchen table."

Even in the dark of the bedroom, he felt her scowl sweep blackly down the hallway. Her gaze would now shift to the neat pile of coins atop the four fanned-out singles. Crisp singles. He had specifically asked for the cleanest, crispest singles in the cashier's check-out drawer. "Oh yes, ma'am, I'm serious," he had assured her, ignoring the young lady's gum-cracking snort of disdain. If there was one thing George Jenkins had learned in ten years of marriage, it was that his wife, Myrtle Jenkins née Morgan, utterly despised crumpled, dirty billfold currency. In fact, George Jenkins had sworn never to iron another dollar bill again.

George knew that his wife's mind would be clicking away right now as she tallied up the groceries—clicking away rather slowly perhaps, but clicking away nonetheless. Dozen eggs, click. Laundry soap ("He better have gotten Tide like I told him and not that faggy All-Temp-A-Cheer"), click. Sixer of Buckhorn, click. Loaf of Wonder Bread, click. Sandwich meat, mayonnaise, pickles. Click, click, click. Subtotal, click. Tax, click. Total, click. Then subtracting this from the twenty she'd left clipped to the fridge, click, she would arrive at a remainder of about five bucks.

George heard the change jingle, her purse snap closed, and the refrigerator open with a shmucking sound. He pictured her standing there beside it, rivalling its bulk. A sharp hiss, five thumping swallows, then a deep belch echoed down the hallway, after which a clang confirmed the empty Buckhorn's entry into the garbage.

George was suddenly glad he's returned all of the change, instead of buying a lottery ticket on number 007 as he had been sorely tempted to do. He prodded his boner tentatively with his fingers. Still there, but softening a bit, like a stick of butter going to the warm. Hurry up, honey, he thought to himself, Come to bed quickly. You've been bowling all night. You've had a few drinks. Come to bed and I'll sink it in you. Then he pulled out the *Playboy* he kept under the mattress on his side of the bed, and peered down at the pictorials in the dim light from the hallway. His boner perked up quite well.

"How did you bowl, honey?" he yelled, his eyes gulping in the full-page picture of Tricia, who was smiling suggestively over her shoulder as she reached down into a sudsy bathtub, presumably for the soap.

"Just fucking terrible!" came the bellowed reply. "We lost to those Lutherans from Berwyn. Those Nazis! Their captain makes me sick. Oh! Smiling like some dainty whore every time I threw a gutter ball. I could have strangled her! The slut is thin as a rail and she bowls with a fuckin' pea, but all she throws is strikes! Oh!" There was a crash as the garbage or something was kicked solidly. "And who does she think she's foolin' with that cheap blond wig?"

"Oh, that's too bad, sweetie," George sympathized to himself. Then, looking up from Tricia, he called down the hall in a voice dripping with carnal possibilities, "Why don't you come to bed, dearest?"

Oh, what a rogue I am, he thought, as he pried up the mattress and thrust the *Playboy* under. Then, in a fit of inspiration, he snatched for a bottle of cologne on his dresser. There was no time to be choosy: Myrtle had grabbed two Buckhorns and was plodding down the hallway. Unfortunately, he latched on to the Lectric Shave. No matter.

The top was off, Lectric Shave splashed onto his chest, the top back on, and the bottle slipped under the bed in less time than you can say, "The name's Bond. James Bond."

When Myrtle reached the bedroom door, George was lying on his back, hands cupped casually under his head, blankets hitched down to reveal his entire nakedness.

But how can we talk about the naked George Jenkins when we don't even know the clothed one? No, it's highly improper. Meet George Jenkins, a man with a boner the size and dimensions of which are best left to the reader's imagination, save that they were known to give full satisfaction to Myrtle Jenkins née Morgan, a woman rather big in the womanly way. The rest of George Jenkins gave full satisfaction to his nickname, "the Wimp." He was a rail of a man. If only he had chosen some respectable enough mouse as role model—say, a Woody Allen or a Don Knotts—he would have done just fine. But instead, he had set his sights upon the impossible gallantry of James Bond. He owned all of the Bond books and made regular pilgrimages to the movies. He knew exactly what it took to be a James Bond: the witty repartees, the steely nonchalance, the vicious karate chops. But he couldn't quite seem to put them into practice. In fact, he was often laughed at. Yet deep down he knew that someday he, George Jenkins, would become that gallant man. In the meantime, he made his living cleaning up dissected corpses at the medical school, and was a devoted husband.

The object of his husbandly devotions was one of those rare specimens of womanflesh cut wholly from Amazonian cloth. Wide shoulders, broad hips, a strapping body with legs solid as pillars. If one word could sum up Myrtle Jenkins née Morgan, it was this—strength. Not some supple, willowy sort of strength, mind you, but solid strength of the tree trunk variety. And topping her off was a face so blunt it seemed crafted by the very circular saws and power sanders she wielded every day as a construction worker. "The face of a rutabaga," George's Uncle Milton had once called it. But it was the rutabaga of George's dreams.

There they were. Myrtle filling the bedroom doorway as snugly as a puzzle piece, George lying on the bed, naked as a rose stem with one thorn.

A flip of Myrtle's arm sent a Buckhorn spinning into the shadows over the bed, where George caught it fumblingly in his hands. "Let's fuck," she said. Two Buckhorns spit and hissed.

Her Barnabas Bombers bowling blouse hit the floor. Her construction boots skidded into the corner. Her blue khaki pants cascaded down her legs. Her left arm curled round behind while her right raised the Buckhorn to her lips. Thump, thump, thump, went her Adam's apple. Her bra snapped open and twin mounds of mammary jello swung pendulously as she shimmied down her panties. Her empty

Buckhorn made a metallic popping noise as it was crushed, then fell atop the heap of clothes. Not once did her eyes leave George's shadowy boner.

George swallowed hard. It wasn't beer he was swallowing. No, it was the prospect of sex with Myrtle Jenkins née Morgan.

She hit the bed like a felled oak, bounced over, and immediately sought out his boner.

"Whew!" he gasped, as her cold hand encased him.

What followed was a flurry of flailing arms and legs. First Myrtle yanked George on top and wrestled his mouth down onto her waiting lips. Then George felt himself being rolled under and smothered with mammary. He nibbled in the prescribed manner, the bed creaking its protest as Myrtle writhed this way and that, all the while working away at George's boner. She never had mastered any sort of jerking delicacy; in fact, she belonged to the stick-shift school of boner tugging. And George must have reached high gear, because she suddenly wrenched him round and wedged him between her gaping thighs, whereupon the bedsprings began to creak a steady beat.

It was then that Myrtle arched her spine with pleasure, wormed her hands up under her pillow as was her habit, and encountered, instead of the usual flat thin crevice between sheet and pillow case, two moist and cold obstructions. Her breath caught in her throat as George pistoned away, oblivious to his wife's sudden distraction. Myrtle's first thought was that George had squirreled away two Buckhorns for their post-coital refreshment. But as her fingers probed these objects, she soon determined that they were not metallic at all, but fleshy, each with a knobby protrusion on the side, as well as two damp and sticky ends. Her eyes popped wide open. "FUUUUUUUUUUUUUUCK!!!" she shrieked. George, taking this shriek as encouragement, came instantly. At the same time, Myrtle Jenkins née Morgan heaved her hips violently skyward, propelling George, who now had no idea what was going on, up into the air, so that he suddenly found himself standing at the foot of the bed, visibly shaken, a thin stream of his precious carnal essence arcing across the intervening space in a perfect parabola.

Myrtle sat bolt upright, a meaty lump clamped in each fist. "You . . . you ingrate!" she sputtered. "What are these?!"

George fumbled for the lightswitch, his mind reeling. Then, as light bathed the room, he stared in astonishment at his wife's hands. To be sure, each held something, but it was difficult to make out exactly what. There seemed to be red flesh and white bone, but there was also pale white skin and a soft down of light brown hair, and his wife's fingers were in the way . . .

"Come on, you fool!" she spat impatiently. Then, opening her hands to look for herself, she groaned with disgust, "Oh my God, they're elbows!"

They were indeed elbows. George's eyes bugged out with horror at the four-inch slices of arm.

But Myrtle Jenkins née Morgan was having none of her husband's horror. "Don't give me that!" she bawled. "Is this your idea of romance, you unspeakable beast?! How many times have I told you? Huh? How many times? Never, never—Oh! you good-for-nothing rapist—never, never, NEVER bring your work home from the lab! And now this!" Myrtle then brandished the elbows so threateningly that George stumbled backwards to the floor.

"B-but my dear, my sweet, my p-precious," he protested feebly, "I've never seen those elbows before in m-m-my life."

Yet even as he said this, a flicker of recognition entered his eyes and voice, for he suddenly recognized these elbows as belonging to the man he assisted at the medical school, Anatomy Instructor Beaurigard Dormouse. In fact, just that afternoon he had seen the Anatomy Instructor scrub these very elbows, then still on his arms, after a particularly messy dissection. So how had they gotten here, under his wife's pillow?

"Hah! Never seen them before, eh?" Myrtle sneered. "You scoundrel! You snake! Who are you trying to kid, you oaf! Maggot, beetle, BUG! You're sick! How did I ever marry you, eh? Answer me that!" George lay silent, quivering. "I could have married dozens. Fred Melnick! I could have married Fred Melnick just like that!" and she would have snapped her fingers, but they were holding elbows, so she jutted her head at him and bugged out her eyes. "He gave me a sledgehammer on my nineteenth birthday. He's a plumber! Does he put elbows underneath his wife's pillow? Oh! You scumbag! You're a maniac, that's what you are. A regular Mr. Potatohead. I think I'm going to call the police, and after them, the funny farm. Oh! I can't believe it. Wait till I tell mother. ELBOWS!"

It was then that a thin trickle of transparent red fluid seeped down onto her beefy forearm.

"Ugh!" she grunted, hurling the elbows at George. Then she wiped her arm and hands with great disgust upon her husband's pillow.

George stepped back against the wall and raised his arms to fend off the two hurtling elbows. But as he blocked one, the other thumped him painfully on the chest, leaving a dull red smear, and both of them tumbled to the floor.

"Get those elbows off of my carpet!" Myrtle bellowed at him, "And not with one of my towels, you fool!"

George, who had been reaching for a bathroom towel with which to handle the elbows, instead grabbed two handkerchiefs from his underwear drawer and wrapped an elbow in each. But when he attempted to sneak them back into the drawer, Myrtle blistered his ears so severely, telling him to "GET THOSE GODDAMNED ELBOWS OUT OF MY HOUSE!", that George pulled on his clothes in a minute flat, shoved the elbows deep into his overcoat pockets, and headed straight for the back door without so much as dragging a comb through his hair. And even as he swung open the door, his wife's scalding words still rained down upon his ears: ". . . and don't you ever come back, you hear?! Do you hear me, George Jenkins?"

But a door is a wonderful thing. Approach one, open it, step through and shut it behind you, and suddenly there you are on the other side. George Jenkins passed through the yellow glow under the back porch light and felt the cold air snap against his cheeks like the bite of tiny castanets. He laughed out loud for no apparent reason, adjusting his cap so the brim angled down just above his eyes. Then he fairly danced down the back steps, turned nimbly on his heel, and headed out front with a jaunty spring in his stride. Hah! Was he not outside? Was he not dressed warmly in this chill night air?

This is good, this little stroll, he was thinking to himself as he shoved his hands down into his overcoat pockets. But the spring in his stride abruptly deflated when his hands jammed against the two handerchief-wrapped lumps.

Oh, what am I going to do with these elbows, he wailed to himself. I shouldn't just throw them away. Mr. Dormouse will never be able to dissect without them. But how can I give them back? What will I say? "Mr. Dormouse, you'll never believe what turned up under the wife's pillow." No, that's stupid. I'd better get rid of them. Over there, behind that tree.

But no sooner did George get them out of his pockets than a scruffy little white mongrel came yelping out from behind a bungalow.

"No! No! Get away!" he hissed, shoving the elbows back into his pockets and glancing furtively at the dark windows of the houses. But the mutt kept yelping and leaping up to nip at his pockets. The pesky thing certainly seemed hungry. Just the sort of mutt to chew up a pair of elbows beyond recognition. "Shhh, doggie! Good, doggie. Here, do you want something to eat?" George coaxed. And he was once again pulling the elbows out of his pockets, when the bungalow's front door cracked open and a sharp voice called out, "Scruffles! Get in here! Bad dog! Come, Scruffles, come!"

George scurried away down the street, hunching his shoulders against the cold. He had nearly reached the busy corner of Cicero Avenue when he spotted the dumpster behind Blarney's Tap. There. The perfect place. The alley was deserted. There was no one on the street. He could hear loud raucous laughter drifting through the rear wall of the bar. But when he raised the dumpster's lid, two startled rats jumped one way, he jumped the other, the lid slammed down with a resounding clang, and his heart didn't stop its wild thumping until he stood on the corner at Cicero, the elbows still bulging out his overcoat pockets.

The light was green, but which way should he go? He glanced uncertainly to his left and froze. Coppers! A blue and white patrol car sat waiting at the stoplight, white exhaust drifting up idly behind it.

He took a quick step forward to cross the street, then stopped abruptly—the Don't Walk sign was flashing. He glanced furtively at the patrol car. They were watching him! His fingers twitched nervously on the elbows in his pockets. He remembered his hat—My God, I look like a gangster—and tipped it back so the brim pointed up in the air. He tried whistling, but his mouth might as well have been stuffed with crackers. To appear more innocent, he repeated over and over under his breath, "I am Henry Fonda, I am Henry Fonda, I am Henry Fonda."

But the light had changed, and George held his breath as the patrol car cruised slowly past without stopping. All of a sudden, several fellows stumbled out of Blarney's on his right. He recognized them: Coach, Shoes, and the Feegs brothers. Arms draped clumsily around each other's shoulders, they began to sing at the top of their lungs under a bright orange streetlight.

"PEG OF MY HEART," their voices slurred out, "YOU THRILL ME!"

George turned away and let his head sink down between his shoulders. He had to get out of there.

"PEG OF MY HEART-my heart," one of the voices echoed out of synch, "YOU-you KILL-kill ME-me!"

He checked the traffic, saw a gap, stooped forward and shuffled out into the street against the light. He had to hurry; three lanes of traffic were bearing down from both directions.

"WHEN WE'RE ALONE, I'LL POP YOU A BONE!"

Perhaps if he hadn't been so worried about getting noticed, George might have paid more attention to the shallow crack just the other side of the median strip, the tip of his shoe might not have struck against that crack just so, and, in short, he might not have tripped.

"Ohhh!" he let out, as he saw the ground rushing up to meet him. He yanked his hands out of his pockets, but these two most-needed appendages were at the moment both clutching elbows. His palms opened to intercept the ground; the elbows flew through the air; he thudded against the pavement; every last scrap of air squeezed out of him with a whoosh; and the rousing chorus of "HANG YOUR RUBBERS ON THE RAFTER, FOR IT'S YOUR HAIRY—" was cut off by a piercing squeal of brakes.

Several horns honked, and a voice cried out, "Are you tryin' ta get yourself killed?"

George struggled up onto his side, feeling an incredible inability to breathe. Then he saw an elbow sitting in the street several feet away, its moist skin sparkling in the bright headlight glare. Good God! And there was the other one several feet further. It, too, had unrolled from its handkerchief casing.

George looked at the row of cars, and could see several of the passengers pointing mutely at the strange red and white objects lying on the pavement. He could already hear the questions of the prosecuting attorney ringing in his head: "Mr. Jenkins, just what was it you were planning to do with these elbow joints you'd been carrying about in your overcoat pockets? And if you would be so kind as to inform the court why you chose not to seek the assistance of law enforcement officers when the opportunity so fortuitously presented itself?"

Gagging and wheezing, George staggered over to the first elbow, weakly wrapped it in its handkerchief and shoved it into his pocket, then did the same with the second.

Suddenly, a drunken voice slurred out, "Hey, ain't dat George Jenkinsh?"

"Where?" another wavering voice asked.

"Ovah dare!" the first one replied, pointing at a skinny figure stumbling over to the far curb. And even though the four of them yelled out "GEORGE THE WIMP!" several times, George Jenkins hustled speedily away and soon heard their fading voices once again break into song.

At the next corner he came upon a mailbox, pulled up short, and stared at it. Did he dare? Surely, it was illegal. But so was carrying around bloody pieces of arm. And who would ever know? Shivering with fear, George pulled open the mailbox slot as if to read the collection schedule and stealthily slipped the elbows inside. He heard them bounce hollowly on the bottom of the mailbox and gave a gay little skip. Gone, gone, gone into Post Office land. Feeling a sudden carefree thirst, George spun about and headed back toward Blarney's.

When the car started up behind him, he paid it no heed. But when the loudspeaker barked out "ALL RIGHT THERE YOU, HOLD IT!" he began to feel very faint.

His thin shoulders drooping, he stumbled over to the patrol car.

"Wh-what can I d-do for you, Officer?" he stammered weakly.

The policeman narrowed his eyes and replied with controlled vehemence, "Buddy . . . you can just open the back door there and get . . . in. You're coming with us." And his partner nodded slowly.

"B-but officers, on what charges? I d-d-d—"

"GET IN!" the cop spat with such surliness that George banged his head on the doorway in his haste to obey.

As for what happened after that, the reports are many and all conflicting.

* * *

Next morning the phone rang and Anatomy Instructor Beaurigard Dormouse awoke sputtering like a horse. "Br-r-r-r-r!" went his lips, "Rr-r-r-r-ring!" went the phone again, and up he sat yelling "I'll get it!" to no one in particular—in fact, to no one at all. The words echoed round his apartment and came right home to roost upon his own ears. He yawned and stretched, swinging his arms up like the vanes of a windmill. They felt unusually stiff this morning. "Must've slept wrong," he mused innocently to himself as he reached for the phone. He grasped only air. Grunting, he looked. His hand was a good four inches short of the receiver. He leaned over, watched his fingers grab the receiver, and casually made to bring it to his ear. Imagine his surprise! The hand would not budge. He tried again, futilely; tried harder still, grimacing with the effort. "Huh?" he muttered, staring as the arm bobbed stiffly up and down, its hand straining absurdly toward him at the wrist. What could this mean?

"Hello?" a tiny voice was saying an arm's length away. "Hello? Mr. Dormouse? . . . Are you there?"

Dormouse glanced dumbly at the phone. What the. . . ? Was his hand somehow closer to him than normal? His arm felt lighter and strangely stiff around the elbow. The Anatomy Instructor looked there, blinked, looked again—the elbow was gone! He stared in amazement. Bicep joined forearm with nothing, not even a scar, in between. But that was impossible. After all, weren't there two bones in the forearm and only one in the bicep? Dormouse, being an Anatomy Instructor, shook his head and laughed nervously. Where was the faint crease? Where was the hollow? Where was the bluish vein from which nurses drew blood? Where was his elbow, damn it? But no matter how hard he screwed up his eyes, the elbow refused to appear. Then he looked at his other arm, and the phone slipped from his fingers onto the bed. His other arm, too, was elbowless.

"Dormouse?" the tiny voice was saying from down on the bed. "Are you okay? Mr. Dormouse? . . . Shit."

Then it hit him. That was the voice of Louella Rosencrantz, the shrew who ran the anatomy department and was always making eyes at him. Damn it! what could she want? He quickly knelt over the receiver as if bobbing for apples.

"Hello? Dormouse here. Sorry about the confusion, but I can't talk now. You see, I'm just . . . pulling a souffle from the oven. It's very . . ." What am I saying, what am I saying? he wailed to himself, then sputtered, "I'll-call-you-back-later-Bye."

What's come over me this morning? he wondered, as his arm lowered like a crane to set the receiver onto its cradle. Was he still sleeping? He pinched himself. No, he was not sleeping. He stood up and walked round to the other side of the bed. He had no elbows on the other side of the bed. He peered out the window at the dreary grey morning. A gaunt fellow in pants several inches too short was pushing a shopping cart full of tin cans down the sidewalk. What a stupid thing to be doing, Dormouse thought to himself, and then glanced back down at his arms. He had no elbows.

After marvelling for a moment or two at this offensive sight, Dormouse did the natural thing—he flew into a rage.

Stiff arms flailing wildly, he searched everywhere. Pillows, sheets, clothes of all varieties, shoes, towels—all of these sailed through the air, draped themselves over furniture, or landed in piles on the floor. All of his books were pulled off their shelves. All of his desk drawers were yanked out and dumped. Marbles hit the floor and scattered in all directions. Sheaves of paper spilled about his bare feet. All the while, he screamed at the top of his lungs, "Why! Why! Why! Where are you? Where have you run off to? EH? Are you hiding in the refrigerator?" The door was yanked open and fresh fruit and cabbages flew across the kitchen. "What if I find you in here? AH-HAH!" And with that, the kitchen cabinets were flung open to reveal boxes and cans, which tumbled to the floor before his savage onslaught. Finally, he stood stock still amidst all this destruction, chest heaving, arms hanging stiffly at his sides.

"I am innocent!" he cried out. "I have no enemies! I've paid my health insurance! What is the meaning of this disappearance?"

His only answer was a steady rapping noise from below, followed by the muffled, heavily accented voice of the lady downstairs yelling, "Do you want me for to be calling police already, do you want me?"

Sufficiently cowed and at a loss for words, the Anatomy Instructor quietly fried himself up some eggs and bacon, his usual morning fare. It was a great stiff-armed struggle, but the two eggs finally lay sunny-side-up on his plate, flanked by four strips of juicy bacon. The toast popped up from the toaster and was buttered an elbowless arm's length away. He sighed pleasantly, inhaling that rich aroma of egg laced with salty bacon tang. He had lifted his fork and poised it over an egg, ready to send creamy yellow yolk spilling across his plate, when he suddenly whispered, "Damn it, I can't even feed myself!" and dropped the useless fork to the table. His eyes stared hungrily at the glistening yellow orbs surrounded by pure, milky white. How could he be so unlucky?

It was then that he remembered the chain letter and gasped. He had broken the chain! He dashed over to his desk and began searching through the papers strewn about the floor. It had only come in the mail last week, and he had meant to send it. He really had! But the more he had thought about it, the more ridiculous it had seemed, and—where was it, where was it? Wielding his arms like brooms, he swept the old gas and phone bills aside.

"Aha! There you are!" he cried in triumph, holding up a wrinkled letter at arm's length in front of him.

"YOU ARE STANDING AT A CROSSROADS OF GREAT FORTUNE AND GREAT CATASTROPHE," the first line announced boldly across the top of the letter.

The Anatomy Instructor felt an empty sensation in the pit of his stomach, as if he were plummeting at great speed down an elevator shaft. He read on, his lips trembling.

"This letter has not reached you by accident. Two flows of luck are now crossing over your head. As always, one is good, the other bad. This letter is the signpost standing at those crossroads. Travel the road down which it points and you will gain riches and your most cherished desires within one month. Travel the other road and you will soon meet with unexpected disaster."

The Anatomy Instructor glanced with horror at his arms.

"To travel the road to good fortune," the letter continued, "take the following steps:

"1. BEWARE! DO NOT GO TO SLEEP BEFORE YOU HAVE BECOME ONE WITH THE CHAIN!

"2. Send a five-dollar bill to each of the four chain links (names) listed below. Do not send checks, the great chain of power only honors cash.

"3. Respectfully retire the top link of the chain and initiate yourself to the chain's profound mysteries by adding your link to the bottom of the chain heritage (list).

"4. Make 20 copies of this document and send them immediately to twenty witnesses, that they may too become one with the chain.

"5. Do not delay! The almighty chain of prosperity is impatient.

"Elliott Scrimshaw sent his letters immediately. He received over $50,000 in the mail, then won $2,000,000 in the lottery one week later. Latricia Puce received her letter and forgot about it. Three days later she burst into flames. Her husband found the letter and continued the chain. He collected her entire $1,000,000 insurance policy later that day. Julius Caesar harnessed the chain and conquered Gaul. When he threatened to break the chain, he was assassinated.

"The chain has circled the globe over 3,000 times. It spans the millennia. The mysteries of its power are overwhelming. Do not hesitate! Join the chain today, and let it carry you to the good life tomorrow."

"I meant to, I meant to, I meant to!" the Anatomy Instructor wailed. But he hadn't, and now his elbows were gone. And to top it off, the name at the bottom of the list caught his eye—Louella Rosencrantz. So this was her way of making advances toward him, was it? No, he would never continue a chain with her. Not even if it meant losing his knees as well. Dormouse crumpled the letter, and with a wild windmilling motion of his arm hurled it into the corner.

Damn it, he needed a smoke! But such a desire taunted him mercilessly, saying, "If only you had elbows, you fool, then you could fulfill me."

Stifling these malignant thoughts, the Anatomy Instructor assumed a dignified expression. It was all a mistake. It had to be. Once the proper authorities were notified, everything would all be straightened out. After all, wasn't this Chicago? There had to be some board or commission, someone who could... Damn it, the whole city was one big bureaucratic wheel just squeaking for wallet grease! He knew how things worked! Why, he'd have those elbows back just as quickly as an alderman can ask, "Where's mine?"

The Anatomy Instructor spent the next twenty minutes under a hot shower, its walls echoing with such phrases as "Perhaps the Board of Health... or maybe Missing Persons... Aargh! I can't even scrub my own scalp!... But where can they have gone to, damn it?... Christ, I need a smoke... No, I'll go straight to my alderman," and so on.

Finally, he emerged pink and dripping, only to confront the dilemma of drying himself. He started with the easy part, pressing the towel against his legs and bending up and down. But when it came to his top half, it was as if his arms were telescopes missing crucial lenses—instead of bringing things closer, they made them seem incredibly distant. He tried flapping the towel at himself, and sent the toothpaste flying off the sink and into the toilet. Swearing hotly, he grabbed an end of the towel in each hand, spread his stiff arms straight out to his sides, and began flapping them up and down, dragging the long blue towel crudely across his torso and head.

He didn't get very dry, and nearly rubbed himself raw into the bargain. Worse yet, when he looked in the mirror he saw a large white pimple sitting squarely on the tip of his nose.

"You sure picked a fine time to show up, didn't you?" he addressed the pimple sarcastically. "I might as well not have a nose at all with you there sitting on it." But then he realized what he was saying and quickly reached a stiff arm over to knock on the wooden toilet seat.

There then followed a series of innovations. He strapped a salad fork to his back scratcher and used it to comb his hair. He clamped the electric shaver to the bathroom door and guided his face across its cutting surface. He laid his long-sleeved pullover shirt out on the bed, then knelt and burrowed his way into it. In short, through hook and by crook, he groomed and dressed himself inside of three hours.

His keys went into his right overcoat pocket, his wallet into his left. Then, out of habit, he grabbed the newly opened pack of Marlboros from the windowsill. A spasm of longing swept through him at their touch and he hurled the fresh pack across the room. Thin white cylinders flew out and tumbled everywhere. He stared at them, trembling with fury, then stepped forward and picked one up. His thumb tapped nervously against the filter. His lungs involuntarily sucked in and exhaled through his mouth. But he needed smoke, damn it. Moments later, he was in the kitchen twisting on a burner. He stuck the cigarette tip into the flame, then whirled round, eyes darting here and there desperately. With sudden inspiration, he set the cigarette on the counter's edge, stooped and grabbed it hungrily between his lips. Warm smoke washed deep into his grateful lungs as he headed for the door.

But before the Anatomy Instructor steps into the street, a few things should be said about him. Yes, there are professors of all sorts, and you might be reluctant to qualify any of them as ordinary, but Anatomy Instructor Dormouse was decidedly out of the ordinary. Moreover, he taught anatomy. Now to cut open live bodies is one thing, but to cut open dead ones is quite another. Those who cut open live bodies... But enough said, enough said. America is a wonderful country just full of sentences, any one of which can land you in a court of law. Someone somewhere reads, "Those who cut open live bodies..." and says to himself, "What's this!? I'm a live body. Damn it, no one's going to cut me open!" And before you know it, he's rung up his lawyer.

The Anatomy Instructor, however, was one of those who cut open dead bodies. He had been cutting them open for so long, in fact, that he had long ago stopped thinking of them as bodies at all. Instead, they had become the canvas upon which he worked his dissecting art. "What a slit!" he would exclaim after a particularly successful cut. And with that, he would dig his elbow into the side of his assistant, George Jenkins, and add, "Eh?", whereupon George would jump in surprise and reply, "Oh, y-yes, sir, an admirable slit," then secretly rub his sore ribs, muttering, "Now why did he have to go and do that?"

Furthermore, the Anatomy Instructor was one of those Americans whose daily toil is in large part justified by the continual upgrading of their living space. If it wasn't a new lamp for the front room's northeast corner that he coveted, then it was a video wall unit, or a love seat for the bay windows. And no sooner would he envision that floral-patterned love seat nestled before the bay windows, than he would envision his dream heiress nestled upon it in his arms. Over the years, this vision of moneyed loveliness had developed to a remarkable degree. When she leaned forward in his fantasies to switch on the torchiere lamp that would one day grace the front room, her loose-fitting cotton dress with the purple and white vertical stripes would spill down from her smallish, cream-colored bust. When she knelt nursing her coffee cup before the fireplace that would someday be restored to working order, the soft orange glow of the flames would play upon the slight crook at the bridge of her nose—the result of a riding accident on her family's landholdings in Kentucky. In short, his dream apartment had become inextricably linked to the woman of his dreams, a woman who, just as soon as that apartment became a reality, would materialize into his arms.

But his dream heiress was the last thing on the Anatomy Instructor's mind this morning as he burst out the front door and rushed off down the street. Arms swinging like pendulums, shoulders thrusting awkwardly, feet stumbling in confusion, he careened down Taylor Street and stopped dead in his tracks as a long black limousine with smoked windows slid over to the curb. The pudgy chauffeur came huffing and puffing around to swing open the rear passenger door with the kind of servile flourish that says, "Yes, I know you're a big tipper." One pinstriped leg swung out, and another joined it. There was a pause. Suddenly, two more identically pinstriped legs swung out beside the first pair. Dormouse peered closer and saw two heads duck side by side out of the door. The chauffeur offered an arm of assistance, and something flashed green into his palm as the two passengers straightened up, then passed right in front of the Anatomy Instructor's very nose.

If you were a bell, and your clapper had just struck, you would know exactly how Dormouse felt when he saw that these two passengers were in fact only one passenger, or rather, two passengers somehow combined into one. Two heads sat atop one incredibly wide set of shoulders, from which hung an expensive tweed overcoat. The mysteries of the body beneath this overcoat were hidden, though it quite clearly had two arms. Meanwhile, below the overcoat's hem, four legs walked crisply in step. But the clapper now struck home again as Dormouse recognized this Siamese pair for what they unmistakably were—his own two elbows.

They swept past him into the Taylor Street Tailoring Emporium. He took a step toward the shop, stopped abruptly, turned around and took a step toward the chauffeur, who ignored him and continued polishing the limo's windshield. He looked up the street. He looked down it. He looked up at the sky, squinted his eyes, and then looked down at the sidewalk, where he spotted his shadow. His whole body vibrated with shock.

But what if they were escaping?! He reached for the shop door, came up short, leaned forward until he could grab the handle, and then stepped backward to pull it open. He walked inside and dodged quickly to his left as a balding fellow in a vest and white shirt unrolled a bolt of dark green cloth, sweeping his arm right into the Anatomy Instructor's path.

"This is our very best worsted, sir. Will it do?" he asked a tall, wan customer in a three-piece suit. The customer soberly replied that it would do just fine, and then smiled ever so slightly, as if a thin layer of glaze on his face might crack if he changed his expression too much.

The Anatomy Instructor moved past them. Everywhere he looked he saw tailors at work. Some labored around torso dummies, others serviced customers, all wore shiny black vests, had sparkling white shirt sleeves, and sported green tape measures around their necks. This plump one here with the washbrush mustache was kneeling on one knee, his round belly resting upon his thigh as he chalk-marked hemming instructions on a pair of pants. That one there with the sunken cheeks and fence-post shoulders was inspecting a jacket's hang upon an elderly, white-haired fellow who was obviously a judge or retired colonel from the way his stern glance seemed to critically assess everything. Another tailor was standing with his arms folded, delivering a few final instructions to a customer who stood tapping his foot impatiently, his new suit slung in its bag over his shoulder. Across the room, two tailors worked in tandem, one pulling pins nimbly from his mouth and pinning untrimmed pieces of a navy blue suit together on a dummy, and the other laying down dashed lines in a pattern meaningless to any but a tailor's trained eye.

Standing amidst all this tailoring flurry, Dormouse saw no trace of his elbows. Had they snuck out? But no, the limo still sat beside the curb.

"May I help you, sir?"

Dormouse turned round to face a short tailor whose balding dome gleamed.

"Um . . . well, I . . ." Dormouse sputtered, raising his arms slightly in a flustered way.

"Ah, I see," the tailor said, noticing that the sleeves of the Anatomy Instructor's overcoat hung down to his knuckles. "You want your sleeves shortened. Well, step over here, please."

Dormouse allowed himself to be led over to a niche lined with mirrors. Yes, shortening the sleeves wasn't a bad idea at all. That is, unless he caught up with those elbows. Now, where were they? He thought he caught a glimpse of four shoes under the fitting room door, but the tailor had finished taking his measurements along the sleeves and was now saying, "Thank you, sir. And may I remove your coat? This shouldn't take more than a half hour."

The coat was halfway down his arms before Dormouse realized what a mistake that was and suddenly clamped his arms tightly against his body, snaring the coat. There was a brief awkward moment as the tailor tugged down and Dormouse clamped tighter.

"Please, sir . . ." the tailor protested, his eyebrows knitting together below his shiny cranium.

Dormouse loosened his grip and felt the sudden draft against his arms as the coat slipped free. Feeling strangely naked, he watched in the mirror as the tailor held one end of the tape measure up to his neck and then extended it across his shoulder and down to the wrist. He saw the smooth, rounded forehead crease briefly beside his stiff arm, then saw the tailor shoot a puzzled glance at it and gasp softly.

"Excuse me, sir," the tailor said breathlessly, and moved off, gesturing silently to the next tailor.

In a matter of seconds, Dormouse was surrounded by tailors. They muttered to one another, shook their heads with wonderment, and stole glances at his arms like scientists examining a rare specimen. One even sidled forward to measure for himself the span between shoulder and wrist, then let out a long, low whistle. "Twenty inches," he hissed to the group, and all around eyebrows leapt skyward like startled kittens.

From every corner of the shop, abandoned customers standing on stools in half-tailored suits glared at the cluster, but felt too awkward to intrude, while at the center of that cluster Dormouse was fuming, especially since he now saw the source of his predicament, his own two elbows, march proudly forth from the back of the shop in a spanking new suit. But the word "suit" cannot begin to describe the garment that clothed this impossible physique. The cluster of tailors let out a collective sigh of awe. Here was tailoring wizardry at its most sublime. Here was line; here was form; here was quadruple-breasted magnificence. But where does one begin to describe... Padded shoulders. Two sets of lapels. Four rows of buttons. Two breast pockets. Two hip pockets. A four-legged pair of trousers with two zippers. And all of this hanging in such a way as to proclaim, "There, you see, this is what centuries of the tailoring art have led up to." Not a seam puckered. Not a thread hung loose. Nothing pulled, bunched, or bound as the debonair occupants of this elegant livery paraded down the middle of the shop with the Anatomy Instructor hot on their heels.

"Where do you think you're going?!" he shouted at their broad back as he caught up to them on the sidewalk.

But the elbows looked neither right nor left and simply ducked into the waiting door of the limo, totally ignoring the Anatomy Instructor's cry of "You won't get away with this!" as they slammed the door shut and swept away into traffic.

from *One Anonymous Mourning*

Paul Carter Harrison

The Medina had begun as a pilot study.

Actually, it came about as a result of the City's capitulation following a fierce armed rebellion by Harlem blacks who broke through the cordon at Central Park South, over-running Broadway and the Fifth Avenue fashion district, gaining momentum, threatening to destroy everything in their path; as they picked up black reinforcements that were scattered among the eastern Europeans of lower Manhattan, the black horde massed themselves at Canal Street for a final crash on Wall Street.

Twelve days of battling cost 700 lives. Most of the dead were whites because they panicked when they discovered that black guerrillas were fighting from alleys and manholes; the blacks sustained their greatest losses on the open fields of Central Park. The Mayor signaled for a truce and called a meeting on neutral territory: Chinatown.

Over tea and barbequed noodles, the Mayor met with the insurrectionist leaders of the P.A.L. to determine just what in hell they were trying to do: "Start a riot?" The negotiations were swift—to everyone's surprise—but the meeting was drawn out because the mincing Chinamen kept serving up food and drink: the City was to pick up the tab. All that the P.A.L. wanted was Harlem. The Mayor was more than willing, since the community constituted an irreparable drain on the City's welfare budget, not to mention its problems of housing development, garbage control and the public health deterioration attributed to drug addiction. Furthermore, where does one find teachers nowadays to work in those crummy schools? Yes, you can have it!

One more thing: the rebels wanted control—for revenue purposes—of the Harlem River Bridge and the East and West highways beginning at 96th Street. This last demand required all of fifteen minutes of cross-haggling to be resolved: the rebels settled for the bridge and the requested section of the East highway.

And now the new boundaries.

The official line would begin at 110th Street and Central Park North from East to West river and extending as far as the viaduct at 155th Street leading to the Bronx. Beyond the official lines would be two buffer zones, also falling under the jurisdiction of the P.A.L. To the south, east and west of Central Park, 96th Street, from river to river, became checkpoint Chico, the main gateway to the Medina. North of the Medina, 168th Street, from the lower Heights to the Harlem River Drive, became checkpoint Bessie. The area within these zones was calculated to takeup the population overflow from the Medina, while at the same time incorporating the drifting Puerto Ricans into a solid front of alliance with the League. The Mayor endorsed the agreement with a sigh of relief—and good riddance: the rebels retreated within the ghostly shadows of the Medina.

The City still remained the central government, thus self-government in the Medina became a study in Machiavellian diplomacy. A peace-keeping force of 300 white policemen was situated inside the Medina to inspect and inform on its progress. A bi-monthly report was required by Division Headquarters downtown. The policemen made regular reconnaissances from their lonely outposts with unfailing tenacity and probity. That was in the beginning, for the League was quite aware that once the economy began to take shape, the most scrupulous reports would become a study in invention: providence would have it that the acuity of a cop's vision was inversely proportionate to the size of the dollar greased in his palm. The watchdogs placed their tails between their legs to show their healthy respect for the Medina's growing economy.

The economy did not thrive, but it did survive. Everybody was required to work; the Puerto Ricans would cooperate too. With every man, woman and child—according to his abilities—out working, the League was able to alleviate the crowding of multiple families into single-family dwellings: they would simply sleep by rotation. And, of course, the bars were open for the overflow.

The cultivation of food was top priority. A mandate was handed down from the League that in every back yard where the walled-in musty gray buildings allowed a single patch of sunlight, a produce garden must flourish.

The populace had no taste for the gummy bleached dough served as bread around the City. They preferred homemade pan bread with natural body and flavored by their greasy hands. And since life was unbearable without a daily staple of hominy grits, two plantations were set aside to grow wheat, corn, barley and oats. Colonial Park produced the barley and oats, and Morningside Park, with the aid of an agricultural Peace Corps composed of City College and Columbia University dropouts, provided the wheat and corn.

In the Puerto Rican quarter, rooftops were screened with wire mesh in order to raise chickens, while the muddy banks of the East River gave root to unpolished rice. The Agrarian Reform was in action and Bethune Row would be its grand market.

Now I recalled a bar—not by name—that Buster had introduced me to when I first returned. I thought if I could find it I might at least get some information. However, the bustling crowds along Malcolm Boulevard did not help my orientation. While searching for clues, I had hoped to see Buster's clean-shaven deportment—clad in silk gray suit —emerge sharply through the monotonous blanket of uniforms, cutting a figure of unmatched confidence and sparing me the troublesome search. Since I could not recall the exact name or location of the bar, my movements appeared unbalanced, as if polarized between nitty and gritty, drawn along a magnetic course of intuition, passing through the hub to the hubbub, then back-tracking to retrace my steps. After many diverse tracings and retracings, I made my way through the throng of kinky beards and woolly heads, ending the journey of distraction on Kenyatta Plain.

The Back Yard. The smells of the joint seemed to confirm its name, so I decided two rights can't make a wrong, thus this must be the place.

As I entered, I received a perfunctory greeting from a group of men standing by the door. HEY NOW, BROTHER!

By now I had learned to return the salutation. Though my gesture often lacked genuine luster, my bravado would at least carry me past the judgment of a hostile eye.

A sudden shrill voice overtook me: "My ba-a-by . . . hey, Big Buster, baby . . . come on over here to your sweet Mau Mau."

I looked around all four corners of the Back Yard at once but Buster was not to be seen through the shoal of heads enveloped in dark places.

"Now look here, honey-cup," came the voice again from the direction of the bar. "Don't be actin' stuffy with me. You ain't showed your face 'round here in days. Jes like you niggers to come sneak off a little bit and then try to igg somebody in company." The men standing around the bar erupted in laughter.

Now we were staring at each other, me and this girl who owned the voice, her mouth drawn taut and her eyelids slapping together indignantly as if peeking from behind shutters to relay her scorn. Head cocked to one side, she was perched up on a barstool. Her gangly legs, concealed in tight iridescent pants fitted snugly into knee-length boots, were crossed in a fit of animus. With both hands fixed at the waist, a fold of flesh was exposed which seemed to roll over at the waist without distorting the contours of her shapely stomach, the end of her short turtleneck sweater rising and falling with each heave and sigh of her breast: her close-cropped bushy hair and fleshy, unpainted lips gave her otherwise feminine audacity a slightly mannish stature. She sat like a lovely black yard-bird waiting to be recognized among the sparrows.

"Now ain't you somethin'," she said caustically. "Standing there with your ass on your shoulders... actin' like you don't know nobody."

"Are you talking to me?" I asked feebly.

"Ain't I lookin' at cha?"

I moved in closer. The men at the bar were anxious to make a little space for me since I had become the object of their unexpected entertainment. Nudging and shoving, they goaded me into position for a front-seat laugh, for the games of the Back Yard were known to be a howl. And how they howled. I suspected that I had been too long away from back yards since I didn't get the joke. My appreciation was particularly low now that the joke was at my expense. But it is said in the Medina: IF YOU GRIN, YOU'RE IN!—so, having little fortitude against the levity around me, I grinned.

"I know who you think I am," I chuckled. "Actually, I'm..."

"No damn good!" she interrupted. "Jes typical, uh-huh, I'll know the next time you come sniffing around this *corner.*" She slapped her thighs. That really got them laughing.

"If I came around that corner, I'd never forget it," I said with some difficulty. "But since I've never been there, I can't say I've had the pleasure."

"You can stop that jive right now, honey," she snapped. "Everybody in the Back Yard knows Mau Mau, huh, you sho' got some nerve bringing your black ass around here without even as much as a 'thanks.' "

I was now becoming impatient with the little scene: "Listen, haven't you ever heard that brothers look alike?"

"Oooh, Buster, you sho' can lie. Look here, baby, you don't owe me no money or somethin'... you don't have to play Mickey Mouse with me. Hell, you must be losing your no-count mind."

Now they were all slapping their sides and spitting up their Medina-sin. My own sense of humor was lost in a hush.

"If you would hold your shutters still," I demanded curtly, "you may have a chance to see just who I am."

Nobody uttered a gurgle or a groan. The arena was muffled in still-

117

ness as if a foul play had been committed and the spectators were trying to determine who was injured. Mau Mau's eyes seemed to brand me for an uncomfortable duration.

Slowly her cheeks began to swell, rising under the force of her spreading lips which, much to my surprise, were taking the shape of a smile, a gesture of modesty that I could not earlier discern. Without uttering a sound, she had broken the silence. I was now inclined to further cool the stagnant atmosphere since I had already proven myself ill-equipped to handle our confrontation, playing the game without a well-timed giggle, missing the chance for a lubricating laugh. I was now thirsty.

"Would you like a drink?" I asked gamely.

"Why, sho'," she replied with a matter-of-fact tone. The men at the bar slowly edged away and turned their attention to some other source of amusement: two men socking out bumps and grinds to a popular gut-bucket rhythm blaring from the jukebox.

One man was in uniform; the other was tucked nattily into snug white trousers with a matching white-on-white V-neck sweater and his head was crowned with the wildest woolly hairdo in the Back Yard: no less could be expected of a local queen. It was not so much the extravagance of the queen's coiffure that caught my eye as much as the absence of the faintest streak of dye, or a hot-combed *page-boy,* or the status challenge to smart femininity, a powdered bouffant.

"Whatever happened to the orange fright wigs?" I asked Mau Mau, as she shook her head with the music's rhythm.

"Been gone out!" she informed with a gusty musical intonation. "That there is the new look, honey. Even the faggots are getting it together for the *image.*"

It seems that the queens were responsible for the *new look.* The League reasoned that once they could get the queens away from the hot-combs and grease, and over to *au naturel,* it would only be a question of time before the women made the change.

"And you know damn well," explained Mau Mau, "that the sisters ain't goin' to let the faggots out-fox them . . . not in this life, 'cause they can get pretty foxy once they get ahead."

I couldn't help but be titillated by this competitive paradox and by how far women would go to preserve their number-one status in a man's eye. Even Mau Mau, with her gangly figure swaying in the stool, her boyish features distorted as she bit into her lower lip with each pelvic thrust made by the dancing partners, would dare any man to say that she was less woman than the queen. Perhaps the only thing they had in common was the *fro,* but so did everyone else, which gave the Back Yard a quality of character, linking everyone communally into one image, much like slanted eyes in Chinatown or the curly-lock sideburns of orthodox Jewry in Williamsburg.

But now that Mau Mau had caught my eye, exhibiting her skill at stationary gyrations, I could no longer acknowledge the truce between her and the jelly-roll, hip-swinging queen. The buns-are-the-buns, one might suppose, but then, comparisons *are* odious.

"Hey Watusi," shouted Mau Mau—that was the queen's name. "You can cut up all you want, but don't you think you're goin' to get out of here without giving me that *fine* sweater."

"What more do you want, Sugar?" answered Watusi, never losing a beat of the rhythm and negotiating now an exaggerated triple deep sunk grind. "I already gave you back that man I took from you last winter." Watusi summarized the point with a quick pivot, turning her fanny up toward Mau Mau while in a deep bend forward, and began undulating with a deliberate counter-syncopated pattern to the music.

The laughter was thunderous—the audience loved it. Mau Mau laughed too. I supposed it was funny so I laughed as well. We were all laughing, but I suspected for different reasons. Now the audience began to pick up the tempo of the music with gusty rhythmic sounds; some would grunt while others would groan. The others got the message.

The partners engaged each other without ever really touching, dancing at that discrete amount of distance which makes salacious intent indistinguishable from a religious rite. People began to clap; Mau Mau also clapped. Almost automatically, I joined in with the felicity. I clapped, but couldn't manage the hoots and howls or the undertones of OOH and AH. I surmised—and probably correctly—that this act of jubilation was no less than inspired, and any false note on my part, amidst the rising spontaneity of the Back Yard, would be detected as sacrilege.

And now the music could no longer be heard over the rhythmic chanting. The crowd encircled the dancers, causing me to strain my neck to see over their shoulders, catching flashes of the sweating figures, rising and lowering, disappearing in motile mesh of heads angling for a better view, up and down, and again lost, if for only a moment, one down, the other up, like a springboard, and it would seem from my vantage point of self-conscious clapping, that the climax was due any moment: with a sudden jolt, the crowd fanned out. Now I could clearly see that Watusi had gone into a paroxysm of uncontrollable undulations, while the uniformed man remained grounded, bracing himself with his arms stretched backward against the floor, his legs flexed and propping up his torso which was angled toward the ceiling, his pelvis pumping up and down in a singular repetitive motion. Watusi broke out of *her* paroxysm like an unstrung bow, leaping into the air and landing directly on the man, both crashing to the floor, bringing the audience down with a crescendo of laughter.

Again I was thirsty.

"Would you like another drink?" I asked, licking my lips.

"I can dig it," she replied. "Jes so that we don't lose our cool."

"I suppose you're doing Medina-sin."

"Hm-mmm! But if you're spendin', I'm always ready to change-up, honey," she said blithely as she dragged on her cigarette and glanced over her far shoulder, leaving a halo of smoke between us.

"Two 'sins,' please," I ordered.

With a flick of her head she broke through the halo. "Now I *know* you ain't Big Buster. You might look like him, but you sho' don't spend like him. Hell, when Buster is in the Back Yard, everybody drinks, and that means top-shelf, believe that! But, what the hell, a girl can make a mistake. It's getting damn hard to tell one nigger apart from another these days."

"If it's really that bad, I don't suppose you know Buster at all."

"Baby, you can't count on knowing nobody once they get out of your bed."

"Oh, I just thought you might still be in touch."

"How you goin' to keep up with all these niggers? Honey, I have a tough enough time keepin' up with Mau Mau. Sometimes you just have to settle for who's around, you know what I mean?"

"Quite right," I agreed, having already given the same possibility some thought now that Medina-sin was doing its best to mellow my mood.

"You spend much time in the Back Yard?" asked Mau Mau.

"No. Only once before when I first came to town."

"From where?"

"Way-across-the-sea," I said apologetically. "Just sort of hanging around, you understand."

"Do you mean places like Paris, Rome, and Chanel?" I simply nodded. "Honey, that's a long way from the Back Yard. Where do you live now?"

"Downtown," I said hesitantly. "But I'm uptown a lot."

"That figures," Mau Mau said. "You go all out of your way to plant your stale oats, but you always end up home for the 'gravy,' not that I want to get into your business," she added derisively. "But don't worry about a thing, honey, as long as you're here, Mau Mau will look after you."

"That's a relief," I said, thinking it could be worse.

"You know, it ain't so bad up here at all. 'Course, us girls ain't dressing up like we used to, but that don't mean we ain't got no fine rags. We got plenty fine rags, and damn cheap on the market, thanks to those blessed 'junkies' . . . but those simple niggers down at the P.A.L. won't let us *tog* until after the Revolution, now if you ask me, that sho' is dumb."

"You're not looking a bit bad," I felt obliged to observe with an overflow of humility, my tongue passing over my lips to soothe the rough edges of the Medina-sin.

"You talkin' good sense now, honey," said Mau Mau. "You ain't tellin' me nothing I don't know," flicking the ash of her cigarette aimlessly in an unaccomplished attempt at grandeur, the ash falling into her drink. I ordered another. "You ain't no bad sport after all," she continued. "I think we goin' to get along fine. At least you ain't got no *attitude*. These so-called brothers around here stay in a *tude*. They can get nasty as they wanna get, but I ain't goin' for that jive about needing to keep a *tude* because of the Movement... hell, I knew these niggers before the Movement and they were always nasty. If you want to make it up here, baby, maybe you'd better get yourself a *tude* too... and *that* you ain't goin' get layin' up with those fair-haired people, now you ought to know that. You got sense. I know you got some smart. I can tell. I can always spot a smart coon from a dumb coon, even though they all call themselves *smart*, hustling and jiving, talkin' trash, but I know my niggers. I should know since I used to teach school. But I gave that up quick when I found out there ain't nothin' a fool can learn in school. It broke my heart to see those kids goin' through those white-eye changes and not learnin' a thing. Jes a waste of time, so I came back uptown where I could make myself useful, 'cause the tricks I teach out here are far more gra-ti-fy-in', you understand, even the dummies up here can appreciate a good trick and sometimes even if it's jes talk. Have you ever read Pearl Buck? Now that's a chick that don't know nothing. I'm goin' to write a book someday, after the Revolution, I'm goin' really tell it, baby, *like it really is,* run down my whole expedition in the funky black Medina, maybe call it Coming of Age in Spooksville, the unabridged experiences of Mau Mau, a *free* girl uptown, and there ain't no hood-winking Laureli with steel-coated panties and nickle-plated titties can tell it better than me, 'cause I really paid some dues for my learnin', but I can't complain, I ain't never lost a trick yet, and every day I figure I'm gettin' hipper, you dig? 'Cause I'm beginning to know where it's at with black men: dress-to-please, cook-some-greeze... lay-on-your-back, and close-your-trap! Now, tell me I'm lyin'! And if you can pick up a few extra dollars to give him, you can really put a nigger through some changes, yes, honey, that's what coming up is all about."

So was the manner in which Mau Mau ran it down.

It seemed to be my invariable misfortune to run into the talky type. Once again, I found myself struggling to suspend any bemused comment which might further aggravate her fanciful chatter and elevate our mutual respect to something more than an acceptable charade. Mau Mau did seem like a bundle of talent—writing or otherwise—in the way she mouthed each word, jutting her lower lip out as if to catch each phrase on a soft, moistened cushion, and while gesticulating madly with one finger, her breast would pulsate proudly as if annotating each new thought, causing the muscles around her bare midriff to stiffen, pulling the hanging flesh into an immaculately taut figure—indeed, anyone might have mistaken this for a serious conversation.

My response to Mau Mau was with the usual mixed feelings I experienced with such girls. I sat on my thumbs without declaring any intentions and uncertain if there should be any. Whenever I met a whore—though Mau Mau was uncommon for the species—I inevitably became the beating-block for countless sordid tales and bits and pieces of professional gibble-gabble. I would muse on their flippancy, sink in their doldrums, but never commit myself to their care. Talk was not necessarily cheap. It could cost several rounds of drinks and, in a particularly vulnerable moment, the payment of some poor girl's eviction notice. The whores I met were voracious talkers and we would become friends if for no other reason than to subdue that tingle in the gonads which urges one to compromise one's principles: how I loathed the idea of paying for a screw.

Even in Spain, where one's concupiscence is often hard-pressed— unspoiled maidens lying primly in their nests—and one is forced down the darkened alleys of the demi-monde districts where gold teeth shine like PAY AS YOU GO signs, even there, I would hold out for a more equitable arrangement: a few laughs, lots of cognac, a sad story or two. In the end—'cause it's getting late—a quick screw for a friend.

Mau Mau's presence had now begun to excite, causing that familiar irritation which I knew she could relieve, but still, I would not tread on the subject. Neither had she, in her endless prolixity, though she did manage to touch my knee with her hand—at least twice.

The afternoon was magically fading into night, and with it, any thought of finding Buster. There would be no trace of him now. He was lost in the afternoon haze, and in the vapors of Medina-sin that escaped from the pores of the Back Yard playmates, inducing the time- less intoxication required to continue the games. Deep in her 'sin,' Mau Mau 'rapped' on animatedly, fanning the smoky atmosphere with her hands. I listened patiently without the slightest hint of my agitation; *now tedium had given way to indifference.*

"You into somethin' tonight?" asked Mau Mau at once, just in time to save our little diversion from sinking completely into diminished desire.

"What did you have in mind?" I was being deliberately coy, not wanting to kick up too much dust and disturb the element of surprise.

"Are you kiddin' me, honey? All I want to know is are you *in* or *out*?"

"As long as I can afford the *'program.'* You see . . ."

"Listen," Mau Mau interrupted. "It ain't goin' to cost you nothin' but time when you hangin' out with me."

"I'll buy that!" It seemed like a fair enough bargain; she advised me that she had two tricks from downtown to *do*. They would come around to the Back Yard to fetch her and if I had nothing better to do I could at least come along for the show: and if her timing was right, maybe we could do a trick or two.

"I jes figure you can't be gettin' the real 'thang,'" said Mau Mau. "Not with all that 'cold-fish' Whitey's handin' out downtown. But when I lay some this juju on you," she said, slapping her thigh, "I jes hope you can still recognize a good *'thang'* when you see it."

I assured her I would.

Mau Mau informed me that we would go to one of the Medina's brothels and in the next breath was off on some tangent about a female's natural role being servitude—IF MEN WERE ONLY KINGS—and how the discovery of something she read about the *collective unconscious* linked her irrefutably with African women. At this juncture I began to lapse into gloating reflections on an escapade I enjoyed in Barcelona with an equally benevolent and mentally adroit Spanish whore.

La Señorita—I never knew her name—had been sitting at the end of a bar which was located in the chic quarter along the Avenida Generalissimo Franco. Six other girls preceded her along the bar, but I completely overlooked them as if magnetically gripped by the dark-skinned La Señorita. She wore a very simple dress, little makeup, and dark horn-rimmed glasses seemed to emphasize her subdued schoolgirl composure.

There we sat at length, *Moreno* and *Morena,* beaming in each other's reflection as if we owed one another some special consideration, some precious alliance which was not possible with a white European, a communion between two black bodies, perversely indulging some well-kept secret, excluding all others from its mysteries, and impressed by our own vibrations which were at least a mutual surprise.

After an hour of benign conversation—tripping over broken Spanish to praise the vigor of the peasants and the wealth and beauty of the Costa Brava, and in the prolix of it mentioning how impressed I was by her knowledge of Little Rock—she finally got around to the critical question: would you like to or not?

I now presented myself as a pathetic student, alone in Barcelona and down to my last *pestas* while awaiting a check from home. She understood perfectly. And, moved by my unfortunate state of student poverty which threatened to abort our desired union, she gratuitously took me in tow—*muy pronto,* she added—and off we went to the bordello, which was constructed with a labyrinth of exits and entrances, up some stairs, around a jigsaw corner, into an elevator which seemed to go sideways. In a poorly lighted corridor we were met by an escort—a pimp disguised as a porter—who directed us to our room, locked the door, and went off with the key. I was terrified. But in a short moment my courage was heated up, for behind the dark horn-rimmed glasses and coquettish party dress was a face as sensuous as a polished seed and a body which seemed molded from the most intoxicating of aphrodisiac roots: the mirrors that lined the walls and the ceiling duplicated her image like a spreading tawny vine.

I immediately summoned mind over matter, deciding to restrain myself out of fear of blowing my whole stack in one quick jolt: no, this would not be a quicky—even though it was free—this would be a divine act, not just a screw, it was a challenge and I had to be up to the task. I would allow no hole untouched—hers or mine—no creases unexplored, and soon she would understand that I was not simply a bum on the run, no, I was not in a hurry and would demand the entire repertoire of her skills.

With subtle calculation, I measured each stroke, every twist and curve, every change of tempo, and at once she began to cry, no! no! no!, sensing the aura of unexpected pleasure, her body giving rise to volcanic tremors. She feared that in any moment it would be too late to suppress them, though she shook and swayed, bucked and buckled as if trying to dislodge her mount, and beat me down to a frazzle before she erupted. Still I persisted, deflecting her efforts with mental reflex, and soon the tremors became more consistent, more violent, eclipsing the sonorous intrusion of a telephone which rang in our ears like an unattended alarm, but would remain unheeded for the duration of the fray, for now the eruption was at hand, the tremors activating a terrifying scream, her legs locked around my waist, and off blew the top—both tops!

"Si, si, todo es bueno," she said through the telephone, assuring the house man everything was fine though she had not expected to be so long. "No hay problema." After hanging up the phone, she stretched out on the bed like a drained wineskin that has given up its last drop, while retaining its shape to perfection, a lasting image of the volume of pleasure its contents had provided: I was glowing with satiety and felt more than grateful.

Having recalled this event seemed inexcusably unfair to Mau Mau, for all desire was now wet in my pants: I had stroked my memory to the point of fatigue, wallowing in the pleasure of an unforgettable moment which discouraged my embarking on any immediate pursuits.

In spite of my dissipation I would go along with Mau Mau just for the ride, just for the show. While trying to relieve my conscience, a vaguely familiar name rang up in my mind, causing me to interrupt Mau Mau's blather:

"Who did you say?" I asked.

"Nai-jah!" said Mau Mau. "That young girl's got a lot of sense. She sho' runs-it-down on you black cats with 'white spots' that go around sniffing for cold-fish while swearin' you ain't givin' up ham-hocks. And that damn sho' is where it's at!"

My hand was in my jacket pocket: slowly my fingers passed along the torn edges of the page I had taken from Doc's magazine, transmitting, almost electronically, thousands of tiny impulses to my mind, which slowly organized themselves into the soulful image of the girl that was concealed within the four folded sections of the page's surface. "Do you know her?" I asked, removing my hand from my pocket without revealing the source of my interest.

"No, I ain't never met her," said Mau Mau fretfully. "But I can read her loud and clear. She might be on another wave length, you know, *deep*, but I know she's real even if she don't hang out in the Back Yard. Sho', she's a little too precious for my kind of 'thang,' but I always say *different yolks for different folks*, we can't all be the same... still, ain't nobody can tell me she ain't no good-doing-sister... that's what all this Revolution and jive is all about... you see, it's..."

Mau Mau stopped short as if trying to catch her breath, drawing her hand to her throat, swallowing, and flashing her eyes repeatedly in a series of blinks as if trying to overcome the smoke which was putting a strain on both of our visions.

"Is she a student or something?" I continued. "Where does she hang out? Does she live in the Medina?" Now that I was gushing forth with talk, Mau Mau was no longer listening. Instead she stared right through me, passing over my vertebrae and out the window, forcing me to yield to the intensity of her stare: my head whipped around obediently toward the window.

The window was vacant.

If there had been something in the window to draw Mau Mau's attention, it was no longer apparent. Still she persisted in her vigil, angling her head constantly, remaining speechless. Again I looked at the window, this time directing my attention out onto the curb where a flashy convertible was parked. A black man—without uniform—was leaning forward talking to the occupants in the rear seat, who were not visible. The driver wore a typical uniform—with fez—and was sitting sluggishly at the wheel which he clung to with both arms, his head braced against the wheel, as if waiting for his passengers to decide on a direction now that they had reached a dead end.

Mau Mau took a cigarette from her pack and lit it without once diverting her eyes from the window. She gaped at the rather unspectacular scene like the faithful movie-goer who attends every run of an old film and never has enough of an old plot: and now for the hundredth time the favorite scene is being played out. She observes now with cold sobriety; however well-known the outcome may be, it never fails to captivate, suspending all expectations. Silence now, for the scene is about to approach its most rewarding moment, just one more moment, please—DON'T LEAVE YOUR SEAT!—you'll see: imperceptibly, a black moon face filled the picture frame window.

It was the man who had stood on the curb. He had moved into full view and was beckoning to Mau Mau. As Mau Mau waved a signal, her mouth formed several syllables, shouting at the man without uttering a sound. It became quite clear that they were discussing me. While carrying on the muted dialogue she offered an ambivalent gesture which seemed to indicate that we were together or that we could be separated. Finally she shook her head, then swallowed down her unfinished 'sin.'

"Okay, Baby," she said. "Let's-take-care-of-business!"

We swept ourselves out of the Back Yard and onto the fusty pavement, making our way to the curb. The man who had appeared in the window now stood by the car, holding the rear door open, measuring my approach with one *evil* eye. Mau Mau instantly jumped into the front seat next to the sluggish driver, who had already started the car. I joined the rear-seat riders—much to their surprise—and the evil-eyed hustler squeezed up front. Not a word was spoken as we drove off; we in the back seat were completely disregarded.

I shared the rear with two white men in business-gray suits. One was hulky, middle-aged, with a doleful crayfish expression on his face; the other, slightly younger, perhaps crowding middle-age, had just enough brawn not to seem fat, shifty eyes and chewed on a wad of gum with confident self-indulgence as if trying to appear to look different. Nobody spoke.

The last part of the trip nearly threatened an end to our unspoken agreement, the young man having pardoned himself three times while trying to reach an ashtray—when he could have chosen his friend's side—which seemed like a tactical effort to communicate. The older man annoyed me the most, furtively examining my presence, forming some opinion or confirming some judgment, then awkwardly looking beyond me, out into the night, as if seeking a faint glimpse of a vision, some lodestar that might brighten the darkness so that he would not miss any signpost reading DANGER! After what appeared to have been a circuitous journey we arrived at a shabby tenement on Pork Chop Hill.

But now that we had arrived, I was no longer certain I would go on, for though the older man annoyed me, the younger man was almost intolerable. The entire trip was spent in his obnoxious chewing with a flawless, gumptious, smack-of-the-gums. The audacity of the gesture seemed to telegraph his cock-sure intentions, working up his appetite as a prelude for a spicy delight: black, succulent *roundei* this time, and only *he* owned the gut for a taste.

The whole scene was written out on his face—MAU MAU, THAT

MOUTHFUL OF JOY—but my reading of it pictured the two unclad men standing before the spread, a juicy black Mau Mau offering all possible choices: OKAY, BOYS, WHAT'LL IT BE? A YANKEE BUCK, A FRENCH SUCK, OR PLAIN OL' BLACK BOTTOM? —to which the young man cries out *Gimme one of 'em!* and the older man asks her to repeat the list. I, not having any appetite, suggest they draw straws.

Mau Mau would begin expertly passing her hand over the older man's paunch, seizing the gobbet between his flabby thighs, and warm it up with her palms, since it fails to rise under its own pressure, perhaps due to the old man's consternation: my being fully clothed, a witness, and aloof, his not trusting the natives if they don't taste their own food.

The younger man, of course, would not be able to stop salivating as he displayed a formidable erection that *he*—at least—could be proud of, and constantly would try to draw my attention to the fact. For now that the wad of gum was sealed securely behind his ear, he would lick the unoccupied palm of Mau Mau, lap up the inner length of her arm, lick at her armpits, and occasionally turn to see if I were looking. Satisfied that I was, he would begin lapping at her navel, smearing her with an unctuous coat of spittle, his tongue tracking the drippings down to her wiry bush, stopping just short of the fold to give me a teasing wink, ease back up to the navel, then past the navel in one glutinous gliding motion; peeking out of the corner of his eye while ascending, catching my eye, he would attack her breast voraciously.

Mau Mau would be prepared for this moment, and take charge of the situation before it got out of hand. She would roll the old man onto his back, his gobbet now warmer, however uninspiring, straddle the old man with her back to him, shoving the withered piece of flesh between her thighs, and nest on it while she summarily let the younger man's awe-inspiring erection cool against the lining of her mouth and he beats on her shoulders as if they were an old chow table, shouting for MORE!, and the older man grimaces as if he's already had enough.

Now Mau Mau would turn a trick of the trade that would really make the younger man blow his cool and the older sample some unearned desserts. Raising her bums off the older man—much to his relief—she would begin to rearrange the younger, setting him on his back so that his head would be lined up just under the older man's spread knees. Mounting the young number, she would fit him in a vice with her legs, locking his 'goodies' inside, brashly announcing NOW YOU'RE GETTING 118 POUNDS OF PURE HOME-GROWN, then with a skillful gymnastic effort, lean forward placing her head between old number's knees and close her mouth around the hopelessly withered gobbet, her head suddenly lost in the hanging flesh which drapes around her shoulders. While the young man stomps his feet wildly, the older grips his head as if afraid to lose it, and I, with callous despair, begin to have indigestion. Their writhing, contorted bodies now seem twisted into the form of a soggy, impalatable pretzel.

They would not be caring a damn as I spring to my feet in order to draw their attention to my obvious disgust, the pressure on my entrails rising and falling, thus forcing me to remove my belt. Neither would they hear my approach, absorbed as they were, gorging themselves in the putrid purée, and I having arrived at the conclusion that the only way to remove its rancid odor was to rid the pantry of its source. Frantically I flail away with my belt, swatting Mau Mau, clapping the old one's bald pate and stinging the younger between the legs, flaying at the flesh and yelling BREAK IT UP! IT'S MAKING ME SICK! Mau Mau would laugh her capricious laugh, never releasing the young man from her grip. And now my belt buckle connects with his eye, that confident eye; and much to his surprise it bleeds. While the older man twitches like a bulky heap of blubber, sustaining the blows and screaming contritely, BEAT ME! BEAT ME!, Mau Mau's laughter incites me on as I vent my disgust with each thunderous clap like Jesus in the Market Place.

Now the younger man would begin to crawl about on all fours, scrambling around with aimless bewilderment, screeching I'M BLIND! I'M BLIND!, desperately searching for the chewing gum which had been dislodged from behind his ear. As Mau Mau dances around jubilantly, the young man's leavings drain from her portal, dripping along her leg like skimmed milk from an eye-dropper, which adds flux to the floor, causing the young man to slip and slide, then sprawl out in a bath of blood and semen—his own. And now, in spite of the old man's utter prostration, he gives rise—paradoxically—to the fullest extension his gobbet had yet owned, as if the protruding red effort belonged to another body. I swat it with my belt and it disappears under a layer of husky thighs, and now I begin to hear sirens in my ears, which heightens my exhilaration to a new pitch of excitement, until suddenly a voice cries out IT'S A RAID! and I am led away with cramps in my stomach and eyes full of tears.

"The coast is clear," yelled Mau Mau from the top floor landing of the building. "Yawl can come on up now."

We walked into a darkened hallway of what seemed to be an unoccupied tenement somewhere in an isolated section of Pork Chop Hill. The older man had become more restless while waiting; the younger man seemed more determined to assert a posture of casual indifference, though he was brimming over with confidence and eager to climb the stairs. "Are you coming up as well?" he asked at last, allowing a wry smile to interrupt his steady gnashing on the gum.

His directing the question as he did caused me to shudder, delaying my response. A void had been created between us that needed to be filled that very instant, for now I was under scrutiny, not only from his grinning eye, but from the other men as well, as if I had been personally challenged and my decision would alter the anticipated folly: at best, I decided to at least close my mouth, which hung open with indecision.

"No," I said at last, raising some doubt in the older man. "I only came along for the ride."

The young man simply shrugged his shoulders and turned jauntily toward the stairs, assuming the lead while the older man clumsily affected a clandestine posture as he palmed two folded hundred dollar bills into the hustler's hand before ascending the stairs. He cautiously inspected each step, aware of being followed by the uniformed man who had turned furtively toward the hustler, nodded his head, and gestured as if saluting.

The hustler tapped me on the shoulder and signaled me to follow; leaving the building we dashed for the waiting car. Sitting in the front seat, much to my astonishment, was Mau Mau, who had just come over the roof and down an adjoining building, poised without the slightest hint of exhaustion. The hustler got behind the wheel and started the car as I slid in on the other side next to Mau Mau.

"What took yawl so long," Mau Mau quipped. "Did-yah get the loot?"

"Watcha think, woman!" replied the hustler with a huff, driving away from the scene with one wide sweep.

"Well, bright boy," she said, grabbing me in the crotch. "Let's hang out!"

I started to inquire about the white-trade, but didn't.

I was all choked up.

from *The Pink Lady Primer*

The Sunshine Inspiration Committee's Guide for True Ladies Everywhere*

Beverlye J. Brown

THE BIRTHING OF PINK

In Which the Sunshine Inspiration Committee (SIC) Introduces: the FLOP, the BOP, ICOP, UCOP, Moral Monitors, Pithy Pinks, The Chatty Kathy News, Pinkie and Blue Boy, Barbie and Ken, W.C. Fields, Shelley Winters, Jockey Shorts, Machiavelli, Carrie Nation, Pygmalion, and Going Dutch—

or in other words

"I know wimmins, and wimmins is difficult."
Ernest Hemingway

Now, Ladies, everyone knows that females without males, especially in groups, are a perennially pesky problem.[PUFF1] W.C. Fields, who,

---

*Unfortunately the *Pink Lady Primer* includes a great deal of information most certainly distasteful to Pink. UnPink unpleasantries concerning Pinkless Emancipated Women (PEW) as well as some Pink pleasantries concerning Pinkly Unconditionally Feminine Females (PUFF) are included as Pinknotes at the foot of the page. SIC says a PUFF will fluff you up when feeling low, but a PEW should be read only on days when you are feeling particularly peppy and in the Pink.

PUFF 1. The gentlemen of London recognized and attempted to overcome this difficulty early on when they issued, in 1547, a proclamation forbidding women "to meet together to babble and talk."

when asked if he agreed with clubs for women, stated, "Only if all other means of persuasion fail," realized the delicate difficulties of female inceptions, receptions and gatherings of all kinds. This does *not*, however, apply to Pink Ladies since the need for Pink is *so* tremendous that stupendous measures (like the Pink Lady Sorority) are what we need to impede the progress of the WHIM.* "I don't want to smoke cigars, or go to stag parties, wear jockey shorts or pick up the check," said Shelley Winters. SIC positively shivers to see the WHIM doing exactly that. Just *think* of them—smoking not only cigars but heaven knows what else, having bachelor parties for brides, wearing designer men's underwear, and going dutch! WHIM Florynce Kennedy advised her cohorts, "Don't agonize, organize," and we Pink Ladies absolutely *must* do *just* the same. Therefore, as soon as Pinkly possible after the inaugural Pink "Tea and See," your area Pinks should call an organizational meeting. The first order of business is to elect a First Lady of Pink, the FLOP, as Administratress. The FLOP will be responsible for calling and containing all meetings, a difficult undertaking as Ladies do tend to giggle and gossip when gathered in groups. The FLOP must also appoint committees, sub-committees, sub-sub-committees, etc., and in general keep the Pink perking happily along.

In addition to the FLOP, your local Chapter must elect a Brigadieress of Pink, the BOP, whose job it is to see that the Sisters are prettily and properly supervised at all times. Moral Monitors should be appointed by the FLOP to assist the BOP so that any Lady who fails to toe the Pink line may be *immediately* criticized and catechized for the good of her Pink soul.[PUFF2] Your local BOP and Moral Monitors must do *everything* in their power to keep the Sisters in prime Pink shape and the WHIM positively agape at all that Pink. Ladies must, of course, learn to accept a little tactfully stated Pink constructive criticism. Thus, as time goes by, the BOP and the Moral Monitors will ensure that each Sister has her very own First Lady of Pink who resides inside as her perfect Pink guide so that like Pink Patron Saints Princess Di and Nancy R., each Sister's conduct will show that she has become pure in thought as well as deed.[PUFF3] This eternal internal

---

*See earlier chapters for discussion of Women's Horrible Infernal Movement.

PUFF 2. The BOP and the Moral Monitors must be deeply and truly Pink. Their Moral Ministry will form the major Pink push for the most persistent pursuit of Pink and reportage of infractions thereof. The Morally Pink Majority must be able to describe itself as dedicated to Pink as Carrie Nation was to the devastation of demon rum and the abolition of "skirts that were too short." Let it be said of the BOP and each Moral Monitor, as was said of Carrie in her epitaph, "She hath done what she could."

PUFF 3. SIC is here reminded of the sentiments of a 19th century gentleman of the cloth: "Happy is the woman who always finds that she *cannot* do what it is improper for her to do as a woman, whose whole mind and feelings are so set against whatever misbecomes her that she experiences a fortunate incapacity to attempt it." Oh happy Pink, more happy happy Pink, forever Pink and still to be enjoyed.

FLOP is our ablest defense against the WHIM and all its Machiavellian maneuverings, and is thus what the entire organizational structure of Pink seeks constantly to nourish with every Pink furbelow it can flourish.

When your Chapter is established, write to the national consortium of Pink, United Chapters of Pink, and the worldwide organization, International Chapters of Pink. Both UCOP and ICOP are Sister "cops" who are simply dying to add you to their rosters and assist in your vigil for Pink. As members of UCOP and ICOP your local Ladies will be eligible to receive the monthly edition of *The Chatty Kathy News,* a noteworthy tabloid they will *not* want to miss. Your Chapter members will also be entitled to use the Pink and Blue Letterhead: a lovely color logo of the famous 18th century paintings, *Pinkie* and *Blue Boy.* This precious pair, a sort of historical Barbie and Ken, will lend your correspondence a *very* special graciousness and charm. In addition, you will have the option to purchase (at Pink discount rates) mugs, fountain pens, glasses, hats, etc., imprinted with a variety of sweet sayings from ICOP's and UCOP's selection of "Pithy Pinks." Currently some of the more popular captions are: LADIES ARE LOVELY; THINK PINK AND MINK; PRINCESS DI COULD NEVER LIE; and SMILE, SMILE, SMILE. "Pithys" are especially important today as they are vitally needed to replace T-shirts and other rude paraphernalia of the WHIM containing such slogans as: "Adam was a rought draft," and "Trust is God, SHE will provide." How, dear Ladies, can we progress in Pink if we are forced daily to contemplate not only the above heresies but such silly slogans as: "You have to kiss a lot of frogs before you meet a prince," "A man's house is his castle, let HIM clean it," and "Liberté, Egalité, and SORORITÉ"! As Professor Higgins remarked when he was, with Pygmalion passion, attempting to redo Eliza Doolittle's unLadylike speech, *"Heavens, what a noise!"*

Dear Sisters, as you establish your own Chapters of Pink, take heart in knowing that the journey of a thousand miles, to our happier and Pinker pasts, begins with one tiny Pink step *back.* Girded with the knowledge that truth is beauty, beauty is truth, and both are Pink, *press back* knowing that Pink is all we know on earth and all we need to know. Remember (paste it on your fridge, embroider it on your hankies, press it to your heart) the motto of Pink: BACKWARD IS FORWARD FOR PINK!

> Organize for Pink today.
> With "Backward is Forward" leading the way.
> Right will make might, and might will make right,
> And Pink will be showered with sweetness and light.

PINKLISTED II - TERRIBLY NASTY TERMAGANTS:
TNT Who Traumatize Instead of Helping to Organize the Pink

Women talking out of turn have always been of grave concern to Pink Ladies. "A whistling maid and a crowing hen are neither fit for gods nor men," but despite such sage Pink proverbs, women have from time immemorial whistled and crowed *ad infinitum ad nastium.* And whenever the WHIM get together to talk, they will *always* trump up imaginary grievances at which they can balk. Their unrestrained chatter invariably convinces them that *something* is the matter with their lives and that they need therefore to ORGANIZE. Female riff-raff full of feminist gaff have organized everything from women opposed to bras to housefraus! Therefore, Pink Ladies Pinklist the following WHIM rabble for their trouble-making babble which is full of serious slips on serious subjects that any *real* Lady would shun.

1. On Physiology:
   "Yes I have a uterus and a brain and they both work."
   Patricia Schroeder, WHIM Wiseacre and Congresswoman from Colorado

2. On Employment:
   "Very few jobs require a penis or a vagina. All other jobs should be open to everybody."
   Florynce Kennedy, WHIM Lawyer and Loudmouth

3. On P.E.:
   "When I really wanted to belt one, I just loosened my girdle and let one rip."
   Babe Zaharias, WHIM Sports Enthusiast

4. On the Economy:
   "We are over-manned and undergirled. If you want more legal tender, hire more of the female gender."
   Helen Resor, WHIM Adwoman and Silly Sloganeer

5. On Dining:
   "There may have been no women at the Last Supper but there damned well will be women at the next one."
   Bella Abzug, WHIM Writer, Speaker, and Busy-Body at Large

6. On Justice:
   "In its judgments on women, sex, and sex discrimination, the justices behaved less and less like nine legal giants and more and more like the seven dwarfs."
   Ellen Goodman, WHIM Pulitzer Prizewinning Blabbermouth and Provocateur

7. On PR and Production:
   "The cock croweth, but the hen delivereth the goods."
   Anne Armstrong, WHIM Undiplomatic Ambassador to Great Britain

8. On Ballroom Dancing:
   "It occurred to me when I was 13 and wearing white gloves and Mary Janes and going to dancing school that no one should have to dance backward all their lives."
   Jill Ruckelshaus, WHIM Politico and Prattler

9. On Brevity:
   "The first section of the ERA is just 23 words: 'Equality of rights under the law shall not be denied or abridged by the U.S. or any state on account of sex.' If that's too many words for you, I'll put it into six: 'Thou shalt not s--- on us.'"
   Eileen Lynch, WHIM Professor and Recipient of the first annual Pink Gross and Gauche Award

10. On Fairytales and the Weather:
    "I used to be snow white but I drifted."
    Mae West, WHIM Philosopher and Immoralist

CONSTITUTION OF THE UNITED PINK LADIES OF AMERICA

In which the Sunshine Inspiration Committee (SIC) Examines: Roses, Rousseau, WACS and WAVES, CPAs, Financiers, Pink Seers, Fish, Bicycles, Spinsters, Benjamin Franklin, Betty Friedan, Isak Dinesen, Ellie Smeal, Jane Fonda, Dirty Fingernails, Diamonds, Smiles and Styles, the ERA, and Harlequin Romance—

or in other words

The Queen is most anxious to enlist everyone who can speak or write to join in checking this mad, wicked folly of women's rights with all its attendant horrors on which her poor feeble sex is bent forgetting every sense of womanly feeling and propriety.... It is a subject which makes the Queen so furious that she cannot contain herself. God created men and women different —then let them remain each in their own position.

Queen Victoria

From Abigail Adams haranguing poor John, who was attending the Constitutional Convention in 1788 to "remember the Ladies"; to the 19th century suffragettes; to the present day ERA-ers the WHIM has blabbed about their supposed plights and organized to fight for their supposed rights.[PEW1] Meanwhile, we Pink Ladies have shivered to see our national defense fall into the hands of wacky WACS and WAVES and National Guardswomen. We have quaked with Pink panic to think our happy homes might crash and burn because they were wired by women electricians with plans from women engineers. And we have positively paled with attacks of the vapors at the rising national debt since women have become cost efficiency experts, CPAs and financiers. Therefore, as part of our Pink organizing, Pink Ladies herewith establish our very own Constitution for the restitution of public and private order and harmony. We do solemnly and Pinkly swear and declare that:

WE THE PINK LADIES OF THE UNITED STATES, IN ORDER TO FORM A MORE PERFECT PINK UNION, ESTABLISH PINK JUSTICE, ENSURE DOMESTIC PINK TRANQUILITY, PROVIDE FOR THE COMMON PINK DEFENSE, PROMOTE THE GENERAL PINK WELFARE, AND SECURE THE PINK BLESSINGS OF LIBERTY TO OURSELVES AND OUR PINK POSTERITY, DO HEREBY ORDAIN AND ESTABLISH THIS CONSTITUTION OF THE UNITED PINK LADIES OF AMERICA.

Article 1 – Ladies should be encouraged to marry between ages 18 and 21. Gloria Steinem says, "A woman without a man is like a fish without a bicycle." SIC says, a Lady without a man has no life plan. The law clearly classifies any unmarried female of legal age a spinster —a word that chills the hearts of all Pink Ladies who know an unmarried woman is a burden to herself and others. (*Always* the odd fellow out for dinner and *never* a partner for bridge.) Isak Dinesen's observation, "A woman who can do without a man can do without God," shows that spinsters may not only lack savoir faire but (heaven forbid) salvation as well!

ARTICLE 2 – Ladies, with the aid of gentlemen, *must* remove women as soon as possible from the maiming responsibility of the professions, any elected or appointed public office, and from any employment outside the home in which they are forced to be *anything* other than a happy helpmeet to a gentlemanly superior. Although a

---

PEW 1. The pernicious and widespread effect of the early WHIM can scarcely be overrated. Virginal young girls threw off their corsets and flirted with dangerous doctrines. Housewives demanded legal rights and society Ladies funded working girls' gatherings. The heiress Mrs. Frank Leslie bequeathed $2,000,000 to Carrie Chapman Catt, President of the American Suffrage Association, for "the furtherance of the cause." Even supposedly sedate little widow Ladies like Mother Jones raced about the country meddling in labor disputes and barking out bunk like, "No matter what the fight, don't be ladylike. God Almighty made women and the Rockefeller gang of thieves made Ladies." That is patently absurd. The Rockefellers made mostly money. Mothers and Gentlemen have made Ladies from time immemorial. (Some women are *so* illogical.)

Lady's only true employment is in the home, gentlemen may feel from time to time that it is desirable either personally (wives may need to help put hubby through school, or contribute a few dollars toward vacation, new drapes, etc.) or for the good of the country for Ladies to work temporarily outside their happy haven. (When duty calls, Rosie the Riveter must do the best she can until Johnny comes marching home.) However, Richard and Rukin in *How to Select and Direct the Office Staff* put *very* clearly the secondary and supportive position in which it is permissible for Ladies to work:

> Many a business depends for its success on some girl who is smart enough to see to it that her boss gets his work done, who sometimes even does his work for him, who keeps everybody satisfied and happy, and who has enough foresight to control new situations as they occur. How do you go about finding such a jewel?

As long as a working Lady *is* such a jewel, she is in little danger of becoming too un-Pink. Part-time work, placed clearly in the context of subsidiary to a Lady's primary duties, is also permissible. Marya Mannes in "Pardon Me, My Mind is Showing" describes such employment quite nicely:

> Nobody objects to a woman's being a good writer or sculptor or geneticist if at the same time she manages to be a good wife, a good mother, good looking, good tempered, well-dressed, well-groomed, and un-aggressive.... Be thin, be smart, be gay, be sexy, be soft-spoken. Get new slip covers, learn new recipes, have bright children, further your man's career, help the community, drive the car, smile. And if you write a best-seller or a Broadway hit too, that's great.

ARTICLE 3 – Ladies, if they do work temporarily outside the home, must be restricted to running *only* the simplest of office machines: typewriters, telephones and such. Computers and other such complex mechanisms are *entirely* too taboo. Females are congenitally best suited to vacuums, washers, dryers, etc. Undomestic machines are clearly a danger to Ladies since even seemingly simple ones may be beyond their manual dexterity, as any girl (like poor Jane Fonda in *Nine to Five*) who has been attacked by a Xerox machine well knows. Certainly *no* Lady must any longer be forced onto the highways and byways, unescorted by a gentleman, as the sole and dangerous driver of such a complex mechanism as a car. What an advance it would be if we could get back to 1908 when the Mayor of Cincinnati very sensibly observed, "No woman is physically fit to run an automobile."

ARTICLE 4 – Ladies' so-called political "rights" *must* be sharply curtailed. Most certainly Ladies must ensure that the ERA or any form thereof, when women attempt to pass it again, as they most assuredly will, *fails.*[PEW2] In fact, if we can vote to prohibit Prohibition, why could we not repeal the insufferable suffrage itself? (Who *really* wants to interrupt a shopping spree or run out in the rain in the midst of cooking dinner to one of those dismal polling places anyway?) Perhaps we shall eventually even get back to *femme couverte,* the time honored legal position that Ladies need not be legal at all, but simply the legal "tenders" (how sweet that sounds) of their fathers and husbands. Now *that,* Dear Ladies, would be a genuinely gentlemanly and Lady-like advance!

ARTICLE 5 – Ladies *must* be shielded from superfluous and disturbing education, and young girls educated to be the wives, mothers, and helpmeets of gentlemen they were intended to be. Girls must learn early that biology is indeed destiny as Freud pointed out. However, that dear man Freud did ask the wrong question. It is *not* what do women want, but what do gentlemen want women to be? The 18th century Romantic writer Rousseau put it most beautifully:

> The whole education of women ought to be relative to men. To please them, to be useful to them, to make themselves loved and honored by them, to educate them when young, to care for them when grown, to counsel them, to console them, and to make life sweet and agreeable for them. These are the duties of women at all times, and what should be taught them from their infancy.[PEW3]

Rousseau's contemporary, Samuel Johnson, put it most practically: "A man in general is better pleased when he has a good dinner than when his wife talks Greek." And the gentlemen of the Washington & Lee campus put it, with an admittedly risque, but *very* firm "nay," when, in 1984, they protested the WHIM lack of maidenly reserve in crashing their previously all-male preserve with the bumper sticker reading:

PEW 2. Ellie Smeal, that dissatisfied housewife and several times president of NOW, stated with true womanly mulishness in June 1982, when the WHIM tried to put a pretty face on the failure of the ERA, "If our opponents think this is over, the fight has just begun." "We'll have it by 1984," predicted Betty Friedan, the dreadnought whose book *The Feminine Mystique* (a volume *no* Pink Lady could peruse without turning scarlet) played a large part in stirring the WHIM into its current tizzy. Tch, tch, don't count your chickens before they hatch, SIC says. The Pink are ever vigilant against the various and nefarious schemes of the WHIM.

PEW 3. The following "humorous" excerpt appeared in the Wells College 1914 *Annual:*
> We found the following extract lying on the floor after a suffrage meeting. A little girl wrote... "men are what women marry. They drink and smoke and swear, but they don't go to church.... They are more logical than women and also more zoological. Both men and women sprung from monkeys but the women sprung *further* than the men."

That a little girl could have conceived such a sentiment, and a group of young women in a college could have thought it amusing, shows that the proper education of young Ladies can *never* begin too young.

Girls in the Hay
Not All Day

ARTICLE 6 – Ladies, like children, must endeavor to be neither too frequently seen nor heard. Poor Pericles, the husband of Aspasia, a noted Athenian run-around, wisely stated over 2,000 years ago, "The best among you is she who is least spoken of among men for good or evil." The modern tendency of women to gad about being seen and heard in an unrestrained and unsupervised manner must be first carefully checked and then promptly pruned. "I can run the country or I can control Alice, but I cannot do both," President Theodore complained of daughter Alice Roosevelt, who in one year attended over 400 functions! Gentlemen may not long be able to maintain their positions of responsibility and trust if they are continually put to such trouble.

ARTICLE 7 – Ladies, whatever their age and stage, *must* have the nitty-gritty of looking pretty down pat. Mary Kay Ash, of Mary Kay Cosmetics, who piled up the pennies helping Ladies not look like ninnies, described her corporation as "a strictly feminine business [where] everyone dresses nice and looks pretty." Mary Kay herself will always be an inspiration to all Pinks. Her beautifully made-up face, her glittering confectioner's sugar-spun blonde coif, her elegantly feminine attire, and her gargantuan diamond sparklers all demonstrate her *very* high IQ, as everyone knows that a good appearance and diamonds always have been, still are, and always will be a girl's best friend. Thus, the cosmetics queen was horribly shocked when two WHIM Harvard Business School professors appeared, as she described it, in "slacks, tennis shoes, short sleeve shirts, short hair, no make-up, and dirty fingernails" to study her company, "flaunting that they were so smart they didn't have to care about how they looked...."[PUFF4] Mary Kay maintains,

> I came along at a time when God knew women were going to get off track. This was about the time women in the 60s were burning their bras.... God needed someone to come along to be a role model for women to stay feminine so He created us.

SIC says we need more Mary Kays to lead the way in saying *nay* to the kooky (and, as Mrs. Ash points out, so often droopy!) WHIM.

ARTICLE 8 – Ladies must all *love* love and recognize romance is designed to enhance a Pink's every waking moment. In how to woo without rue, American Ladies can take a cue from Miss Barbara

---

PUFF 4. Mary Kay would agree with the 19th century clergyman and physiognomist who observed: "Young women who neglect their toilet demonstrate in this very particular a disregard of order, a deficiency of taste, and the qualities which inspire love. The girl of 18 years who does not desire to please in so obvious a matter as dress, will be most probably a strumpet at 20 and a shrew at 25."

Cartland, the step-Grandmum of Princess Di, who has sold zillions of madly successful Harlequin romances. Now Ladies, SIC says this is *l'oeuvre* with verve—troubled romance that *always* ends in happily-ever-after-land as do the romances of true Pink Ladies everywhere. Miss Cartland's heroines have allure but still stay Pinkly pure. Henry Cloud's biography, *Barbara Cartland, Crusader in Pink: The Life Story of the Undisputed Queen of Romance,* explicates her Lady-like, "traditional" theme:

> The Cinderella virgin meets and falls in love with her challenging dark hero in the first few pages. Events occur to mar or complicate the course of true love for the next six chapters. But in the seventh, love wins through, the pair are safely married, and we leave them as the joys of licit carnal bliss are just about to start.

As Miss Cartland, the Harlequins, and Mr. Cloud make quite clear, Pink romances *never* take risqué chances.

ARTICLE 9 – Ladies' brains must take pains *not* to strain themselves thinking dangerous and difficult thoughts. Before marriage a Pink will think what her Papa and Mama approve. After she is wed she lets her husband worry about things over her head while she sticks to things like making beds. If forced to state opinions on matters out of her dominion, she remembers the Bishop of Worcester's wife, who, when asked if she believed in evolution, replied: "Descended from the apes? My dear, let us hope it is not true; and if it is true, let us hope it does not become generally known." An example of the kind of unimpeachably perfect "Pink Think" Ladies should take pains to practice.

ARTICLE 10 – Ladies are *never* cross and crabby or overly gabby. Pink Ladies SMILE. No matter what her daily distresses, ins and outs, bouts and doubts, a Lady's face never shows a trace of anything but the Pinkest grace. She *never* pouts or flouts the basic Pink admonition: It's always in style and *très très* worthwhile to SMILE, SMILE, SMILE.

Now Ladies, SIC knows that the Pink battle is long and the WHIM foe is fierce. As Benjamin Franklin said, "It is hard for an empty bag to stand upright," but the blowhard WHIM have managed, with the cunning of foxes, to, at least momentarily, do so. However, the Pink fair must not despair but bear in mind that the darkest hour is *always* before the Pinkest dawn. Remember:

> Our Constitution without doubt
> Will put the dreaded WHIM to rout,
> And in the end the WHIM may rail
> But Ladies Pink shall all prevail!

SOCIAL OCCASIONS:
FARE FOR THE FAIR TO MAINTAIN THEIR PINK FLAIR

In Which the Sunshine Inspiration Committee (SIC) Describes: the "Bunch and Lunch," the "Chat and Drat," the "Quilt and Lilt," the "Dinner and Skin'er," the "Adept Recept," the "Show and Blow," the "Swing and Ring," the "Chin and Grin," the "Scrunch and Punch," Sophia Loren, Lady Bird Johnson, Scarlett O'Hara, and Nietzsche—

or in other words

"I do not think she has ever been indisposed on a day when there was a party to attend."

Madeleine de Scudéry

Now Ladies, social occasions are absolutely essential for keeping you in the Pink. Thus, never a week should slip away without some kind of Sisterly soiree. Such fun functions are simply indispensable for keeping you Pinkly fit. Compte de Rivard reminds us that "Friendship among women [never true of *real* ladies of course] is only a temporary suspension of hostilities." Therefore, to prevent the Pink ever (like the nasty WHIM) coming unglued, their social calendar must regularly include:

The "BUNCH AND LUNCH" – Pink Ladies gather at a quiet establishment (preferably replete with ferns, flowers, antiques, and sherry) for a quiet tête-à-tête and the lowest calorie repast available. It is mandatory that the bunch be beauteous and the lunch light if this is to be the Pink pause that truly refreshes, restores, and delights.[PUFF1]

The "CHAT AND DRAT" – Two, but never more than four, Sisters (Pink Ladies *always* avoid negative excess and excesses) gather to air the little puzzles and problems of their everyday lives. This is a necessary catharsis for the caterwauling that Ladies are sometimes prone to do and will help to keep you properly in the Pink. It will also ensure that gentlemen, who are particularly put off by carping little complainers, do not have their Blue Boys' ears plagued by Pink-tongued complaints.

The "QUILT AND LILT" – A bevy of Pink beauties gathers for a combination of the old-fashioned quilting party and sing-along. Pink Sisters will find this not only domestically and aesthetically useful but a fabulously uplifting activity for Ladies as it ensures that neither idle

---

PUFF 1. The Victorian girl was described at supper as taking "... nothing but a water ice or the smallest ratafia cake." The value of this mincing delicacy to those concerned with staying in the Pink was perhaps best explained by the immortal Mammy to the rebellious Scarlett before the barbecue, "Ah has tole you an' tole you dat you kin allus tell a lady by dat she eat lak a bird. An' ah ain' aimin' ter have you go ter Mis' Wilkes' and eat lak a fe'el han' an' gobble lak a hawg." (If silly Scarlett had only listened, Ashley might have married her, and she might have lived happily ever after after all.)

Pink tongues nor hands will be in the service of any devilish woman's workshop.

The "DINNER AND SKIN'ER" – Pink Ladies gather for well-mannered and delicate refreshment and edification. Knowing that "Pretty is as pretty does," Pink Ladies may frequently need to chastise their Sisters for the betterment of the individual and collective Pink conscience (and "un" conscience). In agreeing with the philosopher Nietzsche that "Woman learns how to hate to the degree that she forgets how to charm," the Sisters know they also need to heap stern criticism on the heads of any inadequate woman who, though still rudely thundering and blundering along, may yet be persuaded to tread the path of Pink.

Some social events, such as debuts and weddings, will require clusters of Pink Lady functions and should be regularly attended by all Ladies determined to stay in the Pink.[PUFF2] The debut must *always* be graced by the "Adept Recept," in which the harmonious hostess will move at least 500 guests with maximum efficiency in minimal time through "the line"; and the Show and Blow, the coming-out party provided by Daddy for the deb in which Papa's panache as a provider is displayed along with the charms of his darling daughter.[PEW3] Hopefully the deb will also have a "Swing and Ring," one party at which she (no matter what her protests to the contrary about wanting to finish college or join the Peace Corps) achieves her penultimate goal, the engagement ring, from a suitable suitor. The Pink pièce de résistance is the wedding ring itself. Weddings, perhaps the ultimate Pink occasion, will necessitate a "Sip and See" (guests are invited to see the bride's bountiful booty), a "Shower for the Bower" (self-explanatory), a "Princesses Who Couldn't Dance" fete (for the bride's friends who are serving at the wedding reception but are bereft of the

---

PUFF 2. Cornelia Cochrane Churchill Guest has published an indispensable volume for those aspiring to be Pink entitled *The Debutante's Guide to Life*. Cornelia, who was voted "Deb of the 1980s Decade," is the daughter of C.Z. Guest, herself a famous deb who is now a syndicated columnist and accomplished horseLady. C.Z., whose favorite expressions are reportedly "Don't you adore it," and "Isn't it divine," was also once voted "Best Dressed Woman in the World" and was described in *Women's Wear Daily* as "Southampton, Long Island America, Ivy League blonde." SIC says not only Cornelia and C.Z.'s publications but their pedigrees are unimpeachably Pink, and it is clear that staying in the Pink has been no problem for the beautifully dressed Guests.

PEW 3. Paul Mellon erected a replica of Versailles (at the reputed cost of $1,000,000) for his stepdaughter's debut in Washington. Henry Ford, who gave "The Party of the Century" for daughter Charlotte, redid the Country Club of Detroit as an 18th century French chateau replete with antique tapestries, an indoor fountain, and an equestrian statue on loan from a local museum. Brooke Stollenwerck of Dallas celebrated her 1976 debut at the Dallas Convention Center with dancing camels, bears riding unicycles, and thousands of stuffed animals given away as prizes. However, too much Pink panache can be a crashing bore as deb Mary Astor-Paul's parents discovered when the 10,000 imported Brazilian butterflies attached to the ceiling in nets died and fluttered to the floor, when released at midnight, in a heap on the heads of the beautiful people below.

chance to waft down the aisle as beauteous bridesmaids), and a "Pinch and Punch" (a reception given at a *suitably later date* to pinch the new baby and have punch with Grandmama and her proud progeny).[PUFF4]

Part and parcel of the "kick-off," or invitation, to any Pink affair are several "must remembers" vital to the polite pursuit of Pink: a reminder to RSVP promptly, explicit instructions (and reassurances) concerning directions, and admonitions related to medications that will probably be necessary to control the nervous excitability of Pink Ladies before a social event. Such an invitation should be brief (always the briefer the better for Pink Ladies no matter what the communication) but firmly and clearly stated. The following Pink Lady Christmas luncheon invitation is here included as an eeensy weensy exemplar for all those who know that invitations correctly sent are crucial for those bent on staying in the Pink.

> The Pink Lady sorority Christmas "Bunch and Lunch" will be held on Monday, December 15, 12:30 p.m. at Merrybelle Marriwell's little nest at 3296 Lunarcacy. Now Ladies, do mind your manners and RSVP to our harried little hostess as soon as possible. Merrybelle, poor dear, is near distraction what with working (temporarily, of course) outside the home, and trying to do her wifely and motherly duties as well during this busy Yuletide season. Therefore, we musn't keep her in doubt about how many of us will be attending. You may leave a message by phone at her home or in the mail box at her office. *Please* do not call or drop by at work. (Personal chit-chat is so disturbing to gentlemen engaged in their professional pursuits and to the office routine in general.)[PUFF5]

Now Ladies, here is the *really* difficult part—getting to Merrybelle's house. It is all the way to Sunnyville Sanctuary, but don't despair. Although none of us reads maps, and it is difficult

---

PUFF 4. Sophia Loren advises that "Everything I've got I got from eating spaghetti." However, most Pink Ladies, post pasta, do not come out so round, so firm, and so precisely packed as Miss Loren. Therefore, after a particularly strenuous social whirl, some Ladies may need the "Scrunch and Punch," and the "Chin and Grin," exercise classes at which the Sisters may find that staying Pinkly fit is not always as easy as it looks. (But as First Lady Lady Bird Johnson pointed out, it is our patriotic duty to keep America beautiful.)

PUFF 5. Merrybelle knows that "needlework, in all its forms of use, elegance, and ornament, has ever been the appropriate occupation of woman," (*Letters to Young Ladies,* W. Thayer, 1835) and that "A Woman never appears more truly in her sphere than when she divides her time between her domestic avocations and the culture of flowers" (*The Girl's Own Book,* Mrs. Maria Child, 1833). Therefore, Merrybelle has petit pointed (a kind of domestic Pink pointillism so much tinier and more delicately difficult than needlepoint) four new faux-bamboo dining chair seats in the traditional fruit basket turnover pattern and planted an orchid garden in her kitchen window. (Merrybelle has been working double-time at home to stay in the Pink.) Guests absolutely *must* notice and "oooh" and "aaah" with appropriate Pink Lady aplomb over these domestic innovations. (If at a loss for small complimentary talk, "Just Di*vine*," "Absolutely *Mah*velous," and "Fantastically *Fab*ulous" are always handy standard effusions.)

for us to drive, *if* we pay careful attention to the following directions, we will arrive alive:

Go North (some gentleman will point out which way is North to get you started in the right direction) on the Musselman Expressway until you see the flashing green and red "Piggly Wiggly Loves You" sign (*don't* stop for any of those fabulous supermarket specials as you don't want to be late). Just a squiggle past the "Piggly" is a great big plain green (a sort of deep pea green) sign that says: EXIT 30 – GOODMAN ROAD. Go West (stop and ask again if you are confused about which way is West) on Goodman. Keep right on going straight as an arrow on Goodman (there are fortunately no curves or turn-offs or road name changes on Goodman [don't you just hate it when a road changes to another road right in the middle of your driving down it!]) until you see the Golden Circle Shopping Center (many of you will recognize either the twirling "Golden Circles" sign or the "Big Bill Wants YOU to Drive a Seville in Sunnyville" sign) and turn East (stop and ask if you are still confused about East and West) on Lunarcacy. Now all you have to do is drive perfectly straight for two blocks and you are right in front of Merrybelle's happy home.

Be sure to have these directions handy when you set out on your trek to Sunnyville. (Maps are available for those of you with husbands or gentlemen friends to assist you in reading them.)

We will of course all be *so* excited about the festivities that it may be difficult to sleep on the 14th. If so, take a Valium (or two, or three). Remember, regular sedatives and medicinal measures may be necessary for you to maintain that justly famed Pink poise.[PUFF6]

The Sorority looks forward to seeing everyone at Merrybelle's on the 15th. Drive *ever* so carefully. Ta, ta.

Remember now, social occasions for Ladies must be many and merry. They not only maintain the Sisters at peak Pink efficiency but give to each such daily Pink delight. Remember, Ladies:

Plan with elan

PUFF 6. Pink Lady concoctions have a long and useful history. Remember *Lydia Pinkham's Compound?* Your dear Mamas and Grandmamas, who downed it daily, kept it on hand at all times in order to be sure they stayed as in the Pink as possible. (Pinkham's Compound could be stored in large quantities as it reputedly contained 33 percent alcohol as a preservative and thus ran no risk of spoilage.) The motto appearing on the bottle containing the potent potion read, "Young at Sixty Not Old at Thirty." (This elixir undoubtedly helped to Pinkly preserve the youth and energies of its patrons.) Mrs. Pinkham, in true Pink Lady style, not only built, under her husband's watchful guidance, a business that fulfilled some of the Pinkest needs of her day, but contributed amply to her family's maintenance. *And* she was named *PINK*ham to boot. Some Ladies have *all* the luck!

Lest Pink become wan
Pink Parties will do
Pink wonders for you.

PINKLISTED IV – UNFORTUNATE FIRST OCCURRENCES:
UFOs Who Are Foes of the Pink

Being first at anything (unless it is *unquestionably* Pink) is fatal to Ladies working to stay Pinkly fit. History is replete with "Unfortunate First Occurrences"—like UFO Maria Mitchell, the first woman to discover a comet in 1848—in which American women did for the first time what they should *never* have done at *any* time. And SIC simply shivers to remember playguy UFOs like Emily Blackwell, the first woman M.D. in 1840; Antoinette Brown Blackwell, the first woman Th.D. in 1859; and Lucy Hobbs Taylor, the first woman D.D.S. in 1861—all of whom failed to see that practicing their MRS. would have furnished sufficient medical models, heavenly homilies, and daily drillings to keep them happily at home and in the Pink.*

In 1891 Mr. H. Wilson was moved to observe that "Aspiring to the pinnacles of success can cause a woman to experience spells of dizziness and fits of giddiness." Female firsts like giddy Genevra Delphine Mudd, the first woman auto racer, who in 1899 drove her Locomobile in a New York City race knocking down five spectators and stalling in the snow, and dizzy Blanche Stuart Scott, the first woman pilot, who flew two feet off the ground for two seconds in 1901, confirm Mr. Wilson's wisdom. SIC says "Unfortunate First Occurrences" like Harriet Tubman (BAP) leading a military raid in 1863; Victoria Woodhull, described in the Cleveland newspaper as "Mrs. Satan" and "a brazen, snaky adventuress," running for President in 1872; Belva Lockwood arguing, in modified bloomers, a case before the Supreme Court in 1879; and Maggie Lena Walker (BAP), the first woman bank president in 1903, may have been only amusing historical oddities. But clumsy jesting is no joke as the farmer reminded the ass who climbed into his lap, and the Pink have been shocked by "firsts" like Geraldine Ferraro, Sandra Day O'Connor, and Sally Ride who made such enormous WHIM strides. Accordingly, SIC wishes to Pinklist the following UFOs who are prime examples of WHIM who lack the grit to stay Pinkly fit:

1) Frances Perkins – A loudmouth noted for such impertinences as

---

*Of all professional plug-uglies, women in the pulpit are particularly unPink. One early Episcopalian "priestess" got her proper comeuppance when one of the parishioners bit her finger while she was attempting to administer communion. (SIC does not ordinarily condone violence, but some women tempt gentlemen beyond what can be reasonably borne and should, therefore, in all good conscience, accept it as their due lot on certain occasions.) Fortunately, only a few WHIM have actually managed to be ordained, but Ladies must not become complacent as women have been particularly rabid in this area.

"Being a woman has only bothered me in climbing trees," who became, as Secretary of Labor under FDR, the first woman to hold a cabinet position.

2) Clare Booth Luce – A trouble-maker of the first water who became the first woman to deliver a keynote address at a major political party convention and the first woman ambassador appointed to a major posting.

3) Barbra Streisand – A thoroughly obstreperous songstress who was the first woman to write, produce, direct, and star in a major motion picture, *Yentl,* in which she dresses like a man to show that a woman can (of all things) become a rabbi!

4) Marlo Thomas – A supposedly well-brought-up young Lady who shocked the nation when it turned its TV stations to *That Girl* to see the first woman living on her own, instead of staying properly at home, on TV.

5) Jane Byrne – An upstart housewife who turned Chicago politics topsy-turvy as the first woman mayor of a major metropolitan area.

6) Martha Griffiths – A WHIM legal eagle from Michigan who got herself elected to the U.S. House of Representatives and then became the first woman to sit on the Ways and Means Committee and the first sponsor of the ERA in Congress.

7) Janet Guthrie – A frighteningly unLadylike female who varooomed her way to the starting gate to become the first woman driver in the Indy 500. (Just imagine the shock of Pink Ladies present as the starter's voice announced: "In company with the first Lady ever to qualify at Indianapolis, gentlemen, start your engines.")

8) Muriel Siebert – A thoroughly unnatural woman (everybody knows since women can't balance their checkbooks they should concentrate on their looks) who rocked Wall Street and, SIC is *sure,* unsettled the Dow as the first woman broker on the New York Stock Exchange.

9) Sarah Caldwell – A shockingly dressed female who, while wearing a muu-muu, lifted her baton as the first woman conductor at the Met. (If she had been a Lady, she would have *known* that baton twirling is confined to majorettes in cute costumes.)

10) Janice Eberly and Kristin Holderied – Ingenues with *no* due respect for their betters. Janice became the first girl (a mere 19-year-old college co-ed) to become President of the Future Farmers of America. Kristin became the first female to graduate first in her class at, of all places, the U.S. Naval Academy! (SIC could *not* have been more shocked.)

from *Marquette Park*

The Porch

Gary Johnson

Across bar tops, grocery store counters, self-service gas pumps, at chance street corner meetings, and on Sunday morning church steps white with Saturday afternoon wedding rice, you heard the buzz: *Niggers gonna march in Marquette Park!* According to the newspapers, a blue police line with riot helmets and drawn billy clubs would protect black civil rights marchers on a parade through the white streets. And bristling at the threat, the neighborhood firmed up like a wall of hard muscle, like a wet cat, back arched, claws gleaming.

"Hey, I can work with niggers all day long," Claus slurred, "but livin' next to 'em is somethin' else!" Drunk and spouting off whatever came to his mind, knees high, beer can dangling between the open V of his parted legs, in his white T-shirt Claus sat on the top stair of his front porch facing the street, glaring down on the shadowy faces of the three men he had lured from his daughter Carrie's eighth birthday party. "On Fifty-ninth and Paulina in old Englewood—back when it was mostly Micks and Polacks, don't cha know—my old man hadda sell his pride and joy 'cause 'a niggers. And my best buddy got jumped and messed up pretty bad too. What they doin' here anyway? I mean *here*—" And Claus, sweat-faced, furious, jabbed a finger at the square of porch stair between his feet. "Here in this city! Sit around poor as hell collectin' free money 'cause they ain't got no jobs. Ain't never gonna catch up to us. They're too far behind!" he yelled, punching his words.

An orange sunburst, brilliant beyond the peaked bungalows across Fairfield Avenue, had just dimmed to a pinkish glow. Now, tall and bushy above the gleam of parked cars, the drooping trees flung down black shadows from the street lamps; and, in the distance, as the bluish dark erased the final reach of daylight, the sing-song shouts of mothers calling to their children echoed and rolled through the streets. Claus leaned back, his eyes darting glances between the close-set houses, where yellow lamplight glowed in each front window.

"Yeah, niggers lookin' to bust up this 'hood," he said bitterly. "Take over everything. And after all the work I've put into this goddamned house." Suddenly, he jumped down one stair and, leaning into the group, in a groveling whisper added, "Tell ya, first family moves out 'cause 'a niggers, I'm gone the next day!" And thumping his chest, he slugged the last of his beer, and pitched the empty can onto the grass.

"Hey, getting as bad as them," laughed Kramer, who stood big and burly at the bottom of the stairs, smiling through his beard, "throwing your garbage on the lawn!" Sitting on the brick banister to Claus's right, his thick glasses and slick-backed hair shining, Uncle Tony roared with laughter, and slapping his knee, pointed his cigar at Kramer.

"It's my goddamn lawn," Claus growled, "pick it up tomorrow."

Slouched on the brick banister to Claus's left, Larry, wearing a sleeveless Jethro Tull T-shirt, felt an alarmed grin sting his face. Listening to this kind of talk made him uncomfortable, embarrassed. He flicked his longish blonde hair over his ear, then rocked nervously in place on his palms. Oblivious to the kid laughs and women talk filtering out the open screen door to the front porch, Claus lit a cigarette and continued his tirade.

"Wouldn't believe what them niggers did to my old man's house after we split. Trash all over the porch. Broken windows patched with cardboard. Gutters hangin', peelin' paint. Last time I drove past, the grass was so high it swallowed up a whole tricycle. Just the handlebars showed. And all them shops along Sixty-third my ma used to shop at— all boarded up! Nothin' but rats' nests and nigger preachin' halls.

"And that's how it starts," he shouted, meeting Kramer's eye at the bottom of the stairs. "Give 'em an inch, they take a mile. Let 'em come in here to shop the white stores, next thing ya know they ain't buyin' coffee and lunch meat, but your next-door neighbor's house! Then there's a brawl at the Jewel, the whole block fightin' over cardboard boxes to pack up their lives and move away. I mean, I know folks who's moved three and four times 'cause of niggers.

"Two years—that's all I give Marquette Park. What's gonna happen is niggers'll have the whole South Side, and whites the North Side. Two separate cities. We're the last of the pale faces. Bein' squeezed out fast. Mark my word—split right down the middle—North and South!" Claus threw his hand over his head and brought it straight down in a violent chopping motion, and reeling, almost tumbled head-first down the stairs. He chugged another beer, jumped up from his seat, and spit over the brick banister between Larry and Kramer, who leaned in opposite directions away from the spray. "Warm as piss!" he growled. "Need some cold brews."

"That's why I moved to Cicero," Kramer said, throwing his foot up on the bottom stair. "Ain't no niggers there. The one time they tried to move in, they got bombed out!" Pleased with himself, he pinched a cigarette from the pocket of his plaid sport shirt.

"That kind of thinking filled the suburbs," Uncle Tony mumbled, as if uttering a thought.

Suddenly, a station wagon, tires drubbing over the tar patches, whooshed down the narrow lane between the parked cars. Everyone followed the red smear of tail lights, as the scratchy pulse of the crickets floating up from the grass tightened the listening.

"Yeah, we usta chase niggers back in high school," Claus said quietly. "Couple of guys, a car, softball bats with holes drilled in the fat ends, hot lead poured in for extra kick. Yeah, out there past Harlem Avenue on Sixty-third in Argo/Summit. You know, where that huge corn starch plant is. Looks like Cape Kennedy. Somethin' out of Twilight Zone. All these criss-cross pipes, lots of real tall smokestacks like rockets sticking up, and domes hissin' steam. Stinks like hell in summer if ya drive through with your windows down."

Claus heard his own voice very clearly—as if someone else were talking. He jumped down one stair, and sitting with his legs spread wide, he leaned into the group.

"See, every night in Argo at nine-thirty this kind of air raid siren goes off. City folks other side of Harlem prob'ly think it's somebody's volunteer fire department. But it ain't. It's the time for the niggers to get on their side of Sixty-third, and the whites to get on their own side."

"Come on!" Kramer said. "You expect me—? Who you trying to kid? How come *I* ain't never heard of this? I don't believe—"

"Ain't somethin' gets advertised in the papers," Claus snapped. "It's how they keep from killin' each other." Kramer frowned and patted his shirt pocket for his lighter, forever on the lookout for one of the tall tales for which Claus was noted, especially when drunk.

"So if ya wanted to chase niggers that was the only place they lived for miles around," Claus said, then noticed Kramer's frown. "Now you're lookin' at me like I'm crazy. OK, maybe I am. But I know what I know. Chasin' niggers. Yeah, we done it! Things got kinda slow hangin' round night after night by the Wentworth Park fieldhouse. Especially when it got cold as hell and everybody went in early to watch all them sissy TV shows. So we started our own entertainment. Somethin' with some *balls* to it. Cruised around in a nice warm car huntin' down niggers on the wrong side of Sixty-third after curfew. We'd say, 'There's one!'—pointin' like Marlin Perkins on safari—slam on the brakes, jump out and kick that black bastard to the ground. Stomp his face. We was bad. WE WAS BAD. Felt like crime fighters. Heroes. Like we was doin' everybody a BIG favor. I always thought of Spiderman 'back of my mind."

Claus wiggled to the stair edge and spread his hands as if to explain an intricate device.

"Look! We was the last family to leave the old neighborhood. We *gave* Englewood to the niggers. Handed it to 'em on a platter. Right down to the last, my old man really believed he'd wake up one day and find that he could stay in his house. That all his white neighbors who'd moved away would magically reappear. Be bucket-washin' their cars in the alley behind the garage, mowin' their lawns, crackin' a beer on the front porch with a 'How's it goin'?' But he hadda finally give up. Pounded a big red and white FOR SALE sign in the front lawn with the same hammer that kept his house in shape for twenty years!

"Then us kids showed them niggers we weren't pussies—that they couldn't just walk in and take over—by bustin' out their windows. And lemme tell ya it was weird throwin' rocks at the house where your best friend usta live, and where ya usta play in the basement with his Lionel train set.

"Pretty soon *we* was outnumbered! Gangs of nigger kids standin' on the corners home from school. Ya know, showin' off in front of the girls. But ugly nigger kids. Girls with their hair parted a hundred and fifty times so their scalp showed. Boys springin' off the mailboxes like monkeys.

"Then the stores along Sixty-third closed. Sold all their fixtures. Guess they didn't wanna serve no niggers. Kruger's Hardware, Halleran's bar and Dominic the butcher. Ran home from the bus stop for six months straight past those boarded-up storefronts. Duckin' rocks the nigger gangs throwed. Yellin' for us to get outta their 'hood! Stayed home nights. Took to carryin' a blade to school." Waving his arms, Claus bounced forward, talking a streak.

"Then my old man moves us a couple miles west out by St. Jane de Chantel's—*surrounded* by whites. And there's niggers bussed into Kennedy High School! Riots so bad we ripped lockers out of the walls. Flung desks through windows. Cops swarmed the halls in riot helmets with clubs. Just like prison."

Cringing, Larry pulled his neck into his shoulders and swiped his longish hair behind his ears. He heard the same talk at home at the dinner table. His city-worker father, slapping a mound of mashed potatoes onto his plate, complained about "the niggers this, the niggers that," mostly to Larry's mother and two younger brothers. Playing drums on off-nights at South Side blues bars, Larry warned his black musician friends never to telephone him at home after dinner when his old man could answer—all this a secret Larry's mother fearfully kept from her husband. When his old man ranted about blacks, Larry shrank back from the supper table. Arguing would only aggravate his father, and leave hanging an ugly tension that would linger for days.

Just that morning at Sunday Mass the gray-headed pastor, his voice booming from speakers high in the vaulted church ceiling, asked parishioners to stand by their "Christian morals" and "weather the storm of violence sweeping through Marquette Park." The rousing sermon identified as the enemy not blacks wishing to up-grade to higher class neighborhoods and better housing, but realtors, "evil as Satan himself," eagerly selling homes with government-insured loans to poor blacks, who would predictably be foreclosed on in two years and forced off the property. Larry, picturing the neighborhood all boarded up, a ghost town, forgot he was in church. Lumbering down the church steps after Mass, his father complained, "Boy is he outta touch!"

On the dark porch as the others leaned toward Claus, Larry, sitting off to Claus's left, doubled over as if holding his stomach and looked over his knees at his dirty white gym shoes with the purple laces.

"So yeah, we chased niggers," Claus said, drunkenly swatting at a firefly flashing above his head. "Come night, I'd get the call: 'Hey, wanna bust shitheads?' That was Joe Parisi's code word. Cracked me up. He'd roll up front the house, honk, and I'd snatch up my gym bag stuffed with dirty clothes to fool my old lady. Parisi's this little cocky Italian buddy of mine. Maybe you seen him round the house once or twice. Always spittin', scratchin' his crotch, walkin' with his chin up, guess 'cause he thinks it makes him taller. Always had the finest girls. Sharpest cars. Even in junior high. Always knew what was hap'nin'. Like he was goin' through high school for the third time. His cousins coached him. How to screw, how to get drunk, how to box and take care of himself. 'Fact, he made Golden Gloves couple years there. Got so many cousins, they could start their own suburb!"

The boys laughed as Claus wiped the sweat from his eyes.

"Shithead patrols night after night. Became a passion. Then three car blitzes. Guys from the 'hood joinin' in. Reportin' back to the VFW hall parking lot across from Argo High. Whole operation got so serious we kicked one dude out of the car with a pint of whiskey on him. Didn't want no reason for the cops to nail us."

"Ah, go on!" Kramer said. "Suppose yooze guys had badges and walkie-talkies."

"Listen. Went from rocks and bottles to broom handles and brass knuckles to sawed-off pipes and then lead-filled softball bats. Parisi liked the way I handled a switchblade. Papers gave us "gang" status two weeks runnin'. And yeah, Parisi bolted a CB radio in his dash. One night a cousin of his brought along a shiny black .38 automatic, and the car was dead quiet the whole trip. Then Joe got messed up pretty bad."

"Cops?" Uncle Tony asked, flicking his butane lighter to his cigar stub, his glasses glowing yellow.

"Naw, but it was weird. That night the fog was hangin' from the sodium street lights on Sixty-third like huge orange teepees. Me and Joe was cruisin' by ourselves, talkin' quiet and draggin' on cigarettes, our faces glowin' orange. Dressed in black, a kind of uniform that evolved. Said we was guardin' the "last frontier" for white people. Upholdin' law and order and all this kind of stuff. I begged Joe to take a quick run before a party back in the 'hood. All night I was nervous—about school or my old man. Don't remember. But somethin' was botherin' me 'cause I really wanted to kick some ass, and 'cause Joe kept yellin' for me to quit poundin' on his dashboard. Night before was Halloween. Stores still had that twisted orange and black crepe paper looped in their windows. Ducked in and out of the nigger section. Nothin' much goin' on. Joe tole me about his Gram just died. How all the clocks in his house stopped at 5:30—the time she kicked. Even the plug-in ones. Fuckin' creepy.

"Out where Sixty-third comes to a T and bangs into the train yards, and ya gotta turn down Archer Road, out the corner of my eye I see this Electra deuce-and-a-quarter shoot outta that nigger bar parkin' lot on the corner—The Midnight Oasis or Slap Me Five, or Let's Get Funky—some such bull. Always got the door thrown open, flashin' like a Christmas tree, all this funky, faggy disco music rollin' out. Aggravates the hell out of me 'cause I know a bunch of out-of-work niggers are in there gettin' juiced up and jivin' each other with their government checks.

"So this 'lectra with a taped-up headlight cuts us off. I mean this sucker comes flyin' at us head-on like a kamikaze, some nigger yellin' 'Hunkie!' out the window. Joe fishtails 'round the intersection, then jumps on that 'lectra's ass, flashin' his brights. We see two nigger heads in the car ahead. Passenger keeps turnin' 'round to check us out.

"So yeah, while we're cuttin' down Archer Road toward the cemetery where they ain't no lights, and where the ghost of Resurrection Mary in her white sweater tries to hitch rides with lone drivers, niggers pop this big White Castle bag out the window, and it *explodes* in the street—cups and cardboard castles doin' flips in front of our headlights. We swerve, and I grab the dash. (Hey, Joe's *bad* '63 Chevy: c-l-e-a-n, not a *speck* of rust!) The 'lectra whips into this real dark Dairy Queen boarded up for winter. Right across from the corn starch plant that looks like a cloud-makin' factory—all eerie and steamy and pulsatin' in the fog. We chase around the back of this abandoned ice cream joint, sprayin' rocks and skiddin' to a stop 'cause the niggers got their car stalled sideways blockin' our path.

"We're out! I toss a lead-filled bat over the roof to Joe. He snatches it clean, runs at that car yellin' like a crazy man, and busts out a tail light. Nigger driver rolls out from behind his wheel into Joe's smokin' headlights with *somethin'* in his hand—somethin' shiny.

"With *my* bat I dash through the headlights and chop down the passenger, who's staggerin' drunk. Snap that motherfucker's collarbone! And as he's fallin' I step into that low fastball—and BOOM—crack him in the forehead. His head snaps back and I feel me lift him *completely* off the ground! And that sound... that sound... like droppin' a bowlin' ball on indoor/outdoor carpeting."

"Jeez-us!" Kramer moaned, a hint of admiration and awe in his voice, "that's sick!" Uncle Tony covered his head. Larry, flinching his shoulders, rubbed his face with both hands. Standing, Claus towered above his audience, arms held high above his head, holding an imaginary bat in his hands.

"Joe's runnin' at that nigger driver with his bat raised. His black shadow—big as a bear—thrown up by the headlights against the white wall of the Dairy Queen. Three feet away the nigger's all crouched down, almost kneelin', his arm up, ready to block Joe's bat, when *another* set of headlights and that loud gravel crunch sweep in behind our car. Out of nowhere a yellow Nova pulls in. Stops. Nobody gets out or nothin'. For a split second Joe hesitates and turns to look at the Nova. And *that's* when the nigger crouched down in front of him pops up like a jack-in-the-box and knifes him! Whips up his hand like he's zippin' up Joe's jacket! Joe swings his bat like a weak sister and falls, face first, deadweight, on the rocks. I run screamin' at that nigger, and about ten feet away—can still see that mother's gold teeth flashin'—I fling my bat with both hands. Electra's back window shatters. Car doors slam. Voices and shadows and that crunch and spin of tires shootin' gravel all kind of get blurry. We're alone. Nova, niggers, everybody gone in cloud of smoke. Chevy's idling, doors thrown open. Joe's out flat on the rocks, moanin' just beyond our headlights. I don't wanna touch him or roll him over to see his face all fucked up from the rocks.

"I stand there frozen stiff, Joe between my feet, 'til the Sheriff sweeps in, cherries splashin' like huge red antlers floatin' in the fog above the squad car. Cop puts a hand on my shoulder, says, 'What *happened* here?' gut out, voice shakin', scared like."

As if collectively holding their breath, everyone on the dark porch remained still.

Suddenly, two amber porch lights flashed on either side of the screen door, and the laughter of women and children sailed out to the men. Claus's long shadow leaped out ahead of him and tumbled down the stairs. The guys turned to the porch, squinting. Gloria, wearing a terry cloth apron, her blonde hair glowing in the yellow light, stepped out of the screen door leading Ray and Marge, who each held a foil-wrapped piece of leftover birthday cake.

"You guys still yapping out here?" Gloria asked, and immediately noticed a rubbery-legged Claus trying to catch his balance. An odd silence cowed the men. Larry slunk back on his seat, relieved. Timmy and Carrie, their Sunday clothes stained with Kool-Aid and chocolate cake, in an explosion of giggles charged past Claus and scrambled down the stairs into the night. Claus mumbled something and, stooping to grab up a beer can, tripped down a few stairs and collapsed on top of Uncle Tony.

"Whoa! Steady as she goes, Claus!" Uncle Tony chuckled and, grinning stupidly at Gloria, gently pushed Claus away from him.

"Listen, thanks for coming, you two," Gloria said, folding her arms and turning her back on Claus. "The jello mold was great, Marge. I'll get that Tupperware washed up and back to you pronto!" She kissed Marge on the cheek. Ray, smiling weakly, shook Claus's hand. Moments later, after the couple had driven off honking their horn, Gloria, standing inside the screen door, asked,

"Any of you guys want cake? I got tons."

"Just leave us the hell alone," Claus snapped, "and turn off the goddamn search lights, will ya?" The porch went dark. But Gloria's presence had left Claus in a funk. Not until Larry braved a question about the neighborhood did Claus's attention snap back to the porch.

"What if nobody moves out?" Larry asked eagerly, licking his lips. "If whites stay put when blacks move in? Start moving in, I mean."

"Whadeya mean blacks?" Claus growled. "They're niggers. N-I-G-E-R-S. Ain't no blacks or 'fros or nee-grows. They're niggers. Plain and simple. When I say they're niggers, they're niggers, OK?"

"Alright. Alright," Larry nodded, leaning way back with his hands held out before him. "But if, let's say, one or two white families move out of Marquette. Same block. And two black families move in?" Larry watched Claus's face curl into a disgusted look, and said quickly, "Now lemme finish," and took a deep breath. "Those two black families move in. And the rest of the whites stay put. Nobody else moves. Everybody keeps on cutting their grass, painting their garages, stuff like that, just like before. How can blacks 'take over' then? If whites don't sell their homes and move, how can they take over?"

"He's right," Kramer said from the bottom of the stairs, pointing up to Larry. Inspired, Larry continued.

" 'Course, the Nazis with their uniforms and flags and swastikas get the riots on TV. On the news. And because of what's on TV, folks get scared and mad and rush into the street to throw stuff at blacks."

"Hey, *I'm* out there," Claus bragged, thumping his chest. "Makin' sure no nigger don't go walkin' down *my* street lookin' to buy!"

153

Instantly, Larry countered.

"You really think these Nazis *care* about the neighborhood? Half of 'em drive in from the 'burbs to march in front of Walgreens on Sixty-third and Kedzie. They're in it to get on TV, get their names in the papers. They don't have no power. They can't keep Marquette Park white. In fact, it's those Nazi instigators who started all this trouble. Never see them fighting in the street. When the trouble starts, they're miles away!" Larry stopped talking. He realized he was focusing his speech on Claus, and that Claus was hanging his head not even listening. They all started talking at once, until Claus shouted everyone down and yelled to Larry.

"You didn't say nigger! Come on! Say nigger—N-I-G-E-R," he said playfully. "Say it loud enough so all my Lithuanian neighbors hear it loud and clear in their Lugan bedrooms. Get a bang out of it."

Larry laughed, looking away. Claus leaped up from the top stair, fire in his eyes.

"Come on! Say it! What's the matter? Dirty your vocabulary? Say it!"

"I'm not enjoying this at all," Larry pleaded to Kramer.

"Come on, nigger lover. Say it!"

"I'm not a nig—I-am-not—" Larry jumped to his feet to leave.

Claus leaned into him until their noses were inches apart and Larry could smell Claus's beer breath. "Yes-you-are-a-nigger-lover!" he yelled, then backed off, his bloodshot eyes making Larry cower inside.

"Yeah, they're oppressed," Claus said. "And I suppose you're some white knight with all the answers. Well, let me tell you what them niggers do affects *me* and *you* and *every*body on this porch, this block, *any*where you look." Claus reared. "Come on! Say it!" and he shoved Larry on the shoulder, wild-eyed.

"Hey, wait a minute!" cried Larry, taking the shove, arms windmilling to catch his balance. Again, he pleaded to Kramer with a startled look. Standing on the sidewalk before the porch, Kramer threw one foot onto the bottom stair.

"Claus, be cool. Be cool. Sit down and leave the boy alone. He's alright. Just a little confused. That's all. Just a little mixed up. You know—"

Claus stood erect, teetering, eyes burning down on Larry, his jaw thrust out in a dare as if to say, "Come on sucker, hit me." A motorcycle, pipes blaring, ripped down the street between the aisle of parked cars. As heads turned to the racket, Larry fixed his eyes on Claus, who shoved his hands into his pockets, slumped his shoulders and spun away, pacing the porch. Then he stopped and whirled back.

"Jeeze! You just don't know," he yelled to Larry. "Your old man never had to sell the house he was born in and move to a ritzy area and work three jobs 'til he dropped dead of a heart attack. Or checked your pocket every morning before school, makin' sure you had your knife. See some old white lady with a cane—in broad daylight—get gang-banged on a bus stop. See her groceries roll out into the street of a *changing neighborhood.* Haven't found your buddy with his belly sliced open, moaning like an animal. All 'cause of niggers!" Claus spun away, pacing.

"When they move in people start gettin' killed, people start gettin' robbed, raped—you name it. After dark the streets are empty 'cause it ain't no longer safe. And it's gonna happen right here in Marquette.

"One day I'll wake up and hafta pack up 'cause of niggers just like my old man. THEY'RE TRYIN' TO TAKE OVER! Can't you *see* that?" He marked a list on his fingers.

"Jesse Jackson, Muhammad Ali, Luther King, Afro-Sheen, Ebony. Black is beautiful. Man, I'm-sick-of-hearin'-it! Even named a street King Drive 'cause he walked around gettin' rocks thrown at his head. And got himself killed for actin' like a fool. Jee-zus! It's like everything I've said tonight's been thrown to the wind. Ya didn't hear a damn *word* of it!" And shaking his hands over his head, Claus took two giant steps across the porch, ripped open the screen door, and disappeared into the yellow glow of the house.

Larry sat stunned for a moment, half expecting the other porch sitters to take up for Claus. As he strained to hear the goings-on inside the house, a tingly sweat crawled down his back. "Didn't know he was so touchy," he said rather quietly, staring at the screen door.

"Aw, don't worry yourself about it," Kramer said. "It's the beer talking. Nothing against you personally. He gets that way now and then."

Kramer lit another cigarette and twirled down into a sitting position on the bottom stair facing the street. Half turning while blowing a plume of smoke, he added, "The man feels he's gotta fight for what he believes."

from *Act of God*

Zoe Keithley

Saturday was her day off, but somehow Mother Adelli felt drawn to the dining hall and her student charges even so.

Through the windows the sky was almost black; rain drops the size of quarters collided with the glass. Lightning stitched the churning clouds; thunder cracked and made everyone jump, then laugh.

Talk was unusually exhilarated—probably, the nun concluded, the result of the false alarm late in the afternoon which had sent everyone trooping out, single file, to the driveway and tennis courts—everyone except the new girl, who had been sent to the dormitory to unpack and had fallen asleep there.

"Did you think we left you up there to be smoked like a ham?" Mother Adelli stood between CeeCee and Helene, a hand on each girl's chair.

CeeCee giggled deliciously. "Yeah," she turned to the new girl, "didn't you hear the alarm? Didn't that scare you?"

Helene pulled a blank face and stared at her a long moment, then shook her head from side to side.

"Well, I would have been SCARED TO DEATH. You would have heard ME running all over the building like a MADWOMAN!" CeeCee raved her arms through the air, illustrating. She and the new girl exchanged looks, each, for a different reason, disgusted with the other.

"So, how long has your father dumped you in here for?" It was Debbie's voice, obviously directed toward the new girl.

Talk at the end of the table dropped suddenly into silence.

"I'm not DUMPED." Helene's voice was loud and she was on her feet. "You poor saps may be dumped, but I'm not." Now silence spread to the whole table.

"Well, what do you call this," Debbie refused to back off, her eye gleaming with satisfaction at the sight of the new girl's red face and clenched fists, " 'vacation time in Hawaii'?"

"You don't even know my father," Helene shouted at her. "He's one of the best surgeons in the world. Maybe he'll do you a favor and sew up your mouth, you cow!"

Mother Adelli, who had already wandered away, was back.

"That's enough, Miss! Sit down!" she said sharply to Helene. The girl remained standing, swaying back and forth.

"That's enough from you too, Deborah. You know better than this!" Abruptly, the dining hall slid into an alert silence.

"You young ladies will apologize to one another," the nun continued. "There is no place in a community like this for unkindness," she said to Helene, "or for thoughtlessness," to Debbie.

"She doesn't know anything about my father!" Helene spat at the nun. "She should apologize to my father!"

"Well where IS he?" Despite the consequences, Debbie couldn't resist temptation. "I'll be GLAD to apologize to him."

"An apology is all I care to hear from either of you," the nun said, hushing Debbie.

"I apologize," Debbie countered cheerfully, tiring immediately of the game, and spearing a piece of meat.

Mother Adelli turned to Helene. "Apologize to Deborah, Helene."

The table chewed in silence, watching. Helene's face hardened.

"A simple 'I apologize' is sufficient." The nun waited.

Still rigid as a pole, Helene sat down. She crossed her arms over her chest and stared straight ahead.

Mother Adelli waited. "Please," something in her mind said to the hard, hurting face, "don't start out this way." A grinding seemed to the young nun to have started up in the atmosphere around the girl and herself.

"Helene?"

A curt nod, finally.

Debbie smirked up and down the table over the dripping piece of meat.

The new girl said nothing. She picked up her fork and began toothpasting her potatoes through the tines. But her eyes gleamed. Something inside her, something like a dark, hard coal, and exactly in the same deep spot turned icy and aching by her father's leaving, now ignited and quietly burned, low and intense.

*****

Tea. Mother Adelli looked at her watch. 7:25. Not too early for a cup or two before evening prayers and dormitory duties. An extra treat for her day off! She slipped the book of devotions, recommended by Father Dousten in the confessional last Wednesday, back onto the bookshelf.

From the kitchen doorway she saw Soeur Josephine, sleeves rolled above her elbows, a large white apron tucked at the waist to form a huge pocket for rags, and her Working Sisters' veil pinned back. She was scouring the cooking grill, her final chore of the day.

The muffled chatter of Mother Adelli's rosaries alerted the little Puerto Rican sister, who turned on her a shy smile and then immediately dropped her eyes and made a half-curtsy.

"Good evening, Mother."

Now here, Mother Adelli reflected, was meekness personified. Tonight's devotional reading had preached meekness.

"Can I trouble you for a pot of tea, ma Soeur?"

Soeur Josephine blushed. "Oh, but it is always a happiness to serve you, Mother. I put the hot water now!"

But how, Mother Adelli went on to herself, was she to be meek and responsible at the same time? The scene in the dining hall, which had hardly left her mind since it happened, loomed again. This was the first real flare-up in her short five-month career as Mistress of the Middle School. The questions the incident raised left her anxious, perplexed and irritated. And Frances de Sales' *Wise and Loving Counsels* tonight (very much against her desires) exacerbated everything for her.

As she watched Soeur Josephine rinse the teapot at the sink and clink two heaping spoonfuls of tea into its belly, the nun suddenly noticed through the serving window the darkness in the students' dining hall, and then felt it behind her in the corridor, and before her in the Cloister dining hall to which she would carefully carry her tray.

By contrast the yellow lights of the kitchen warmed the wood of the baker's table and sent soft color through the metal of the mammoth institutional stove and refrigerator, gaily lighting the scoured bottoms of the copper pots, patient on the wall.

Soeur Josephine, now gathering a few cookies, kept her brown eyes respectfully to her task.

"I'm sorry to say there has been an incident with the new girl," Mother Adelli began in her mind, as though Soeur Josephine had looked up and asked a question. "It will mean an 'assez bien' at her first Primes. I know that seems harsh, but I don't see how I can do anything but treat her like all the others—though I feel very sorry about it."

She went on addressing an audience in her head which included the Sister. "It is my duty to keep order no matter what the circumstances." A cup and saucer rattled onto the tray, followed by a plate of cookies.

"Mother." Soeur Josephine's eyes were modestly downcast.

"Thank you, ma Soeur. This is so nice." She took the tray and its chiming china.

Really, she didn't want to go off into the dark like this by herself. She wished she could have, instead, sat down with Soeur Josephine and poured out the events of the day to her compassionate ear. But being together in such a way would have been unthinkable to either of them. Not the Rule, but common custom in the Cloister frowned on it. So instead she must take herself off to the Cloister dining hall. Sacrifice, if painful, was so much the more sweet and fragrant an offering, she told herself, freighting the tray and her feelings into the darkness.

* * * * *

"Just as you would guess from the word," Mother Adelli explained to Helene after breakfast, in the hall, "it means 'first.' 'Primes' is a kind of report we make to ourselves, first thing in the week, an evaluation to start the week and to keep track of how close we came to our ideals last week and to catch ourselves in case we might have been going off the path—both academically and spiritually. It's an old custom in our schools all over the world. Just follow the other girls. You'll catch on."

The nun drew a breath. Now she must say the part she didn't want to say.

"The incident in the dining hall Saturday night, I'm afraid, must be registered against both you and Deborah in your evaluations this week. While I understand that it is upsetting to come into a new situation—"

Her voice, to her ear, developed a thin, nasal quality. The words were unaccountably hard to say. Helene's eyes, gone flat, shifted lazily over the nun's face, then past it and down the hall behind her.

"—we must all learn to live together in peace and good feeling," she finished, unconvincingly.

The girl swung from her dumbly, like the automatic arm of a phonograph, and went through the double doors into Study Hall, where everyone was arranging desk chairs in a double-row semicircle. Reverend Mother, or her representative, with Mother Adelli alongside, would sit at the apex. Mother Adelli would give an oral evaluation of the academic and social behavior of each student. Marks given out would be as follows: "trés bien," very good; "bien," good; "assez bien," well enough (not so good); "rien," nothing (bad).

She had no choice about it, Mother Adelli told herself again as Helene Rhenehan's name came up on the list.

In response to her name, and following the example of the other girls, Helene rose and came forward to the center of the semicircle, where it broke apart to make an aisle, and stepped ahead one more pace, directly in front of Reverend Mother. Her eyes fixed on a knothole just peeking out from under the Superior's shoe. Mother Adelli waited for the new student to curtsy to Reverend Mother, but the girl remained stationary.

"Assez bien," Mother Adelli said finally, as the pause became awkward. Surely she had not forgotten to explain something so basic as the curtsy to the girl!

Reverend Mother looked up, surprised. She straightened, glanced at the notebook open on Mother Adelli's lap and then looked closely at the girl. The Superior didn't like the feel of it.

"I'm sure this is not an accurate picture of your stay here with us, Miss Rhenehan. We will not expect to hear such a report again. Many find the first days in a new situation unsettling."

Helene stood with her chin raised scornfully. Behind her, thirty girls held their breath a little. How did she continue to stand so starchily, Helene's fellow students wondered about her with admiration, and never even give Reverend Mother a glance? Nobody liked Reverend Mother's attention, although almost everybody got it at least once. Some—like Debbie and CeeCee—got it regularly and seemed to even develop a callus of sorts. But not the first time!

"You may sit down, Miss Rhenehan."

Reverend Mother wanted to move on. The girl turned.

"A curtsy first, Miss, as a sign of respect for the occasion and the persons involved in it. Perhaps your Mistress has not had time to instruct you in the use of the curtsy here. I'm sure the oversight will be corrected at her first opportunity."

Mother Adelli colored at the correction.

Helene put a foot behind her and bobbled on it clumsily. A snicker snagged the air but was quickly muffled in answer to Reverend Mother's sharp snapping of her wooden clapper for order. Angered, Helene turned to reclaim her seat and, as she did, felt something in the air, a subtle change, an energy, from her fellow students. Respect, she decided. It was respect for her because she hadn't crumbled.

In a flash the vision came to her of how it would all be! She would get back at Mother Dilli and make her pay for all this—for not making Cow apologize about her father, for making HER say she was sorry when she had NOT been in the wrong, for giving her a bad mark she didn't deserve in front of Rancid Mother and embarrassing her with the stupid curtsy thing. She slid onto the base of her spine and crossed her arms in satisfaction, watching the remainder of the girls, one at a time, bob, receive a grade, bob again.

After Primes, Reverend Mother stopped Mother Adelli in the hall.

"Show the Rhenehan girl about the curtsy. See that she knows how to use it."

"Yes, Reverend Mother."

"If—." The Superior stopped herself. "I'm sure everything will be all right now? The girl is going to be very happy here?" she inquired with a raised eyebrow and strong, lingering question marks.

"Yes, Reverend Mother." Mother Adelli's mouth was dry as sandpaper.

* * * * *

"Mother Adelli!"

Mother Durban's slender black figure fairly flew across the nuns' lounge. Bonnet-framed faces turned in little groups as she reached the couch and several chairs where her brown eyes had spotted Mother Adelli talking with Mothers O'Rourke and Crewelman.

"The new girl, Mother—" Mother Durban started, sinking into a chair and lowering her voice almost to a whisper. Mother Adelli's two companions automatically bent forward, like fingers on a hand, closing.

"I—I'm sure it doesn't mean anything, but I thought you should know because it DID involve fire—"

Mother Adelli's eyebrows rose suddenly and she gulped air.

"Oh, not a lot of fire, Mother. Very controlled—to a little place on the tennis court. Still, where would the girls get matches, I thought."

Mother Adelli searched the nun's worried face. She would have liked to have taken up one of her fluttering hands to hold.

"I'm sure whatever it is can be straightened out," she said instead.

The little Mistress of the Minims nodded, ran her tongue over her lips and told the story.

She had taken them—minims (grades 1-4) and middle school—to the tennis courts after "goûter," their afternoon snack. They were deep into Red Rover before she'd noticed the new girl and several others off by themselves and hunched over something in a far corner. Squinting out of the brilliant September sunlight into deep shade, she didn't for a moment see the thin column of smoke. She called, "What are you doing, girls?" and, as she hurried over, heard the new girl chant fiercely, "Burn! Burn!" while the others scattered.

"I—I saved what they were burning, to show you." From between the square folds of her large white handkerchief she drew forth a paper doll, charred at the bottom. Clearly it was a Religious of the Sacred Heart and a small, dense black circle rode the face just above the end of the mouth. Automatically Mother Adelli fingered the dark mole hovering on the lower crest of her right cheek.

* * * * *

"Do you like to be called 'Lene or Helene? Here you've been with us four days already and I'm just now asking about your name." Mother Adelli mustered a cheery tone.

There was hardly room for one person, much less two, in this former storage closet. Against a window of opaque glass sat three grey file cabinets; a fourth squeezed itself into a front corner and left just enough space for a wooden chair where the new girl sat trimming cuticles with her teeth and peering under the desk at the nun's two black shoes.

Against the front leg of the desk lay a coiled jumprope, not yet returned to the sports closet. The girl reached a brown oxford forward, caught a strand of the rope and began raising it on her toe and letting it fall to the floor. The little slap, slap amused her. Catch a fish, throw it in a ditch; catch a fly, poke it in the eye; catch a toad, squish it in the road. Her game of rhymes blotted out the nun's voice.

"Well," the nun went on, "I guess we'll call you Helene then, unless you say differently."

Slap, slap, slap went the rope. Just below her fingertips on the desk top and right through it, Mother Adelli was conscious of the paper effigy in the drawer, as if it were burning there, but the nun's discipline kept her voice moving. Nothing she said gained the girl's eyes or unlocked her tongue. She heard her own voice crossing the desk, remote and mechanical. Suddenly she knew that she had never expected to confront the girl with the charred doll and something in her chilled at the realization.

"I never wanted to come here." Helene's voice, blunted and flat, unexpectedly broke the air. "I only have to stay six months," she added definitively. Then, as if she had explained everything, she stood to leave.

"Just a moment. Sit down please."

Heartened by this communication, the nun shifted gears. Perhaps the girl just needed to get her anger out. Mother Adelli pressed the opportunity: the time would go fast; so many changes were difficult, but, with our Lord's help, Helene would feel at home soon. The girl, bent over, continued fiddling with the rope as the nun tried bravely once more to hack an opening to her.

Still, something about this girl repelled her, drove her back, and that feeling made her, inexplicably, want to cry. It was as though a kind of fate had been sealed of which she was ignorant and against which she was helpless.

Then the dinner bell plucked softly at the air. Mother Adelli heard it with gratitude.

"The dinner bell."

The girl made no reply. The fiery mass of her hair still hovered over the rope.

The nun started to rise. Unexpectedly, compassion for the girl stirred in her. Now she wanted to reach across the desk and embrace her, warm her until the hardness in her face, especially in her eyes, melted. But, "Nole me tangere" said the Rule: "Do not touch me."

"Is there any way I can be helpful to you, Helene?" she asked instead.

The girl's head popped up suddenly, above the desk top, face grinning. One clenched fist rose up next to the face. Swinging from it was the product of her industry—a section of jumprope ingeniously tied into a hangman's noose.

Mother Adelli felt her heart stop, then sink. But something in her sternly gathered composure.

"Bring the rope with you," the something said crisply. "I'll show you where to put it away."

But behind the nun's dry eyes her head swam.

* * * * *

The large old ceiling fan in the nuns' dining room, complaining softly, stirred the air. Fragrances of dinner mixed with the clatter of serving dishes and the high-pitched buzzing of feminine voices. Twenty-two graceful black arches of nuns' heads, broken by the occasional white veil of a novice, moved to and fro with dishes and talk like clusters of flowers.

"The carrots please, Mother? Mother Adelli? The carrots?"

Outside the wind rattled the tall windows along the wall.

"By the way, Mother, whatever did you do about the paper doll?" Mother Crewelman helped herself from the dish.

Five or six pairs of ears turned immediately toward Mother Adelli, who dusted her fingers and prematurely swallowed a last chunk of biscuit still steaming at its center. Tears leapt to her eyes.

"Is something wrong, Mother?" Mother Byrne, on her right, asked, concern on her delicate and aging face.

Mother Adelli forced a laugh. "No, no. Thank you, Mother. Just a piece of biscuit. Too hot." But something at her center pulled itself away into a rigid column.

"Whatever DID you do about the paper doll, Mother? About the new girl?" Mother Crewelman pressed.

A babble followed; most had heard nothing of the incident. Mother Crewelman's voice cleared the air like a study hall clapper as three raspberry jello molds and plates of Mother Concepcion's anniversary cake were set along the white cloth.

"It was a paper doll the girl made and tried to burn on the tennis courts. Isn't that right, Mother?" This time Mother Crewelman turned to Mother Durban, on the far edge of the discussion.

Mother Durban nodded. Like her small charges, she had an intuitive intelligence which counselled her now to caution.

"It was a silly thing," she soft-pedaled, "but since a *very little bit* of fire was involved—"

"Did you determine whether the drawing was of a particular nun?" Mother Crewelman cut Mother Durban off and turned back, eyes sparkling keenly behind her glasses, to Mother Adelli, who was staring into a large round dish of gleaming, undulating and brilliantly raspberry jello. "Was it you the girl was drawing, Mother?"

The surface of the jello was like a gorgeously moving ice pond, shimmering which lights all the way to its center. Mother Adelli eagerly allowed the brilliant colors to mesmerize her and shut out the faces with their questions around her.

"Oh, I wondered about that too—with the little mole—. Was it you, Mother, do you think?" Mother O'Rourke's voice yanked her attention back to the table. The room suddenly felt raw with light and chatter.

Then she saw it. Just as Soeur Josephine reached from behind to replenish her coffee, Mother Adelli picked up the jello dish to serve herself and saw the dead fly at the edge of the gleaming lake. It was on its back, legs bent askew, wings laid out like veils from its plump hairy body and huge sectioned eyes looking both right and left. Rigor mortis had set in.

Disgust and rage rose in a torrent into Mother Adelli's face. Her hands began to shake. She dropped the bowl on the table and wheeled on Soeur Josephine, just withdrawing the coffee pitcher.

"A fly!" she squeezed through her clenched teeth. "There is a fly on this jello, Sister!"

That was all she said, and all she needed to say. Soeur Josephine, paling, whisked the offending dish into the kitchen. The nuns at table stirred uncomfortably.

As if standing just behind herself, Mother Adelli watched the scene, stunned. It was totally uncharacteristic of her to criticize a Working Sister, whom she considered to have a naturally purified vocation.

"Oh. Have some of this jello, Mother," Mother Durban broke in hurriedly. She reached to pass a different bowl.

"No. Thank you. Food is not that important." Amazed, Mother Adelli saw herself stand up. "I'll excuse myself. I have work to do downstairs."

"You wouldn't leave before grace, Mother?" Mother Crewelman leaned forward over the sparse cake she had served herself.

The question was like a hand slapping Mother Adelli from a stupor. She blinked twice, hesitating. "No, of course not, Mother," she said and sank back into her chair.

Conversation among the nuns began again in little leaks and dribbles, about the startling changes in the weather—sunny and warm one minute, dark, cold, rainy the next. And that awful wind, coming out of nowhere, throttling the trees until they hardly had a leaf left!

from *A Chocolate Soldier*

Cyrus Colter

Alone on the street corner under the bleary light—it is past midnight—he stands waiting. Has he missed it? he wonders—the final bus back to campus. He painfully hopes he has not—his fatigue is too real for the interminable journey on foot. Also the threat of rain hovers in the night air. He yawns. Suddenly then it is as if some sepulchral bodiless voice from out of the black void, or escaping from some far-off ominous cave of winds, addresses him in tones both admonitory and sad: "Cager, Cager, for shame. Why—though you call it a job, your mealticket—why do you continue squandering your days and nights in a bawdy cabaret, run by that chief harridan of the world's proprietresses, when your neglected books, to you once so precious, now pitifully cry out for both your reform and return? Or have you no more capacity for shame?"

He wishes to mumble some feeble defense, cite some extenuating pretext, like: I have, yes, to eat, live, somehow hang on; the crummy job is my sole means. True, it is low, menial, exclusively flunky work, e.g., scrubbing pots and pans, mopping floors, unloading heavy supplies, but—no matter that I too often get carried away with the place's raunchy, exciting entertainment fare—what alternative is there? He feels utterly trapped in his present life and at times considers giving it up completely and returning home to the Virginia tidewater—only then to recall the high, if now futile, mission that had first brought him here. Now he leans heavily against the light pole and tries to shut off the grating tumult in his head—until the bus in fact arrives at last.

He boarded, dropped his coins in the fare box, and in long, weary strides made his way down the aisle past the moveable "white/colored" sign and on into the mandatory rear—in the process passing the four lone sleeping white men passengers, one of whom was snoring. Almost at once, in deep self-communion again, he sat staring out the window at the night ghosts and shadows of what seemed an unending, a worldwide, nighttime. The bus now stopped again, to take on two more passengers—a white woman and her seven- or eight-year-old son. The strange child had soon utterly monopolized Cager's attention. It was first the bizarre way the boy was dressed, entirely in macho adult-looking clothing: Tyrolean hat with feather, leather jacket, its green plastic belt almost as wide as a sash, plus sharply pressed little trousers and tiny highly polished jackboots. He seemed at times not a child at all but some freak fascist midget out of a circus or movie, until the rosy, cherubic face was observed.

After paying their fares, his mother, a tall, pale woman with lantern jaws, brought him over halfway back into the white section where they sat down. The child at once climbed up on the seat, faced to the rear, and curiously studied lone Jim-Crowed Cager. The two for a moment looked at each other, before suddenly the boy brought up both arms, as if holding an imaginary rifle, took dead aim at Cager, and, feigning pulling the trigger, cried out exultantly: *"Bang! Bang! Bang!"* He then went into gales of childish laughter. The behavior so completely stunned Cager that he did not at first react at all. The child soon fired three more phantom rounds, all the while crying, *"Bang! Bang! Bang!"* —then, still laughing, turned to his mother for her commendation. But, appearing tired and bored, she only went on staring straight ahead.

Cager reacted at last. Jumping up, he seized the moveable Jim Crow sign in front of him and went and affixed it directly in front of the mother and child. Then, heedless of whether or not the bus driver or other riders had seen this insurrectionary, unthinkable act, he returned to his seat and, grinding his teeth, whispering to himself, plopped down again. Suddenly the mother, realizing what had happened, that she and her son had just been gerrymandered into the "colored" section, blanched even paler, then opened her mouth, gaping with shock and incredulity, yet somehow could not speak. At last, though, after frantically darting her eyes up front for help, but where apparently no one had yet noticed, she turned furiously on Cager, under her breath spluttering a string of racial epithets just as her son again trained his ghost gun on Cager and, squinting down the barrel, repeatedly squeezed the trigger—*"Bang! Bang! Bang!"*

Astonishingly now, Cager let out a series of strange manic laughs, not strident, not even loud, but which almost at once changed into a menacing growl. The woman, however, had jumped up, grabbed the Jim Crow sign in front of her, and, muttering more imprecations on Cager, returned it to its former place in the rear—her son all the while covering her actions with the withering fire of his imaginary automatic weapon until his mother was safely back in her seat. *"Bang! Bang! Bang!"* he cried out again and again.

The commotion had finally now awakened the riders up front, who were turning around to stare. Also, the bus driver, at last glowering into his rearview mirror at the ruckus, hollered back to Cager: "Boy, you better stay back there where you belong before I git the cops on here!" Strangely, though, Cager was so fascinated, so engrossed, by the child's actions he seemed wholly oblivious of everything else. Finally, pointing up front toward the white passengers, he said to the boy: "Hey, my man, why don't you shoot up in *that* direction once in a while?" Whatever anger he may have felt before seemed somehow now to have vanished, supplanted, however, by a deeply serious and conscientious curiosity.

But the child had all but lost interest now and was looking around for something new to occupy him. Finally, though, he replied: *"If I shot up there, they'd shoot back."* Then, bored, he glanced idly at his mother. Cager stared at him in awe, until soon the bus approached the mother's destination, whereupon she pulled the signal cord and herded the boy forward to leave. But not before Cager had leapt to his feet, raised both arms high as if he too now held a powerful firearm, and aimed it straight at the departing pair. *"Bang! Bang! Bang!... Bang! Bang! Bang!"* he shouted hoarsely at the top of his voice.

The passengers up front now had spun around scowling, as the bus driver out-shouted Cager: *"Set down!*—you damn drunk nigger, befoh I pistol-whip your head myself!" All this as he slowed the bus and finally stopped.

The child then, just before alighting ahead of his mother, turned around to Cager and, calm, composed, doubtless sleepy also, raised both hands high above his head in the classic gesture of capitulation, surrender. Then he and his mother stepped down and disappeared into the night.

The bus went on now. Cager, quiet, subdued, in a deep study, almost a trance, sat staring through the window out into the blackness. He had been so absorbed in what had happened, but most of all by the child's hands-over-head submission in surrender, that the bus driver's slurs had not fazed him, had hardly registered. Soon he was moving his lips, though not quite silently, murmuring in a kind of grand, wondrous affirmation: "Yeah, yeah..." he breathed, almost in an awed hush. "Clausewitz, ah... yeah, he was so right, wasn't he?—I can see it now plainer than ever. Oh Lord, I got to try to get myself together again, somehow. *I got to.* Even that little bastard, just a baby, but already wearing jackboots—even *he* knows what it's all about. You heard what he told you, didn't you? Whew!—those folks sure learn early, don't they? Yeah, and that's why they're where *they* are and we're where *we* are. Huh? Lord, Lord, help me, won't you? ... help me ... help *us*. ..." Emotion had closed his throat. He could no longer even talk to himself.

* * * * *

It was not Wednesday afternoon's rain that had caused the postponement. Far from it. There were no plans that day anyway to use the big vacant lot for drill practice. Rather, the arrangement had been to move indoors for an evening session. But now, just after dark, throwing off his dripping poncho as he entered Shorty George's little restaurant, Cager, in frustration and disgust, had to explain to Shorty the actual, and highly unsatisfactory, situation. "The lodge hall's not available. And I only just now found out about it. They've cancelled us out. They could at least have told us sooner!" His anger flared. "But you know them simple lodge niggers! They're an ignorant bunch of clowns. Bad as it's got for us in this town lately the only thing these backward-ass fools can find to do is meet in their hall and go through a lot of childish gibberish and lodge ritual like some kind of ignorant voodoo—flashing crazy signs and signals, winking, giving each other 'the grip,' and all that shit. It's pitiful, man! Jesus Christ!" He was walking the floor.

Shorty, worried about the four customers in the place, pulled him over to a sequestered table in the corner. "Keep your shirt on, Cage," he said.

"Instead, then, of letting us hold our meeting like they'd booked us to do, and for a fee, they revoke us till some other night so they can get together and go through all that crazy irrelevant rigmarole like a bunch of coons in a minstrel show! It's a damn disgrace! What they oughta be doing is coming to our drill sessions, learning what's *really* going on, what our people have to put up with in this cracker burg!" He took a deep breath. "Well anyhow, we can't meet tonight. So the unit's dismissed till Friday over in the lot again. Will you get the word out, Shorty?"

Shorty was glum, disconsolate. "Yeah," he finally said. "But it's just as well, for I got worse news for you. Togo Jackson's lost the new uniforms."

"*What?*" Cager took a step back almost as if reeling.

"Somebody stole 'em out of the trunk of that pile of junk he calls his car."

The waitress, Shorty's long-suffering wife, came over to see if Cager was going to eat. "Hold it," Shorty said to her. "Later."

Cager was still staring incredulously at Shorty, then began wringing his hands in utter anguish. "What the hell're you *talking* about!" he at last shouted at Shorty, as the latter's wife looked on in alarm and the few customers stared.

"You oughta know," snapped Shorty. "Togo was your idea. We all told you he was dumb as hell, a moron, but you wanted him in the organization anyhow, said we needed everybody we could get. Why would anybody but a moron leave twelve brand new jackets to our uniforms out in his car all night less'n he's dumb as a fence post? They wasn't even paid for yet, just the down-payment. We still gotta pay Nate Goldberg for 'em."

Cager heaved a heavy sigh, sank into a chair at the table, and stared out at the rainy darkness.

The "organization" did not even have a name yet. Presently it was still what Cager, its founder and leader, with Shorty as early financial backer, called the "drill unit." But, with Shorty's concurrence, he had already designed a uniform and matching cap for the members—gray-green jacket and trousers with red and gold accouterments, including a gold forked-lightning bolt on the left sleeve and crossed Ashanti spears on either lapel. The trousers, with red and gold stripes down each leg, would come later when the money was available.

The "unit" nevertheless met at least one evening a week to drill and confer—in either the customary vacant lot or the Negro lodge hall. In the latter, in addition to an hour or so of close-order drill, much time afterwards was devoted to what Cager referred to as "briefing sessions." These, invariably led by him, included discussions of subjects like the town's physical lay-out, which they sedulously studied, including the location, even floor plan, of the courthouse, its situation and distance from the police and fire stations, the armory (and its contents), the radio station, gas works, electric generating station, and sundry other sites, all referred to by leader Cager in his briefings as "strategic installations." His eyes fairly shone as he told the seventeen or eighteen men usually present: "It's all in case any trouble starts. *We* won't be starting it. It's in case *they* do. We got maps of everything. We know just about all that's going on, too. That's the job of our intelligence section. Shorty here and I have also designed a uniform for us even though they're not over twenty-five of us as yet."

This brought some affirmative nodding among his hearers and smiles of gratification.

"Speaking of Shorty," Cager said, "we sure wouldn't be much without *him* and what he's done for the 'unit.' He's showed how important *he* thinks it is. He's put his *money* in it, ain't he? That's the best proof there is. He came up with most of the down-payment for the uniform tunics, didn't he? I know you'all know that and are going to come up with your part when you can. But he'll get every nickel he's put on the line for the 'unit'—we'll see to that. My hat's, then, sure off to Shorty. Now there'll be more guys than ever coming into our army, you mark my words. We're building from the ground up—solid. When we get a couple hundred or more of our troops signed up, and all of us have our complete uniforms, we'll march down Main Street to the courthouse on a Saturday at *high noon,* man!"

"Tell it like it is, Cage," somebody said.

"It'll be a warning to 'em, I'll tell you," said Cager. "It's the uniforms. Don't forget, we're no damn lodge, or club. We're not just some marching unit, either. *We're an army!*"

That had been four or five months before. Now Shorty George pulled out a chair across the table from Cager and sat down. He spoke in a low, earnest voice. "But, Cage, forget about the uniforms for a minute, will you? Nate Goldberg ain't pressing us. He's sympathetic—for a white man—and the only one around here making uniforms that wouldn't run blabbing to the white folks on us. He's almost one of us, says so himself, and I believe him. So skip the uniforms for the time-being, Cage. I been meaning, though, to talk to you about some other things...just in general like." Shorty swallowed. He was clearly having difficulty tackling the subject. "I been thinking a lot about what we been trying to do all these months. Sure, I've put a little money into it but I ain't making no big deal outa that. The organization was your idea, from the beginning, and you're due the credit. Nobody's gonna take anything away from you on that score. Back then we all thought it was a helluvan idea and long overdue. But lately—and this ain't got nothin' to do with the bad luck with the uniforms—I been thinking a lot about what's down the road for us, for our organization. Is there any honest-to-God future for what we been callin' our 'army'? Is it practical? Does it make any sense at all? See what I'm sayin'?—or askin'?"

Cager, already struggling to control his incredulity and deep offense at this startling heresy, indeed apostasy, sat studying Shorty for a moment, hard. "Yeaaah," he finally said, his fierce irony dripping, "it's practical, it makes sense—if, that is, being *strong* makes sense." Soon, however, he was glaring furiously at Shorty. "You believe in *strength,* don't you, man?"

"Sure, Cage. Only thing is, how strong does it look like we're gonna get? Strong enough to do some real good? Or are we just gonna go out in the street in a bunch of monkey suits and get our heads whipped and throwed in jail again like when you whipped them two cops and locked them up only to have the judge put you *underneath* the jail—we just gonna do that? See what I'm tryin' to get at? Sure, strength is practical, *if* you're strong enough to win. But seems to me you gotta think about what your chances are, too. Am I right? The thing is, though, I ain't seen no big surge of people tryin' to come join up with us, and we been recruitin' for these many months now. Tell me, what's on your mind, Cage? How do you see this thing shapin' up? I need somebody to tell me somethin'."

Now, in the struggle to control himself, Cager was writhing in the chair. He liked and respected, almost loved, Shorty and abhorred the thought of losing his friendship by treating him unjustly or speaking rashly any more than he already had. "We ain't going to get strong just overnight, you know," he said. "It takes time. It takes a lot of work, too. But look, Shorty, if you're getting fed up, if you want out, there won't be any hard feelings. Honest." But his emotions were overwhelming him, making his voice falter, then quaver. "You've been our friend and backer. *My* friend, too. You've put your money into this thing that I know oughta been going into your business or to your family. On top of that I know how lucky we been to have an old ex-army sergeant like you around to teach the men how to really drill and learn discipline. How're we ever going to forget these things, any of 'em? We can't. You're sure entitled, then, to a voice of your own. But getting strong—I'm talking about *militarily!*—ain't easy. Nobody said it would be! Good God, Shorty!" He was writhing again.

"By 'militarily' do you mean with an army, Cage?"

"How's anybody gonna get strong without *eventually* having some kind of army? Look at history, Shorty!"

Shorty seemed to have lost patience now. He looked at Cager, shook his head, and tried to smile. "Cage, you really believe that, don't you? Lord have mercy. And you had me believin' it, too. We was both nuts. But you're the one that's nuts now—not me no longer. But you've always had your head so high in the clouds on this thing it wouldn't never let your feet touch the hard ground. Lord, *an army!* Why, it don't make no kinda sense. I think we oughta just throw it all outa our minds and chalk it up to bad experience. No, no, I ain't all of a sudden lettin' you down—I hope you understand that. I'm just askin' you to think about it, study it a little, and see if I ain't right."

Cager would not even look at him now.

"Some of the other guys are thinkin' the same way as me, too, Cage. Even talkin' among themselves."

Cager bristled. *"Who?"*

"Never mind who. But they're gettin' bored, losin' interest-like. Most of 'em, anyway. Cage, we gotta face up to it, all of us. It's a crazy idea. Christ Amighty—*an army!* Always was. Like kids shakin' a bare crab apple tree at Christmas—with nothin' comin' down. Where we been all this time? Good God, I don't know. You had this vision, I guess, and we went followin' along."

Cager took another deep, deep breath, then observed his erstwhile colleague. Finally, swallowing all words, he reached for his poncho.

"Don't you want something to eat?" said Shorty. "We got ribs and collards tonight."

Cager, now grinding his teeth, made no reply. His eyes were glazed over, slightly wet, as he finally shook his head in the negative. Then he rose from the chair. At last, though, he tried to speak, to argue, his eyes flashing fire. But he was unable, and soon, swinging the poncho around his shoulders, averting his gaze, walked out.

* * * * *

Directly from Shorty George's, still fighting tears, he stormed out of the rain into Ma Moody's place—talking to himself, also reviling himself as well as the whole world and all mankind in it. "Oh, Shorty, Shorty!" he thought. "How'n the hell could you do it? You were my right-hand man!" He was heading to find Ma now and wondering about her mood, though well knowing that Wednesdays were slow business nights even in good weather, and that the pouring rain now only made customer prospects even bleaker, invariably sending Ma into one of her mean, dyspeptic tempers from which she might not recover until next day and then only when she had finally seen some sun.

His poncho still dripping, he found her in her "office," a tiny partitioned-off cubbyhole wedged in between the dining room and lounge, and in tones both suppliant and demanding, the words gushing, told her of what he characterized as his "bound obligation"—to Shorty George. This of course was a grave tactical error, for the moment Shorty's name was mentioned, Ma mashed out her cigarette, picked up a pencil, and, all the while keeping her eyes away from him, began a dry, impatient—vindictive—drumming of her desk. Shorty was a business competitor, even if a pitiful, almost negligible, one. Ma, though, in such matters was relentless. "In other words," she said, "you want money from *me* to give *him*, is that it?"

He was impetuous, reckless. "Shorty made a helluva sacrifice, Ma! He didn't have much money, hardly any, but he came up with what he had! He's poor as Job's turkey—you know that. His place barely takes in enough to stay open. I don't see how he takes care of his family. As it is, he's the cook and his wife's the waitress! But I couldn't have started the organization without him. He even scraped up the down-payment for our uniforms. Now *they've* been stolen! Oh, Lord! He'd siphoned that money off his business, Ma! The organization was my idea but right away he jumped in and helped me. But, sad to say, he wants out now. He didn't ask for his money back, though. He's written it off. But he's entitled to get it back—he can't afford to forget it. You can see that, Ma! It was *my* idea!"

Ma's eyes flashed angrily. "You don't have to tell me that! *I* know it was your idea! Who else could come up with anything that simple-ass and dumb?—a bunch of grown niggers out marching in a vacant lot!"

"But he wouldn't be out this money—about a hundred and seventy-five bucks—if it wasn't for me!"

"Of course he wouldn't! Which shows he dumber'n you—which ain't easy to be!"

"I gotta see that he gets it back, though, Ma! If you could let me have it, I could pay you back in no time—I could put in more hours here, some days now as well as nights. So you'd be *guaranteed* your money back!"

"Oh, now, would I? Boy, when the Lord was handin' out brains, you musta been behind the door, or out to lunch, or some place." Ma had already resumed studying a stack of invoices on her desk, merely adding, casually, "Y'better let me think about it some more and get back to you." She did not look at him again. He stood waiting. Finally, though, regarding it as hopeless, and knowing protests would do no good, he left helplessly muttering to himself. Soon he found himself in the adjacent dining room ordering a sandwich before returning to Gladstone.

As he now sat waiting for his food, his frustrations and fatigue seemed to have settled painfully in his neck and shoulders, even down his spine, though he yet dreaded the thought of having to return to campus and all its ecology of blasted hopes where his string of comedies had now all but been played out and himself consigned to utter nadir. Soon his sandwich and milk were brought but they at last seemed to him as having little taste. Yet, he slowly masticated the food and tried to confine, narrow, even hedge in, his thoughts in order to make them somehow more manageable. This too in the end remained equivocal.

It was then, as he still ate, that the girl entered the dining room. "Cage, baby!" she cried, swooping over to his table. He sighed. It was Hortense Bangs. Embarrassed, he wanted to look around to see if any of the mere dozen other diners had noticed. Hortense was somewhat notorious. Even Ma cared little for her patronage.

"How you doing, Hortense?" he finally said.

She was standing over him now. "I'd join you, sweetie," she said, "but Silky Thomas is meeting me here to eat." At this he tried to grin. "How're things, baby?" she went on. "If you ask me, you look like you just got back from your mama's funeral or somethin'—and I *don't* play the dozens! Ha-ha-ha!" She passed on to another, yet nearby, table.

Although loud and brash, she was not bad-looking—slender, neat enough, young, her facial skin slightly pitted yet a pleasant saddle-brown. It was her eyes, however, that were most arresting—alert, intelligent, with a definitely worldly, brassy and brazen, almost defiant, glitter. She was, alas, also known for vending her considerable charms for cold cash.

Before long Silky Thomas, a "colleague," duly arrived—a laughing, boisterous, lighter-skinned (squash-colored) girl—and within minutes, abetted by some bonded bourbon whiskey, the pair were off on a flight of loud, hilarious talk and gossip, comparing notes on a variety of escapades, including every recent male encounter either had had or could remember, all of it, though, heard not only by nearby Cager but by the other diners in the place also. As time went on and Hortense had disposed of her third Manhattan he noticed her occasional neglect of her conversation with Silky in eyeing him. Again embarrassed, he looked away. But when she—obviously the lavish hostess—ordered T-bone steaks for herself and friend he was impressed.

Now Spats Smith, Ma's live-in boyfriend and Midnight Club straw boss, ambled in. "Spats, baby!" cried tipsy Hortense. "Come over here, honey—*look!*" She opened her purse, took out a double-sheaf of ten and twenty-dollar bills, and waved them at Spats. Cager's mouth fell open. "Come on, Spats, baby!" said Hortense, "I'll buy you some of your favorite Vat 69!" Spats, habitually smiling and courteous to all customers, at first hesitated, but at last then, obligingly, came over. "I'm flush tonight, Spats!" Hortense said. "Set *down,* I say!"

Spats still smiled his gold-toothed smile but remained standing over her, saying, "Lemme take a rain check on it tonight, will you, baby—I'm workin', y'know. And why don't you stop wavin' all that cabbage around? That ain't good. Ain't you got a boyfriend that takes care of business matters like this for you?"

The two steaks arrived now. But not before Hortense, by way of reply to Spats, let out something resembling a high, shrill, almost braying, horse laugh of derision. "Spats, you got better sense than that! Ha! Ha! Ha! Christ! Do I look that simple?—to have some damn nigger pimp spendin' my hard-earned money for me? Don't believe it for a minute, baby! Like last night, I caught me a real live pigeon. Didn't no damn pimp help me do it, either. This drunk cracker came to see me just after he'd left a big poker game he'd cleaned out! Ha!—and promptly got *himself* cleaned out! I bet when he sobered up this mornin' he wished he'd gone straight home instead of first comin' to my flat! I changed his luck, all right! Now, how come I need some damn pimp to help me spend this money? You tell me that, Spats baby! Ha, ha, ha! What?"

"Okay, okay," grinned Spats, anxious to quiet the uproar, "but just stop wavin' that wad around and put it back in your purse. There's a lotta people around, y'know, that'd like to get their hands on some of that loot."

Cager almost winced. He watched Hortense with feverishly burning eyes. At once, catching him in the act, she gave him her strident, lascivious laugh and again stuck out her quivering tongue. It as quickly aroused him and immediately he hated himself for it. Spats Smith had moved on now. It reminded Cager that he too should long since have left. He seemed powerless to move, though. He lingered indecisively, as if somehow waiting to do something he dreaded. But Hortense, in the euphoria of her bourbon, misread his mind and stepped up her flirting. It made him sick, more desolate than ever. But smiling, she still watched him, her manner ridiculing him; then, laughing, she made more faces at him. Now he would not look at her.

Yet, when she and Silky had finished their steaks and were eating dessert, Hortense tipsily called over to him. "Cage, I been watching you ogling me all night—I ain't blind, you know. But when I start ogling back, you act like you wanta get up and run somewhere. What's the matter with you? What you scared of?—Ha! Ha! Ha!" Silky laughed too. He could only grin though it seemed a grimace. Shortly Hortense called the waitress over for the check and once more, his eyes popping, he saw the tremendous wad of bills she ostentatiously pulled out of her purse. "Come on, Silky, honey, let's go," she said, rising after she had paid and had heavily tipped the waitress. "And that means *you too,* Cage baby! Come along, now—you're goin' with me. Ha!—Silky's got a car out there and she'll drop us off at my place. Then you and me are gonna have us a ball—*all night long!* Hey, hey, now!" She raised both hands and, snapping her fingers, did a raunchy little dance.

"I can't! . . ." he tried to say. "I've got to get back out to campus!"

"Don't hand me that! You've had an hour to start back out there. Instead, you been setting there undressing *me.* So don't act so upset now." She gave a high, excited, unsteady laugh. "I've had my eye on you ever since you started workin' here! Ha! Ha!—yeah, I've had you slated for a killing a long time, old string-bean Cage! You come on home with me and I'll learn you some things them damn professors out at Gladstone ain't never heard of. 'Cause what I'm talkin' about ain't in any damn *book!* Hey, now!—I'm talkin' about the *sweet* life!" In attempting to give her little dance again she reeled and almost stumbled. Cager was trembling with shame. He was also thinking of that huge wad of money in her purse. Soon, therefore, drooping, limp, his gaze downcast, he got his poncho and left with them out into the driving rain.

The moment he and Hortense were alone in her flat, she threw off her coat and, smiling, stood triumphantly before him. "What's the matter, baby?" she tried to coo. "You didn't say a word all the way here. Now you look scared as hell. I sure don't know why. What could a little woman like me do to a big handsome galoot like you? Ha!—except maybe take him in that bedroom there and ring his bells for him right good! *Ding-a-ling! Ding-a-ling!*" She reeled back on her heels laughing and again almost stumbled. "You oughta be lookin' forward to me," she said. "Yeah, shakin' with excitement like I sure know how to make a man feel. But instead you stand there lookin' like a ghost or like you just took poison. Lord, baby, tell me what's the matter." He only observed her and said nothing. "Let me fix you a drink, then, Cage. You sure need *somethin'* for whatever it is that ails you."

"That's true," he said. "But it's not whiskey." He finally sat down on the sofa.

"Well, *I'll* have a drink," she said, and left the room.

He sat gazing around him and hating the oppressive, cloyingly sweet smell of the living room deodorant. The apartment, though tidy enough, was small and boxy and reeked of this weird incense in the midst of which were a half-dozen subdued multi-colored lights strategically placed to create "atmosphere." When she finally returned with her drink he saw that she had also changed out of her street clothes, reappearing now in a negligee so sheer he could make out, even in the incense-laden murk, her stark naked figure underneath. His blood jumped, then began furiously pounding. He wanted to run over and grapple with her, kiss and caress her—the smooth tainted young body, the protuberant breasts, the wiry pouting muff between the thighs, her sweet musk. But at last, drink in hand, she sat down beside him on the sofa, though not yet close to him. "To save my life I can't understand you," she smiled impishly, seeming now, despite the new drink, to have somewhat sobered. "You knew when you came here what the deal was. 'Cause I told you. You knew I was goin' to be a bad influence on you—*college boy!* Ha! Ha! So why're you now acting so damn innocent—or plain scared? I didn't bring you here to turn a trick with you, you know. This is *my* night to howl—and yours. If I was workin' I sure wouldn't be drinkin'. That's dangerous. In this business you got to keep your wits about you—*all the time*—or you'll end up some night dead." She sipped the drink, lit a cigarette, and sat back observing him. Both were silent for a time.

Finally she said: "I told you I been watching you like a hawk, didn't I? Well, I have and you know it. What do I care about you and old Flo Ransom? Hey, you didn't know I knew all about you two, did you? But that woman's another story. Ha!—another whole *book!* But I won't get into that—what she does is her business. Only thing I can say, though, is that you're as naive and 'country' as they come, Cage baby. You need somebody to wise you up, look after you, somebody that's hip to the tip—like *me*. You need protection. What can Flo Ransom do for you? Nothing. That's why I brought you here—at least one of the reasons—to talk. About *us*. I need a boyfriend, Cage. And I don't mean no damn pimp. And you need somebody to look after you that knows the ropes. I *will* say, though—ha!—that Flo Ransom knows 'em better than a lot of people give her credit for! But *you* sure don't know 'em, Cage honey. Lord, have mercy, no. But as for me, I need a man I can like for what he is, somebody I can look up to, like you, an educated young guy—and I bet I ain't two years older'n you. What I *don't* need—and don't want, and won't have—is some roughneck bastard that's only thinkin' about takin' what little money I get ahold of now and then, like last night. They forget I'm flat broke sometimes, too. But that's when a pimp wants to start mistreatin' you, beatin' up on you, when you ain't producin' for him. None of that for me. I want somebody that needs me as much as I need him. Y'know what I mean?"

Cager at last solemnly nodded, then took his eyes away.

Hortense bridled. "Why don't you *say* something, for Christ's sake! You sure get on my nerves! You ain't all that damn dumb. I hear at one time you was smart as hell out at Gladstone. Well, you at least must've been able to *talk!*"

He frowned, shook his head, then spread his hands futilely. "I don't know what to say, that's all. . . ."

Yet, before long, she had moved closer to him on the sofa, her voice somewhat softening now. "I didn't mean to scold you, Cage honey. That's my trouble, I run my mouth too much for my own good. I've been talking to you like I was putting some kinda big business deal to you. I don't feel that way about it at all. It's more like a nice warm feeling that I've got—I'm tellin' you the honest-to-God truth, Cage. It's like the way you feel when you really like somebody. And need 'em, too." She raised her face toward his and looked at him. "I'm a girl —no, a woman, I guess"—she laughed—"and have got feelings like anybody else." Suddenly then, nervously, she leaned over and tittered in his ear: "Would you like to have sex with me tonight?"

He started. Frightened, he looked bewilderedly at her. But at last, his eyes staring now, piteous, afire, he could not speak. Yet, he longed to say, to cry out, to her, *"Yes, yes!"*

Soon she moved still closer to him, until now their shoulders and hips touched. "Honest," she said, "I ain't trying to make a customer outa you, or anything like that, you know." She gave another uneasy laugh. "I *told* you it ain't business. That it won't cost you nothin'. I just want to have sex with you, that's all. What's wrong with that? I want to see if you like me like that. I *am* a girl, or woman, and I'm healthy. And I also like you a lot, so it's natural, ain't it, that I'd want to sleep with you. Have I got to tell you again you're my type? It's because you're intelligent. And a good guy. You're not rough-acting, either, like a lot of these clowns I know. *Ha!*—yeah, you can be *my* pimp any time! But ain't you got the least bit of feeling for me? Ain't you just a little bit excited, setting close to me like this—Ha, ha, ha!—and us rubbing asses?" Then without any warning at all, before he could possibly have known what was happening, she slid her hand along the inside of his thigh to his genitals. They were throbbing hard.

He jumped straight up. Then stood before her quivering and mortified.

"What'n the hell's wrong with you?" she cried. "Do you get all upset about a little foreplay like that? You act like you've never been to bed with a woman! I know, though—I can tell—I excite you, all right. I could feel—for a second or two there at least—that you was hard . . . or was somethin' . . . Lord, I don't know what, to tell you the truth. What kinda guy *are* you, Cage?" Then, as he still stood before her, numb, speechless, quaking with both confusion and desire, she shot out her hand to touch him again. He jumped back as if she had had a white hot poker in her hand. "Cage baby, I swear before God I've never run into anybody like you before in my life. You sure got me up a tree. I've seen all types—at least I thought I had—but nobody like you. You like women, don't you? You ain't a faggot, are you?—tryin' to put me on. You don't think I ain't met a lot of them, do you? Two of my closest buddies—Art and Sammy—are flits, what're you talkin' about? Tell me, are you one of *them?*"

He scowled, then glared, at her.

"Okay, I take it back. On the other hand, though, don't be so quick to lose your cool. It don't look good—like you're over-reactin' or somethin'. There's a lot worse things you can be than a sissy, I'll tell you that. But what *is* your problem, then? Good God, let me in on it—if you know. Which I doubt."

"I *am* a pimp!" he finally blurted. "I came here only to get some of that money you were flashing around at Ma's!"

She gaped at him. "Cage honey, I know you're dumb about some things," she said—"Not all, but some. But, Lord have mercy, I didn't know you could be *that* dumb. This thing's gotten outa hand. It's crazy. Money? What kinda numbers are you talkin' about?"

"A hundred and seventy-five dollars."

"That ain't a fortune but it's still money—somebody else's, mine." She had scooted back from him now, to her original place at the other end of the sofa, and sat staring at him as if baffled. "I guess I ain't as surprised that you'd want money from me as I am that you'd think—just for half a second!—that you could *get* it, talk me out of it. You sure don't know *me,* honey. I never gave a damn man a quarter in my life. Even if I do say it myself, you're dealin' with one of the hippest, hardest-hearted, most street-wise women you'll ever come across. I'm young, sure, but I started early. I've dealt with every kinda no-good type there is, every one of 'em—and, yeah, right here in this hick town. Niggers and crackers alike. Crackers that after they screw you, want to kill you, or tell you they gotta mind to. Or while they're screwin' you call you all kinda dirty coon-breeding, filthy nigger bitches, saying all niggers oughta be burned alive, all this while they're gruntin' and carryin' on, fuckin' you, gettin' their nuts off. I tell you, they're crazy, they're sick. People to be really afraid of. Oh, sure, they're mostly drunk when they're sayin' all these things but, oh yeah, they're speakin' their sober thoughts right on."

Although Cager now seemed strangely to have little interest in what she was saying, the words, he still somehow watched her face with awe, and finally revulsion.

"Then of course," she said, "there's the niggers—oh, my God. They're just as bad, in other ways. Some big filthy black ape, drunk, or right off a garbage truck, will want to screw half the night for five dollars. When you tell him no dice and cuss him out and order him to *git,* then he wants to beat you up, cripple you. I've coped with all kinds, I tell you—black and white—and all of 'em are the same, a bunch of low, no-good, horny dogs. They're all dogs, yeah—animals. Still they think they can look down on you, talk to you, or treat you, any damn way they want to—just because you happen to be a whore. It *is* happenstance, you know. Well, there you are, that's what the scene's like, and I been dealin' with it, too. So here comes old country boy Cager that's gonna take advantage of *me,* talk *me* outa some money. Right?" She was not smiling.

"Why do you live this kind of life?" he said abruptly, frowning. Then the horror and disgust returned to his face. "Good God, *I've* got sisters. I'd shoot one of 'em first. How can you live this way?"

"Because it's how I was cut out to live. I told you it was happenstance. You ain't got any choice. You gotta play the hand you was dealt and not bellyache about it—just hope things will be better next time around, in the next life. I'm a religious gal, you know, even if I don't go to church—where they wouldn't want me anyhow—and pray all the time. Ha! Ha!—I mean *all* the time. Maybe it's because I'm plain scared—scared that some night one of these misfits will cave my skull in, or cut my liver out. See what I mean? Sure I'm religious—I *better* be! If I had *my* way, though, I'd be a *queen,* settin' on a damn throne somewhere—cool! Ha! Ha! Ha!"

He gazed morosely at her, then said something not quite audible.

"So what's your story, Cage baby? How'd you think you was gonna con *me* outa some money?"

"I was up against it," he finally said, almost apologetically. "I needed the money bad."

Hortense smiled. "Why didn't you go to your old girlfriend Flo? She's a big shot around here, ain't she?—my, my, works for the *State.*

Now, don't make me have to tell you how she *got* with the State, sweetheart—ha, ha! But where was she?—old green-eyed, freckle-faced Flo."

Except for grinding his teeth he sat mute and would not look at her.

"Oh, but maybe she wouldn't have had the kinda money you're talkin' about, eh? Right, Cage baby? Wow, a hundred and seventy-five smackers. You ain't knocked up one of those little gals out at Gladstone, have you?"

"I wanted the money for Shorty George," he said. "He put it up when we were starting our organization and ain't been paid back yet."

"Christ, I thought that dumb outfit had gone bust by now. I sure don't hear about it any more."

He stiffened, almost bristling. "We've had a temporary setback, yeah," he said. "Shorty's probably dropping out—that's why he oughta get his money back—but we *ain't gone bust!*" He glared at her.

"Oh, Cage, come off it. That outfit was a joke. Instead of protecting us it was the laughing stock of the town—and most of all by these rednecks, the ones you was tryin' to scare. How'n the hell did you'all dream that thing up? It was a scream, Cage—honest. You'all out there trampin' up and down that empty lot like a bunch of clowns, people passing by laughing their asses off—even the niggers."

He jumped up. "That's a lie! Don't you say that about Negroes! It's not true! It was a good idea—a *great* idea!—I don't give a damn what you'all say! Ain't you got any pride? To hell with all of you! . . . . You don't deserve any better!" He had grabbed up his poncho and was running to the door.

Suddenly she pursued him now, trying to intercept him, head him off.

"Get to hell out of my way!" he said, his arm throwing her aside.

"Now, you just wait a minute, there, Mr. Cager!" she cried. "I'm sorry I said that, even if it was true! I'm sorry, I say!"

But his hand was already on the doorknob.

She tried to jerk it away and then they struggled. "You can have the money! . . ." she said, panting. "Hell, that's no sweat! I'm sorry for what I said. Don't you leave—I'll go get my purse right now! Do you hear? You wait, now, Cage!" She was pleading as she turned him loose.

"Come back!" he said. "I don't want it! I won't take it!"

She returned. "You listen to me, Cager!" Her pleading had strangely turned to panic. "What money I handle is all bad—bad money! It comes from the bad and as soon as I get it, it goes right back to the bad! Can't you see that? I want you to take that hundred and seventy-five bucks and give it to Shorty like you said. For once money of mine will be goin' for something that at least has good intentions! I told you I was wrong, didn't I?" She had now become hysterical. "Give me this one chance, won't you? *Oh, Cage!...*"

But he opened the door and fled down the stairs.

Next morning she went to the Post Office and sent Shorty George a money order for a hundred and seventy-five dollars. The sender's name was stated merely as "Cager," for she knew neither the real first name nor any version of his last. Only "Cager." But that was enough. Cager, though, did not know that she had done it.

Two days later, with clearing skies, Ma Moody called him in and, in one of her rare better, indeed generous, moods, returned, of her own volition, to the subject of his recent request for a loan. He glumly thanked her but, lying, said he no longer had need of it.

* * * * *

Spring, authentic spring, though late, had arrived at last—with a warmer sun, fledgling grass, honeysuckle, hydrangeas, azaleas, the sweet perfumed air, and garter snakes. Impishly, chauffeur Sampson stood in the door of the garage behind the Dabney house smoking a cigarette and chewing cloves. He would not, however, let himself get near officious cook Phoebe (of the two hundred fifty pounds and balloon derrière) coming from the smokehouse with a side of bacon. He was determined today not to give her the opportunity to detect his breath. He knew she suspected the usual—gin—even if he had only had a taste, certainly not enough, to himself he argued, adversely to affect the performance of his duties.

"Why don't you get yoh big ass on back in that kitchen," he thought but of course did not say to her, "instead of hangin' around out here in the backyard tryin' to smell my little gin so you kin run in there and tell her I'm at it again and not to let me git her kilt in some accident, which I ain't about to do 'cause I ain't had but a thimbleful, and it don't hinder me none—do it, now? You kin see I just got back with her, didn't I, from takin' her to make a talk at one of her Confedacy meetings. Ain't that right, now? How kin I be high, then? But, Lawd, wouldn't she skin me alive if I was and she caught me. Wow!"

Phoebe watched him, then came closer. "Hummph, just like I thought," she said. "I can tell by your eyes wobblin'. That's your gin, I don't care how many cloves you done chewed. You better watch yourself, Mr. Big. You better watch *her,* too." She spoke as if she were reading his mind off a ticker tape. "Yeah, but not only her," she said. "There's somebody *else* around here you better be watchin'. That old boy Rollo's catchin' on fast, you hear me? *She* sees it, too—I can see it by the way she watches him, just like a hawk. And never gits after him about his work, like she does you, which is some kinda world record for her. He does his work, don't fool around none, and keeps his mouth shut. Besides, he's a college boy. Long as she's been puttin' up with your carryin'-on she just might be gettin' him ready for somethin' else, who knows?—like drivin' her big car for her. You guessed it—*he* don't drink nothin' but milk."

"Haw!" uttered Sampson. "You must think I'm the world's biggest chump. Well, I ain't. First thing I done when he come here was check out his drivin'. He kin drive, all right—a span of mules. So what's he goin' to be doin' behind the wheel of a great big long new shiny black Cadillac that ain't even got any numbers of the license plates, just letters—L-E-E! Tell me that."

"I ain't tellin' you nothin'," said Phoebe. "Can't nobody do that."

Meanwhile, inside the house, Cager, on his knees, was vigorously buffing the oak floor of the portrait gallery—when suddenly M. E. F. Dabney came up behind him before he saw her. "Rollo." He almost jumped. "Are you registered for the draft? I've been meaning to ask you why it is you haven't been called into the military service."

He straightened up, though still on his knees, then, seeming to himself to be kneeling before her as if she were some monarch, he awkwardly got to his feet and, shiftily, looked at her. "No'm," he said. "I'm not registered."

She frowned. "Don't you know you could go to jail for that? If you want to continue working here you'll have to obey the law and go downtown and register. The country's at war—I don't have to tell you that. My grandson, who is your age, just arrived overseas, in Europe, to fight. But you wouldn't even be required to fight for you'd doubtlessly be sent to one of the service supply units—far behind the lines. So the least you can do is go register."

He reflected on this. And finally said nothing.

"What about all those other boys out at Gladstone?" she said. "Have any of them gone?"

". . . Some have." He spoke tentatively, though.

"But not many, I'll bet. Well, tomorrow you go down to the draft board in the Courthouse and do your duty—get on the rolls." She turned to go on.

He stopped her, though, by pointing up at one of the portraits over them and asking, "Who's that, ma'am?"

She looked. "That's General Jackson." But she was impatiently sidling away as she spoke, though adding, "General Thomas Jonathan Jackson—'Stonewall' Jackson."

". . . Oh," he said, his eyes widening in awe, "*that's* who that is, is it? I know about him but never saw his picture. He's from Virginia. He was killed at Chancellorsville—yeah, yeah." Next he pointed to the adjacent portrait which hung directly below the long, gleaming bayonet fiercely affixed to the interminably long Enfield musket. "He's from Virginia too," he said eagerly—"General Lee. I know quite a bit about him."

She at last returned and, reverently, gazed up at Robert E. Lee's white-bearded, unruffled countenance. Suddenly then she turned and said, "You studied about him out at the *college?*"—her voice harsh, unbelieving, though also as if a yes-answer might in her estimate somewhat redeem Gladstone.

"No'm," he said, "in high school—back in Virginia."

She stared at him. "*I'm* from Virginia," she finally said. Then with a quiet dignity yet a slight arch of the chin—"My forebears have been there since, you might say, almost the time of Captain John Smith and Pocahontas." She did not smile. "One should always be proud of being a Virginian. It's had such a long and fruitful history, and produced so many great men—including more presidents than any other state in the nation. Then of course there was General Lee. . . . Ah, no more can be said after him. What part are you from?"

"The Tidewater."

"Well . . . indeed. So was my father." She spoke gravely. "He was born near Elberon. And my mother in Smithfield."

"My father sharecropped on a place between Rescue and Moonlight," he said. "That's not too far out from Smithfield. We were closer to Cook's Grove, though."

She sighed. "Most of those names are no longer familiar to me. It's been such a long, long time."

Leaving him standing there with the piece of buffing wool in his hand, she continued toward the library. He followed her. But unaware, she entered, sat down at her writing table, and reached for a sheet of stationery and her gold fountain pen. Meanwhile, as he could never refrain from doing whenever in this room, he stood staring around him in wonder, amazement, at the four great high walls of books—most of them in some respect or another about war. They hypnotized him. She looked up now and, startled, saw him standing almost directly over her. Instant displeasure showed on her face—at both the intrusion and the presumption.

"Ma'am," he said—it was almost an accusation—"you got more books here than we got in our whole library out at Gladstone."

She bridled and reddened. "Your trouble out there is not the paucity of books! It's the kinds of books they are! Impractical, foolish books—*French,* my goodness! And Shakespeare. Greek mythology, social etiquette, the so-called African 'civilizations'! That's what's wrong out there—and not only the library but the whole college. Now, please leave me—I've got work to do. And don't you forget about going to the draft board—tomorrow!"

Somehow he did not move. Rather, he still stood looking at her, not challengingly, not defiantly, only knitting his brow as he wrestled with the problem, also as if debating whether or not to articulate it. Finally —"Yessum, I'll go register, but to tell you the truth I'm not too interested in *this* war." He stopped and swallowed, as if to garner strength, indeed the daring, to say more. "This war," he said, "is not the one I carry around in my head all the time. Sure, ma'am, I think about war, all right, the past ones and the future ones, too, but not much about the present one. This war's for other people—you folks." He spoke quietly, sincerely, even confidently, as if what he was saying was so patent, so logical, it was unarguable, something she would see at once if only he took the time to spell it out. "We're not like you'all," he said —"We don't have much stake in this war. That's why we got to start raising an army of our own. I hope I, or somebody that's got more on the ball than I got, will be able to do it. We'll fight *our* war, then. Do you know the writings of General Karl von Clausewitz? Do you get what I'm saying? I'm dealing with how my people can get the wherewithal, and the know-how—the *power* is what I'm talking about—to wage *our* war, wage it to victory. *You* can see that, ma'am!" He was almost pleading now.

The utterly shocked and dumbfounded expression on her face had first caused it to blanch. But as the anger, then outrage, hit, it flushed an engorged ruby red, almost purple. Now, her jowls quivering, she snatched off her pince-nez. "What in heaven's name are you talking about! Where on earth did you learn such absolutely stupid drivel! Out at that Gladstone? No, I don't know that German's writings—I never heard of him! And, no, I don't get what you're saying! Or maybe I *do* and see how dumb or insane you are—really both! You talk of raising a nigra army, fighting your own war, winning some kind of silly minstrel-show victory, I guess! Is that it? Good God! 'Wherewithal'! 'Know-how'! 'Power'! 'Victory'! Have you lost your childish mind? Well, let me tell *you* a thing or two! You've already got your 'power'! You've already won your 'victory'!" She was pointing wildly toward where they had just come from. "You got them when those generals out there in that hall-gallery could no longer hold off the Northern hordes that so outnumbered their barefoot, starving men and overran our prostrate Southland!" She was shouting, almost shrieking, now. "They destroyed our way of life, completely and forever, and impoverished us till this day! *That* was your victory! And it was won *for* you, not *by* you! Your fancy notions, wherever you got them, are asinine! Absurd! Actually, they're laughable if it weren't for the gall they show. So now you—and 'your people,' as you call them—are living on the fat of the land and in the greatest civilization that ever existed at any time or in any place! And you—and 'your people'—are here only because you were brought here and placed down in the very midst of all of it!

Certainly, a little of it was *bound* to rub off on you—not much, but a little! Yet that's when you began getting all your fancy, highfalutin' ideas!—that you could demand the rest, or go about raising an army of your benighted shirttail nigras and take it—instead of thanking your lucky stars you'd been exposed to any of it! Otherwise today you'd be running around somewhere over there in the African bush in a loincloth with a bone in your nose!" She stood trembling. "Now, you listen to me! My grandson is over there somewhere in the very thick of the fighting, while you, and those others out there at that Gladstone like you, are whiling away your time reading Homer and Voltaire and playing squash! Well, I won't have any of your preposterous nonsense in *this* house!" She was shouting again. "You get down there to that draft board tomorrow and register or else take your clothes and leave here now! At once! I mean every word I say! *Now, that's all!*" Apoplectic, she waved him out—as frightened Phoebe and Sampson, even old Caleb, peered around the corner from the base of the stairs.

Sampson finally turned and grinned triumphantly to Phoebe, "Don't look like to me she got him in mind fuh anythang—'cept maybe lynchin'."

Cager left the library. But he had been strangely numb, could not feel anything. Her sudden savagery had surprised him, left him limp and ineffectual. At last as he had left her presence he was stooped, his head bowed, and he shuffled as if partially paralyzed. He seemed less resentful than bewildered, then finally numb again, though soon once more utterly confused, as if, due to his own fault, he had somehow failed to get his point—a point to him so clear, logical, so rational—across to her, convince her he was right. The anger, the bitter hurt, and then the fury, like the delayed fuse of a time bomb, would come only later.

Contributors

Andrew Allegretti was awarded Illinois Arts Council Artists Fellowships in 1985 and 1987. A portion of his novel, *Winter House,* appeared in the Chicago issue of *Tri-Quarterly*. He has also won two Illinois Arts Council Literary Awards—one for a short story in *Privates,* and another for a novel excerpt in f^2. He teaches in the graduate Creative Writing Program at Columbia College (Chicago).

Beverlye Brown, who currently teaches at Eastfield College in Dallas, Texas, has taught courses in writing and literature in high school, university, graduate school, and private workshops. Her fiction has recently been published in *Texas Writers* and the f^2 issue of *F Magazine.* Her story, *The Silk Kites,* will appear in the story anthology of *Dallas Writers* this fall.

Bill Burck recently read an excerpt from his novella-in-progress, *The Elbows,* on public radio station WBEZ in Chicago. His stories and articles have appeared in several issues of the literary anthology *Hair Trigger* and in *Esprit Magazine.* As a judge for the Coordinating Council of Literary Magazines (CCLM), he helped select the best undergraduate literary magazines of 1986.

Cyrus Colter is the author of *The Beach Umbrella, The Rivers of Eros, Night Studies,* and *The Hippodrome.* He is a lawyer, a former Illinois State Official (Commerce Commissioner), and an emeritus professor at Northwestern University, where he chaired the Department of African American Studies and held the Chester D. Tripp professorship in the Humanities. He lives in Chicago.

Paul Carter Harrison, Rockefeller award winning playwright, director, and essayist, is author of numerous plays and essays, and *The Drama of Nommo* (Grove), a collection of essays on the aesthetics of black theater. He is co-author with Chuck Stewart of *Jazz Files* (New York Graphic Society Book/Little, Brown). *One Anonymous Mourning* is his first novel.

Charles Johnson is a 1987 Guggenheim Fellow and recently received a PEN-Faulkner award for his story collection, *The Sorcerer's Apprentice* (Viking Penguin). He is author of two novels, *Faith and the Good Thing* (Atheneum) and *Oxherding Tale* (Grove Press), and the 1986 Writer's Guild Award winning PBS drama, "Booker." He is Director of the Creative Writing Program at the University of Washington and fiction editor of the *Seattle Review.*

Gary Johnson teaches creative writing at Columbia College (Chicago). His work has appeared in *Hair Trigger II, The Best of Hair Trigger,*

Privates, and the *f²* issue of *F Magazine.* In 1980, he was a judge of the nationwide college literary contest of the Coordinating Council of Literary Magazines (CCLM). He is a 1981 winner of the Edwin L. Schuman Award for fiction at Northwestern University.

Zoe Keithley is currently the coordinator of the Tell-Your-Story Writing Project for the City of Chicago's Sesquicentennial. She teaches at Columbia, Wright, and Calumet colleges. In 1982, she won second place in the adult division Joanne Hirschfield Poetry Contest. Excerpts from her novel-in-progress, *Act of God,* appear in the anthology *Hair Trigger 6/7* and in the award winning *Hair Trigger 8.*

Nathan Lerner's cover photograph "Closed Eye" (1940) is part of the permanent collection of the Metropolitan Museum of Art, New York, and the Museum of Contemporary Photography at Columbia College, Chicago. He has taught at the Illinois Institute of Technology and the New Bauhaus, which became the School of Design of Chicago. Currently, he is preparing a show of photographs taken during his many trips to Japan.

Harry Mark Petrakis is the author of thirteen books and has twice been nominated for the National Book Award in Fiction. His work includes the novels *A Dream of Kings* and *Days of Vengeance* and the autobiography *Reflections: A Writer's Life, A Writer's Work. Collected Stories* was recently published by Lake View Press.

Glen Ross teaches in the English and Creative Studies Departments at Central State University, Oklahoma. His novel, *The Last Campaign,* was published by Harper's. Excerpts from it appear in the anthology *American Men at Arms,* by F. Van Wyek Mason (Little, Brown, republished by Pocket Books), and in a creative writing text, *Successful Writing.* He also has published stories in *Army Magazine* and *New Mexico Quarterly.*

Betty Shiflett's stories and articles have appeared in numerous magazines and literary quarterlies, including *Life Magazine, Evergreen Review, College English, Privates,* and the *f²* issue of *F Magazine.* She received an Illinois Arts Council Fellowship for her full-length play, "Phantom Rider." Her one-act, "We Dream of Tours," was twice produced by Dream Theater at the Body Politic Theater in Chicago.

Shawn Shiflett teaches Creative Writing and English at Columbia College (Chicago). He was awarded an Illinois Arts Council Artists Fellowship for the first chapter of his novel, *Hey, Liberal,* and his stories have been published in magazines and literary quarterlies, including the *f²* issue of *F Magazine.* He was featured in the 1985 fall issue of *Chicago Single Magazine.*